The
Twenty-One-Year
Contract

by

L. B. Griffin

a sequel to
Secrets, Shame, and a Shoebox

The Twenty-One-Year Contract

Contact Information: info@thewildrosepress.com

Cover Art by *The Wild Rose Press, Inc.*

The Wild Rose Press, Inc.
PO Box 708
Adams Basin, NY 14410-0708
Visit us at www.thewildrosepress.com

Publishing History
First Edition, 2022
Trade Paperback ISBN 978-1-5092-3972-6
Digital ISBN 978-1-5092-3973-3

a sequel to *Secrets, Shame, and a Shoebox*
Published in the United States of America

After a glass of water, Jack made himself a cup of tea and returned to the job in hand. This was going to be much harder than he could ever have imagined.

Working deep through the night, Jack methodically sifted through volumes of paperwork until light inched its way through the curtain. Though he felt thoroughly ready for bed, he continued searching, his aim to find at least a smidgen of information about his niece.

Randomly tidying up as he went, Jack noticed an encyclopedia oddly extended over one of the top shelves. He tried pushing it back into place. It was jammed. It looked awkward. Pulling it out to check the depth of the book, Jack found a box file hidden behind. Upon the side panel was one word, capitalized in thick bold lettering:

KATHLEEN

As the hazy sunlight grew, Jack pulled the curtains to lend natural light, took the file off the shelf, sat back in Henry's chair, and looked inside.

Dedication

Dave, thank you
for all your encouragement and support.
Without you this would all be
a distant dream.
With love.

Acknowledgements

Special thanks go to Nan Swanson, my editor, who has guided me throughout this wonderful publishing journey. Nan has not only offered her patience and wisdom, but she has also made it fun. My thanks also go to The Wild Rose Press for taking me on. And to the fantastic artist who created such a superb cover.

Also special thanks to my children—Sam and Kelly—who have been unwavering in their help, even when I haven't asked, and to Jac Forsyth and Chris Heywood, who gave me the final push to get it out there. To writers and friends—most of whom have been there right from conception and have given their time, patience, and guidance—I couldn't have done it without you: Cindy Beadman, Barbara Compton, Peter Dixon, Paul Fines, June Foster, Jonny Griffiths, Jae Monroe, Dianne Preston, Davina Rungsamy, Katherine Tanko. I have listed you in alphabetical order because I see it as the fairest way of saying thank you with equal appreciation.

Finally, to you, the readers, who are important to every writer and especially to me. You have been truly amazing in your support. Not only have you purchased my novel, but you have taken the time to write great reviews. Thank you.

Prologue

3 September 1939

As the radio crackled into life, Molly reached for her daughter's hand, and they listened as King George VI addressed the nation in a speech that would last five minutes, forty-four seconds and change the course of history forever.

"...my people at home and my peoples across the seas. I ask them to stand calm, firm and united in this time of trial. The task will be hard. There may be dark days ahead..."

"Oh, dear God, not again." Molly scrubbed the heels of her hands into her forehead as if trying to rub away the King's message. "Nothing good comes of war, only devastation and death."

Cassandra looked down at her taut belly. She had missed another period, and that weighed more heavily upon her mind right now.

Chapter 1

February 11, 1954

Pops winked at Kathleen in the rearview mirror as he reversed their brand-new Morris Minor into the Latimers' drive. Excited, Kathleen wriggled impatiently around on the back seat that hung with the scent of leather. Beside her she had a small overnight bag and a bunch of delphiniums cut fresh this morning from their garden.

"Now, Kathleen Gray…" Her mother turned around from the front seat, with baby Bobby sitting on his mother's lap, gurgling. The words began to drift over her and out the window. She'd heard it all before. Great Aunt Jane was ill. They would bring her home to look after her. York was a long drive. All Kathleen could think about was staying over with her best friend, Lucy.

"Please stop worrying, Mum. I'll be fine, really."

Lily Latimer, Lucy's mother, waited at the front door, and Kathleen handed her the flowers.

"They're divine, Kathleen, thank you," said Mrs. Latimer, and breathed in their perfume. "Now, remember to call me Aunty Lily. It would never do being called Mrs. Latimer. It makes me feel so very old."

Kathleen smiled, and, remembering her manners,

waited whilst Mr. Latimer came through the hallway. He looked every inch the newly elected local MP, so very proper. So proper, in fact, Kathleen had to resist the urge to curtsey, though she never did, and not wanting to embarrass Lucy, never spoke of it.

"Kathleen." Mr. Latimer offered a polite, reserved nod as he walked past to join the group at the door. Kathleen listened to Pops speaking with Mr. Latimer, thanking them for their help. She loved Pops' voice, deep, gentle, easygoing, just like him.

"They could be hours and hours droning on," Lucy whispered, and dragged her upstairs to her room, grinning. "You can wave goodbye when they leave."

Kathleen half smiled. Once upon a time her shy little friend would never have said boo to a goose, but now, at last, she was coming out of her shell. Lucy had already settled Kathleen's overnight bag on a beautifully decorated chair.

"Well, what do you think?" Lucy proudly threw her arms wide and spun in a circle. Kathleen studied Lucy's bedroom with a keen eye. She knew all about the changes as they were made and had helped her own mother make the curtains and swags.

"Groovy," said Kathleen, using their most recent new word, something Lucy's mother had heard in one of the latest films from America.

"Woah!" Kathleen gasped, staring at a massive movie poster advertising *Gentlemen Prefer Blondes*. "GroOOovy," she said, still trying to get the word out without sounding forced.

"She's beautiful, isn't she?" said Lucy.

"Sexy, I'd say!"

Lucy immediately pinked.

Kathleen gazed at the poster.

"Mummy said I can't see the film until I'm older. Probably because they're kissing or something."

Kathleen laughed and immediately began to brag she knew all about kissing, as Christine Patterson had told her to practice on a mirror. Lucy prodded her lips, questioning. Mirrors were hard and cold, whilst lips were soft and warm. Kathleen shrugged, giving an exaggerated wobble-headed demonstration, wrapping her arms around her body and swam her hands up and down her back. The girls burst into a fit of giggles, and both jumped as Aunty Lily peered around the door.

"Your parents are going, dear. I'm sure you would like to say goodbye?"

"Yes, Aunty Lily." Kathleen had dropped her arms by her side, feigning innocence, and looked over her shoulder at the wide-eyed Lucy, mouthing, "She didn't hear, did she?" Lucy just bit her bottom lip with the slightest shrug of her shoulder, and Kathleen trailed back downstairs after Aunty Lily.

"Look after Mummy and Pops, won't you, Bobby dear?" Kathleen tickled her little baby brother's soft chubby cheek and kissed him fondly, saying goodbye.

Bobby babbled happily, and with drool dribbling around fat creamy white knuckles, gave her a little wave, like he'd just learned to do. Kathleen felt an overwhelming rush of love. She loved everything about Bobby, right down to his soft curls tumbling around his ears. He was a beautiful little miracle. Especially as her adoptive parents had been told they could never have children of their own.

"Now be good, won't you?" said her mother, hugging her goodbye.

"Bye, Mum." She sighed contentedly as her father bear-hugged her one last time, and she saved just one last kiss, for Bobby, and they were off.

That night the girls were treated to supper in Lucy's bedroom. Napkins were prettily arranged in neat triangles on filigree plates, with cold milk in fluted glasses. Kathleen looked at the plates of ham, tongue, and one cherry tomato nestled inside a crisp cupped lettuce leaf, amazed Mr. Latimer allowed such decadence, and in the bedroom of all places.

"Look," hushed Kathleen once Aunty Lily left. She locked the door. "I've brought us something a tad better than milk," and she produced a jam jar filled with red liquid.

"What's that?"

"Cherry juice." Kathleen chuckled, draining the milk, and rinsing their glasses in the bedroom sink.

"Chin-chin!" Kathleen grinned widely after sharing the contents between them. "Down the hatch in…three, two, ONE!"

Lucy swallowed the lot—and gagged.

"Cherry juice?" she shuddered.

Kathleen laughed. "Now, how about a ciggie, darling?"

Lucy's eyes popped as her friend produced a packet of cigarettes and matches.

"Come on!" Kathleen opened the bedroom window and let the freezing air in. As she lit the cigarette she leaned out, took a deep drag, spluttered, and handing it over said, "Here."

"But what if Mummy or Daddy…"

"Just stick your head out the window, Luce." The tobacco had made Kathleen lightheaded, and she didn't like the sensation at all.

Lucy took a quick puff and coughed all over the place.

"What are you trying to do, kill me?"

"It's *so grooovy* staying over, darling." Kathleen laughed.

Lucy waved a forty-five vinyl in the air, forgetting the cigarette in her hand.

"I have a new Comets record, and look what Daddy bought me. I'm so lucky!" At first glance it looked like a small handheld suitcase, but the inside revealed a record player.

"Goodness, Luce!"

She took the black gem from its sleeve and switched on the record player. The turntable began to spin, and she gently guided the needle to the vinyl, but it slid across, scratching the surface. She caught it quickly and replaced the needle at the edge. Seconds later music burst into the room. Kathleen clapped her hands in delight and started swinging her hips. Lucy joined her, wheeling Kathleen under her arm and spinning her around.

The girls danced to virtual exhaustion, playing the record over and over. By the time Lucy's mother collected their trays, they were so excited it took all her effort to contain them.

"It's rather cold in here," said Lucy's mother, her eyes narrowing as she sniffed the air. Lucy held her breath.

"We were dancing, Aunty Lily, and it got so hot, we just had to open the window." Kathleen answered with ease.

"Hmm. I see. Very well. Now, girls, it's time for

bed. Remember to clean your teeth, and then lights out."

"Yes, Mother," said Lucy.

"Remember, Lucy, Father would be very unhappy to have his sleep disturbed." Raising her brow and glancing at Kathleen, she added, "No more noise, or music, or anything else!"

As the door closed, the girls, stifling their laughter, threw themselves onto their beds. As the evening wore on, they settled into whispered hushes. Kathleen having secretly borrowed torches from her father's garage, they lay in their beds, searchlights crisscrossing the ceiling as if hunting for wartime doodlebugs, until eventually sleep won over.

****

Six forty-one a.m.

Propping herself on her elbow, Kathleen peered into the breaking light and exhaled, "Groovy."

Lucy was curled into a tight ball, blankets tucked right up around her chin, sound asleep. Pulling on her dressing gown and tiptoeing to the window, Kathleen inched the curtain open and peered out. Her eyes popped as she saw scattered ash had stuck to the frost on the window. There would be hell to pay if Lucy's parents found out.

Lucy snuffled and turned, mumbling something, while Kathleen scraped away at the incriminating evidence until it had gone.

"Phew!" Kathleen's breathing returned to normal as she gazed out the window. The frosted road sparkled; the avenue of brand-new houses spelt wealth. She stood a while watching a bird flit between manicured bushes, acknowledging this must be the perfect home for

Lucy's father, though she doubted he understood the lowly constituents of his borough. After all, he didn't seem completely in tune even with his own family, not at all like her wonderful Pops. Kathleen suddenly shivered as if someone had walked over her grave, and she decided to snuggle back under her covers until Lucy woke.

****

Seven fifty-six

"Wake up, lazy bones!" Lucy bounced up and down on Kathleen's bed, tugging at her blankets. Kathleen yanked them back, desperately trying to stay asleep.

"I don't want to, thank you very much, Luce!"

"Come on, come and see. There's a police car outside the house. Come on!" She pulled Kathleen out of bed, and they poked their heads through the gap in the curtain. Sure enough, there was a police car parked in the same spot where Kathleen's father parked only yesterday.

"You don't think anyone saw us smoking, do you?" Lucy's eyes were fearful and wide. "Or found out about the sherry?"

"Don't be stupid."

At a knock on the front door, they fell silent. There was talking. Then, to their dismay, a female began to cry.

****

Seven fifty-eight

"Mummy?" Lucy moved toward the bedroom door, listening, hesitating. Kathleen instinctively reached out a hand. Moments later, a door closed, and the sounds disappeared. The girls flung on their dressing gowns,

8

shoved feet into slippers, and crept downstairs. Even though the study door was tightly shut, they could hear muffled voices, and intermittent sobbing. Without warning, the door opened. Light flooded into the hallway. Two gargantuan uniformed policemen stepped from the study, followed by Mr. Latimer. The girls looked guilty, as if caught in the act of stealing.

"Mummy?"

"Lucy, you are to come with me." said Mr. Latimer, taking charge. Kathleen curiously noticed his voice held a warmer edge than his usual formal, clipped British.

"But…Mummy?" Lucy's eyes were large and round.

"Your mother is fine," Mr. Latimer said with finality, nervously smoothing down his moustache. "It's Kathleen they have come to see."

The girls gasped. Kathleen released Lucy's hand, shrinking against the wall. The three men filled the hallway, eyeing one another awkwardly. Mr. Latimer nodded toward his wife and propelled Lucy toward the kitchen. From along the hallway, over the radio airwaves, came the familiar voice of the newsreader delivering the eight o'clock news.

"No! Don't leave me, Lucy!" cried Kathleen, watching her friend disappear. Aunty Lily tenderly placed her arm about her and gently encouraged her into Mr. Latimer's study.

The room smelt of stale tobacco and old leather. A large desk, almost central to the room, held piles of artfully arranged paperwork. To Kathleen, it looked how a judge's court room might be. The sherry? Cigarettes? Surely not? The door closed behind them.

Aunty Lily asked Kathleen to sit in an enormous, padded chair, and as she sat, she felt it could swallow her up. The adults stood uneasily as she stared up at them with her hands clenched upon her lap.

Kathleen, scared half to death, now wondered if maybe they really did find out about the sherry, or the cigarettes. None of it made sense, though. Aunty Lily wouldn't be in such a state over that, would she?

Aunty Lily crouched beside her, eyes red, swollen with tears. When she spoke, her words came choking out in tiny pieces, unravelling themselves like a horror story.

Kathleen sat in rigid disbelief.

"Kathleen?" Aunty Lily's voice came from a distant planet. "I'm so sorry, Kathleen."

The room pressed in on her. Judgment day. Her beautiful parents were dead? Her gorgeous little baby brother Bobby, dead? Great Aunt Jane, dead?

"No! Never! Liar!" Kathleen screamed, furious Aunty Lily could say such things, oblivious her arms were flailing, striking everything and everyone. One of the policemen caught her and held her tight, his armor wrapped around her, until she could fight no more.

Aunty Lily collapsed to the floor. Kathleen folded, sobbing, weeping, disbelieving, in a heap. Eventually, using her last ounce of energy, she threw herself at Aunty Lily, crying, "Make it better, please, please, please, make it better."

And together they hugged one another on the floor of that office, in wretched misery.

Chapter 2

Jack Matthews had time to assemble his thoughts into order as he flew across the Atlantic, but the news was devastating. His mind numbed. Nothing made sense. Raking his fingers through his hair, Jack beckoned to the pretty stewardess and ordered another double whiskey, his fourth in less than two hours. He normally would be receptive to her charm as she handed him a fresh glass and nibbles, but his thoughts were elsewhere. The plan, as always, was to be there for Kathleen's birthday. But now his beloved twin sister, poor sweet little Bobby, his great pal Henry, and Great-Aunt Jane were all dead? Surely, someone had made a terrible, terrible mistake?

Seventeen hours after stepping into La Guardia airport and onto the transatlantic Pan Am flight, Jack stood on English soil, luggage in hand, with a four-hour drive ahead. He scratched his chin and went to the washroom. He would never normally allow his face to show stubble, but his five-o'clock shadow had turned ten. He wanted another drink. He thought better of it. Maybe a good strong coffee would be best, but England had no idea what a good coffee was. He swore. He sighed. The car rental arranged by his secretary would be waiting outside the terminal.

****

Exactly three hours and twenty-nine minutes later,

Jack checked his watch as he pulled into the drive. He sat there looking at Westfield, the home of his sister and brother-in-law. How he wished he had taken his time. He remained sitting in the car, engine running, heart in mouth, staring at the large, detached house, passed down by Henry's ancestors. Westfield, the complete opposite to his smart, up-to-the-minute New York apartment—which was seldom lived in and cleaned by staff he never met. Westfield was a rambling joy, in need of repair. To him, it spelt warmth, family, and love, where during the war Maury, with Henry's wholehearted agreement, took in a menagerie of evacuees and cared for the little waifs and strays until they could safely return home. They had always opened their door, and hearts, to anyone who needed shelter.

Jack wound the window down and switched the engine off. The cold morning air drifted in, along with the distant echo of cows and a barking dog.

Wafts of grief enveloped him. His eyes watered as he watched the film of early morning mist lift. A beautiful red-gold glow cast itself across the porch. The driveway circled a small patch of grass surrounded by a border filled with bushes. Even the crocuses were already nosing their way back to life. He could see the thick woody clematis growing up one side, still too early to splash color, reminding him of the photograph he took with the family, the day they planted it. Kathleen's fifth birthday. He drew a deep breath. There would never be enough air in his lungs to get rid of the feeling of utter loss.

A tractor rumbled its way up the lane and stopped outside the gate, engine rattling loud as a tank.

"That you, Jack?" The farmer's weather-worn face

peered toward the car as he shouted above the noise.

"Hello, Chaz," Jack replied, halfheartedly getting out. He recognized this would probably be the norm now, having to deal with a succession of people and their condolences. He was glad in a way to see Chaz's friendly face, but still felt awkward.

Chaz flicked off the engine; it lent a moment's unnatural silence to the air. Clambering from his seat, Chaz held out a rough hand.

"I'm so sorry. I couldn't believe it. Still can't." Shaking his head, he wrapped a strong, kindly arm around Jack's shoulder and drew him in along with the smell of good honest hard work and earth. "You know, anything we can do." Chaz hitched himself back onto the tractor and fired the engine.

"Thanks," Jack mouthed, raising a hand while also appreciating the man's brevity.

Chaz rumbled on down the lane. Jack groaned, rubbed his eyes, and stood a while longer before pulling a cigarette from its packet. Time passed before he stubbed the butt out and watched it gasp its last moment. Jack grabbed the two bottles of whiskey that had been rolling around in the passenger well. Then he found the key under the doormat and jammed it into the lock. The door flew open and slammed into the hallstand.

"Sorry!" he shouted apologetically into the empty house, and flicking the light on, he waited a moment, listening, with infantile hope his family would jump out from behind a door and shout, "Boo!"

Jack's face fell. He lit another cigarette and walked into the lounge, drinking directly from the bottle. The warm liquid eased his throat. His head fuzzed into a welcome anesthesia. The ground took on a life of its own. He searched for an ashtray, eventually pinpointed one, and managed to stub the cigarette out. The bottle fell from his hand, and he watched it roll along the floor.

"How could you do this to me? How could you leave me?" Jack staggered to his room, and he gave way to oblivion.

****

When Jack woke, he found the sun streaming in through the window. His head and eyes hurt. He stunk of travel, and booze hung heavy on a dog-hair tongue. Marveling he'd found the bedroom, he wandered into the bathroom, took a leak, and looked at himself in the mirror. A short, spikey, dark beard peered back. His eyes and cheeks were gray and hollow. He knew Maury would have told him off for getting drunk.

"Sorry, Maury," he whispered, his eyes misting, but also knowing his sister would roll her eyes at the sight, hand him aspirin, and give him a hug.

Splashing water over his face before searching for pills, he grabbed a towel and checked his watch. To his surprise, it was way past two. He went straight to the rental to gather his bags. The sun seemed exceptionally bright, almost painful. He squinted to see an enormous cat on the bonnet, sunning itself. The car door was wide open. Surely, he hadn't left it like that. Half the wildlife in the neighborhood must have had a party inside. There were feathers and droppings everywhere.

"Bloody hell! I guess this was all your doing?" he mumbled at the cat. Cat cocked his hind leg and licked its fur with a pink tongue and a carefree attitude. Jack growled. It was wasted—the cat didn't budge.

Jack trashed the kitchen in search of something to settle his stomach. He could only find tins of something or other, and milk turned lumpy green. The smell made him retch as he threw the contents down the sink. Fishing out his last cigarette, he cursed.

"Bloody stupid time to try and give up!"

A jar of coffee sat on the draining board, but the smell of chicory made him heave. He never relished it, even when cold stone sober.

"Hello, Jack, are you in there?"

A shaft of light caught the floor. He instantly recognized her voice and quickly wiped his mouth with the back of his hand. Treenie. She with the huge breasts and great butt. Jack often wondered how Chaz, the old goat, had snared her.

"Yup, here, out back."

"Oh, Jack." Chaz's wife stood there, her face glum, one hand on her hip and the other holding a basketful of goods in the crook of her arm, her hair wrapped up in a time-warp scarf of land army style.

"Treenie, I…" For lack of words, Jack threw his hands up despondently.

"Chaz said you were here." She put the basket on the floor and gave him a hug. "I guessed you wouldn't have time to think about food." She glanced at the stale loaf.

"That certainly won't do," she sniffed, put her hand deep into her dungarees pocket and, pulling out a handkerchief, blew her nose.

"I'm sorry, Jack. I try to stop myself, but I just can't. It's so bloody well awful."

Jack liked the sound of her voice. It was eloquent, even the occasional swear word sounded like she was saying grace at the dining table. He pressed his lips together to prevent his emotions from spilling out. Instead, he just nodded as she wiped her eyes.

"Poor Kathleen. I haven't seen her yet. She's with Lily Latimer, isn't she?"

Jack nodded.

"Look…" Treenie sounded businesslike, trying to control the quiver, and placed the basket on the table.

"There's a steak and kidney pie. Just needs heating through, and some other bits and pieces. I thought you might need some time to get your head around things. But make sure you come around, whenever you like. I don't want you starving!" She waggled her finger.

"You're wonderful, Treenie." Jack hugged her. He meant it. She and Chaz had been good friends to the family for years. Treenie stood a while in the embrace and pulled away, attempting a smile.

"Now, don't you get ideas. I'm a married woman." She wiped her nose, trying to laugh. "You *can* manage to warm things through, can't you?"

He nodded.

"Good. I'll let myself out, then."

****

Jack gratefully ate a slice of bread and cheese and felt a little better. He left the pie for later, when, he hoped, his stomach would feel more settled, if he could face more food. With the kitchen still in disarray, he grabbed a bottle of whiskey. His heart had sunk when Treenie mentioned Kathleen. He knew just how selfish he was being. He twisted the cap. He needed to be selfish for just a while longer.

As Jack wandered around the house filled with happy memories, it offered a sense of normality.

Cheerful black-and-white photographs of the family peered out from their frames. Boots and shoes of all sizes stood at the back door, and hats, scarves, and macs hung on a peg, giving the cruel illusion that all was well. His face screwed up. Nothing would be normal, not anymore. He swallowed a lump, and as he turned, he saw a shopping list written in his sister's distinctive loops pinned on the notice board.

"Oh, Maury." Jack took the bottle back into the lounge and sank into a chair. Just one more swig. He remembered he had something important to do, but a few moments later he passed out.

****

He was freezing. It was dark, and the front door was open. Did he leave it like that? Jack got up and shut the door, shivering, before putting the kettle on. He made himself a cup of black tea and took more aspirin. He would phone Lily. His plan was to collect Kathleen in a couple of days. Lily would help him out, especially as all the legal stuff needed to be sorted. Jack raked his fingers through his hair. It was about time he started getting their affairs in order.

The only place to find any official paperwork would be in Henry's study. His brother-in-law's filing system seemed arbitrary. Academic books filled shelves. More spilled onto the desk, and as he stepped between the miniature hypocaust of school files stacked in neat piles across the floor, he found the desk drawer was locked. There was a key in a chipped saucer, next to a tea-stained cup with dusty, green-gray mold crusting the bottom. Sitting in Henry's chair, Jack felt the full weight of the situation on his shoulders.

All at once he felt both angry and sad—his

emotions were running riot. He shouldn't have to be here. This wasn't his reality! But he knew he was being selfish. He needed to be there for his niece. Reluctantly, Jack picked up the key, and twisted it over in his hand, hoping it would open a door into another world and let him out of his misery.

Huffing, Jack grabbed the last of the whiskey and two glasses. Giving them a cursory wipe around with a tea towel, he returned to the study. He poured equal measure of the golden malt and, raising one glass to the heavens, he left the other for Henry, beside the teacup.

"Here's to you, Henry buddy." Swallowing the contents, he poured himself another.

"You were my very best friend." He took a swig. "The best husband my sister could wish for." He finished off with, "And a wonderful father!"

Jack read poetry, which he hated. Tidied the kitchen…well, kind of. And watered a dead plant. He knew it was a distraction. He scrubbed his head as he hunted around in drawers hoping to find one more cigarette, all the while knowing the real issue bothering him. Kathleen's future. Reluctantly, Jack began his search again by unlocking the desk drawer. He found nothing more than bills ready to be paid. He took out his cheque book and proceeded to pay outstanding invoices, ready to post.

In the left alcove, Jack found a large box, next to Henry's briefcase, piled high with school papers. Doubting it could hold anything relating to Kathleen or her future, he gave it a cursory check. Recently completed but unmarked homework spilled out onto the floor. Jack moaned softly, bile rising in his throat. It was more than he could bear. Henry would never get to do it now. After a glass of water, Jack made himself a cup of tea and returned to the job in hand. This was going to be much harder than he could ever have imagined.

Working deep through the night, Jack methodically sifted through volumes of paperwork until light inched its way through the curtain. Though he felt thoroughly ready for bed, he continued searching, his aim to find at least a smidgen of information about his niece.

Randomly tidying up as he went, Jack noticed an encyclopedia oddly extended over one of the top shelves. He tried pushing it back into place. It was jammed. It looked awkward. Pulling it out to check the depth of the book, Jack found a box file hidden behind. Upon the side panel was one word, capitalized in thick bold lettering:

KATHLEEN

As the hazy sunlight grew, Jack pulled the curtains to lend natural light, took the file off the shelf, sat back in Henry's chair, and looked inside. There were two envelopes. One held a copy of the adoption papers. Rubbing his head, he mused, "Strange. I thought things like this would be a bit more businesslike." He turned the pages over. The adoption papers looked more like a draft, hastily cobbled together.

The simple statement identified the adoptive parents, and the adoption was for a female infant. At the bottom of the page there were three counter signatories, the Registrar, a Miss C. Moore, Social Worker, and Mr. & Mrs. H. Gray, along with the date. Nothing indicated the birth parents or provision of an original birth certificate. Puzzling, he put it to one side and studied the next envelope that bore a London frank mark. Jack slid the contents out and began reading.

The header, gold embossed, quickly told him that it was from a firm of London-based solicitors, Gilbraith and Son. The name gave him an unexpected jolt. Jack put his hands in his head, closed his eyes, and gave a low, agonized moan. Moments later he pulled himself together to read on.

Though there were very exacting instructions contained within the document, by the time he reached the bottom of the second page, he was still none the wiser.

Chapter 3

The receptionist at Gilbraith and Son answered the telephone promptly, professionally, and after a moment, transferred the call to Mr. George Gilbraith.

"It's good of you to speak with me, Mr. Gilbraith. Please allow me to introduce myself and state my purpose."

As the solicitor listened to Mr. Matthews, he felt sickened to his stomach. A call from a relative was far from any scenario he'd considered all those years ago. Mr. Matthews's voice broke his trance.

"…You see, Mr. Gilbraith, Miss Kathleen Gray was adopted by my sister and brother-in-law some fourteen years ago. Mr. and Mrs. Henry Gray?"

The solicitor listened quietly.

"You see…" An anguished sigh across the line. "They perished in a car crash five days ago."

George Gilbraith, stunned, fell silent.

"Mr. Gilbraith?"

His hands trembled. The guilt, the shame, never far from his mind. He needed to think, he wanted to distance himself, to gather his thoughts. If only he could turn back time.

"And Miss Gray?"

He instantly regretted asking and quickly covered his query, and feigned ignorance, yet he knew every detail of the contract as if he had signed it only yesterday, not fourteen years ago. "You must be in complete shock. I am very sorry for your loss."

"Thank you, Mr. Gilbraith. At the moment my niece, Miss Gray, is staying with friends whilst I try to put the affairs in order. I hoped you may be of assistance. There is little information relating to my niece, and I wondered, as circumstances have changed, if there may be information we should be aware of?"

Moments passed before the solicitor spoke. "Mr. Matthews, I understand your concern. Sadly, as you say, circumstances have greatly changed." He composed himself. "Of course, you understand I will need to thoroughly investigate your claim and will need time to consider how to proceed."

"Absolutely. I wonder…I would like to apply for guardianship. Perhaps I could make an appointment. Maybe we could discuss this matter at the same time?"

Mr. Gilbraith carefully considered his response before agreeing and asked he make the arrangement with his secretary.

As the line went dead. George Gilbraith swiveled in his chair, reached across his desk, and lifted up a photograph. He ran his thumb across the frame, it sparkled just like the person behind the glass used to. His eyes misted as he replaced the framed picture and remembered the day his son Johnnie presented his mother with tickets to *Swan Lake*. Marjorie was delighted with her birthday gift, and how surprised they were when they were introduced to the rising star and cast afterward. Soon after, Johnnie told them he planned to marry the girl. He could easily see why his son was entranced. He too had been captivated by her charm and beauty. Why, even Marjorie reluctantly accepted the fact that the girl was more than "just a dancer." That was, until she found out about her background. George Gilbraith bowed his head in shame. Why he never had the nerve to stand up to his wife's bigotry he never knew, but he knew what sealed the deal.

"I'm so sorry, Johnnie," he whispered, "I really can't believe how I could have been so weak when you were so very brave." And for the very first time in fourteen years, he buried his head in his hands and allowed tears to fall. If only he had possessed the wisdom of King Solomon, things might have turned out very differently. Disgusted with himself and the role he played, he asked himself over and over how he could have been so blind, so stupid, and so very cruel. Slamming his fist upon the table, he cried out, "Enough!" He reached for the telephone and flicked a switch.

"Yes, sir?"

"No more calls today, Miss Fry, and please arrange a taxi." Then, more softly, with a hint of apology, "I'm sorry, Elizabeth. We will have to cancel our three thirty."

"Yes, sir." Then she whispered in return, "Are you *sure* you wish to cancel your three thirty?"

"Yes, perfectly sure, Elizabeth. I have no choice in the matter."

Chapter 4

Having confirmed his appointments with the solicitors and with Kathleen's school, Jack telephoned the Latimers with the hope of speaking directly to Lily. Nigel answered.

"My Lily is out getting some medications for Kathleen. The child is overwhelmed with grief. Of course, if you were here taking care of her, you would know."

Jack clamped his teeth shut, angry at the comment. He could never understand what Lily saw in the tactless, obnoxious turd. But what Nigel implied was true. The guilt stuck in his throat.

"I really appreciate all Lily is doing, Nigel. I really do, but if she could manage to take care of Kathleen for two more days, I will be forever in your debt. There is so much to do. It would be unkind to try to look after my niece whilst making the funeral arrangements. Just two more days is all I need."

"Very well." Nigel did have the grace to sound at least marginally embarrassed. "Two days."

Jack gritted his teeth, expressing eternal gratitude, and replaced the receiver. He needed air. He felt he was suffocating. A walk might give him the impetus he needed to make his last call.

Slipping on stout boots and pulling the Barbour off the coat peg, he remembered the last time he wore it.

The rain fell in torrents during his visit during October half term last year. They were all going stir crazy. When the rain eased, Henry insisted they go for a walk. Kathleen had climbed a tree, confident as a monkey, and looked down upon them, laughing loudly when he slid backside into a ditch, taking her father with him.

"Fuck!" he yelled at the four walls. "Didn't Henry give enough of himself in the fucking war? Didn't we all?" He felt his head would explode.

After their last mission, Henry had been left with a shattered leg and a permanent limp, and himself with deep scars on his back. He knew it could have been so much worse. But he would never forget the bravery of that young man. If it weren't for him, who knew...

Taking a deep breath, Jack stepped out into the cold, crystal-clear air.

The rear of the property was mainly laid to lawn with perennial borders. His face crumpled. How he missed his big sister. She always teased him, she being just four minutes older. He turned his gaze back to the house and tried to get rid of the long-hanging headache by rubbing his forehead as he walked around to the front of the property.

Jack knew his sister and Henry had wanted to fill the place with screaming, happy children. Maury was devastated when she was told she couldn't conceive, so they decided to adopt and were blessed the moment Kathleen arrived. Then, much later, a miracle happened. Maury fell pregnant with Bobby. Poor, dear, sweet little Bobby, an innocent taken before his little life had barely begun. Jack angrily bunched his fist and punched the wall. There couldn't possibly be a God. Breathing heavily, he looked at his bloodied knuckles.

L. B. Griffin

This type of behavior wasn't going to help Kathleen. She needed him to be strong, but at this moment all he wanted was a drink and oblivion.

A Labrador padded up to him and wiped a wet nose into Jack's hand.

"All right, Buddy?" He rubbed the dog's soft black ears as a tractor rumbled along the lane.

"Hey there, Jack!"

He raised a hand. "Hi." He hid his hand in his pocket. "I thought I'd go for a walk."

"How about coming for a brew first? Treenie will tell me off if you don't."

Jack offered a brief smile. "Okay, thanks, yes."

Chaz got back on his tractor and trundled up the lane, heading toward his farm.

Dogs barked from somewhere out the back as Jack entered the property through the five-bar gate. Tell-tale chunks of mud were left in the tractor's wake all the way to the cow shed at the rear of the property, but the front part of the grand farmhouse remained clean and welcoming. Treenie arrived at the door. "You took your time!" She held out her arms and held Jack in a warm embrace.

"Treenie," he returned, "I've been looking around Westfield. It needs quite a few repairs here and there. I guess Henry had it on his to-do list."

"Probably." Treenie smiled fondly at him. "Come on." She slipped her arm into the crook of his and guided him through to the kitchen. "I have fruit cake that needs eating before it goes stale. And the tea's been brewing for a while. I guess you like it sweet and strong 'cause that's how you and Chaz are going to get it!"

An Aga constantly kept the kitchen warm. The

kitchen floor with flagstones and a huge wooden table heaved, laden with jams, bread, butter, and the promised fruit cake. Chaz, just about to help himself to a slice, hailed their arrival.

"Glad you made it, me old mucker." Chaz spread his hands wide. "I would have to eat this lot myself if you didn't give me a hand." He patted his Buddha belly. Jack smiled.

"Sit yourself down, then," Treenie ordered.

"Thanks for this, Treenie." Jack unconsciously thrummed his fingers on the table and began sharing his experience with the solicitor.

"I'd be careful, Jack," said Chaz. "Solicitors are bloody legal bandits, in my opinion. Banks are the same. I say keep the money under the mattress, and me business to meself." Chaz brushed crumbs off his stomach and onto the floor. The Labrador instantly vacuumed them up.

"Get out of it, you greedy blighter." Chaz shoved the dog to one side with his foot. "He's getting fat. Just look at the size of him, Treenie!"

"Away with you. I like spoiling my boys." She eyed their empty plates. "I guess you could manage some more?" and she cut them each another slice without waiting for a response.

Jack smiled and realized how comfortable he felt around them and their banter. A comfortable room, with comfortable people. How he wished Eve were there with him right now. The thought brought him up short. He hadn't thought about anyone like that for a very long time.

"Well, that's me done. Work waits for no man." Chaz popped his mug into the china sink and gave his wife a wink before leaving with, "Bye, Jack, don't be a stranger."

"I'd better be off as well, Treenie. Thank you. For everything."

"Chaz is right. Don't be a stranger. Anytime you want to talk, or need a bite to eat," Treenie said giving him a hug before he left.

Jack, grateful for the short time spent in their company, was now keen to be alone out in the fresh air to blow away the cobwebs. He headed out over the ten acres of undulating land that belonged to Westfield and took the simplest route to the lake. First through West Woodlands, then over the stream via the cradle bridge, and eventually along the well-worn path to the lake where he often enjoyed fishing with Henry. As he drew closer, he could see herons having a feast, and began to run the hundred yards or so full pelt, pounding over dried earth, yelling and waving his hands at them.

"Stop stealing the fucking fish!" The offenders took off in a Jurassic flight before he could wring their necks—well, that's what he wanted to do, or at least wring someone's bloody neck for allowing his family to die. He kicked at tufted grass in fury. He hated himself. He hated what happened, and wondered how he could possibly take care of his niece? He wished he could, but his life just did not allow for children. Not ever.

The telephone rang shortly after Jack's return. It was Miss Fry. She delivered a message from Mr. Gilbraith. It was short, formal, and in no way helpful other than arranging to discuss guardianship. He replaced the receiver and scratched his head. Whatever was going on, Maury or Henry had never divulged a word.

Chapter 5

"Lily," Nigel Latimer called out. "Jack has just phoned. He'll grace us with his presence in a couple of days. Not before time, I might add." Lily arrived at the office door.

"Nigel!" Lily closed the door, hushing him. "Kathleen might hear!" She wrung her hands together. "Are you sure we couldn't offer to keep Kathleen for longer? Maybe…permanently?"

"Now, we've talked about this, Lily. It's simply quite out of the question."

With a shrug of her shoulders, she realized just how things could have been so very different if she had not played Nigel and Jack against each other all those years ago. Perhaps, then, her husband would not be such a controlling arse.

****

Two days later Jack arrived at the Latimers' house. Lily answered the door. She noticed immediately how his face looked pale, and the remembered sparkle in his eyes was now lost. Even though they had not seen one another since school days, they comforted one another, as if they had never been apart. Lily felt the hard press of muscle against her with surprise, and regret. Jack was no longer a shy, gangling youth. He was strong and—was it possible?—even more handsome.

She gently pulled away, briefly thinking about

what might have been. Here was the man, no longer a boy, with a quiet confidence and purpose, but his face still held the kindness she knew so well.

"Jack, come in. I'm so sorry. It's simply awful. Kathleen has been fretful for days, not eating, not drinking, and the medication, well, all it seems to do is make her listless." She glanced upstairs. "I thought it best to move her into the guest room. To give the girls some space, you understand?"

"It's a nightmare, Lily." Jack shook his head. "I'm so sorry, putting all this on you. It wasn't my intention, but I'm so grateful."

"I'm not complaining, Jack. You know that, don't you? I just needed you to understand Kathleen's state of mind. Besides, there's no way I would allow the authorities to get involved."

Jack spread his hands, in an act of submission. "What do I know about children? How can I possibly look after her? She needs her mother."

"I know," Lily breathed sadly. "We might be able to have Kathleen stay over some weekends. But I'm afraid, what with Nigel's work…"

"Thank you, Lily, that is really kind. I don't know how I would have coped without you."

Lily, marginally thankful for his generous words, upon seeing his expression touched Jack's arm. "I'll go get her."

****

Kathleen turned away as the door opened, and hid under the blanket. Lily lifted the cover and began stroking her hair. Dark circles ringed her eyes, and it was evident she had lost weight.

"Darling, Uncle Jack is downstairs."

"He's here?" Kathleen tried to sit, but she was like an empty shell of her former self, nothing like the robust child she once was.

"It's probably a good idea if I help. You haven't eaten lately. It's made you weak."

Kathleen looked at Lily, a wan smile on her lips.

****

Jack stood at the bottom of the stairs with undisguised shock. Reaching out, he wrapped his arms around her and held her steady. He felt the lightness of her tiny frame, her frailty, her vulnerability. They stood there and hugged one another for what seemed an eternity while Kathleen's tears fell, unchecked. Lily awkwardly suggested they go to the lounge, and Jack took the hint.

Lily decided to give them some time together but stood behind the closed door feeling like an interloper in her own home, a spy listening. She debated what to do. She heard muffled exchanges and Kathleen sobbing. Her heart went out to the child, she felt useless. How could she possibly make it all better? If only her husband were more reasonable. It might not be the best solution, but it would certainly help. Kathleen needed a family and stability. The only thing she could do right now was make tea, hot and sweet, but that simple task gave her purpose.

****

Jack loved his niece. Even though she was not Maury's natural child, there were so many similarities she could easily have been—her wild hair the shade of burnt umber, her skin almost translucent, and the tiniest of freckles sprinkled across her nose, even down to the way that nose wrinkled up when she smiled. He noticed, not for the first time, her eyes, charmingly green. He only knew of one other person who had eyes like hers, and briefly, sadly, wondered where she might be now. When Kathleen's sobs began to subside, Jack spoke to her, carefully, quietly, like an adult. After about half an hour, Lily tapped at the door with a tray of tea and sandwiches, looking flustered. Jack smiled at her encouragingly. Kathleen squished next to Jack, so close they looked glued together.

"We have decided it's time we went home."

Chapter 6

Pulling into the driveway, Jack drew a deep breath and gently caught Kathleen's hand.

"We will get through this together, Kathleen." As he opened the front door, she froze. He held onto her, a gentle reassurance, and together they stepped over the threshold.

The house was quiet. Impossibly still.

Kathleen could see the telephone table, as usual arranged with a notebook ready to take messages. Someone had been using it—there were screwed-up balls of paper on the floor, and for one heartbreaking second there was a glimmer of hope. Everyone had made an awful mistake. They were wrong. Her eyes traveled to the coat stand, and her heart gave way to another huge wave of grief. Pops' umbrella poked out from under his mackintosh almost as if he were about to bound out of the kitchen, put his coat on, and rush off to school. A wail escaped her lips.

Kathleen felt her uncle's warmth wrap about her, comfortingly, holding her close.

"It'll take a while to get used to being here." He gulped. "But if you want to leave, just say. We can always find somewhere else."

She shook her head.

"I want to be here, with you, Uncle Jack."

Jack strode into the kitchen, mumbling something

about having to clean up. Kathleen followed quickly behind, scared he would walk out the back door and leave forever, only Jack turned to her, red-faced.

"I'm sorry, I just didn't think. I guess I've been so used to others tidying up behind me." Kathleen looked about. Cupboards looked as if they had been raided, and used crockery filled the sink.

"I'll do it now." He looked disgusted with himself and turned on the tap, filling the sink with water, attempting to make amends. As he began sloshing a cloth around the cups and plonking them onto the draining board, Kathleen grabbed a tea towel and helped.

With the kitchen a little tidier, and Kathleen worn out, she sat on a chair. Jack rubbed his forehead.

"How about I put the kettle on, now we have some clean cups. I just need to do something first." He winked and hurried out of the room. Frightened he was going to disappear forever, she followed him so closely she almost tripped him over.

They were in the lounge. A pink broadsheet carpeted the room. Two empty whiskey bottles lay drunkenly on the floor, and a glass lay buddy-like on its side.

Uncle Jack's arms telegraphed wide. "I'm such a slob," he declared. When Kathleen gave him a look his sister might, he could have cried.

"No more drinking for me, my girl." He nudged Kathleen. "And none for you, either." Gathering the debris, he stuffed it into the bin, then stopped what he was doing to wrap his arms around her.

"Look. We need to work out how I can take care of you. Do you think you can help me do that?"

She rested against him. The top of her head just reached chest height. He placed a kiss on her hair. It smelt of stale shampoo and something girly. They both needed to clean up. "I'll switch on the immersion heater, maybe a good long soak and some of Treenie's home cooking? What do you think?" As Kathleen remained leaning into her uncle, she was so glad he was there—how much she loved him! She thought about their times spent together. They were legendary. Six months, a year might go by. Then he would arrive, dump his suitcase in "his" room and stay for a couple of weeks or sometimes a month, and other times, just a long weekend.

As swiftly as he came, he would disappear off to another country. Kathleen understood he worked hard for an American company, but all she really knew was that he was an engineer, could fly aeroplanes, and traveled across the world. The job obviously paid well, but she never actually knew what he did. Not properly anyway. She had never really been interested in the boring stuff.

Kathleen sighed inwardly, remembering there was always joy in their home, but when Uncle Jack arrived her mother always seemed lifted by her twin brother's appearance. She could see it in the smile in her eyes and hear the happiness in her voice. Her Pops was just the same, slapping him on the back and taking him to the pub as if he were the prodigal son. Kathleen remembered fondly the gifts her uncle brought and how he acted like a playful, naughty, brother who no one could fail to love and no one could resist. His antics often turned the house upside down with games he insisted they play inside or out in the garden, or the woods, it didn't matter.

She remembered Pops, often unable to stop himself from joining in, became worse than all of them put together. She recalled how her mother would deliver mock disapproval and then disintegrate into fits of giggles. She remembered how the geese once chased Uncle Jack into the ford and pecked him soundly on the bottom. How he acted up for days, saying he could not sit down.

Uncle Jack always teased that because of her, he was the confirmed bachelor. He said he would never be able to find anyone quite as beautiful or as smart. In Kathleen's heart that made Uncle Jack even more special.

"We will be there for one another. Like the musketeers, all for one, and one for all."

Kathleen nodded as tears began to trickle down her cheek. He'd read aloud the abridged version of the musketeers' story when he last visited. They'd all sat in the lounge, Bobby curled up with her mother, sucking on a bottle of milk. Her father, with his arm draped around the back of the sofa, and herself, on the floor, propped between Pops' legs. The story had been easy to visualize—the glamour of Paris, and handsome men swashbuckling their way through life. Not only did her uncle have a great storytelling voice, but the sheer romance and excitement of it all enthralled her. Kathleen snatched for air between sobs, nodding, and repeated, "All for one, and one for all."

Chapter 7

The day was windy and gray. Mourners arrived in flapping black coats, like ravens circling death. The family were well known, popular, and the church was full to bursting; the congregation vied for space at the back and spilled out the doorway.

Lucy and Jack flanked Kathleen like her protectors. Lucy held her hand, and Jack pressed close to her as they walked down the middle aisle to their seats. Kathleen's eyes were instantly drawn to the tiny box. She nearly collapsed.

When the congregation were seated, the vicar began his sermon. Kathleen buried her head in her hands and wept. She couldn't imagine her baby brother in that tiny box, or any of her family encased in coffins. It was just too cruel. Too much to bear.

Lucy stayed close, comforting, pressing a handkerchief her way. Kathleen caught the quiver as her uncle sang the hymns, and he lightly touched her shoulder as he left the pew to give the eulogy.

Kathleen listened as he described their lives. He stood at the lectern reminding everyone of the love and fun the family shared. His tribute was beautiful, just like him. He even managed to make the congregation smile and laugh. She found it difficult to look at her uncle for long. He was so handsome, so strikingly like her mother.

When he returned, she saw his eyes were moist. Kathleen stood up, took his hand, and held it tight in unspoken solidarity.

Chapter 8

Treenie called two days after the funeral, bringing homemade and all manner of wonderful, farm-fresh foods. They were in the kitchen, just about to prepare a meal. Jack looked worriedly at Treenie, and she stepped in.

"Why don't I give you a hand, Kathleen." She grabbed an apron. "Seems Uncle Jack needs some lessons." She found a couple of sharp knives, and with a little light banter they all finished the job together.

****

Jack deliberately avoided them being inside for long. He was thoughtful, not demanding of his niece. He made sure Kathleen got up every morning at a reasonable hour and structured her day. When the weather was right, he showed her how to use his camera, and how to search out interesting shots, find the best angles, and best frame a picture. They pulled weeds, flew kites, and ate meals out in tiny cafés far from home. Jack knew his cooking was abysmal, and in fairness, Kathleen's heart for eating was limited. Treenie called, inviting them around, but understood they could not face extra company, so instead she brought homemade casseroles, pies, bread, and cakes.

Jack planned to go through the rest of Henry and Maury's personal effects when Kathleen went back to school, but it was evident that the notion of her returning to school was becoming problematic.

They were in the kitchen, and Jack was putting the potatoes on the boil. He glanced across at Kathleen, who was standing, staring into space, carrot in one hand, knife in the other. Her face probably bore the same expression as his own, but he could not begin to imagine her inner turmoil. How was she going to cope? He felt so desperately ill-equipped, not remotely parent-like. How could he take care of his fourteen-year-old niece in balance with his hectic work schedule? He could not think of a good answer. Every time they spoke of normality, Kathleen resisted. He knew the job of looking after her would be difficult but had not envisaged any of the reality. Soon, he thought, soon he would have to take control.

On the tenth day, as they sat together on the floor, warming themselves in front of the fire, burning bread on toasting forks, Jack broached proposals for her future, hoping, praying, she would understand.

Kathleen sat there, propped against the sofa, the long-handled fork in her hand, a plate by her side, silently staring into the flames. Testing the slice of bread for crispness, Kathleen pulled the toast off and put it on the plate ready to butter. Her eyes were glistening as she turned to look at him.

"I think I'm ready to go into my mother's sewing room. Will that be all right?"

"Of course." His voice warmed to the theme. "Would you like me to come with you?'

"No, thank you, Uncle Jack. I would just like some time alone. Is that all right?"

"Kathleen…" He smiled kindly. "Together, alone, whatever you need. Yes?" Jack watched as she left the room, and held his breath.

He knew this was a huge step, an important step. Maury and Kathleen shared a love of sewing. Maury excelled in her work and had built a good business from early on, and Kathleen was her little rising star. He could only hope this would be a start of the healing process. For a second, he pondered, wondering whether he should follow, to make sure she was okay. A few minutes went by, and he decided to respect her wishes. If Kathleen needed him, he would only be a shout away. Then an idea sprang to mind. He went straight to the telephone to tap up a few favors.

****

In the most precious room of the house, the place only she and her mother shared, Kathleen imagined her mother was out on a job, measuring up the next order. It was a wonderful room, and like the rest of their home, well ordered.

Remnants of material were diligently folded into appliqued boxes. Bales of cloth were stored neatly on racks. Patterns, homemade and shop bought, were stored in cleverly disguised shoe boxes. A treadle sewing machine sat in one corner. Her mother swore by the consistency of the Singer's stitch and would not purchase another. The large cutting table with walk-around space held drawers stocked with tape measures, needles, pins, pincushions, scissors, and cottons. There were two comfortable rocking chairs facing one another, giving them a chance to chatter as they worked.

A manikin, an important extravagance her mother had purchased for two shillings from the rag-and-bone man, stood next to the fabrics. Upon it was one of

Kathleen's creations. A full-length silk gown made from half a parachute and almost complete. Kathleen stroked the material and studied the design. How she loved the feel of silk. Not only did it feel wonderful, but it hung beautifully. It was going to be stunning. Her lips pinched to parenthesis as she remembered the day she haggled with the market trader, knowing her mother looked on, proudly watching the exchange, as she eventually wore the poor woman down and bought the complete parachute for half the original price.

As they left the market, they discussed how they could make two garments from the material. One would be a beautiful wedding dress, and the rest would be for her. Kathleen's mother knew she dreamed of being a dress designer, working for the stars of Pinewood or, just as fantastic, Hollywood, and she always encouraged her ambitions.

Kathleen sat absorbing the stillness and peace, waiting—praying—for her mother to rush into the room with an exciting new order and start discussing how to complete the gown. She exhaled and stared out the window, not seeing—angry, hurt, furious, hating the world. *Why did they have to die? It just wasn't fair.*

Losing her wonderful adoptive family had brought unimaginable grief, but soon she would be facing another loss. Her beloved uncle would be moving on. His life was not here, with her, and whilst there was never any doubt how much she was loved by her parents, there were always those unanswered questions about her natural mother. Now, with her family gone forever, she could never ask, and as the sense of loss, abandonment, and rejection grew deeper, it began to envelop her very soul.

****

The girls in the playground watched in stunned silence as Jack Matthews strode toward the teacher on yard duty. Everything about him oozed film star—his looks, the cut of his suit, and something about his assured manner.

"Can I help you, sir?" The teacher on yard duty fawned over him, acting like an infatuated schoolgirl. When he introduced himself, she gathered her wits and summoned the Head girl who swung her hips seductively and flashed conceited smiles at open-mouthed pupils as she showed Jack to Miss Wray's office.

Jack glanced about the room. Educational books lined the walls, interspersed with framed photographs of past students with cups, shields, and medals. He held out his hand with a light smile—his niece had described the headmistress perfectly. A plump, aging spinster sat behind a huge desk. She stood as he entered. Her glasses dangled from a cord to her breast-line as she held out her hand.

"Mr. Matthews." Miss Wray said kindly, "This is a very distressing time for all concerned." She encouraged him to sit. He found himself pleasantly surprised at the sensitive way Miss Wray conducted their meeting. She provided an opportunity to discuss boarding school and a way to gently introduce Kathleen to the idea. "It would be helpful to show your niece around the dormitories first, meet some of the gals, whom I am sure she will already know. Then I would suggest she stay for a weekend or two, to get her used to the idea, before moving in more permanently?"

"That sounds very reasonable, Miss Wray, I feel

any change is going to be extremely difficult. She is so fragile right now."

"Quite." Miss Wray paused briefly. "It's good to know you understand these things. Mrs. Fuller, the housemistress, takes all the gals under her wing. I really couldn't think of a better person to look after your niece whilst you're away. I could introduce you to her today if you wish?"

Jack instantly liked Mrs. Fuller, a pleasant, matronly woman in the kindest, sparkly-eyed way. He could almost imagine his young niece being cuddled by her when feeling low.

"So many children with so many challenges," said Mrs. Fuller as she showed him through the small homey dormitories lined with three beds either side. "We arrange the girls by age, six girls to each dorm, and each room is allocated an older girl who is their 'go to.' You see, we like to encourage the girls to look out for one another. They may spot things that one might otherwise miss."

Jack liked the idea of the girls taking care of one another. He noted the rooms were well lit and decorated to a good standard and smelt fresh. Each bed had been personalized with a little bedside table, a lamp, and a teddy bear or doll sitting on the bed. Though the room was empty, as school was taking place, Jack got a sense of wellbeing, and that made him begin to feel more at ease. It was going to be difficult enough to leave Kathleen, but if he knew she would be taken good care of, it would help.

"And here is our sick bay." The door, painted in white with a red cross upon it, was closed. Mrs. Fuller knocked and waited for a reply and then made the introductions. Nurse Gibbons had been tidying her room and immediately held out her hand at the introduction. "Nurse takes on all the medical treatments and other ailments that girls might need help with." Mrs. Fuller gave him a knowing look, and Jack, for the first time in his adult life felt a little embarrassed. Jack's first impression of Nurse was a no-nonsense type—her smartly starched uniform appeared to reflect her personality. Surely, he hoped, that could only be a good thing. Kathleen would need a balance with the firmer touch. They returned to Miss Wray's office, and he stood a while staring out the window before sitting.

"So, Mr. Matthews, have you drawn your conclusion?"

"From what I've seen, I have to say I am impressed. Thank you. Of course, I prefer to discuss it with my niece and put the suggestion of weekend trials to her first. Also, I would like to know if there are any conditions. For example, if I wanted to take Kathleen on holiday, or see her at the weekends?"

Miss Wray adjusted her spectacles, her voluminous breast-line inching a gap off her desk.

"Of course, I would not expect the gal to miss her education. But if you let us know in advance, we can prepare her with the appropriate clothes, et cetera, et cetera." Miss Wray waited for his reaction, which seemed suitably positive, and then she became more businesslike. "There is of course the topic of the fee."

"I can see no problem, Miss Wray. You have been most helpful providing those details, and as discussed, I can arrange to pay a year in advance, if that would be helpful." The issue of finance was of no importance. He could easily afford twice the price and would, if it meant Kathleen was happy and given good support and the right amount of care. "So, to the issue of Easter, I have arranged a trip for my niece during the break. Something I hope she will enjoy, and if it goes well, I hope thereafter to return to work. As said, I'm based in America. Hopefully, I will be able to visit in between." Jack looked at the headmistress. "Thank you once again for all your help. I will consult with Kathleen and be in touch shortly."

Chapter 9

Two weeks on, Kathleen arrived for her first stayover. Mrs. Fuller, the housemistress, welcomed her warmly, suggesting they go straight to her dormitory. Kathleen was secretly amazed to find her uncle right behind them and felt heartened; he appeared every bit as nervous as she did.

"It's marvelous to have you back, Kathleen," said Mrs. Fuller with a warm welcome. Kathleen smiled graciously and followed Mrs. Fuller out of the room. Her uncle trotted quickly behind them, and Kathleen felt another sense of relief that he was not going to dump her, yet. They arrived at the dormitory. The curtains had been drawn back, letting in ample light, and three girls were lined up in a row by the door as they arrived.

"You obviously have a talent," said Meg, who introduced herself first.

"Why do you say that?" Kathleen asked, glancing over the basic coverlets and thinking of her own room back home and the pretty embroidered bedcover she had completed.

"Simple. Anyone who stays in this dorm is talented." Meg grinned. "Beth is an absolute whiz on the piano—we all think she'll be a concert pianist one day, don't we, girls?" They all nodded enthusiastically, but Beth just smiled shyly. "I'm not that good, but I do enjoy playing. Do you play piano, Kathleen?"

"Chopsticks, and badly." She gave a flicker of a smile, then a flash of memory caught her breath. Her father first taught her the basic tune when she was around six or seven, and they had laughed themselves silly at their mistakes.

"Perhaps we could play together and have some fun then?" Kathleen slowly nodded, but her attention had already been drawn to a petite girl who looked, at most, ten. Puzzled, as it was a senior school, her heart went out to her. She looked so very vulnerable and wondered why her parents saw fit to board her.

"This is Amy," said Meg. "This is Amy's first term with us. She is incredibly talented. Her artwork speaks for itself." Meg proudly pointed toward Amy's wall over her bed. It was covered in superb images of setting sunsets and people in cafés.

"They're wonderful, Amy. I noticed them straight away. They brighten up the whole place."

"Thank you, Kathleen," said Amy, immediately warming to her.

"I believe we can leave Meg to show Kathleen around, don't you think, Mr. Matthews?" Jack glanced at Mrs. Fuller, then looked to his niece waiting for permission. She nodded, but felt bereft. Another loss was imminent.

"Perhaps I could collect you around four tomorrow, what do you say?" Uncle Jack smiled, conveying safety and reassurance.

Meg instantly hooked her arm into Kathleen's and encouraged the other girls to join them.

"First, we will find Cook." She looked over her shoulder at Mrs. Fuller and smiled. The girls giggled as they left the dormitory. Meg grinned from ear to ear, and once out of earshot said, "Cook is the best person in the world, especially if you want to have a midnight feast."

"Midnight feast?"

"Yes, it's ours and Cook's little secret. We've never been caught so far, but we have to be careful," and as the girls talked animatedly about their little tricks, Kathleen's mind churned over what would now have to be her new, hateful, unwanted life.

Chapter 10

Her first full day back, Lucy met Kathleen at the school gates. Kathleen spied a gaggle of girls trying hard not to drool at her handsome uncle.

"You may need to do a Roger Bannister," she told him.

"Pardon?"

Kathleen sighed. "You'll have to run the four-minute mile? I think you're about to get mobbed."

"What on earth do you mean?"

"Goodbye, Uncle Jack." Exasperated but loving his modesty, she gave him a hug. Then, with a backward glance, one arm linked in with Lucy's, she waved, and he watched them climb the front steps to school.

"Bogey has asked to see you before first period." Lucy heaved the school entrance door open, exposing a long, tiled hallway the color of dark chocolate. She sniffed. The hallway smelt strange. Yes, it still stunk of sweaty socks and toasted buns, with a hint of disinfectant. It instantly reminded her this world had not changed. She hesitated. Lucy encouraged her forward.

The door to their form room was ajar. Bogey Edmonds looked over the top of round spectacles, a loop of cord attached to them. Her cameo brooch was pinned at neck height, centered. They caught her just as her finger inched toward her nose. No, nothing had changed there either.

Wooden desks with filled inkwells formed orderly queues of four lines, six deep. The blackboard highlighted the date, scratched out in chalk, and on her desk a dusty blackboard rubber sat in line with two new pieces of white chalk and one worn down to a nub. No, definitely nothing had changed there either.

"Good morning, Miss Gray. Please close the door behind you, Miss Latimer."

The instruction could be misinterpreted without being rude, so Lucy stayed close. Miss Edmonds turned her attention back to Kathleen.

"Miss Gray, I'm sure you're aware that you've missed a great deal of education whilst you've been away, and what with examinations upon us you will need to be on top of your game. I suggest every evening is set aside for revision and weekends are spent in the same vein." She reached for a folder, and then with a light cough said, "I've taken time out of my busy schedule to ensure that you have the opportunity to catch up." She paused the briefest of moments. "You could do well if you set your mind to it. Focus. Try to put the recent events of your life to the back. Move on. Make your parents proud."

Kathleen, trembling with rage, stormed out. How could Bogey possibly understand? Her parents were dead. They would never know if she did well or not. Not at school. Not in life. Not ever! What was the point?

"Kathleen!" Lucy quickly caught up. "Don't take any notice of the old fart. We all know she's bonkers."

"Oh, Luce. It's as if nothing has changed. But it bloody well has!" Kathleen furiously blinked back tears.

Lucy gave her hand a comforting squeeze.

"I guess I'll get detention now, not that I care!"

"Come on, we're a team, remember?"

Kathleen dragged her fingers across her cheek, wiping away salty drops, shaking her head, knowing in her heart another loss was imminent. "Yes. But it's just not that easy."

****

At the weekend, Jack collected Kathleen from school. He could see all was not well. Worriedly opening the car door, she slid in and sat in stony silence all the way home. He knew he had to be more than just an uncle. His niece was grieving. He had to be strong, calm, patient.

"Come with me." He directed her to the kitchen. "I think you're going to have to show me how to peel a spud. Look at the mess I've made." Kathleen took one look at the potatoes the size of marbles, and her shoulders shook. Then she giggled. Such a simple, normal, stupid reaction meant so much to him, relief spread across his face.

"How big were they to start with, Uncle Jack?"

"Ooh, I'd say…" He expanded the distance between the palms of his hands, until they measured the width of a table. Kathleen shook her head.

"Here. Mum always uses this." She picked up a weathered paring knife, her eyes traveling over the blade as if for the first time. She drew a deep breath and looked him straight in the eye.

"Mum *used* this knife. It *was* her favorite."

A lump caught in his throat. She sounded so much like Maury.

"My sister was a sensible woman, that's for sure. I'll keep practicing until I get it right."

"Better still, Uncle Jack, do them in their jackets. You can't go wrong." Kathleen gave him a half-hearted nudge.

"Smart Alec." He nudged her back, amused at her wit. Pouring his love out, he gave her a cuddle.

"All for one, and one for all?"

"All for one, and one for…" Kathleen's voice trailed off into a world only known to herself, and Jack could see the distant, sad, lonely child emerging again, and prayed his little treat would be appropriate.

****

Lily and Treenie jointly agreed to call on Jack. They wanted to give him a little moral support, especially as Lucy reported to her mother some of the difficult moments Kathleen encountered at school. They found Jack in the front garden, a saw in one hand and wood clamped in a work bench. He was sticky with sweat. His hair was ruffled, and the front of his shirt had become trapped half in and half out of his trousers. Clearly pleased by Lily and Treenie's arrival, he immediately downed tools. "Sorry, about the state I'm in. I wasn't expecting visitors."

"Away with you," said Treenie. "A bit of honest-to-goodness hard work doesn't do any harm. Anyway, we just popped over with cake to see how things are going."

"Perfect timing as always, Treenie. Cake sounds just the ticket. I was feeling rather peckish. I'll put the kettle on."

They sat around the kitchen table waiting for the kettle to boil, whilst Treenie cut up large wedges of fruit cake and Lily began discussing school.

"I know this may sound rather glib, Jack, but time is a great healer."

"Absolutely," Treenie readily agreed.

Jack picked up a dessert spoon and stirred the teapot.

"I went to London a couple of days ago," he began. "You remember I said, Treenie? The solicitor involved in Kathleen's adoption."

"Yes, I remember."

Jack exhaled. "You know, I didn't say, but I couldn't believe it when I met him. Gilbraith, that is. The shock of it. I just had to ask." The women sat there politely waiting for him to continue. "When Mr. Gilbraith kindly showed me a photograph of his son, I knew I was right." Jack looked between the women, a mixture of sadness and pain stamped across his face. "I still can't believe the coincidence."

He rubbed his forehead. "His son, Ginger Gilbraith, was in our squadron. A new recruit, ready to start out in life. Full of vim and vigor." Jack's mouth drew into a pencil thin line. "Because of his unwavering bravery he saved my life and Henry's too." The women gasped. He shook his head. "It's such a small world, isn't it? Who would have believed it, me turning up at his father's firm?" He stared at the table before looking back up. "It was good to talk to Mr. Gilbraith. In a strange way I think it helped us both a little bit, to talk about the past."

They sat a while before Lily broke the silence. "Does Kathleen know that you plan to leave for America after Easter?"

"Yes. Only in general terms, though." He looked

bothered. "I wonder, might I have an opinion? You see, I've arranged a bit of a treat for Kathleen before I leave for America. I'm hoping it'll give us a chance to talk properly, and to get her away from the reality of here…" Treenie and Lily listened expectantly.

"I don't know if I'm doing the right thing, but I've called up a favor." This time he gave a half-hopeful smile. "I'm taking her to Paris, for a short stay."

"Paris?" Lily sounded astonished but enthused.

"Yes. A friend works at one of the big fashion houses there and has agreed to give us a tour." Lily and Treenie were astounded.

"Oh, my goodness, Jack! How fabulous! Kathleen will love it!" said Lily.

"You don't think it's a silly idea? You see, since I got my secretary to book everything, I've begun to doubt myself."

"It's a simply wonderful idea," said Lily wistfully.

"Well, that makes me feel a whole lot better." He looked thoughtful.

Treenie had begun refolding the ribbon of scarf taken off her head. "It's a brilliant idea, Jack. Kathleen will most certainly love it." She tied the scarf tight, cupped her jaw line, and lifted her shoulder in a Marilyn Monroe pose. "What I know about style is no one's business. Boo-boo-be-do!" Treenie sang, smiling widely and winking at Jack. "Kathleen will be in her element, trust me."

Jack winked back, a look of relief upon his face. He took a sip of his tea and prayed Kathleen's reaction would be just as positive.

"Well, not a word, then, please. I don't intend to tell her about the fashion house until we're there."

Chapter 11

Easter half term, 1954

Kathleen arrived at the bottom of the stairs nervously holding a small leather suitcase in her hand. Jack looked at her, astonished.

"Will I do, Uncle Jack?"

"Will you do! I don't think I've ever seen you wear anything other than school clothes or dungarees before. You look...beautiful."

Kathleen blushed, showing off her outfit by parting her coat to reveal a shift dress with its reverse colors of green, with a blue trim.

"What do you think?"

"I think the Queen would approve. Did you know she's off on her maiden visit to Australia? Where exactly did you buy your outfit? Maybe I should pass on the name of your dressmaker?"

"Buy it?" she scoffed, but at the same time delighted. "The material came from Mrs. Mortimer's, and Mummy..."

For one happy moment she forgot the shocking truth. Tears stung her eyes, and guilt betrayed her lips.

"It's all right. You're allowed to be happy," Jack soothed. "We will never forget. Not ever."

Kathleen sniffed back a tear.

"Well, madam, Paris is waiting. I just hope they are

ready for you."

****

Paris greeted them like old friends, bathing them in the golden glow of early morning sun. Jack hailed a taxi and quickly gave instructions to the driver while Kathleen, mesmerized, sat next to him in the back seat. She leaned across, whispering, worried, "He's a terrible driver, Uncle Jack. Are we safe?"

"Don't fret, he knows what he's doing." He patted her hand trying to reassure her.

"But they all seem a little crazy, and they drive on the wrong side of the road."

Jack laughed, and began to give her a potted history of Paris, his aim to take her mind off things as they sped along the huge expanse of road leading toward the Arc de Triomphe to join the ever-swirling tide of cars.

Not much later they safely pulled up outside a grand hotel close to the Louvre.

"Monsieur Matthews, Mademoiselle," greeted the concierge, then pinged a small brass bell on the desk. "It is a privilege to have you return so soon, Monsieur."

A bellboy, in a smart blue uniform and wearing a pillbox hat, arrived and almost clicked his heels before he escorted them to their rooms.

"You're likely to catch a fly, young lady." Jack gently bumped against her.

"Surely this can't be just for me?" Kathleen stared at the suite. "It's massive!"

"I'll be right across the hallway," replied Jack, as he tipped the bellboy. "I need to freshen up. But perhaps"—he checked his Rolex—"we can meet up and take in some of the sights. Let's say one hour?"

"Uncle Jack?"

"Yes?"

"I don't think I need to go anywhere else. This room, all of it, it's wonderful."

"Trust me, Miss Gray. I know you of old. Ten minutes from now, you'll be bored and climbing down the drainpipe."

Her mouth turned up at the edges. She hugged him tightly.

"Uncle Jack?"

"Yes?"

"Thank you. Really, thank you."

Once alone, Kathleen investigated her suite. Fresh flowers filled a low circular table flanked by two armchairs facing toward French windows which opened out onto a balcony and overlooked the museum. The door from the lounge led to the bedroom. She found to her sheer delight a four-poster bed and immediately flopped onto it and began angel-winging her arms across silky satin sheets.

Moments later, she rolled over and went through to the next room. She couldn't believe it—a bathroom all to herself? Thick, luxurious bath sheets with delicately packaged products placed on the lip of the bath. Turning on the taps, tempted by the choice, she added half a sachet of rose crystals and watched them cascade into the water.

As the room began to steam, Kathleen laid her clothes on the bed, glad she'd listened to Treenie's advice, and, knowing they were going out, placed a pencil and small sketchbook into her bag. Now with the bath filled, she dipped a toe to check the temperature. Perfect. Then after finding a head wrap, she slid into the soft, fragranced waters.

Not once had her mind strayed far from her family, and even enveloped in the comfort of warm water, tears fell. She whispered, "I love you, Mummy. I love you, Pops, and I love you, Bobby. I know the angels will take good care of you. Wherever I am, and wherever you are, and however old I grow, I will never forget you."

Chapter 12

They were walking through the charming Gothic quarter of Paris with its myriad of streets, small quaint restaurants, and boulangeries when Jack suddenly pulled her in tight.

"Stay close!"

"Why? Is it dangerous here, Uncle Jack?" She clutched at his sleeve.

"Yes. French men are particularly dangerous, especially around beautiful young women." He waggled his eyebrows at her.

"Stop teasing!" She relaxed and grinned.

"Seriously. Haven't you noticed the Parisian wives tugging their husbands in the opposite direction when they see you? Trust me, they *are* dangerous!"

"Don't be silly." Kathleen flushed deep red, giggling. He smiled but knew he was right. His lovely young niece would break men's hearts soon enough. Kathleen quickly became distracted as they walked by a restaurant, its doors open, and a welcome aroma drifted on the air. She sniffed. "Gosh I can smell fresh bread, but there's something else I don't recognize. Goodness, its strong!"

"It's most probably the cheese you can smell, or maybe the garlic, they love the stuff, so do I, though it's not so wonderful on the breath…"

"Look, Uncle Jack!" Kathleen pointed excitedly

toward a young artist. Upon his head he wore the fabled beret, and as he crouched beside a box of open paints his long gray overcoat caressed the cobbles. A couple of paces away stood an easel and a painting of the cobbled street, a wonderful replica of the area.

"May I ask the artist a question?" she asked. Jack nodded, gesturing her forward.

"Look, Uncle Jack, can you see the artist's brush strokes? There are thousands of them, like tiny perpendicular flicks." She stood back at a distance. "It's simply stunning!" Her eyes shone in appreciation at the artist's skill. Jack listened with interest, not only pleased that his niece was able to complete her exchange in French with a quiet confidence, but also with her interest in the arts.

"Do you wish for the painting?" asked the artist casually as he continued easing paints onto his palette.

"I wish…" She stopped. "No. But thank you."

"You like me to paint you, no?"

Kathleen blushed and caught hold of her uncle's arm, ready to move on.

"What did I tell you?" Jack whispered, once out of earshot. "You can't trust a Frenchman. Give them an inch, and they'll take a mile."

Kathleen gave him a poke. "Don't be daft." She laughed, but it betrayed her pleasure.

"Right, then, young lady, next stop the Eiffel Tower. I hope you're wearing sensible shoes, my girl, because we are walking the seven hundred and four steps to the second floor."

"Easy." She scoffed. "Isn't there a third floor?"

"I think you will be satisfied with just the two. The steps are quite an experience, and then of course there is the view."

Kathleen was thrilled as they began their ascent and she timed the walk, pushing Jack to move more quickly.

"The caging around the stairs seem so flimsy, Uncle Jack. Do you think anyone's ever fallen off?" She had been looking at the images of the elegant ladies in long flowing gowns with bustles that did the same walk all those years ago.

"I'm not sure. Maybe we'd best keep to the middle?" He winked. "Come on. We've a challenge to beat. Fifteen minutes, wasn't it?"

"Fourteen minutes and twenty-one seconds!" Kathleen announced when they reached the second platform and dragged a puffing Jack over to the side to look at the view.

"My goodness, Uncle Jack! Look at those people— they look just like ants." He nodded, amused. "Why, from this height even the buildings look like miniature models. This is amazing!" Jack smiled, watching her flit between other tourists to look over the sides, unable to contain herself.

"I guess this wasn't such a bad idea, then?" Jack asked, pulling her back and pointing out places of interest.

"You are joking, aren't you? This is absolutely incredible."

****

They took a break on the lawns below, and while Kathleen began sketching, Jack took shots of her against the backdrop of the Tower, until his stomach gurgled.

She chuckled. "Are you hungry, by any chance?"

"Starving! Come on. Let's go get something to eat."

Jack took her to visit his favorite brasserie, where the terracing provided a wonderful view of the Seine. He took obvious pleasure in explaining the simple menu, then relaxed back into his chair and watched Kathleen as she began to sketch again. Her hair kept falling across her face, and she kept scrubbing it back behind her ears. The action illuminated her youth and innocence, but he knew it hid depths of sadness. He understood her pain and meant it when he said, "All for one, and one for all," and hoped she would have the maturity to adjust to the plans he was forced to make. He wanted to talk to her about her future, but he suppressed the notion. The timing wasn't right. She stopped sketching, turning to him, and gave a half sigh.

"I was thinking how Mummy would have loved all of this." She batted away tears and reached for a handkerchief.

Jack nodded, and squeezed her hand, having thought the same. He allowed himself to think about Eve, his girlfriend. It would have been good if she could be here, to support Kathleen, or, at the very least, get to know her.

"You're right." He coughed the emotion away. "Anyway, I'd better not take all the credit. All the hard work is mostly down to my secretary, Gracie. She's a marvel."

"Well, if she's not already married, and Gracie is sweet and pretty, you should marry her straight away."

Jack laughed, deep, rumbling, and infectious.

"Gracie is pretty, but she's about to marry one of my buddies. I don't think Eve or my buddy would take too kindly if I made a move on her."

Kathleen suddenly brightened.

"Who's Eve, Uncle Jack?"

His cheek twitched. Her name had unintentionally slipped out.

"Um, I guess you could call her my girlfriend. A New Yorker. You'd like her."

"A girlfriend, eh?" Kathleen elbowed him.

"Maybe I'll tell you about her another time."

Kathleen took the hint. "Well, do you think your friend would mind if we bought Gracie a present, as a thank-you for all her hard work? I have a little pocket money."

"I think that's a marvelous idea. In fact, how about getting something for your friend Lucy, and for Aunty Lily and Treenie, at the same time? They've all been so exceedingly kind."

"Oh, yes, please."

He eyed her plate. "Well, young lady, you'll have to finish your meal first."

Kathleen didn't need telling twice and ate every single morsel.

Chapter 13

Stepping out of the taxi and into Boulevard Haussmann, Kathleen gasped. Her artistic interest was piqued by the fantastic window displays. By the time her uncle led her into Galleries Lafayette, she was beside herself. The store was enormous, stylish, nothing like she had ever seen back home in the backwaters of Somerset. Her eyes immediately traveled keenly up the wide sweeping staircase, then to a stunning stained-glass domed ceiling. She began to dreamily imagine a hundred debutantes with flowing gowns descending the stairs, with one of her creations as the centerpiece.

"Catching flies again?"

"Sorry." Kathleen quickly clamped her mouth shut.

"Do you think you may be able to find something appropriate here?"

Kathleen nodded enthusiastically. "Tell me a little bit more about Gracie."

"Like what?"

Kathleen exhaled. "Well, for example, what color hair does she have, and what color clothes does she favor?" Jack scratched his head in amusement. "Um…"

By the time Kathleen poked and prodded him for every little detail and examined every counter for the perfect gift, Jack was completely bemused, and exhausted.

"Are you happy with your selections now,

mademoiselle?" He looked worn out. Kathleen tutted as he paid the assistant.

"We have to get it right, Uncle Jack. I just hope the scarves meet with everyone's approval." Kathleen stifled a yawn through a smile, watching the assistant wrap the gifts in wonderful packaging.

"Sorry."

"No need. I'm ready to call it a day. I never knew how hard it would be to select a few gifts!" His eyes twinkled. "Just kidding." He nudged her. "Tomorrow is another day. I need you to be ready by nine sharp tomorrow morning. Not a moment later. Agreed?"

"Of course, Uncle Jack, you know me."

"Hmm. That's what I'm afraid of."

Once they were safely back at the hotel, Kathleen promised fervently she would be ready by nine the following morning. Then, throwing herself onto the bed, for the first time in ages she slept soundly.

Chapter 14

Jack deliberately studied his watch as Kathleen arrived for breakfast. He knew his niece was a terrible timekeeper, and pointedly tapped the face of his Rolex, with a look of disappointment.

"I'm not sure we can make it now. I said nine o'clock sharp. Not nine thirty-two."

"I'm really sorry, Uncle Jack. Really, I am. I slept so well…" She hungrily reached for a croissant and took a sip of hot chocolate. "But what is it we can't make, exactly?" Jack pointed to the chocolatey moustache on her upper lip before answering. She sheepishly took the hint, dabbing her mouth with a napkin.

"I have a friend"—he gave her a sideways glance—"who has kindly agreed to give us a private tour of the fashion house where she works. I don't suppose you've heard of…" As the name left his lips, Kathleen jumped out of her chair, nearly knocking it over in her disbelief.

"What! I mean, pardon? Really? You're joking!"

Jack put his hands up.

"No. I'm not joking." Glancing around the room, he added, "Please, sit quietly. The other guests look as if they are about to have a nervous breakdown." Kathleen immediately returned to her seat and sat on her hands.

"I don't understand."

"Why? Would you be interested *if* we could still make it?"

"Interested! Seriously? Of course, I would!"

Jack raised a brow. "Well, maybe we could grab a taxi…just in case…"

"Oh, my goodness. Really. Now? Am I dressed appropriately?" Her face fell. "*Can we* still go?"

Jack shook his head in amusement. "What you're wearing is much more acceptable than…"

"Acceptable than what? Tell me!"

"Those awful dungarees you're so keen on."

"Uncle Jack! As if I would."

He glanced at his watch. His notion of getting her to breakfast earlier than needed had been a sensible move.

"You've precisely fifteen minutes to make sure you have everything you need, and don't you dare be late!"

****

As the taxi drew up, Kathleen noticed a petite young woman standing outside the huge doors. It struck her immediately how model-like she looked. Her skirt nipped in at the waistline, and full shoulders created the illusion of impossible proportion so very different to the hangers-on of utilitarian clothing from the war years. It was then she realized the woman was smiling, and not just at anyone, but at her uncle. She watched shyly as they gave one another an affectionate hug and kissed cheeks in the French traditional way.

Jack turned to Kathleen.

"Kathleen, this is my good friend Mademoiselle Françoise Pavey."

"It is good to meet you at last, Kathleen. I have

heard so much about you." A light frown crossed her brow. How well did her uncle know Françoise, exactly? He'd never mentioned her before.

"I love your outfit. Where did you get this?" Françoise asked, with obvious interest, but Kathleen remained unusually lost for words.

"Kathleen is too modest," Jack stepped in. "She wouldn't tell you, but this is one of her own designs." Jack sounded so proud Kathleen wanted to hug him.

Françoise stood back, stroking her face. "The colors, chosen well." She ran her fingers over the fabric and paid careful attention to the quality of stitch, and asked, "You *designed* and *sewed* this?"

Kathleen nodded. Françoise paused again and slipped her tiny hand into the crook of Kathleen's arm. "We will see you later, Jack." With that, she guided Kathleen into the building. "I am thinking you are a good seamstress, Kathleen Gray, niece of Jack Matthews. I am even more pleased to show our work. Come."

An enormous photographic portraiture of the famous designer stood at the top of the flight of stairs.

"Is that who I think it is?" Kathleen found herself whispering.

"Oui, how you say, life size. Gorgeous, no?"

Kathleen just stared. She thought him quite handsome, for an older man, and his statuesque height was certainly impressive. "Is this life size, Françoise? Uncle Jack is six foot two, he looks even taller!"

Françoise smiled. "Oui, life size, and taller than even Uncle Jack." And she guided her on, pointing to photographs of famous women.

Kathleen stopped and gazed at her most favorite

actress. Her pretty, imp-like face innocently peered back.

"She is very cute, and so lovely." Françoise smiled. "We are designing the outfits for her new film." Then she pointed out a photograph with a beautiful model and explained the feted blouse named after her.

All the while, Kathleen thought of her mother. As they walked from room to room, each with their own purpose, she noted how everything was immaculate, fresh, and surgically spotless. There were rooms filled with cabinets housing every color of thread and silk imaginable. One room stored rolls of fabrics stacked under huge tables and along walls. The familiar tailor's chalks, scissors, and tape measures were hung militarily neat, and she was amazed at the hundreds of swatches pinned on boards alongside braids of all descriptions.

"For inspiration," Françoise said, as if she could read her mind, then put her fingers to her lips indicating silence, as in the next room fabrics were being measured and sliced with the utmost precision. They moved on, and Kathleen was shown specialists in toile making as they trialed their designs on mannequins with pale, fine linens. She was given an opportunity to speak to the designers, and when they stepped back outside into the sparkle of sunlight, Kathleen had a lump in her throat.

"I can't thank you enough, Françoise, for making this happen. It has been such a wonderful opportunity. I am so very grateful." Kathleen still refused to believe her family were gone forever. She knew her mother would have loved this experience, but she knew for certain now that this was where she saw her own future. She would make her mother proud.

Chapter 15

Nigel Latimer declined to get out of the car at the airport, making a feeble excuse that he needed to write up some ideas for his campaign. Instead, he sat tapping an irritated beat on the dashboard, thinking about Jack and his wife. Nigel would never explain himself to Lily, but he wanted Jack out of their lives, and as quickly as possible. Nigel witnessed the change in Lily since his arrival, and furthering opportunities of her being alone in the company of his old adversary would never do.

Standing in the viewing area, Kathleen, Lucy, and Lily waved as Jack stepped onto the airplane. He turned for a moment, and saluted.

They watched the plane taxi along the runway, lift off the ground, and disappear into the clouds. All the while, Kathleen's mouth twisted in a desperate attempt not to cry. Lucy intuitively squeezed her friend's hand, but nothing could, or would, remove the deeply rooted sense of loss and fury. Kathleen tried hard to console herself that her uncle was leaving for good reason and would return, hopefully soon. But then, her parents had promised they would come back in time for her birthday, and they didn't. The thought terrified her. Lucy slipped her arm around Kathleen's shoulders, and they walked back to the car in silence.

They found Nigel tapping the remnants of tobacco from his pipe onto the grassy verge. Nigel watched Lily as she ushered the girls back into the car, and a wave of love and guilt washed over him. Lily looked lovely today, as she did in high school. He twisted the pipe back into his mouth, and absently filled the bowl with his favored tobacco. He wished he had the confidence and ease that Jack appeared to have around women. He steeled himself to tell Lily how sorry he was, and how much he loved her, but never got the chance. As the girls got into the back seat, Lily turned and hissed into his ear, "Well, I hope you're pleased with yourself? At least we will be less cramped in the car, now Jack's gone."

A wave of anger played Nigel's hand. "Kathleen got to say goodbye, didn't she, and don't forget we didn't *have* to take him to the airport." Nigel regretted it the moment the words were spilled. This was not what he wanted at all. Lily looked at him despairingly, shook her head, and turned away to stare out of her side window.

****

Kathleen sat alone in the dormitory, having returned late. The rest of the girls were having supper in the dining hall. While the girls were lovely, she had decided to keep herself to herself. She needed time to think, but deep down, all she really wanted to do was shout and scream at everyone. This wasn't her life. She hated it. She hated everyone. She hated her uncle for leaving her there. She hated her family for dying. How could they? She hated Lucy for having a family. She hated her mother for abandoning her.

Kathleen pulled out her small sketch book and for a second looked fondly over the drawings completed in Paris. A wave of grief caught her short. It did that, and mostly when she least expected it. She threw the sketch book across the room in her temper, then trashed her bed, throwing the blankets and mattress onto the floor. Exhausted, she sat upon the springs, breathing heavily, then hated herself for being so completely selfish. The sketch of the Eiffel tower had been torn in two. She shrugged. So what.

She calmed a little. The decision had been made the moment her uncle left her to go to America. She chewed at the inside of her lip and found the list where she had already begun to outline a brewing plan. First, she would need to check the figures against her monthly allowance. Next, she would try to calculate how much she might need, and how to legitimately get her hands on all her money without attracting attention to herself.

She tidied up before Mrs. Fuller could find the place in uproar, then licked the tip of the pencil and jotted figures down, and, working out each scenario like a game of chess, each move was carefully thought through, three steps ahead. She considered Lucy. They always shared everything. She realized how crazy she was acting, but also knew it would be unfair to put such a burden on her best friend. No, this plan would need to be kept completely secret.

Chapter 16

Miss Wray walked around her office with a letter from Mr. Matthews in one hand and her walking stick used for support in the other. She was worried. Mr. Matthews quite rightly required a progress report on his niece, but the news she received from staff was not good. Kathleen Gray's results were poor. A stark contrast to the intelligent pupil who had gained A level standards long before her year. Miss Wray expelled a sigh. She would support a grieving child through her misery, but she would not tolerate insubordination. Kathleen had all the makings of going to university, which was an accolade for any girl in this male-dominated world, and by Jove, she would expect nothing less.

"Hmm." She tapped the letter and then re-read the reports from staff, all were similar, except one.

Lessons had been finished an hour before. The headmistress summoned three key staff to her office. As the women walked along the corridor together, it was evident that none of them knew why they were required. The moment they arrived, the school secretary showed them in. They found Miss Wray pacing.

"Good afternoon, ladies, please take a seat." Miss Wray immediately began to read the communication from Mr. Matthews aloud. Mrs. Fuller kept adjusting her glasses nervously. Miss Edmonds sat there, arms folded with an "I told you so" expression, but Miss Wray saw she had Mrs. Sellers' interest. There came a knock on the office door. "Come!" Miss Wray tapped her stick impatiently on the ground, and her secretary entered with a shorthand book and pencil. "Thank you, Dora. Please, take a seat." Turning her attention back to her teaching staff, Miss Wray's face spelt concern. "I'm sure you can appreciate that we do not want to tell Mr. Matthews we are failing his niece. Furthermore, I will not allow a blemish on our otherwise perfect reputation."

She turned to Kathleen's form tutor. "And what's your appraisal of the situation, Miss Edmonds?"

"Miss Gray in my mind has become lazy and belligerent." She looked the headmistress square in the eye. "She refuses to put her mind to work, and it is all I can do to contain her behavior in class." She hastily added, "Of course, I have made an example of her. There have been many instances of detention, as you are aware, and for good reason."

Miss Wray shook her head. "Kathleen is exceptionally bright. Do you think detention is the answer? As you say, there have been *many* instances." She allowed her words to hang.

Miss Edmonds stared at the headmistress, astounded, and folded her arms even tighter across her chest. Her tone became more defensive.

"Detention, I find, dissuades gals who are becoming 'difficult' as sometimes wont during puberty. Though I confess I have never had a child quite like Miss Gray before."

"Miss Edmonds," said the headmistress more gently, "have you spoken to Kathleen? Privately, say, one to one, during these detentions? Perhaps ask her what the issue really is?"

The notion of an actual discussion with a pupil obviously floored Miss Edmonds. Knowing all eyes were upon her, she flushed an angry red. "I may be form tutor, Miss Wray, but I am primarily a mathematics teacher. I expect children to follow instruction without challenge, and should they become obstreperous, I follow school protocol." She muttered almost under her breath, "Talking to children, discussing things with them, whatever next?"

"Thank you for your thoughts, Miss Edmonds." Miss Wray noted her discomfort, and her focus turned to the housemistress. "Mrs. Fuller, what is your view of the situation?"

"Miss Wray," she began, "it appears Kathleen has gone more into a decline since her uncle left for America. I have of course called the doctor, but it is his opinion that the girl is still grieving and that with time she will improve, and I agree. However…" At this point, the housemistress took her glasses off her nose and polished them, as if searching for the right words. "I would also like to add something positive about Kathleen. As we are all aware, she has always been a popular girl. She is kind, caring, and considerate. It has come to my attention on more than one occasion she has supported girls who are struggling, even when she is struggling herself. I firmly believe, given the right amount of continued support and given time, her attitude in class will improve."

"That is good to hear." The headmistress nodded. "Thank you." She turned her attention on the sewing mistress. "Mrs. Sellers, would I be right in thinking

Kathleen is way beyond the level of making aprons and caps?"

Mrs. Sellers picked a fold of her skirt between her fingers before speaking.

"Kathleen is already a gifted seamstress." Her words were diplomatically couched. "There is not a moment of doubt in my mind about that. Mrs. Fuller is right. Kathleen has always been supportive. She motivates and encourages the girls in my class. Even now, when she so obviously feels low, she shares her skills and takes time to demonstrate how things are done. Why, sometimes…" Mrs. Sellers paused, a bubble of excitement welling in her throat. "In fact, I have a suggestion, if I may?" She asked for permission to continue and found herself standing, enthused. "It's only an idea, you understand, but I'd go as far as to propose we give the girl some additional responsibility, such as becoming a sewing assistant."

Miss Edmonds gasped at the suggestion. Her teacup rattled upon the saucer in response. Mrs. Sellers smiled soothingly, half expecting the reaction. "You see, I feel that Kathleen requires focus away from her loss. She needs to feel valued and listened to, much like all of our pupils who are going through difficult times, as Mrs. Fuller pointed out." The last words were suspended upon the air before she cast a curious look at the mathematics teacher. Mrs. Sellers returned to her seat, but it was clear Miss Edmonds did not approve. She raised her head haughtily, her arms remained tightly folded, and her lips were pursed firmly together.

The headmistress's expression betrayed nothing. Instead, she sat quietly at her desk, her cane placed within reach, her fingers loosely linked. The seconds turned into long minutes before she spoke.

"Mrs. Sellers, I think all things being equal, your suggestion is not without merit. I have a proposal, born primarily from your innovative idea. How say you, if you were to develop the curriculum alongside your plan for Kathleen as a sewing assistant?'

Mrs. Sellers was astounded, to the point of being speechless.

"Well? Do you think you can rise to the challenge, Mrs. Sellers?"

"Yes, yes, of course, Miss Wray. Indeed, I do!"

"Miss Edmonds. I also believe there is plenty of scope for mathematics to support Mrs. Sellers's class. In fact, it would link perfectly."

Dismay crossed Miss Edmonds' face.

"Let me give you a few examples, ladies." Rising from her desk, Miss Wray began outlining her plans. As she walked around her office, there was a spring in her step. She was now in her element with the sudden realization that such a simple concept had never been thought of before, and the ideas flowed along with her enthusiasm.

"Ladies!" she said, slapping her walking stick upon the desk, making everyone in the room jump. Her mind was racing. She knew it would take creativity and hard work. The women looked at one another, astonished, as she outlined more thoughts.

"Miss Edmonds, you are a conscientious and much valued member of my staff. I trust you will work closely with Mrs. Sellers to achieve the goals set out. These will be exciting times. We can do something to be proud of. Something that will put us on the map of academia, and way beyond others in our field. We will be the flagship leading the way forward. What say you?"

Mrs. Sellers, also enthused, looked as if she were about to hug the headmistress. Mrs. Fuller clapped her hands in delight, but Miss Edmonds looked at her in disbelief.

"But Miss Wray, can you imagine it? We will have anarchy…" She stopped, eyes wide, blinking. It was evident from Miss Wray that there would be no argument accepted.

The women spent the next hour discussing how and when the strategy would be implemented. Now confident with her proposition, Miss Wray summoned Kathleen to her office.

Chapter 17

"Ah, Kathleen," said the headmistress from behind her desk. "Do come in."

"Good afternoon, Miss Wray." She saw Mrs. Sellers as she stepped into the office, wondering what kind of punishment she might receive today. Detentions were already mounting up, but she didn't care.

"Please take a seat. There is something we need to discuss."

When Kathleen left the room and closed the door behind her, there was a lightness in her heart, and something she had not felt for some time. Hope.

The moment Kathleen left, the women looked at each other with satisfaction.

"I suspect you have been wanting change for some time, Mrs. Sellers?"

"I confess it's rare to find such skills in one so young." Mrs. Sellers blushed.

"I agree. I think the gal would make a fine teacher one day. Maybe more, with the right guidance." Miss Wray continued to smile. "I will compose a letter outlining our program to Kathleen's uncle. I believe he is a progressive gentleman and will be glad of any interventions we put in place."

Three weeks after discussing her plan with the headmistress, and with positive response from Mr. Matthews, the sewing mistress watched Kathleen's progress with quiet pleasure. At the end of the first week, Mrs. Sellers asked Kathleen to stay behind—she had another idea in mind for the girl.

"I believe you often helped your mother, Kathleen, with her business?"

"Yes, Miss." Kathleen flushed at the thought of those days, her heart heavy with the memories.

"Now, tell me, is there something you would really like to tackle, something special perhaps?" Kathleen's eyes glistened at the thought of her mother at home and their time together sewing.

"Would you like some time to think about it?"

"Yes, Miss."

"Very well, come and see me after last class tomorrow." That night Kathleen went to bed thinking about her mother, and about Mrs. Sellers' suggestion. Would she? Could she?

By the morning she had her answer.

Chapter 18

Kathleen sat next to Mrs. Sellers as they drove along the familiar lanes toward her home, her fists clenched so tight upon her lap her knuckles turned white. The first thing she saw as they pulled into the driveway was the clematis. She gulped. The sight of it took her straight back to happier days. The climbing vine, which had wrapped itself right around the doorway and burst into a profusion of purple, was something she had never truly appreciated before.

Treenie and Chaz came out of the house, she with her hair tied up in her usual scarf. Treenie held a duster and Chaz a broom. As soon as the car pulled to a halt, Kathleen jumped out and rushed to embrace them while Mrs. Sellers watched the display of affection between them with a small cry of pleasure.

"My goodness, young lady, you are certainly growing up." Treenie held Kathleen closely, laughing in her friendly way. "Why, you're up to my nose already!" She gently pushed Kathleen away to arm's length and gave her the onceover. "And you're losing weight, young lady. I always thought you were always a skinny thing, but look—you've all but vanished."

"First things first," said Chaz, stepping forward and giving Kathleen a pat on the back and winking at Mrs. Sellers. "I think you need to earn your keep, young'un. I need your help to milk them camels."

"Camels?" Kathleen laughed, shaking her head. Chaz had always teased her from a very young age that his cows were in fact camels.

"Of course, camels," said Chaz looking serious. "What else would they be? And afterward I expect you to come around for tea and cake."

Kathleen grinned. "Oh, Chaz!" And to her surprise she suddenly realized her fears about returning home were beginning to melt. She looked between the couple who were always so dear to her family. It would be good to go to their farmhouse with its creaking floors, low beams, and the range that was forever hot and full of good things to eat. And all at once she felt hungry.

"May we, Mrs. Sellers?" Mrs. Sellers saw a brightness in the child's eyes, something that had been missing for so long.

"Well, that is a most kind offer. It sounds simply marvelous, and I would love to see how you milk camels." Everyone laughed.

Treenie held out her hand, and Kathleen took it. "Come on, Kathleen, let's go and see what you plan to take back to school."

Mrs. Sellers, grateful, followed behind.

Treenie had made sure the place was well aired and cleaned before their arrival. It smelt of heavenly lavender, and as they walked through the door a sense of wellbeing filled the house, lifting Kathleen's spirits further. Instead of feeling anxious, she felt able to let go of Treenie's hand, and, for a moment, stood at the bottom of the stairs looking up.

"May I have a few moments alone?"

"Of course," said Mrs. Sellers.

Kathleen went straight to her bedroom filled with

wonderful memories. She looked around her room that seemed somehow smaller. A photograph of her family sat on the dressing table, and a white-and-gold embossed prayer book lay beside it, given to her the day she was confirmed, along with *Anne of Green Gables*. She opened the book and read the inscription from her parents—given to her on her eighth birthday:

"For our darling daughter Kathleen—like Anne, you are filled with kindness, spirit, charm, and have the inner strength of a warrior. With much love, Mummy and Daddy."

A sob caught in her throat. It looked like the books had lain there waiting for her return. She quickly gathered up everything and pressed it to her chest. Turning, she walked back out and called, inviting them into her mother's workroom. Mrs. Sellers glanced at Treenie, who gave her an encouraging smile and whispered, "Thank you for doing this, Mrs. Sellers. Her uncle is very grateful, and it is so lovely to see Kathleen again."

The sewing mistress touched Treenie on the forearm. "It's a pleasure. Let's hope everything we have planned works for her."

Mrs. Sellers made appreciative noises as Kathleen proudly invited her into the workroom, and her eyes immediately fell upon a silk gown.

"Gosh, Kathleen, this is beautiful. Your mother's work?" she said, walking toward the manikin with the creation displayed upon it. Kathleen colored.

"That, I believe, is Kathleen's creation," said Treenie at the door.

"Really?" Mrs. Sellers turned. This was far more than just a girl with a natural ability—she was truly gifted. "It's superb. Would you consider bringing this to school, to show the girls and maybe…" She hoped she wasn't pushing things too fast. "Perhaps you might like to finish it?"

Chapter 19

Jack Matthews' workload was relentless. He desperately needed sleep, but the time zone on his Rolex indicated he should phone Lily as planned. He put a call through to the operator and waited.

"It's great to speak to you, Lily." His voice traveled warmly over the miles. "Kathleen's been telling me she is looking forward to staying over this weekend."

"That's good to hear." Lily paused. The line crackled and hissed. "Sorry? Can you still hear me, Jack? The line's pretty poor this end."

"It's fine here. Go on."

"I was thinking"—Lily spoke louder, just in case—"that Kathleen might like to join us in Cornwall during the summer break next year. What do you think?"

Jack, astonished, asked about Nigel's view on the matter.

"I've spoken to Nigel and checked with the hotel—there is availability. The girls can share a room, and on a selfish note, Lucy will have company her own age, and it'll take pressure off Nigel."

"Are you sure?"

Lily heard the guilt in his voice travel through the line, but almost cracking with relief.

"You're a real lifesaver, Lily. Thank you. I know Kathleen will be thrilled." As Jack replaced the receiver, a sultry voice called out.

"Are you coming back to bed, Jack? I'm missing you already."

"I'll be there in a moment, Eve. I just need to write a couple of things down." He took the top off his pen, added the dates to his diary, and hoped Eve would like the thought of spending Christmas in England. A little muscle in his cheek twitched. Next year's contracts, trying to balance his busy schedule with visiting and taking care of Kathleen. At least Kathleen would be away with Lily for a week during summer next year. He tapped the pen on the diary. It might just work…

"Jack?"

Eve stood in the doorway. She looked stunning, as always.

"Please, I just need another minute…"

"I can't wait." Eve slipped her negligee off one shoulder, exposing a full, rounded breast. Jack felt himself harden. He chuckled. She was insatiable.

"Oh, God, Eve, you are so…" His mind now held only her. He began softly kissing her forehead, her lids, her tiny nose, her full lips, whilst trickling his fingers gently down the whiteness of her smooth throat toward her breasts. And with a pleasured moan, he swept her up into his arms and into his bed.

****

Midmorning the following day, whilst Eve showered, Jack made a pot of coffee and poured himself a mug before reading through the school itinerary. The list covered the academic year, September through mid-July. It also included a list of activities for boarders during the summer vacation. Even with the program they had so thoughtfully set up,

L. B. Griffin

reading between the lines of communications from Kathleen and reports from the housemistress, there had been a definite decline in her mood. Only to be expected, he thought gloomily, what with Christmas looming. Jack rubbed the bristles along his jawline, chastising himself for not being more organized. Screwing up his eyes, he thought about the contract in Africa and commitments in Asia. He could see no way out.

Drumming a beat, he began cross-referencing the timetable, marking off the first week of next summer, when Kathleen would be away with Lily. That would be a great start, he thought, wrestling with his conscience. He was still trying to convince himself that Mrs. Fuller's options looked interesting when Eve pulled up a chair, smelling citrus-fresh, her hair wrapped in a turban. She looked and smelt gorgeous, even without makeup.

"It's a shame they don't do summer camp like here in the US, Eve." He smiled thoughtfully, about to reach out for his coffee, and pushed his thoughts on paper toward her. "I wonder if you might take a look. Maybe you have some ideas?" He hoped she would cast her eye over his plans and help talk them through.

Eve swiped the mug from him and pulled a nail file from her gown pocket, pursing her lips. He tried gauging her mood as she glanced over the sheet. She seemed slightly irritated. Eve liked romantic gestures, the more expensive the better. He, on the other hand, preferred spontaneity, and the simpler things. But first he had to be honest. Kathleen remained his priority.

"Eve…" He poured a fresh coffee. "I need to talk to you about the Christmas holidays."

Chapter 20

Christmas 1954

Trudging up the lane, laden with gifts, Jack and Kathleen were wrapped up well against the cold. The snow crunched underfoot, while a heavy blanket of white in the sky promised more. Kathleen hoped she would be able to cope. She didn't want to feel sad, but most of all she didn't want to let her uncle down. She swallowed as they neared the farmhouse. Christmas would never be the same.

The dogs were barking somewhere out back, and the moment they arrived, the front door, burdened with a huge holly wreath, opened, and Treenie appeared on the doorstep. Instead of her usual farm gear, she wore a figure-hugging dress, and her shining hair hung in soft waves to just below her ears.

"Welcome, welcome, come on in." She drew them into a warm hug.

"Treenie, you look stunning," said Jack in an instant.

"You look really glamorous," added Kathleen, honestly unable to believe the transformation.

"Why, thank you." Treenie quickly closed the door behind them to shut the cold air out.

Kathleen saw the Christmas tree, set inside the hallway, just below the staircase. It smelt of fresh pine, and the branches were strewn with sparkling colored glass baubles. The normality of it all struck her so deeply, it cut into her heart. How she had once loved to help decorate the tree at home. The feelings she held were so alien to her. She felt so very low. So very sad.

"Hello, you two!" Jessica, Treenie's daughter, arrived, jostling Kathleen's thoughts.

"Come on, let's get you toasty warm and a hot chocolate inside you."

"You're looking well, Jessica." Jack loved the whole family and couldn't wait to catch up with his old buddy, Jessica's husband, Archie.

"Fat, you mean," she said, rubbing her pregnant belly.

"No Jessica, I mean it. You look beautiful."

"You're such a charmer, Jack." She tutted happily and turned to Kathleen. "Why don't you give us a hand in the kitchen?"

Kathleen nodded, giving a pinched smile, while Jack looked over the top of his niece's head, mouthing grateful thanks. The women linked their arms into hers and immediately tasked her to polish the dinner plates.

"When you're finished, can you please take them through to the dining room?"

Kathleen managed another nod, and once done gathered them up, but entering the room, a moan caught in her throat. Christingle oranges, spiked with cloves, lined the mantelpiece, and they sent her straight back to the last Christmas with her family. This would be it from now on. Only Uncle Jack could really understand, but even he seemed to be getting on with his life.

"All for one," Jack whispered in her ear, suddenly by her side, as she fought back tears. It was as if he read her mind. Chaz popped his head around the door.

"Hello, me old muckers."

"Shoo!" Treenie had arrived with a large plate of freshly sliced bread.

"Go and get that mucky stuff off, mister, and wash your hands, or you won't be getting any goose!"

****

The invitation to join the family for Christmas had been kind. Kathleen knew she was being selfish. Uncle Jack had told her there were children in the world who had nothing and were literally starving. It upset her to think all of this was going on and here she was being so ungrateful. She needed to be kinder to everyone. To her uncle. Maybe even to herself. Maybe she should try to find out more and decide how, in a small way she might help those children.

Kathleen watched the festivities bleakly. Best china laid. Cutlery and glassware shining. Grace imparted. Everyone chatting, helping themselves to a wonderful meal. It could be anywhere, but nothing removed the fact her family were gone, forever. She distractedly watched her uncle dollop a spoonful of mash on his plate. She could barely lift a hand to eat.

"This mash is absolutely delicious, Treenie. You should open your own restaurant, or at the very least give lessons, and you should definitely write a cookery book." He glanced at Kathleen. "Shouldn't she, Kathleen?"

"Don't Americans do mash?" asked Treenie.

"Yes, but it tastes somehow sweeter over there, good, but not a patch on this."

"I think we're getting the hint, Jack. Here." Chaz laughed, passing the dish back.

"Leave some for me, mate!" Archie bumped him in the ribs. "So, what's your plans after the New Year, Jack?" Archie asked, as he plated roast parsnips.

Jack swallowed slowly, a frown furrowing his brow. "I've a contract with an African diamond mine."

"Chaz, you're hogging the roasts. Kathleen hasn't had a look-in yet," interrupted Treenie, seeing the look of dismay upon her face.

Kathleen forked a potato politely onto her plate but left her food untouched. She couldn't face eating. Jessica caught the mood and flashed a ring strung onto her necklace.

"This belonged to Archie's great-grandmother. It's beautiful, isn't it? Trouble is my fingers have got so fat I can't wear it."

"May I?" asked Jack, taking a closer look. "A Burmese diamond, if I'm not mistaken?"

"How on earth?" Jessica looked impressed. Jack shrugged.

"The cut, color, clarity—all give a clue. I believe they'll be a rare commodity soon, so look after it."

"Well, should you find a super-large diamond, I'm sure Kathleen wouldn't mind one, would you?"

Kathleen attempted a smile. Picking up his napkin, Jack dabbed his mouth, winking at her. "Trust me, I'll be on the lookout."

After the meal and a plethora of board games, the women cleared the table, whilst the men went to finish work in the barn. Jack trudged past the kitchen window, listening to the women singing carols along to the radio, and allowed himself a relieved smile. The day seemed to have gone far better than he could have hoped for.

"Here you go, Jack, me lad," said Chaz, handing

him a pitchfork. "If you can toss hay into the stalls?"

"You got it," said Jack, happy to help. His hands, mostly soft from lack of recent physical labor, quickly began to blister, but as he forked hay and filled troughs with pails of fresh water, he felt satisfaction in the work. His mind turned to Eve. Someone he'd believed at last might be the one to spend the rest of his life with. How could he have gotten her so wrong?

"You okay, Jack?" Archie elbowed him. "Looks like one of the cows farted in your face."

"Oh? No." Jack glanced at Archie with a quirky smile. "No farts, buddy. Not yet anyway. Just worrying about Kathleen. I've seen the way she looks. So desperate. So…lost. Trouble is, I just can't see a way forward. My work…"

Jack flung the last of the hay over the top of a cow, and it stumbled, mooing at him from the stall.

"I'm no good for her, working abroad. Kathleen needs someone who can hold her hand when she's sad and give her a cuddle when she cries. My work doesn't allow for that. I'm rarely here." He leaned on a pillar, wiping his brow, and cast his mind to the girl in the photograph, always close to his heart. Cassandra. A lost love, now a distant memory. When Eve came along, he knew she would only ever be second best. Jack frowned. Maybe that was why Eve was so difficult. Perhaps she knew, deep down. She must have felt insulted by his answers, and then when she found the keepsake, well, she was right. He had felt awful.

"You need a wife," said Archie, matter of fact.

"Huh, had that plan quashed…"

Outside the cow shed, Kathleen had just arrived with a flask of mulled wine and caught the last bit of the conversation. She gulped back a wail. Uncle Jack had someone to marry, but not now? It must be her fault, getting in the way of his life. She fell against a shovel outside the barn. The men stopped talking. Putting on a brave face, Kathleen went in and handed them the flask, pretending she had not heard any of it, and gulping back tears disappeared back into the house.

Later that night, Kathleen watched her uncle run ahead, deliberately skidding along the icy lane, pushing her to beat him. He ran again, like a huge child, slipping and sliding. She joined in the activity halfheartedly, until they reached Westfield and dashed inside to strip off the warm layers.

Uncle Jack flung his coat onto a chair. It fell to the floor, and she gathered it up and hung it by the front door, next to Pops' coat. Neither of them could bear to remove that coat. Kathleen watched her uncle busy himself with the fire. Uncle Jack was a businessman, flying all over the world. Coming to England just for her was stupid. Unfair. A burden. She was right all along to make plans. In a way, she had hoped they would come to nothing. But now, after hearing that conversation in the barn, there was no way she would become Uncle Jack's problem, not now she knew the truth. How could he ever have a life, having to be responsible for her? How could he find a wife and have a family of his own, with her around?

"Fancy some toast, m'lady?" Jack poked at the grate, moving the coals around to burn more evenly.

She started. She had previously fretted. At least now she could satisfy herself her plans were right. He tilted his head at her, a frown crossing his face. He still wore the knitted bobble hat she'd made him.

"Aren't you going to take that off?" Kathleen's eyebrows wiggled as she tried to keep a lid on her thoughts.

"Never! Not even when the sun shines." He grinned.

"Well, you might look a little silly wearing it in Africa. Perhaps I should make you a pith helmet!" She looked at the fire, hiding her feelings. "And yes, I would like some toast please, and maybe we could have a game of chess after?"

Her uncle, looking surprised, raised a contemplative brow.

"Toast, tea, and chess, in that order." He leaned over the back of the settee and lifted a rectangular object from behind. "But first things first. This is for you. I know it's not a patch on your wonderful gift to me, but I hope you find it just as pleasing."

Kathleen studied the package, trying to assess what the gift might be. From its size and shape, it suggested a large jigsaw puzzle. So, sitting cross-legged on the floor, she placed it on her lap.

It didn't feel like a puzzle box. With her curiosity growing, she quickly untied the string, and the paper peeled away.

"How? When did you manage to do this?" Kathleen exploded in complete surprise.

"You were so taken with it. And I seem to remember the artist was taken with you." Uncle Jack winked. "Do you still like it?"

"Like it? I love it! Thank you."

Kathleen was already on her feet studying the detail. Paris in the spring, the light dancing across the cobbled street. "You are really spoiling me, Uncle

Jack."

"Nah, it's my way of bribing you to get you to do the cooking for the rest of the week."

"I would have done it for free, as well you know!" Kathleen grinned, picking up the painting again. This time she placed it at an angle on a chair, so it could be looked at from almost anywhere in the room. Glassy-eyed, Kathleen hugged him.

"It could go over there." He pointed to a space on the wall. "There used to be a lovely painting of the ford and geese there. Not sure what happened to it, though." He looked thoughtful. "What do you think?"

"Yes." Kathleen went to the spot and held it up. "I think here would be perfect."

****

They sat by the fire, playfully knocking knees, toasting forks in hand. Jack decided it was time to broach the issue of next Easter, and next summer. It seemed so distant it shouldn't matter, but he needed to see his niece's face, not talk over the telephone, or write a letter.

Kathleen listened carefully as he told her about the coming year. He watched her every expression, wondering, waiting. Her reaction was remarkable. She gladly accepted the proposition of going away with the Latimers and seemed perfectly happy with the summer school arrangements.

"There are lots of other girls staying during the break, Uncle Jack. Do you know, I'm looking forward to it already?"

"Kathleen, you truly are amazing!" At best he'd expected tears. "Are you absolutely certain?"

"Seriously? Stop fretting. I'm all grown up now. I

don't need babying."

Kathleen couldn't believe it. It seemed a penny had slotted into the jar, so perfectly matching her plans she almost blurted it out loud.

"Why don't you write to Mrs. Fuller, the housemistress, and I'll give her the letter?"

"When exactly did you become so smart, kiddo?" One side of his mouth curved up, his right cheek dimpling, and he added, "Perhaps if I wrote out the cheque as well?"

"All for one?" Kathleen nodded enthusiastically, hoping, praying, the phrase would prevent her secret from spilling.

"And all for one." Kathleen caught a flash of relief across his face. Guilt was all she could feel. Her uncle was so adorable. She hated herself for lying, but it was necessary. He needed to get on with his life. A life without her.

****

Jack was thinking briefly about Eve. His decision had been right. Kathleen was worth more than a thousand Eves. He would pull out all the stops to be back before October next year.

Chapter 21

February 1955

Alone in her dorm at last, Kathleen retrieved a piece of paper, hidden safely from inspection, taped behind the small cupboard next to her bed. Poring over the growing list and chewing the end of a pencil, a little piece of the wood fell away, leaving the bitter taste of graphite in her mouth. She spat it out into a handkerchief. Her mouth pursed into thoughtfulness. It would take a great deal of creative thinking to pull this bit of her plan off. She would need to start with her trusted ally, Mrs. Sellers, the sewing mistress.

At the end of the next school day, Kathleen peered through the viewing pane of the sewing room. Yes, she was there as hoped. She knocked and waited.

"Come?"

"Mrs. Sellers, I wonder…"

"Yes?"

Kathleen took the cue. "I understand you are wardrobe mistress for the local amateur dramatics group?"

"Yes, that's right." Mrs. Sellers immediately placed the material and pincushion to one side.

"Well, I wondered if I could offer an extra pair of hands at the weekends?"

"Indeed, that would be most helpful!" Mrs. Sellers

was clearly surprised and pleased at the suggestion. "However, I will have to check with Miss Wray, and of course your guardian, first."

Kathleen smiled, sure there would not be an issue, and in her head, she moved another pawn in her imaginary game of chess.

****

It was early evening, before supper. Kathleen arrived in the dorm expecting to find a little peace and hoped to jot a few more notes into her formulating plan. Usually the girls were busy, finishing off homework or out playing tennis or joining in some other activity, such as knitting, board games, or reading in the school library. Only Kathleen found Amy, alone, sitting on her bed, her back to the door. Kathleen could hear quiet sobs. Amy must not have heard her enter.

"Amy, what on earth's the matter?" She went straight over and looped her arm around her shoulders. Amy cried even more at the touch. "Mummy promised I would be living back with them after a couple of years. Now it seems I must stay here. Forever."

Kathleen felt dreadful. All this time she hadn't taken on board just how vulnerable the other girls must feel. It brought her up with a start to think she had been so selfish. Of course they would be struggling. After all, they were all boarders. There had been no choice in the matter. She knew her poor behavior had been a kind of defense mechanism yet she hadn't wanted to think about it. She wanted only to focus on her own issues. When the girls in her dorm avoided her, she felt only relief. How could she explain not only were her parents dead but she had also been adopted? Embarrassed by the fact, she'd kept the secret throughout her whole life.

No, she couldn't deal with the humiliation of it. Children and adults alike could be cruel if word got out. It was obvious from the start that all the other girls were from good backgrounds. But little Amy? Poor girl, totally alone and, in a way, not unlike herself, was in bits. How could she have been so selfish not to have noticed before?

"Come on. Let's find Cook. Perhaps she'll make us hot chocolate?" Amy's sobs were subsiding. It was then Kathleen saw the photograph and a letter in her hand.

"Is this your family?"

"Yes."

"And who is this?" Kathleen pointed to a small boy by his mother's side, holding her hand. "He looks adorable."

"That's my brother, Cyril. He's going to board when he turns eleven. Next year. We've been communicating. This is from him." She waved the letter in her hand. "He's so unhappy." Amy sniffed. "Mummy has never really been keen on children. We have always been looked after by a nanny."

Kathleen winced. Her own mother obviously didn't want her, but she was given away for an entirely different reason. She really wasn't wanted. But this wasn't about her. Kathleen shook herself. How thoughtless not noticing the signs right in front of her.

"Cyril seems sweet, Amy. He obviously loves you as you must him. But I don't believe your parents don't care about you. From what I understand, they have a life that doesn't call for children—aren't they always moving? You said once your father is in the Armed Forces."

"Yes. He's got a new commission. I don't

remember ever being in one place for very long. It was always hard work adjusting to new schools, making new friends." Amy blinked, a lightbulb moment. She looked at Kate with renewed attention. "Maybe you're right. Maybe by the time I reached ten, they thought moving me into senior school where I didn't have to move again would be a good idea. The trouble is that now it's Cyril's turn. He sounds so desperate. I just don't know what to say to him to make it all better."

Amy seemed more in control now, thoughtful. "Our nanny once said Mummy was worried about us, about how unsettling it was, moving us from one school to another all the time."

"Well, there you have it, then. Your parents care for you, and this is their way of making the best out of a bad deal." Kathleen rubbed Amy's back in little circles, and with a light sob Amy nodded agreement. "Maybe you can help Cyril come to terms with another move, possibly a more permanent one?"

Amy brushed her tears away with the back of her hand and sniffed.

"Come on, let's get chocolate, not just for us, but for everyone. They should be back soon, right?" Kathleen suddenly remembered her book, safely stored inside her bedside table. "Have you ever read *Anne of Green Gables*, Amy?"

"No. Why?"

"Well, let's get the chocolate first, and then I'll tell you."

Cook really was the dream Meg had told her about when they first met, and the rest of the girls were herded in by the promise of hot chocolate and biscuits. As they settled in, Kathleen took out her book from her drawer. "May I read you the first chapter from *Anne of Green Gables*?" she asked. Meg was thrilled. "I haven't read that one for ages. Yes, that would be lovely, Kathleen."

The girls by now were tucked up in bed, the lights low, and Kathleen found her voice. She had listened to Uncle Jack's stories over the years and loved the way he spoke, the way he brought everything to life. To her surprise, it seemed she had the same natural ability to read to an audience, and as she began to read the first chapter, girls were instantly encapsulated in time...

"*Mrs. Rachel Lynde lived just where the Avonlea main road dipped down into a little hollow, fringed with alders and ladies' eardrops and traversed by a brook that had its source away back in the woods of the old Cuthbert place...*"

As Kathleen read on, she began to realize just how right her mother had been. There were hints of Anne in her. In fact, she thought soberly, there were traces of Anne in all the girls in her dorm. They all shared common ground. By the end of the first chapter, and just as she was about to close the book, the girls were clamoring for more. Mrs. Fuller arrived, hushing them to sleep and lights out, but Kathleen agreed she would read one chapter every night. Kathleen made another discovery about herself that night and broke down one of her own barriers. She hoped to make up for her aloofness with the girls, but in the back of her mind the plan continued to brew.

****

Kathleen became a familiar sight to the aging postman, passing pleasantries, befriending him. Quickly realizing his delivery times every day, Kathleen deliberately coincided her walks, meeting the postie halfway down the steep hill. Mr. Prince made no bones that he struggled up the hill to the school. Today, the bitingly cold wind froze her face. She found the postman gasping, puffing, pushing his bike. His cough sounded dreadful.

"Good morning, Mr. Prince. You don't sound very well." She felt sorry for the old man, who tried to stifle his next phlegmy cough without much success.

"There's mail from abroad, but it's not marked for your attention," he said, knowing she always waited for news from her uncle.

"Never mind. Look, why don't I take the post to school today? It'll save you the journey."

"Thank you for the offer, young lady, but the Royal Mail should be delivered by a bona fide postman. It's my duty to the Crown."

"Perhaps you could make me honorary postie?" began Kathleen persuasively. "If anyone asks, you handed it to me at the school gates?" As she spoke, his cough racked his body.

"How about I meet you tomorrow? At the same time, but at the bottom of the hill. Just until you get better?"

"It's very kind of you, miss," Mr. Prince said doubtfully, with his postbag straddled across his shoulder, holding his bike steady. "Honorary postie, is it? Only until my cough goes."

"Honorary postie. Until your nasty cough goes. It will be our little secret, Mr. Prince, and my pleasure. I promise."

To her delight, tipping her a grateful wink, the postman pulled out the bundle for school.

"Our little secret."

"Get well, Mr. Prince," she called, as he climbed aboard his bicycle and allowed it to freewheel back down the hill. Kathleen knew that at least she would be helping the poor man as well as herself.

****

Monday morning, Mrs. Fuller summoned Kathleen to her room.

"I have a letter from your uncle." She held it aloft.

Kathleen provided a look of surprise. Mr. Prince, the postman, would never know his complicity in her deception.

"I confess I am a little disappointed," continued Mrs. Fuller. "Your uncle requested you were to be involved in the activities we provide here during the summer break." She sniffed, re-reading the letter. "It appears there has been a change. You have been invited to spend a month with the Latimers, instead."

"I have, Mrs. Fuller?"

"Is there anything you wish to say on the matter?" She peered over the top of her glasses.

Kathleen's heart flipped. Her palms moistened with anxiety. What did she need to say? Had she been found out?

"I'm not sure what you mean." Was this it, game over before it began? Think! "If it would please my uncle, Mrs. Fuller, I would love it."

"Hmm. Very well. Mr. Matthews does sound keen on the idea." Her face relaxed into a thin smile. "Very well, I believe a letter of thanks from yourself to Mr. and Mrs. Latimer would be appropriate."

Kathleen's heart raced as she tried to control her breathing. In for a penny, in for a pound. She looked at the housemistress pensively.

"There is something else, Mrs. Fuller. My uncle has arranged an extremely generous allowance." Mrs. Fuller placed her glasses carefully on the table.

"I wondered if it might be sensible to open a savings account?"

"Preparing for the future is always a good idea." The housemistress looked suitably pleased.

Placing Kathleen's forged letter on her desk, she pulled a foolscap ledger off a shelf, and, sitting down, slipped her glasses back on her nose. With each turn of the page, the housemistress licked the tip of her forefinger.

"Aha, here we are." Dragging her finger down the entries, humming and hawing, she wrote numbers down on a separate sheet of paper.

"It's good to see you have not been frivolous with your allowance." Her eyes flicked up and down the column again, then looked through her diary.

"I'm not sure when I might find the time to take you to open an account."

Kathleen's heart sank. She had no intention of anyone being involved in opening the savings account. If her plan were to work, she would need to be able to access cash without question. Thinking quickly, putting her hands behind her back, crossing her fingers tightly against the lie.

"Actually, Mrs. Fuller, Lucy spoke of opening her own Post Office account, and it gave me the idea. I wonder, as I'm with the Latimers this weekend, if I could do it at the same time?"

Kathleen stared straight ahead, unable to meet the housemistress's gaze, convinced she would be struck dead for telling so many lies. Mrs. Fuller looked marginally relieved. Noting the sum into her ledger, she agreed to arrange twenty pounds to start with, and said she would notify her uncle of her plan. When Kathleen left Mrs. Fuller's room, it was all she could do not to burst a blood vessel. It was perfect. She could not have hoped for a better outcome. Now, with twenty pounds in her hand, and no plans to see Lucy over the weekend, it was time to put her acting skills to the test.

Chapter 22

Kathleen found the perfect spot. The library was a good place to hide herself from prying eyes and allow herself to read the jobs vacant and rentals without awkward questions. Opening her Post Office account, under the name of Miss Abercrombie, had been surprisingly straight forward. She allowed herself a brief smile, thinking about her performance as the absent-minded spinster. Managing to fool the strait-laced Post Office mistress in the next village was no mean feat.

Kathleen folded in half the newspaper full of Mr. Anthony Eden the Prime Minister. She put it in her satchel and pulled out her sketchbook. Looking through her developing portfolio, she began to feel guilty. Up until now she had been so engrossed, carving out each move for her planned departure, she had deliberately avoided thinking too deeply about Uncle Jack or Lucy. Trying to convince herself she was right, she whispered, "You will come to understand, I promise."

****

Lucy twiddled her hair distractedly. "I've got something I want to ask." She looked nervous. "You can say no if you want to."

Kathleen sat beside her on the school bench, swinging her legs, scrubbing the tips of her shoes on the schoolyard.

"Gordon Andrews."

"What about Gordie Bordie?" Kathleen answered, mildly irritated by her friend's interest in the spotted nitwit. She turned her focus on a couple of the younger girls learning to play two-ball.

"He asked me out!"

"Bloody hell. Don't tell me you've been going out with Gordie Bordie behind my back? Thanks for telling me."

"Well! That's rich. You do as you please!" They were looking at one another square in the face. Lucy went all boss-eyed.

Kathleen hooked her fingers into her nose, dragging it upward, making a face like a pig and snorted. They both squealed with laughter. Neither could argue with the other for more than a second.

Kathleen tilted her head to one side. "You're serious, aren't you?" She nudged her friend so hard she nearly fell off the bench.

"How about us going out as a foursome?" Lucy blurted out. "I've got a bit of pocket money saved. We could go to the flicks. Gordon has a friend who is sweet on you."

"Are you mad? I've no interest in spotty boys."

Lucy's right brow shot up, puzzling. "So you have a man friend, do you, Miss Gray?"

"Well, not yet, but I will."

"Oh, go on. Please say yes. Mummy would go all ballistic missile if she knew I had a boyfriend. You've got to come, to give me an alibi."

"All right." Kathleen sighed. "But Gordie's got to bring a decent friend. Not a clod. There is no way I want to play gooseberry with a bloody clod."

Lucy threw her arms around Kathleen excitedly, ignoring her request.

"*Calamity Jane*'s on at the Gaumont."

"I don't think you'll be seeing much of the film," said Kathleen flatly. "But just make sure Gordie's friend is clear—I'm only there to make up the numbers. *And don't bring a bloody clod.*"

****

The girls spent hours Saturday morning titivating. "A blind date" was all Lucy would say. Kathleen felt a tad excited, and a bit nervous. By one o'clock, they were waiting at the train station for the boys, in drizzling rain. Kathleen was keen to see her date. When Gordon came swaggering toward them, all hair cream and shaving rash, she privately conceded he was a bit better-looking than she remembered.

But when her eyes turned to his friend, a step behind Gordie, her heart did a little flip. Philip was nothing at all like the shy, spotty youth she remembered. He had outgrown his friend by at least four inches and looked more like a rugger player than the gangling boy of just a few months ago. Philip's hazel eyes cast an appreciative look over her. Her stomach fluttered uncontrollably.

Lucy whispered, "Is Philip okay? He's not too much of a clod, is he?"

"No, surprisingly." Kathleen quickly lowered her tone, pleased she had taken time to dress up.

Gordon confidently wrapped his arms around Lucy's waist, pressing himself against her while Lucy tried twisting away out of his control, clearly shy of his vigor.

"Well," said Gordon sarcastically, Lucy still firmly

in his grip. "Little Miss Gray agreeing to come along? Now, there's a page turner."

"Good to meet you," said Philip, holding out a broad hand. Gordon roared with forced laughter.

"Bit formal for you, Phil mate?"

"Shall we get out of the rain?" said Philip, offering to carry Kathleen's umbrella over her head. Trembling, but pleasantly surprised at his manners, she stopped herself from biting back at Gordon, and the couples naturally fell into step. Gordon kept showing off, speaking loudly enough for the whole street to hear.

"I don't have much time for the pictures, but the back row, now that's a completely different matter." And with that he grabbed Lucy's hand. "Come on, let's get a wriggle on." And Gordon began running and laughing, dragging Lucy with him.

Once inside the cinema, Gordon, ignoring the usherette, made a beeline for the back row, engineering Lucy into the farthest corner. Philip steered Kathleen in after Gordon and settled down beside her. The organ played until the lights went out, and then Kathleen heard the rustle of Gordon's sleeve snaking along the back of the chair, presumably around Lucy's shoulders.

As the advertisements burst onto the screen, from the corner of her eye she saw him leaning in to Lucy. Within moments they were kissing. They kept on kissing right through to the end of the Pathé News and right through the supporting film. Kathleen squirmed, wondering how on earth Lucy knew so much and seemed so relaxed about it all. In fact, she was amazed she could breathe.

"I need to stretch myself out a bit. Do you mind?" Philip whispered in Kathleen's ear, flopping his arm casually along the back of her seat. She waited with a thrill of excited anticipation. But Philip didn't make another move, and she wondered if maybe he didn't fancy her after all.

The main film was part way through, and Gordon was breathing heavily. Embarrassed, Kathleen jiggled around in her seat, turning away from them, and Philip twisted a little toward her, shifting in the confined space, and whispered in her ear, "Is this okay?"

Kathleen didn't have a chance to reply. Leaning forward, he planted his soft warm mouth over hers, and she instantly melted. It was the most delicious sensation she'd ever experienced. With every touch she felt her pulse rising. She was just wondering if they would ever come up for air when Philip's knees thumped the chair directly in front.

"'Ere, I'm gettin' fed up with your antics! I've come to watch the film. I'm gettin' the manager," said a bald man, twisting around from the seat in front, glaring.

"Sorry, sir," began Philip, apologizing, having swiftly pulled out of the embrace. "My legs, you see, they're just so long."

"I've known the likes of you all my bloody life," the bald man retorted, already standing, shuffling along his row past seated filmgoers.

Kathleen began to giggle, but the more she tried to stifle it, the more it grew.

"Something funny, young lady?" said the woman who had been seated next to Baldy. "You should be ashamed of yourself."

Suddenly a light flashed in their eyes from along the end of their row just as Doris Day's voice poured from the screen, singing "Whip-Crack-Away," and Kathleen hooted with laughter.

"Out!" They couldn't see who was behind the torch. "Out!"

The picture froze with the star on screen, her mouth wide open, brilliant white teeth gleaming. The audience gave a collective groan.

"Sorry, it was just an accident," said Philip, rising, immediately apologetic again. "It's my knees, you see." He caught Kathleen's hand.

"Out!" said the male voice again, now with two torchlights blinding them. Phillip, pulled a laughing Kathleen along with him, squeezing past other courting couples.

"And don't try coming here again!" They were ejected out into the rain. Kathleen, although laughing loudly, was a little annoyed her bubble of pleasure was so unceremoniously cut short. Lucy and Gordon were right behind them.

"Come on, let's find a café where we can get out of this awful rain," said Philip. And together they splashed their way through puddles, on a mission.

It seemed like everyone else with the same idea had headed for shelter. The café was really busy. They managed to find a table for four near the toilets. They sat down and ordered a pot of tea. The toilet door kept banging with an unseen draught, and Kathleen began to shiver.

"Are you up for a challenge?' said Gordie, looking at Lucy keenly as she tried to warm her hands around the cup. "Philip has a little place we could go to. Without interruption. Interested?"

"Of course!" said Kathleen, agreeing before Lucy

had the chance to say no. Life was too short. The anger, hurt, and grief at the death of her family still firmly tied her in knots. Anything remotely outrageous she would do, just to try and forget, even though she hated herself for being unreasonable.

"Great. Drink up, then!"

As Philip and Gordon paid the bill, the girls tidied themselves up in the tiny toilet. Kathleen and Lucy stared in the mirror together. "Don't look so worried. It'll be fun, Luce."

"I hope you're right." Lucy scowled back.

"Come on, let's live a little, Luce." Kathleen didn't care what she might be getting them into. They stepped outside the café. The rain had stopped, and the boys were grinning.

"Ready?"

Chapter 23

"Where are we going?" asked Lucy.

"You'll see." Gordon cockily grabbed her hand, and they walked to the bus stop, where the number twenty-nine was just pulling in.

"Perfect timing!" said Philip and helped an old woman with her shopping get onto the bus, whilst Gordon dragged Lucy past, uncaring. They were on the top deck and headed for the back seat where the bus conductor followed them along. Philip paid the fare, and just five stops later he caught hold of Kathleen's hand and guided her off the bus.

"We'll go in the back way. Don't want the neighbors nosing in on our business." Puzzled, she turned back, only to see the bus pull away with a gush of oily black smoke pouring from behind, and gave a half smile at Lucy.

"Come on," said Philip, and she followed single file along a back lane, picking their steps between muddy puddles and rangy weeds. He stopped outside a low wooden gate. "The coast is clear. My parents won't be here until six, so we have plenty of time to get to know one another better," he said, and for the first time in her life, Kathleen felt doubt.

"Hey, wait for us, Phil!" Gordon shouted, lagging behind.

"Shut up!" hissed Philip, putting his fingers to his

lips. Kathleen saw Lucy's face—it was a picture. Her hair flew wildly in the breeze as Gordon hurried her along, but she was smiling and looked so happy Kathleen wondered what she was worrying about. Philip tipped up a plant pot by the back door and produced the key. Once inside, he insisted they take off their shoes and hold on to them. Leading Kathleen once more by the hand, he walked them through the kitchenette, along a small hallway, and up the stairs.

"You go in that one, Gordon. It's my brother's room, so don't mess it up or I'll get the blame."

Kathleen was trying to decipher if Lucy felt this was all right, but all her friend did was glance at the floor, avoiding eye contact.

"It's okay," said Gordon. Lucy bit her bottom lip. "I've got Johnnies," he said pulling a pack of three rubbers from his pocket. "Here's one for you, Phil." Philip had the good grace to blush.

"Are you okay with this, Kathleen?" queried Lucy.

"Stop messing about. We haven't got all day!" Gordon snapped, and hustled Lucy into the bedroom, closing the door firmly behind them.

"Come on, let's just fool around for a bit," said Philip, and with that he opened his bedroom door and led her inside. She looked about, surprised at the tiny space with a single bed crammed against the back wall and a chest of drawers on the opposite side allowing just a small walkway between.

"It's not the Ritz, I know." He loomed large in the cramped space, looking embarrassed. "But it's home, and I won't do anything you don't want to, I promise," and with that he began kissing her. This time they spent a long time just kissing, first sitting on the bed, then attempting to lie down together, adjusting their positions to make themselves more comfortable. Then Philip moved so he was on top of her, but as he tried to undo her blouse they ended up in a heap on the floor. They both burst out laughing, and for a moment their eyes locked. It was getting serious. It was then Kathleen heard a cry. She froze. It was muffled but she felt sure it was her friend, and she sounded distressed.

"Did you hear that, Philip?" She pushed his hand away.

"What?" He was slowly undoing her blouse and kissing her neck.

"Stop." She put her fingers to his lips. There it was again, a shrill pleading—"No, I don't want to."

"Philip, I'm sorry, but you said *you* wouldn't do anything I didn't want to. But what about Gordon? Would he be the same with Lucy?" Philip's face said it all. Kathleen pushed Philip off and jumped up to make for the door. She felt his hand upon her shoulder.

"Let me. I brought you here. Gordon can get a bit fresh at times, but I can handle him." A small sigh of relief escaped her lips, and as she quickly did up a button she noticed Philip checking the time. Worried, she pushed past him.

"Lucy?" said Kathleen, banging on the locked door. Philip gently manhandled her out of the way.

"I said I would handle this. Gordon. Mate. Open up." He knocked on the door loudly. The air was still, not a sound could be heard. "Gordon, open up quick!"

"Just a minute!" There was a rustling, and Gordon came to the door, filling the gap. "What do you want? You're spoiling our fun." His face was red, and he stood there still trying to drag his trousers up from around his ankles.

"Are you all right, Lucy?" Kathleen called, trying to see around him.

"Sorry, mate, I got the time wrong," said Philip quickly, cutting her off. "Just realized my parents will be back by five, not six, so we need to get out of here." Gordon looked at him furiously.

"Damn it, Phil, we were just getting to know one another and having a bit of fun. Weren't we, Luce?" There was a small whimper from behind him.

"Let Lucy tell me that herself," said Kathleen, anger getting the better of her. She forced herself in front of Philip.

"We need to get going, Gordon," said Philip firmly, and with that, as Gordon stepped to one side, Lucy rushed out, disheveled, tear-stained, straight into her friend's arms.

"Off you go, and don't forget your shoes." The coolness of Philip's voice betrayed the look on his face.

"Yes, off you go, then, little girls." The sarcasm in Gordon's voice now occupied the landing. "You're nothing more than a tease, Lucy Latimer. Wait till I tell everyone how easy you were." He began sniggering, still attempting to do his trousers up. With that, Lucy burst into tears, but before Gordon knew what hit him, Kathleen gave him an almighty shove. He fell backward onto the floor, knocking the wind right out. She pointed directly at his crotch.

"If you say one unkind thing about my friend, trust me, I will tell everyone your penis is smaller than the size of a peanut. Which incidentally matches the size of your brain!"

Gordon gasped. "Bitch!"

"Trust me, peanut penis. I can do far worse." Her eyes narrowed. "Just one word."

Philip turned away, smirking, as the girls quickly let themselves out the same way they came in.

"Oh, Kathleen," wailed Lucy as they picked their way back along the muddy lane toward the main road, tears dripping down her cheeks.

"Did he?" Kathleen looked at her anxiously.

"No!"

Kathleen exhaled, relieved. "This is all my fault. I'm so sorry, Lucy. I really am. Come on, now, don't cry." She put her arm around her friend's shoulders. "He's simply not worth your salt."

Lucy turned to her, wiping away tears with the back of her hand, and gave a half-hearted smile. "Peanut penis?"

"And don't forget peanut brain," said Kathleen, privately thankful they were safe, and they walked arm in arm toward the bus stop.

Chapter 24

Summer Break 1955

The amateur dramatics society went on summer break just two weeks before end of school. With rehearsals resuming at the end of August, Mrs. Sellers planned to do an inventory and tidy the costumes. Instead, Mr. Sellers arrived to speak to Kathleen, with a note asking if she would like to make a start at it on her own. Reading the instructions, Kathleen took the key.

"Of course, Mr. Sellers, I'd be happy to. Please tell Mrs. Sellers I hope she gets well very soon."

"My wife said you wouldn't let her down," said Mr. Sellers, pleased. "I'll drop you off at the hall. It's the least I can do."

Kathleen rushed back to the dorm to collect her jacket, bag, and money, leaping along the hallway. It was as if fate loaned her a gift. Now she could find the perfect place to hide her disguise.

****

Lucy and Kathleen were sitting on the swings in the park. All week it had rained, that fine, misty, never-going-away type of rain that soaked you to the skin. But today the weather had changed. There was a smattering of pellucid sky where the sun managed to poke fingers of warmth between the clouds. Children were running around, making the most of their freedom, screaming

L. B. Griffin

excitedly. An older boy, much to his own amusement, pushed the witch's hat faster and faster, trying to bounce smaller children off, leaving one child crying and tearful. Kathleen got up and gave him a piece of her mind. The boy stopped when he saw she was bigger and looked every bit ready to thump him. Kathleen returned to her seat, chewing her bottom lip. How normal everything looked, but nothing felt normal anymore. Soon, soon all this would be left far behind.

"Are you okay, Kathleen?" asked Lucy. "It's not because Philip hasn't been in touch?"

"Nope!"

"Is there something you're not telling me? You look…" Lucy squinted at her sideways.

"What?" Kathleen glanced at her, alarmed. "What do I look like?"

"I don't know, but something's up." She looked worried. "You look sad, Kathleen. Really sad. Just like you did…after." She couldn't bring herself to say *loss of your family*. "I can't bear you being sad." Lucy gave her friend a squeeze. "You know you can tell me anything. We're best friends. *Aren't we?*"

Doubt was already growing in Kathleen's heart. She would remember Lucy in so many ways, and she had been lying for so long now, it almost seemed like fact, but it didn't stop her fretting. There would be nothing better than to be able to share her plans. Perhaps she could?

"Don't you want to come away with me to Cornwall? Is that it? You only have to say," Lucy looked on unhappily, unwittingly breaking the moment of truth.

"Spots!" It was all she could think. They both

hated them, after all. Boys or spots were hated in equal measure, and the topic for discussion most days.

"Liar, liar, pants on fire."

"I'm not lying, Luce, honest."

"Spots?" Lucy suddenly giggled with relief. "Well, you do happen to have a huge one growing on your nose, Kathleen Gray. So big in fact, even Pinocchio will be a distant memory."

"Ha, ha. Very bloody funny."

Kathleen walked around to the back of Lucy's swing and began pushing her, not daring to let her friend read her. It would be all too easy to tell her everything. But Kathleen's sensible voice reasoned that if Lucy knew even the smallest detail, she might accidentally—or even deliberately—manage to put a stop to it.

"Tell me all about Polzeath again. It sounds great. I can't wait," she said, but with a nugget of fear gnawing away. Though her plans were meticulously carved out, there was still the unknown. What if she had forgotten something really important? She pushed Lucy higher, and with each push went through every detail. She had enough money to survive for two months, and a bogus Post Office account, in the name of Mrs. Abercrombie. Lord knew why she chose such a stupid name. Lucy shrieked in delight as Kathleen pushed her harder. Now all she had to do was disappear the week after they returned from Cornwall.

Lucy shouted, "Enough!" but as Kathleen gave her one more hard shove, jumping up, catching the bottom, and pushing the swing, it jolted and twisted, swinging Lucy in all directions.

"Sorry, Luce!" She stepped away, watching Lucy

holding tight until the swing righted itself.

Of course, there was still the issue of finding a job and somewhere to live. She puckered her lips. That might be a bit of a problem. She began pushing the swing again.

Chapter 25

The first week of the summer break arrived. Kathleen could hardly believe the time was almost upon her. She could think of nothing else. Packing for the holiday, she knew her future relied entirely on absolutely everything falling into place.

Already five moves ahead, she checked and double and triple-checked each scenario. She looked back through her list.

The key to the village hall was safely stowed in the bottom of her bag.

Check.

Two suitcases, one safely hidden behind the bric-a-brac in the village hall.

Check.

Letters written, ready to post.

Check.

Tickets to London.

Check.

Post Office book and confirmation of the Post Office box.

Check.

She looked at her copy of *Anne of Green Gables*. It was precious, but Amy loved it as much as she did. She put it in Amy's drawer along with a note to keep it safe until she returned.

She puffed out her cheeks. Everything was in place

except one simple thing—the solution as to how, where, and when the letters could be posted. They lay at the bottom of her suitcase, ready stamped, concealed within a larger envelope. Straightening her back, she went to meet Mrs. Fuller.

Mrs. Fuller stood at the front door, dramatically tapping her watch for Kathleen's benefit.

"The taxi has been waiting ten minutes, young lady. I thought I would have to send a search party!" But she said it with a smile in her eye, knowing just how terrible the girl was for timekeeping. "Right, Miss Gray, enjoy yourself and have a lovely time."

"Goodbye, Mrs. Fuller, and thank you."

Kathleen felt the guilt rising in her chest at having already managed to fool so many people. Poor Mrs. Fuller and Mrs. Sellers had been totally duped, and in a moment of madness she threw herself at her, repeating her thanks. As the taxi sped away, taking Kathleen to Lucy's home, she glanced over her shoulder and took one last look at school and prayed none of the staff would get into too much bother.

****

The alarm clock jangled—four fifteen in the morning, still as dark as night. Lucy fell out of bed and flicked on the main light, sleepily rubbing her hands through her hair. It stood up on end. Her eyes closing, she obviously wanted to go back to bed more than anything.

Kathleen rolled over in bed, groaning, pulling the covers over her head. "Tell me again why we must get up this early?"

"The sooner we leave, the sooner we get there." Lucy found a wave of energy and began bouncing up and down on top of Kathleen. "Come on!" She jumped off the bed, taking the blankets with her.

"Oh, bloody hell, Luce!" Kathleen squealed, trying to pull them back. But Lucy won the tug-of-war, and they began dressing and talking in a jumbled, sleepy, drunk-like stupor.

"I hope we get good weather." Lucy put her jumper on backwards. It felt odd, the neck stuck high under her chin. She looked in the mirror, saw the problem, tugged the jumper off, tripped over her shoes, and fell headlong onto the floor. Kathleen burst out laughing.

"Serves you bloody right!"

****

Mr. Latimer checked the kitchen clock against his watch. It was precisely four thirty a.m. He liked order and began re-checking his list. Lily had boiled the eggs the night before. This morning, she made two rounds of tinned pink salmon sandwiches ready for the journey. Trying to rid himself of the lingering pong of fish and eggs, he left the kitchen door wide open, letting cold air in. Nose twitching, Mr. Latimer twisted salt into waxed paper, placed everything into the picnic hamper, and stowed it all in the boot of the car.

"Come along, girls, let's get cracking." He gathered up their suitcases.

Mr. Latimer had an unusual lightness to his voice, thought Kathleen. Why, even his face seemed younger when he smiled at his wife. Aunty Lily was clearly on a high, even at this ungodly hour. It seemed nothing could dampen her spirits. She apparently heard the radio promising good weather, and with that, combined with the delivery of their brand-new Rover P4 this week, she was beside herself.

"Ooh, I feel like the Queen," she said, sliding into the passenger seat. The scent of new leather hung as strong as that of the salmon sandwiches.

"Do you think I could drive, Nigel?" He finished putting the last of the luggage inside the boot and slipped into the driving seat.

"Hmm, we can talk about it."

"Oh, Nigel! What's the harm? I passed my driving test first time. Not like someone I could mention." Lily waggled her eyebrows at him.

"How about on the way home, Lily?" He put the gear into first.

"Did you hear that, girls?" Lily turned toward them. "I might get to drive this little beauty!"

Two hours later, Mr. Latimer, on the lookout for a comfort break, had found a hedge with a five-bar gate, and pulled in. As the sun began to rise over the hill, the girls clambered out of the car and sat on top of the dew-covered gate. Lily unwrapped the eggs and handed them out, offering the little salt wraps as well.

"Thank you, Aunty Lily. Breakfast in the open air, simply divine," said Kathleen, peeling her egg, the odor unmistakable.

"You're most welcome, dear." Lily smiled at her fondly. "Another hour or so and we just might see the coast."

Mr. Latimer finished his tea and, flicking the dregs away, advised everyone to be on the lookout for farmers, dogs, and cows whilst he stretched his legs in the field.

Kathleen grinned at Lucy. Mr. Latimer was human after all. Lucy smiled back. Aunty Lily busily rearranged the picnic hamper and checked if they needed a comfort break. Mr. Latimer by now was climbing back over the gate, looking awkward.

"There's a clearing off to the left. I can safely report there are no bulls." He shook his foot, grimacing. "But you have to be on the lookout for cowpats."

"Oh, Nigel!" sighed Lily, exasperated. "We can't have you in our new car smelling like a farmyard, now, can we?"

"Thought it was meant to be good luck, old girl."

Mr. Latimer joined the girls on top of the gate, winking whilst his wife found a rag to clean his shoe off.

Kathleen smiled. Lucy's father was rising in her estimation.

"Do you fancy driving the rest of the way, Lily?"

"Why, I'd love to, Nigel!" said Lily, evidently surprised. Nigel sat beside his wife whilst she adjusted her seat, and the girls clambered into the back.

"Don't forget to check your rearview mirror, darling."

Kathleen's mouth dropped open, and Lucy whispered, "They get like that on holiday. All lovey-dovey." She grimaced, going boss-eyed in disgust. Kathleen covered her mouth, fighting giggles.

****

Around an hour later, cornering a bend on a hill, they saw a Georgian hotel come into view. It stood proudly on the clifftop, sentry-like, the eyes of the windows overlooking the sea. As Lily pulled the car up outside and put the handbrake on, they were greeted with a polite reverence by an older man in a smart pinstriped suit.

"Good morning, Mr. and Mrs. Latimer. It is so

good to see you again. I trust you had a good journey?"
He turned to the young male beside him.

"Eric, please see the luggage is taken straight to
their rooms and ensure everything is in order."

"Yes, sir." Eric, smiling, picked up the cases whilst
discreetly giving the girls the onceover. They turned
pink with delighted embarrassment. It was all they
could do not to snigger.

Eric showed the Latimers to their room before
swiping up the girls' luggage and strutting down the
hallway, motioning toward the amenities as they went.
He flashed a broad grin at Lucy and, checking over his
shoulder, tapped his nose and dumped their luggage
inside their room.

"If I can be of any *extra* service, there's a small
annex at the back of the hotel." He wiggled his hands in
his pockets suggestively. "Whenever you feel the *urge*,
I can show you what a cloth-eared elephant looks like."

The girls burst into fits of giggles and ran into their
room.

Maroon walls and two single beds greeted the girls
as the door closed behind them. Kathleen grimaced. It
was so dark, so dismal. She immediately pulled the
heavy drapes back and pushed up the sash window to
lean out. "Hey, come take a look, Luce. Groohoovy!
We've got a sea view. Come see. Wow. The waves are
enormous!"

"You know I hate heights. Come back in, please,
Kathleen, before you fall."

"Aw, come on, Luce." Kathleen was laughing, but
Lucy worriedly grabbed her arm, tugging her back.

"Stop it. Come on, back inside where it's safe. We
can get unpacked and sorted, and you know Daddy will

expect us to be on time for lunch."

****

The Latimers were already seated in the dining room. Kathleen caught Mr. Latimer glancing at his watch as they arrived.

"I'm sorry, Mr. Latimer, it's my fault we are late," she apologized, immediately claiming responsibility. "We have a sea view! It's fabulous. Thank you so much. I couldn't get enough of it, could I, Lucy?"

Mr. Latimer melted just a little.

"Dining times are very exacting. I was beginning to become concerned lunch would be over and you would miss out." He shook his head, smiling as they sat down. "That would never do."

"Now, girls," said Aunty Lily. "We thought we would go for a stroll along the cliffs this afternoon, build up an appetite for our evening meal."

"We've got our cossies on already, Mummy," said Lucy keenly. "I could take Kathleen to the beach. You don't have to look after us *all* the time."

"I dare say you're right." Lily's love for her daughter spread across her face. "What do you think, Nigel?"

"Absolutely, dear. These young things don't want to be hanging around the old folk." He folded a napkin on his lap. "There is one stipulation, though." He looked his daughter straight in the eye. "I'd like to be certain where you're going, and that you'll be back in good time, ready for the evening meal."

"Of course, Daddy," said Lucy, quickly outlining their plans. Her mother clapped her hands in delight.

"It's settled, and don't forget to wear your sunhats. We'll see you in the lobby, all spick and span, at five-thirty sharp."

****

The girls set off with hats and towels, their hair flying in the warm breeze as they chased one another.

"I know a shortcut. Follow me." Lucy took them across the road into a narrow sandy track. Five minutes later, the lane petered out, bringing them onto a smaller road just wide enough for one car to pass another.

"We're here!" she cried excitedly. All Kathleen could see was a pub, a small village shop-come-post office, and a church.

"I can't see a beach, Luce. Have you got the right place?"

"Come on." Lucy tugged her by the hand, pulling her on down the road and around the corner. "There. What do you think of that?"

Grass-topped cliffs embraced a huge expanse of beautiful golden sand that stretched toward a rolling sea.

"The beach is divided by the cliff over there." Lucy pointed eastward. "Behind the headland is a cove. The one you saw from the hotel window."

"It really is beautiful, Lucy. I never imagined this." Kathleen was already kicking off her shoes and dropping her belongings in a heap. "Beat you!"

"Never!" Lucy, pushed her shoes off and ran after her.

Sand flicked up their heels as they sped toward the sea. A large dog bounded up beside them, joining the race. A man whistled and shouted for him to come, but the dog stayed, happily leaping alongside. The girls, still in competition, were level and entered the water together, shrieking, laughing as it splashed over their feet and swooshed up their calves, freezing them to the bone. Still screaming in delight, they jumped over the swells, and the dog followed suit, tail wagging, mouth smiling, tongue lolling.

"Last one in is a sissy!" shouted Kathleen, running back toward their belongings. Lucy called after her, chasing, following her trail of imprints in damp golden sand. With the heat from the sun already beginning to warm them, they peeled off their clothes and once more headed back to the water, the dog still in tow.

Kathleen dove headfirst under a breaker that thundered toward her and came up for air, then swam strongly toward the next wave. She ducked under again, surfacing, gasping, shivering, so cold her bones were already frozen. Treading water, looking for Lucy, she could just make her out on the shoreline, along with the dog leaping around beside her.

Lucy had managed to force her hair into her swimming hat and had just clipped the band under her chin when she saw the oncoming wave. Fear filling her heart, she rushed into the sea shouting, waving her arms with a warning.

"Come on!" Kathleen shouted, treading water and pushing back her hair, which hung like seaweed around her face. Suddenly a dark shape shot past. Something flew high above her, blotting out the sun. Her voice was instantly lost in the sudden roar of an enormous wave crashing right over her head. Caught by surprise, she went under, all air knocked from her lungs. Foam rushed up her nose and into her ears. She gasped for air but swallowed a lungful of sea. Kathleen fought back, trying not to choke in response, the urge to breathe so great. She kicked hard to reach the surface, and her arms continued to strike upward. Another wave crashed over her, pushing her back under. She floundered. Ever down, down toward the seabed. Her heart pounded, her chest hurt, and her lungs were on fire. She felt weak. Empty. A few bubbles escaped her lips, and a sense of peace began to envelop her. She would be with her parents and little Bobby now. Uncle Jack would be able to move on.

Chapter 26

Suddenly something grabbed her. A yank. Then another. Then another. She was being tugged upward. Her eyes dragged open. She could see light. So distant. Then another tug. Daylight brighter. Not far. Her chest felt as if it was being crushed. All her energy had been spent. She could do nothing to help. Her eyes closed.

It felt like hours but must have been only moments before she surfaced with strong arms wrapped about her and under her shoulders. She snatched at air, coughing, choking, spluttering. A dark-haired girl was mouthing, "Idiot!"

Kathleen, still straining for air, was unable to respond. Seconds later, another thunderous roller headed their way, with a surfer riding inside the white foamy curl of the crest and right at them.

"Breathe in!" the girl yelled, still holding her tight.

****

A surfboard slid to a watery halt along the shoreline, gluing itself on the sticky sand. With the distraction of the dog now gone, Lucy began frantically pacing, staring into the waves, her heart pounding with fear. She'd seen a surfer come off his board. Kathleen had disappeared under a wave. There was no sign of her. The friendly dog irritated her now, barking, leaping up around her. She saw two people standing together farther down the beach. One body, bent over, curled up on the sand, retching. Lucy peered, praying, heart in mouth. Yes, maybe. With tears streaming down her face, she ran hell-for-leather toward the group, hoping she was right.

"Kathleen!" cried Lucy, puffing, exhausted, frightened, seeing her friend's face red and blotchy, still snatching at air. "I was so worried. I thought you'd drowned!"

An older girl close by, wearing a wetsuit, pushed her fingers through her dark hair, creating short, spiked turrets.

"She nearly did. And she got me and our Artie knocked off our boards. Could have been nasty." Kathleen had the good grace to look ashamed.

"You're obviously not from these parts," said the girl. She held out a hand. "I'm Morven." She jerked her head to the male next to her. "This is Artie. We were just telling your friend here how important it is people know the rules of the sea. Don't want people drownin', now, do we?"

"Nope, we don't, and that's for certain," said a sun-bleached blond Artie. He pulled the top half of his wetsuit down to his waist, displaying a superbly toned, bronzed torso. Lucy blushed, momentarily distracted from her friend's plight.

"It's not good for business!" Artie smiled. He turned back to the coughing Kathleen. "Are you feeling a little better now?"

Kathleen nodded, more than a tad embarrassed but glad to be alive.

"Good." He pointed out a small shack nestled in the cliff at the top of the beach and close to the road. "That's our surf shack." The side of the building was painted in delightful abstract art imitating sea and surf boards. "We give lessons in *safe* surfin' and swimmin'."

"Groovy," Kathleen mouthed, still gathering in lungfuls of air and feeling a complete idiot.

Artie and Morven shook their heads, groaning.

"Safety is key, Kathleen," Morven said firmly.

She gestured toward the shack. "Come 'n' take a gander when you're passin'. Now, are you okay?"

Kathleen nodded.

"Good. If you're interested, we'll give you one free lesson. Each."

"When you're passin'." Artie grinned. "I need to go and get me board back." He was scratching the side of his face thoughtfully. "We'll be cookin' fish on the beach with our mates tonight. If you're stayin' and feel like it, why not join us?"

"Groovy! We'll be there, count on it." Kathleen was trying to get back to her usual self, and ignored the worried gasps from Lucy.

"Around sevenish? No rush."

****

"Are you quite mad?" said Lucy, once out of earshot. "You nearly drowned! Isn't that enough for one day?"

"Don't tell your parents!" was all Kathleen could muster, just as the friendly dog bounded up around her ankles, nearly bowling her over. Lucy laughed, pushing her friend on the shoulder.

Kathleen shakily picked up her towel and for a second buried her face to conceal just how scared she really felt. Patting herself dry, she took in a deep breath of welcome air, grateful for life and full of relief

Morven had come to her rescue. She turned to Lucy with forced enthusiasm.

"Come on, Luce, we need to live a little. Let's go tonight, have some fun."

"You know my parents won't allow us out at night. Let alone to stand around a bonfire on the beach, eating fish with a bunch of strangers."

"Luce, relax. We'll bring your parents as well."

"What? Daddy will die of apoplexy!"

Kathleen smirked, knowing what the response would be before it left her mouth.

"Just kidding, Luce. I'll think of something."

"Huh. I just can't wait to hear your plan for tonight then, Kathleen Gray. You know just how strict my parents are."

Lucy picked up a piece of driftwood and threw it along the beach for the dog to give chase, privately thanking the heavens she was still alive.

"No problem, Luce. I've just had an idea."

Chapter 27

The Latimers met the girls outside on the terracing for pre-dinner drinks.

"I do like punctuality." Mr. Latimer took a sip of wine, having already ordered fizzy bitter lemon for the girls. Lucy grinned. It had been a major coup getting Kathleen ready on time.

"You look lovely, Aunty Lily." Kathleen was genuinely impressed by the simple but elegant pale-green outfit her friend's mother wore.

"Why, thank you, dear. Did you have a good day?"

"Groovy. Lucy really knows the area well. And we've had such fun. We have met so many friendly people. Haven't we, Lucy?" Kathleen smiled benevolently.

"Uh-huh."

"Jolly good show." Mr. Latimer had an indecipherable expression on his face whilst repeating the word *groovy* to himself.

"To happy holidays," he said, lifting his glass and chinking it against his wife's.

A waiter arrived and escorted them to their table by the window with an excellent view of the sea. As they sat down, Kathleen saw a couple of surfers catching the waves way off in the distance. She yawned widely, quickly covering her mouth with an apology, and by the end of the meal she had stifled another yawn.

"I'm so sorry!" Kathleen mumbled, looking mortified. "I don't want to be a bore, but would you mind if I went to bed? I'm really tired."

"I'll join you, Kathleen. If that's all right, Mummy?"

"My goodness, Lucy. I never thought I'd hear you say you wanted to go to bed early. Very well, girls, we'll say goodnight," and she kissed them on their foreheads.

Lucy hugged her father. "Good night, Daddy."

"Good night. Oh, yes, I almost forgot to say. I thought we would go to St. Ives tomorrow. It's supposed to be Cornwall's epicenter of art. I believe you gals might like it."

"Nigel!" exclaimed Lily. "What a wonderful idea!"

"Breakfast, eight thirty, sharp? Good night."

Lucy nudged her friend as they climbed the stairs. "Are we really going to bed?"

"Are you bloody nuts? Of course not. I told you I'd think of something."

Once in their room, Kathleen picked up a pillow, dressed it with a nightie, and placed it strategically under the blankets along with another.

"See? Covered with a blanket, and the curtains pulled, should your mother come to check on us, we'll look like we're in bed, asleep." Lucy copied the example.

"Now what?" Lucy stood back, a little unsure her pillow did justice to the shape of a body.

"You said you can only see the smaller bay from the hotel." Kathleen chuckled. "While you were in the bathroom, I went on a reconnoiter."

"Seriously?"

"Uh-huh. First, let's get out of these dresses and back into shorts!"

****

Giggling, they crept back down the stairs and out through to the rear garden. A gate was set into the hedge. It led to the back road, where three bicycles were parked.

"Now!" said Kathleen, grabbing her friend by the hand and dragging her across the road toward the sandy track. Having succeeded in getting across the road unseen, laughing between gulps of air, they ran until they reached the bottom of the lane.

Finding Morven and Artie was simple enough. There was a group of ten, laughing and joking. Artie played at being chef, with skewered mackerel on sticks layered across the heat of a bonfire. The girls were all similarly dressed in shorts and thick knitted blue jumpers, whilst the males wore shorts and heavy cotton shirts. For the first time in her life Kathleen felt envious. The Cornish girls looked so completely at ease in their skins, and with their lives.

"Glad you could make it," said Morven, first to spot them. "Come on, I'll introduce you."

The group, five males and five females, made them feel instantly welcome. It turned out they belonged to the Baptist Church Project. Morven pointed toward the cliff where a small hut was silhouetted against the sun.

"If it rains, we go in, but we prefer to stay outdoors if we can." Lawrie, probably the eldest of the group and the evident leader, had his arm looped around Sadie's waist. As Kathleen looked more closely, she could see her jumper had three rows of tiny buttons stitched along one sleeve in the shape of a wave.

"That's really clever," commented Kathleen, also noticing Sadie's hair, braided with baby feathers and earrings to match.

"Thanks, kiddo. Obviously, you have an eye for detail, unlike Lawrie here. He'd only notice if I walked around stark naked." Lucy gaped. Sadie twisted the feathered silver earring between the tip of her index finger and thumb, then unhitched herself from Lawrie and strolled sexily toward the fire. "Come on," she said, looking over her shoulder. Lawrie watched her every move. "I don't know about you, but I'm starvin'!"

Eric arrived with a guitar strung over his back and sat down on a rock and began strumming a catchy rift. Instantly two girls wandered over and started singing along.

"Come on, Luce." Kathleen pulled her along, excited, loving the music, wanting to be a part of it.

"It's you!" He looked up, amused, confidently changing chords, not missing a beat. "I'm surprised you're allowed out."

"We can do anything we want, can't we, Luce?" Kathleen tried to look poised and sound nonchalant.

"So you won't mind me if I accidentally tell Mr. and Mrs. Latimer I saw you tonight?"

Lucy gasped.

"If you do, we'll deny it!" Kathleen flashed back.

"Thought so."

"You wouldn't tell, would you?" Lucy nervously wrung her hands.

"It's okay." He laughed. "Grab me something to eat, and I'll forget you were ever here," and Lucy, true to form, immediately did as asked.

After the last of the food was devoured, the boys

set up a game of quick cricket, insisting they all join in before it became too dark to see the ball. Then, as the last of the flames and heat from the fire slowly died, Morven shouted, "Surf's up. Who's comin'?" They all immediately came to life, whooping and grabbing their surfboards. Kathleen watched their shadowy figures in amazement, rushing to the shore, heading out into the whiteness of waves, still remembering just how thankful she was to be alive.

"It's time I went," said Eric, stringing his guitar back over his shoulder. "It's beginnin' to chill. I'll walk you back, if you want. They'll be out there for hours, and I can't have you gettin' lost on my watch."

"Thank you," said Lucy gratefully.

"Don't you surf, Eric?" Kathleen called, chasing him along the beach.

"I do. But I have to be up at four. I'm picking up a guest from the station. The manager is all of a puff and being all cloak-and-dagger like. Someone famous. Told me not to breathe a word."

They reached the bottom of the sandy path. Without Eric's torch, the lane would have been virtually impossible to navigate.

"Come on, I've said too much already." He stuffed the torch under his chin with a ghoulish grin, deepening the mystery a little more. "But between you and me, she's a writer with a French-sounding name, and she's coming to see my cloth-eared elephant."

The girls, blinded by his torch light, exploded with laughter.

Eric, for all his bravado, was thoughtful. He knew the terrain well, helped them when they stumbled, and flashed his torch along the lane to guide their steps.

When they eventually came close to the hotel, he checked the coast was clear before escorting them through the kitchen and up the back stairs reserved for staff.

"Remember, no talk of special guests, and I won't mention you being out tonight." The girls nodded their quiet thanks and quickly stole into their beds fully dressed. Kathleen lay in bed plotting. Eric would be the ideal answer to posting her letters. She would seek him out tomorrow.

****

Mrs. Latimer's muffled voice came from the other side of their bedroom door. Kathleen immediately drew her blankets tightly up around her chin, glancing at the clock. It was seven thirty.

"It's Mummy!" Lucy's eyes were boggling.

Kathleen scooted out of bed, "Start brushing your hair and follow my lead." Lucy looked scared out of her wits.

"Come in," called Kathleen.

"The door's locked."

"Just a minute." In one swift motion Kathleen unlocked the door.

"Good morning, Aunty Lily." Kathleen peered sleepily around the door.

"Ah, I see you're dressed already. Well done. It's time for breakfast." Aunty Lily's voice filled the room with light and excitement. "It looks like another glorious day. Perfect for our trip to St. Ives."

Chapter 28

Kathleen threw her arms around the couple. "I've had a simply wonderful time. You have no idea." And she meant every word. The family had looked after her as if she were their own and helped her slot into their world with ease. Kathleen understood Lucy's father better now. The pressure of his work, the long hours, clearly played a role in how he presented himself. But in the short time they were away he'd managed to relax, showing his softer, kinder, more thoughtful side.

They were parked outside the school gates. The high gray stone wall surrounded the grounds, and Kathleen prayed they could not be seen. Mr. Latimer lifted her little leather case out of the boot of the car.

"Perhaps next year, young lady," he began, "perhaps you could join us for longer?"

"Really? That is very kind of you, Mr. Latimer."

Next year. Where would she be? Reaching for the suitcase, she quickly played her hand.

"You've driven so far out of your way already, Mr. Latimer. It would make me feel so much better if you were able to get to Lucy's grandfather's before dark." He placed a kindly hand on her shoulder.

"If you're absolutely sure, Kathleen? I will personally write to your uncle and tell him what a pleasure it has been having you stay with us." And with those kind words ringing in her ears, she threw her arms around him with an overwhelming sense of guilt and gratitude.

"You have been so very kind, all of you. I've had the most wonderful time. Really I have."

Kathleen remained exactly where they dropped her off, waving at the disappearing car.

This was it!

Amazed and pleased the Latimers had gotten her back so early, Kathleen knew if she moved quickly she could catch the first and only train to London. Far better than hiding away in the back of the church hall overnight. Far better than she could have ever hoped for. Racing back down the hill, she searched for the gap in the hedge on the opposite side of the road. The fence, managed by the farmer and meant to keep his cows from straying, proved a difficult obstacle, but on her many trips to meet the postman, she'd found one small gap, just wide enough for her to get between. On the opposite side there was a dirt path, just the width of a single step there between the cow field and the bush, leading toward the church.

Throwing her suitcase over the hedge, she waited to hear it land. The dull thud rewarded her. She sucked in her stomach and stretched her legs gingerly between the gap, trying to avoid being caught on the barbed wire and hedge. But as her toe touched the other side, a long spiny hawthorn caught her unawares, slapping her hard across the face. The whiplash stung; worse still, a thorn viciously embedded itself in her face. Trying hard not to cry, she gently eased the needle from her skin, rubbing her sore and bloodied cheek. Taking a deep breath and collecting her suitcase, she put the experience down with positivity. At least with all the sunny weather of late, the bridle path was bone dry and her suitcase *had* avoided a cowpat.

Timing was all important. The church bells were calling Sunday worshippers to prayer. At the bottom of the path, she crouched low by the stile. It led straight into the church grounds. Soon everyone would be inside. Rummaging around inside her bag, she found the copied key to the church hall. There would be tea and biscuits immediately after the service. She had to be quick. Bobbing from behind the fence, she heard the muffled pipes of the church organ, and watched until the last of the worshippers closed the doors behind them.

Climbing the stile, Kathleen skirted her way around to the church hall. It was risky, but there was little time to waste. The next train was due in one hour, and if she had to wait, the last one the following day would not be until four. The congregation would be out in twenty minutes. She turned the key in the lock and closed the door quietly behind her. Kathleen was forced to wait a few precious seconds whilst her eyes adjusted to the change in light. Quickly, she made her way toward where she had hidden her range of clothing. With no time to lose, Kathleen pulled on the stockings and suspender belt over her socks, achieving the look she desired. The light brown hosiery hung loosely and, over bunched-up socks, gave the illusion of varicose veins. Next, she pulled on the large droopy-breasted armor, made from kapok, and put on a floral print dress over the top. She looked in the full-length mirror. It did the job perfectly; she looked at least four sizes greater than usual.

Kathleen began to sweat. Having made the outfit in

the winter months, she hadn't considered the heat of the summer. Wiping her brow, she forced her feet into scuffed, buckled shoes. She wanted to look like she just came from church, but first makeup had to be applied. Not too much to draw attention, but enough to age her.

Kathleen pulled the mirror toward the window. She had to get this right. Theatrical pancake cosmetics were hard to apply. She had perfected the technique, practicing over and over in the bathroom at school, discovering also in the process how to rid herself of it as quickly as possible. Makeup done, she donned the small felt hat, pinning it at a jaunty angle. Mrs. Abercrombie stared right back at her.

"Well, my lovely. We'd best not be 'anging about in this heat. Come on, let's get to this 'ere station." Kathleen laughed. It worked every time at the Post Office. Hopefully, it would serve her well again.

With two suitcases, one in each hand, and a handbag looped over her wrist, Kathleen checked no one was around, and locked up.

****

The train was miraculously on time. As Kathleen boarded, a man offered to help.

"Thank you, dearie." She kept her sentences short, deliberately looking away, concerned her makeup might be sliding down her face or she might quite possibly slip up with her accent.

"There," he said putting the suitcases on the rack.

"Very kind." The man smiled and found himself a seat, opened a newspaper, and began reading.

At Paddington Station, the busy terminal was filled with oily fumes, dust, and grime impossible not to inhale. She tried to ignore it as she descended the train carriage steps.

"All aboard!" A guard blew his whistle and waved his flag. The train she'd just left chugged its way out of the station, followed by stinking, eye-watering smoke billowing above and behind. A wonky tannoy system echoed across the vast expanse of the terminal, impossible to understand, yet confident travelers hurried toward their next destination. Though the underground would need to become her best friend, she decided to arrange a taxi.

Soon they were cruising swiftly in traffic. Kathleen stared out the window, enamored with the hustle and bustle of London. The people here were different. Marvelously different, and it wasn't just their difference in attire from the backwaters of the countryside where she lived. It was a whole new style. They seemed modern, exotic, and appeared to be moving in the fast lane of life. "How simply groovy." She whispered to herself.

"We're here, luv." The hackney cab pulled alongside the curb. "The White Horse, you said." A sign swung on a rusty hinge. The street was filled to bursting with market vendors and customers. Kathleen swallowed, her nerves racing all over the place. "Are you quite sure this is where you are staying?"

"Yes."

"You sit tight, luv. Can't have a woman going into a pub on her own, now, can we?"

"Thank you." She gratefully accepted, and feeling overwhelmed, rooted around for a large tip. Moments later, he emerged looking pleased with himself.

"We have to go around to the side entrance. The landlord sends apologies, they're really busy right now, but I've got the keys, and I'll bring your bags."

"No need, really, thank you. I can manage."

"I insist. I want to be sure you're safely installed." He took the bags from her, and they trailed upstairs. He placed the key into the lock and opened the door.

"Thank you. You've been most kind." She handed him a large tip. He stared at the sum of money.

"I can't take this."

"Don't want to offend an old woman, do you?"

"Well, if you're sure, and should you ever need a cab, ask for Bert White." And with that he put her luggage into the room and was gone.

****

Kathleen stood in the tiny bedroom, absorbing all it offered. The small bedside table had a china wash basin with a jug of water, and under the bed, poking from beneath the faded coverlet of embroidered daisies, a china potty. Gasping for fresher air, she pushed the sash window open, leant out, and breathed in.

Distracted momentarily by the view, she watched in amazement. The street market was doing a bustling business, with women squeezing the produce and clearly bartering with the vendors. Her mother would have loved it, though Mr. Smith, the greengrocer, would have keeled over if anyone tried that back home.

The notion brought her back to earth with a solid thump. No Mother. No Pops. No sweet, dear little Bobby. Tears welled. Stupid thing! She was sniffing into a hanky when the door opened.

"Hello, luv, sorry we couldn't be there to escort you to your room. We're always busy on market day, should have said when you booked."

A woman with bright red lipstick and coiffed

mousy hair smiled brightly.

"Me name's Mrs. Foster. I'm the landlady. Me husband's managin' the bar. I just wanted to make sure you're settled and wondered if you'll be wantin' the room for longer than a week?"

Kathleen, gathering her wits, confirmed that one week would be sufficient to see around the capital.

"Will you be wantin' supper tonight, Mrs. Abercrombie? We've got pie, mash, and mushy peas, or fish and chips from around the corner." The landlady eyed her queerly.

"Pie and mash sound lovely, Mrs. Foster, thank you." The mere mention of food made her stomach grumble. "Is there any chance of something to drink?"

"We've got stout, or would you prefer a cuppa?" The woman continued to run an appraising eye over her.

"A cuppa sounds good," she mimicked the strange way the woman spoke.

"Shall I make you up a tab, for the food?"

"Tab?"

"You know, luv. Give you the bill at the end of the evening, or pay as you go?" Mrs. Foster, arms folded, waited.

"I'll pay as I go, thank you."

"Good. That'll be a bob for the meal and thru'pence for the char." Mrs. Foster cast her eye over her luggage, still on the bed, then whispered in her ear, "Incognito are we, luv? Your secret's safe with me. I've 'elped plenty of women gettin' away from their bleedin' brutish 'usbands. You won't be the first, nor the last."

Kathleen stared in horror.

149

"You're safe here, trust me." Mrs. Foster pulled away. "Anyways, ladies always use the snug. Ain't nice havin' men disturbin' you while you eat," and she gave Kathleen instructions to come via the back stairs. "The lavvie's next on the left, and it costs an extra bob for a bath if you want, but considerin' your predicament, I'll make it thru'pence."

Kathleen was instantly transported back to Paris with Uncle Jack and the wonderful selection of bath oils. "Thank you. How kind. I'd like to take a soak tomorrow morning, please, and would supper be all right in an hour?"

"Aw, la-de-da. Supper, is it?" Kathleen found the landlady grinning broadly. "Very well, supper at six it is, and a soak for the lady tomorrow."

She disappeared, chuckling to herself. "Supper, whatever next."

Kathleen found a mirror from her handbag and discovered her wig askew and, under the heavy makeup, a huge welt just under her eye. It felt sore to the touch, and remembering the argument with the hawthorn, she wondered if that was why Mrs. Foster assumed she had been beaten? How awful.

As she descended the back stairs, the reek of tobacco grew stronger. Men's voices drifted on the air, their language melodic, deep, lilting, strange to her ears. Curiosity got the better of her, and lifting a dark brown curtain draped for privacy, she was taking a sneaky peek when a cavernous voice from behind startled her.

"I guess yer the lady me wife's been talkin' about."

Kathleen spun on her heels, astonished to find a huge beer-bellied beast of a man behind her. His nose looked like it had been flattened in the middle and pushed to one side, but his eyes were sparkling with amused kindness.

"Mrs. Foster's explained the *situation*." He held out a large, calloused hand, at least twice the size of her own.

"I'm Mr. Foster. No need to be scared, luv. Come on through." He indicated toward the end of the corridor. "Don't mind them in the bar. They won't hurt yah."

The landlord guided her through to the snug, saying, "Bullies are just cowards," and adding quietly, "With so many Eye-tal-yuns frequenting our establishment, any unwanted English visitors wouldn't be clever enough to think to look 'ere anyways."

"You're not Italian?"

"State the obvious, luv!" His chest rattled as he exploded with laughter. "Before the war, this place were owned by me father-in-law, Gawd rest his soul. But when the war come…" He paused before coughing up brown phlegm and spitting it into a nearby bucket.

"Lucky the pub never got blown up, but then the Eye-tal-yuns came 'ere and settled. It's me wife's pub, an' she reminded me their money is as good as the next man's." He shrugged, rubbing his nose, grinning. "So long as they pays their way, they cause us little trouble."

The snug was tiny, and though just a second away from the main bar, it was separated by wood dark as ebony, topped with mullioned glass windows. The divide made it impossible to view the other side and kept the noise to a minimum. The snug housed just three small dark oak tables, each having two chairs. Two women already occupied one of the tables, talking earnestly. They stopped the moment they saw Kathleen enter, warily eyeing her up. She did as Mr. Foster suggested, taking a back table, and Mrs. Foster was out in a flash, bringing her a cup of tea and a plate of pie and mash.

"Here you go, luv," she said, placing the food in front of her.

"Right, ladies, another 'alf, is it?" They nodded, resuming their conversation in lowered tones, and Mrs. Foster brought them two halves of watery-looking ale. Kathleen dug her knife and fork into the suet pudding. It was thick, laden with lard, nothing like the light fluffy ones her mother made. Finding her way through to the center, there were a few bits of minced beef glued between gravy so dense it could hold up a spade. Beggars can't be choosers, she mouthed, remembering her mother's favorite quote, and ate every tasteless morsel as if it were the best meal of her life.

****

They were sitting in the tiny back yard of the pub. Mrs. Foster smoked a roll-up whilst her husband worked alongside the potboy sorting out the delivery. The sound of kegs of beer being shifted inside the cellar echoed into the yard, but even with the noise, Kathleen felt a strange kind of peace and normality.

"The mark is going down," said the landlady, blunt in her approach, referring to the welt on Kathleen's face. "What did you do, cook his potatoes until they went to mush or not get the food on the table quick enough?"

"I really appreciate your discretion, Mrs. Foster." Kathleen knew she reddened, as if embarrassed, feeling the flush. "Would you be offended if we didn't talk about it?" She couldn't keep lying to this kind soul, and it would only put her in a difficult position if she knew her age and the truth of her background.

"'Course, luv, didn't mean to be nosey. Tell me to mind me own business, but if you need somewhere safe, you can stay 'ere as long as you like. Promise. I'm right 'ere, okay? I won't charge ya the goin' rate." The suggestion was so kind, so genuine, that Kathleen gulped back a tear.

"You have been extremely kind, and please don't think I don't appreciate your offer…" She paused, then asked, "Have there been many women?" Mrs. Foster stubbed out the butt with her toe, and in the shade of the yard Kathleen caught an expression of sadness crossing her face. She began rolling another cigarette expertly between her thumb and forefinger.

"Me sister…" A fat tear rolled down over her cheek, she swiped at it, but the salty liquid soaked into the cigarette paper. "Lovely, sweet, innocent Dolly. Never said a word. Then it was too late. Twenty-five, dead in the ground and never said a word." She shook her head. "I never read the signs. The bruises was brushed away with simple explanations, like bumpin' into a door, fallin' down a step. Then she stopped comin' to see us."

Another fat tear rolled down her cheek. "I were too busy with the pub to realize how much time passed. But she were me only sister, and she couldn't talk to me. Why didn't she come and talk to me? Why didn't I see what was goin' on?" Mrs. Foster wiped the tears away, and Kathleen gently caught her hand.

"You mustn't blame yourself, Mrs. Foster, but what became of her husband?'"

"The stinkin' pig got away with it!"

They sat quietly in the part shade of the tiny yard for some time, Mrs. Foster with her thoughts and Kathleen with hers. Eventually the landlady rose. "Whilst your company is good, I need to get on."

"Mrs. Foster?"

"Yes, luv?"

"Before you go, may I ask a favor? I stink, I know I do. Even having a bath hasn't done the trick. This disguise has been hanging for days—is there anywhere I could give it a wash?" The landlady laughed out loud. "That wig's foolin' no one, either, specially when it slips. I didn't like to say. Come on, let's sort you out, and in return you can clean the bar and the loos before me customers start driftin' in. Deal?"

"Deal!" and they shook on it.

Chapter 29

One week later, Kathleen placed a note on her bed addressed to Mr. and Mrs. Foster with her sincere thanks and final payment for her stay. Early that Saturday morning she left the White Horse pub for good. There was not to be a trail. The kind Fosters should not be implicated in her deceptions. Having already visited a variety of bedsits, she had placed a deposit on one to secure the room.

Stepping out into the side street with her portfolio tucked under her arm, and with a carpet bag swopped with Mrs. Foster for her luggage, she had transformed herself.

Gone were the long wavy titian locks. Instead, her hair was black and spiky short, just like Morven's. She wore clothes of her own design, and as men wolf-whistled at her in the street as she headed for the tube, she felt completely liberated. Once installed in the tiny bedsit, she re-read the Jobs Vacant columns. There was one job that stood out from the rest. It sounded perfect. She sighed. She would need to find a telephone box and call the Latimers. Now everything was down to her.

****

Kathleen stood outside an atelier on Kings Road, Chelsea, checking her watch. For the first time in her life, she was early. On the front door, a discreet sign stated: "By appointment only." She tried peering past the huge display of fresh flowers filling the window but found it impossible to see inside. Pleased the rain had stopped, she smoothed down her suit. Her reflection in the glass caught her eye and her breath. She looked so different, so much older than her fifteen years. With a slight quiver of nervousness, she pressed the doorbell. Moments later, a young woman answered.

"Good morning, madam?"

"I have an appointment. I believe Madam Raines is expecting me." She proffered a hand-painted business card. "Miss Kate Westfield." There, she breathed her name with a quiet confidence, her carefully thought-through keepsake of home, Westfield. She prayed she wouldn't forget and revert to her old name.

"Please step inside, Miss Westfield." The girl could only be a few years older than herself, her manner convivial, professional. "My name is Sarah. Please take a seat. I will inform Madam Raines you are here."

Kate took in the ostentatious furnishing and décor of the waiting room. Up-to-date copies of *The Lady* and *Vogue* were perfectly arranged on an Italian coffee table. Smart, elegant, but most important, welcoming, the three golden rules her mother always swore by in her life and work. She was right.

Madam Raines appeared from the back, oozing class, her clothes cleverly hiding a fuller figure. The proprietor had no hesitation in appraising her new candidate, running her eye over her suit as Sarah made the introductions.

"Where did you purchase this?"

"It's my own design, Madam Raines." Kate noticed the proprietor's lips twitch, hinting at pleasure.

"If you would like to follow me, Miss Westfield."

Madam Raines walked two paces ahead, leading her through a wide, mirrored corridor into a large room, and Kate gasped at the fabulous display of haute couture. But the next room, to her delight, was the heart of everything, the work room. Two girls glanced up from their sewing. They smiled and resumed their work. Madam Raines slid a sample of fabric onto the cutting table, but as she did Kate could not help but notice how the poor woman's fingers were beginning to gnarl, much like old Mrs. Weatherspoon's, in Church Walk. Madam Raines would struggle to cut cloth, let alone hold a needle and thread.

"The instructions are on the notepad. You have one hour."

Madam vanished, leaving Sarah close by, working on a fine garment.

Kate, quickly read the instructions, studied the material, exchanged a brief smile with Sarah, and returned her focus to the job at hand. Forty-five minutes later, she held the material aloft, giving it a little tug. Pursing her lips, she checked her work once more, and nodded with quiet satisfaction.

"You've finished?"

"Yes, I believe I have."

"Would you be kind enough to remain here?"

Kate folded her hands on her lap, waiting for the verdict.

Madam Raines studied every inch of the finished article. The pleasure in her face could not be disguised, and with the subsequent offer of a position, it took all Kate's effort not to jump for joy.

****

Two weeks later, Kate, dressed for business in a

157

soft, easy-to-wear outfit, arrived at the atelier at exactly seven forty-five. Sarah opened the door, eyes wide and blinking.

"She's coming here!" Sarah sounded excited and terrified at the same time.

"Who?"

"The client."

"What client?"

Madam Raines arrived, her face set authoritatively. "I wish to speak to you both, privately." She took them into her office.

"My client requires the utmost discretion, Miss Westfield. I've already clarified my expectations with Sarah. Whilst my other girls are competent, I believe yourself and Sarah would be best suited to this particular task." Madam Raines quickly outlined the work required, and the time frame to complete the alterations.

"Don't fail me, or there will be consequences. She is one of our most important clients."

Kate's heart pounded. There could be no misunderstanding Madam Raines' message. With what-ifs running through her head, Kate looked at Sarah, their expressions mirroring one another's worry.

"You really don't mind doing the fussing around her bit, Sarah?" Kate asked, out of earshot of Madam Raines, hating the thought of treading on her new friend's toes.

Sarah shook her head, smiling. "I'm more than happy to fawn. Whatever it takes."

By nine thirty they were presented to a pretty, dark-haired woman. Even though she wore sunglasses, Kathleen needed no introduction, and immediately bobbed a curtsey.

"We are off to Monte Carlo tomorrow. I've been guaranteed you can finish by three."

Kate quickly assessed the exquisite cocktail dress.

"Yes, of course, madam." It would require very careful alterations to fit the client's diminutive but expanding figure.

Much later that day, Kate returned to her tiny room full of new beginnings and her mind all over the place. She didn't care how small or smelly her room was, how lumpy the mattress, or how mentally and physically exhausted she felt. This was her day. The client would have no idea just how difficult and delicate the task of adjustments had been, but Madam Raines most certainly did. At the end of the day, her employer had asked to see her portfolio.

"Yes!" she shouted at the four walls. "Yes!"

****

Kate soon learned Portobello Market might be the place to find some much needed items for her flat. With the limited information she gleaned, she soon found it, surprised the market already heaved with potential customers. Stalls stretched either side the cobbled road, offering a mish-mash of goods. From paintings to brass candlesticks, from china to clothing, it was a display of the world of everything needed to furnish a home—well, pretty much. She passed an old man wearing a battered bowler hat upon his head. She smiled at the scrap of paper stuck to the side with the word sixpence upon it. It reminded her a bit of Alice in Wonderland's Mad Hatter. He had an old gramophone player perched on an old tea chest, and he tried flogging it to every passerby. A child, no older than ten pushed a pram, filled to the brim with an assortment of bedding and suitcases. At first glance, she thought it might be his home, but he began calling out, offering his wares. Already shocked and saddened at her previous thought, this was almost as bad, a child being set to work at such an early age. Kate stopped him and bought a pillow and a blanket. He seemed to look right through her as if he were already identifying his next customer. With her purchases under her arm, Kate began her search again and found what she was after. Misshapen cutlery and dishes and plates of all kinds were stacked in a heap. Her bargaining skills from a previous life had not been tested for a while, but she eventually managed to strike a good deal. As she left, she heard someone singing, his voice, accompanied by a guitar, was broken by a vigorous cough. Her mind whirled back to the holiday spent with Lucy. The busker had a certain talent, but he was being ignored. She dropped a coin and went on her way, but not once did the image disappear from her mind.

Chapter 30

South Africa, 1955

Van der Valk, known as the Dutchman, looked formidable standing there, arms folded, watching Jack Matthews' arrival at the diamond mine. His neck sprang straight from his shoulders, his girth every bit as wide as his height. He tapped a Smith and Wesson handgun impatiently against his leg.

"About bloody time. You'd better be as good as they say you are." His English was perfect, though hinting a light guttural accent. Jack, irritated by the man's manner, kept calm and nodded.

"Providing the equipment I've ordered is here, and you've arranged five good, strong men, I'll get on with the job straight away."

"It's all here, and the men have been selected. Just you keep your mind on the job and out of my business, and there won't be a problem."

Jack frowned and put his rucksack on the dusty earth, studying Van der Valk.

"Fine by me." Even at ten paces Jack could smell the stench of sour tobacco and body odor. "Perhaps you can introduce me and tell me where I'll be staying?"

"The Kaffas are over there." Van der Valk jerked his head toward a group of men. "That's your billet." The Dutchman pointed a ham-sized fist toward a tent. Whoever had tried putting it up had failed dismally.

L. B. Griffin

Jack, having taken an instant dislike, guessed the Dutchman wanted to get a rise, but he played him at his own game.

"Thanks, very thoughtful."

Poker-faced, aware the Dutchman was watching, Jack picked up his kit and strode across toward the gang of five. Jack introduced himself, and the self-appointed leader, Naidoo, who spoke English the best, tried explaining the problem, pointing to the earth, and drawing in the dust and the heat. Jack nodded, rolled up his sleeves, sweating as he issued instructions slowly, carefully, using the stick and the earth to confirm understanding.

The work was dirty, hard, and treacherous, and to the gang's evident astonishment, Jack buckled down, working every bit as hard as the next man. He stepped in when dangerous situations arose and never expected them to do anything he wouldn't do himself. Naidoo proved to be a good listener as well as communicator, and as they discussed the next stages, the men heeded his directions well.

Throughout each day, Jack, appalled at the working conditions, held his tongue. He was upset to see tiny children, no more than scraps of humanity, part of the workforce. He spoke to Van der Valk about it, only to find him erupt into anger, telling him to mind his own bloody business, but Jack had already begun cataloguing events and taking photographs.

"How long have you been here, Naidoo?" he asked casually, whilst calibrating the equipment and adjusting a piece of turned metal into a rod.

"Since I was five, Massa." The name came without an explanation. "I came with my parents. They drown, I

162

stay." His words, so dry and matter of fact, he could have been discussing the weather.

"Do you have other family?"

"No, Massa. Just the mine." His eyes drew toward the shaft. "I still close to family."

"How old are you?"

"I fifteen, Massa." Shocked, Jack compared Naidoo to his niece and thought he looked twice her age. Nothing could hide the lines on his face, or the yellowed whites of his eyes.

"And you've worked here since you were five?" Jack asked in disbelief.

"We need to live, Massa. We work, we sleep, we eat, we have shelter, we live." Lowering his voice, he said, "We paid less than white men, and do most dangerous work. People disappear. Watch Dutchman. He steal. You see."

****

Jack gave the children little sweet treats, or did magic tricks, making them laugh in astonished delight, and they began hanging around him as if he were Father Christmas himself. Their huge brown eyes, though dulled by life's hardship and poverty, blinked with thrill, gratitude, and surprise every time at the small kindnesses he showed.

And every day Jack took photographs, each shot telling a story.

As the temperatures soared, thick, oppressive heat scorched lungs, and sweat slathered Jack's hair and rolled down his neck. His clothes were saturated the moment he dressed, and there would be no let-up until nightfall. He'd spoken to Van der Valk more than once, but it was clear the man became agitated at any practical suggestion or offer of improvements. As an engineer, Jack could fix almost anything mechanical. He scratched at his stubble, growing into a beard, thinking over the conversation with Naidoo. A little muscle in his cheek twitched. The man was undoubtedly corrupt, yet there was so much potential, so much available wealth that could so easily change everyone's lives.

At the end of the shift, Jack walked the stifling journey across to the Dutchman's hut, knowing from previous encounters he needed to tread carefully, but he would try one last time.

Jack knocked on the side of the shack. He could see the Dutchman sitting at his desk, drinking a beer. The man filled the room. The stench made it hard to breathe.

"You chose well, Van der Valk. The men have worked hard," began Jack.

Van der Valk responded by pulling another beer from a bucket of water and twisting the cap with two sausage-fat fingers. He took a slug.

"I'm almost done," Jack continued, jerking his head to outside. "But I've one other idea I'd like to run past you before I leave."

Jack spread a sheet of paper across the table.

"See here…" He pointed to the sketches of the second shaft. "I can add a couple of safety measures for next to nothing. It'll reduce the risks for the more dangerous jobs."

The Dutchman looked bothered.

"What do you think? Naidoo's gang and I could work on it before I leave?"

"So it's Naidoo's gang now, is it, Kaffa lover?"

Van der Valk snarled. "I told you, stay out of my business!"

The Dutchman licked his lips, took another slug of beer, and wiped the back of his hand across his mouth, ending the conversation.

With icy politeness, Jack left. One more day and he would be going home. In his tent, Jack sighed. Without his skills, he would not have made his fortune, but if he didn't do anything, he would be just as corrupt as the next man.

****

Having finished his work, Jack was crouching beside a group of children, playing a little game of stones. The routine of the Dutchman continued at the end of the shift as the miners were frisked. Van der Valk, with his henchmen either side of him, glanced across at Jack, and waited. When Naidoo came out of the shaft, he told him to strip. The whole site watched, their fear tangible. Naidoo covered himself with embarrassment.

"I am a good boss?" he roared.

"Yes, you good boss."

Naidoo was instantly rewarded by being struck across the head with the butt of the gun. It sent him flying, like a bird struck by a car, into the dirt face down.

Jack flew at Van der Valk just a second too late. The Dutchman's lip curled, and, snarling, jabbed the gun into Jack's neck and palmed uncut diamonds in his hand.

Van der Valk licked his lips salaciously. "He knows the punishment for stealing. You best keep out of this."

L. B. Griffin

Jack didn't believe for one minute Naidoo was guilty. He twisted and threw a punch. Useless—the man was a room full of blubber. In return, he received a crack across his head and fell unconscious to the floor. When he woke, he found he had been dragged inside his tent. His head throbbing, he peered out. Naidoo was strung naked against a pole. Stealing meant certain death, if lack of water or the heat didn't kill him first. Jack managed to catch the eye of one of the gang of five. Quietly they came up with a plan. Hoping to God it would work, Jack handed over three bottles of whiskey. Now he would wait until darkness fell.

The sounds of the night, quiet, eerie, menacing, filled Jack's senses. Sudden rustling outside his tent sent prickles down his spine. Danger lurked in every crevice. Soundlessly, instinctively, in the pitch black, he reached for his revolver. He would be the most likely target now. Jack listened intently. Nothing. He shook his head. Perhaps his imagination was running away with him. There it was again. A swish so soft that if he had been sleeping, he would never have woken. Lightly, silently, Jack slid onto his belly.

"Massa?" Jack remained on the floor, throwing a whispered voice to the back of the tent.

"Who's there?"

"Pillay." One of the gang, his voice low, urgent.

"Come." It was even darker inside the tent than out. Jack could see the man's silhouette lifting the flap.

"Where you?"

Jack jammed the revolver straight into his groin.

Pillay froze.

"Why are you here?"

"I see much. Hear much. You make very bad

166

enemy. We go. Dutchman make you vanish."

"Naidoo, is he all right?"

"Yes."

Pillay, surefooted as a goat, showed Jack the safest route through the face of the valley. His Jeep was still there, parked behind a mound, as he hoped. The rest of the gang of five, including Naidoo, were quietly waiting, gathered like dark rocks set into the terrain.

"What the—! Naidoo?" The men surrounded Jack. He could feel their heat, their tension. His plan had been that once the guard was drunk, they would help Naidoo escape.

"You risked your life. We brother now." The men fist-pumped the air in solidarity. It had been only a few years since Jack last felt true brotherhood, in the RAF. Now these men, whom he barely knew, astonished and humbled him. Jack, with a resigned sigh but thankful Naidoo was safe, poked him.

"You are really getting on my nerves. Do you ever listen?"

Jack pulled on the choke and twisted the key. The engine kicked in. They gave a quiet whoop, mixed with relief. Fifty miles before they would get to the airstrip, and the embassy at least a hundred more. With only the stars to guide them, it would be fifty long miles to work out what to do.

Chapter 31

New York City 1955

Jack came out of the dark room in his New York apartment and began flicking through the mail. His new secretary, Patti Davis, had been on the phone confirming his appointment with the board. Two more hours and the information would be shared. He felt unusually tense. A letter from Kathleen promised light relief. He smiled, knowing it would most probably be full of her usual youthful imagination. He found a postcard of St. Ives and a letter in the envelope. The card read, "Wish you were here," encompassed within a smile.

The letter, as hoped, was full of joyful recollection. He put the whiskey glass to his nose before taking a sip, then began reading.

Dear Uncle Jack,

I hope this letter finds you well. I have had a simply wonderful time in Cornwall with Lucy. It really was the best. Lucy and I got sunburned, but Aunty Lily put yoghurt on our skin to make it better! It was yeuky, and it dried out all crusty, like chamomile lotion. Aunty Lily says ladies are not meant to have a tan, but I think it suits me well.

Jack chuckled. He read on.

Mr. Latimer was really kind, and funny. He took us

to St. Ives; it is SO GROOVY! There were some amazing artists—it reminded me of our time in Paris.

Mr. Latimer took us to a pub. Lucy and I had to sit in the car when he went inside to get the drinks. He bought us all a Schweppes bitter lemon and a packet of Smiths crisps and brought them out on a tray!

She had drawn another smile alongside a packet of Smiths crisps. Jack took another sip of his malt.

Lucy and I went swimming. The sea was simply freezing, but we made of new friends, and later we had a barbeque on the beach. One of the boys, Eric, plays a guitar, and he is very good. He is thinking of forming a band. I think there is every chance that he will become famous one day.

Jack sat up. It was the first time Kathleen had mentioned boys. It sent alarm bells ringing. Boys had needs. He frowned. Lily hadn't mentioned boys or a barbeque. It was unrealistic to expect Lily to give a blow-by-blow account of everything they did, but boys? Perhaps they were there with them?

Taking another sip of whiskey, remaining unsettled, Jack leaned forward in his chair and read on, scanning for any other mention of this confounded Eric.

We will be putting on a play in October and a Pantomime in January next year. I have been helping Mrs. Sellers with the wardrobe. The costumes smell like moth balls, so I hold my nose. Do you happen to know of anything that would take the dreadful smell away?

Jack smiled, a little relieved with the mention of boys gone, but he would still speak to Lily, and possibly the housemistress.

I hope you like the postcard I have enclosed. Lights out now. I will write soon. Promise.

L. B. Griffin

All for one and one for all.
With love, your most fabulous groovy niece,
Kathleen x

Chapter 32

The Latimers' home

Lucy read the letter from Kathleen two weeks after their holiday in Cornwall. It had been tucked very carefully inside a small, zipped pocket in her handbag. At first, Lucy thought it might simply be a thank-you note, but that wasn't Kathleen's style. In her bedroom, she sat on her bed and tore the envelope open.

Dearest Lucy,

You are my one true friend. I know you can be trusted with a secret, but I didn't want to put this burden on you. By now some people may be wondering where I am and asking all kinds of questions. If that is the case, I am really sorry, but you can truthfully say that you knew nothing.

Uncle Jack never knew, but over Christmas I overheard him talking to Archie. He said it was difficult trying to take care of me and he needed a wife. How can he do that with me hanging around? So I have decided to leave. I have money put aside, I have a lovely flat, and I have secured a job.

You see, Lucy, I am not in the least bit unhappy. I am safe and making my own way in the world.

I also have secured a P.O. Box. The number is twenty-nine, so you can keep in touch. I will find a way of contacting you.

All my love, Kathleen xxx
Enc. Postage stamps.

Lucy was already on her feet, pacing her bedroom. Kathleen should be staying over next weekend. Conflicted, Lucy wondered if she should tell her mother. In the end, she decided not to. Kathleen trusted her to keep the secret, and so she would.

Three days later, the telephone rang. Lucy could hear one half of the conversation.

"You sound simply dreadful, dear," said her mother. "You have tonsillitis? Oh, you poor thing. No, I completely understand. Of course you need bed rest. Pardon? Oh, yes, of course, Kathleen, but not long." She passed the phone over to Lucy.

"Now, don't keep Kathleen talking. She has a dreadful sore throat."

As the girls spoke, Lucy tried to covertly relay the message that her mother was standing close by. Turning, smiling, her mother took the hint and disappeared.

"Are you coming home?"

"No."

"Are you quite mad?"

The conversation lasted all of two minutes before her mother came back into the hallway.

"I think that's enough, Lucy. We want to encourage Kathleen to get better, don't we?"

Lucy hissed goodbye before her mother took the receiver from her hand.

"Kathleen? Ah, yes. Now, dear, back to bed and get better soon."

Lucy was furious. She hated the deception and wanted no part of it. With Kathleen's lies, her parents would not expect her to stay the weekend, and that took her right up to the end of the school holidays.

Chapter 33

End of summer, 1955

Miss Wray, the headmistress, looked between the summer itinerary planned for Kathleen in one hand and a letter from Mr. Matthews in the other, puzzling.

"As you can see, Miss Wray, the letter is quite clear." Mrs. Fuller, the housemistress, was all of a fluster, explaining Mr. Matthews had changed his mind at the last moment.

"And you say Mr. Latimer dropped Kathleen off at school? Have you spoken with Mr. Matthews?"

"No. Only his secretary, in New York. Mr. Matthews has been working abroad."

Miss Wray knew Mr. Matthews took extraordinary pains to ensure everything was in order. His communications with the school up to this point had been exemplary. Mrs. Fuller lost her composure and let out a wail.

"Mrs. Fuller!" Miss Wray snapped. "That type of behavior won't do at all. If we are to find the child, we must all pull together. Are you absolutely certain that Kathleen is not with Mr. and Mrs. Latimer?"

The housemistress held a chair to steady herself.

"It appears rather than spending a month with the Latimers, as we were given to understand, Kathleen spent only one week with them."

"What!"

"From all the information we have thus far, Kathleen has been missing the whole of the summer break."

Shocked, the headmistress rhythmically tapped her walking stick. Her tapping stopped abruptly, and she asked her secretary to notify the police.

Mrs. Fuller slumped in the chair, mumbling, just as Mrs. Sellers flew into the office.

"Apologies, Miss Wray. This is urgent." She waved a letter in the air. "You need to read it."

Miss Wray read aloud,

"Dear Mrs. Sellers,

It was a difficult decision to make, but I knew that I could not continue being a burden to my uncle. I am sorry if I have made life complicated for you or have worried you unduly. I hope you will understand and that, in time, you can find it in your heart to forgive me.

Please would you thank everyone from the very bottom of my heart for being so kind and supportive during a very sad and lonely time in my life. Please know that I am safe, and that one day I will make you proud.

Yours most sincerely,

Miss Kathleen Gray

P.S. This is very important. Would you please keep a closer eye on Amy? She was so distressed about her brother being boarded for the first time this year, and Amy is missing her family dreadfully. With grateful thanks."

"When did you receive this, exactly?"

"Second post, today, Headmistress."

"Did you suspect anything?"

"No, not a thing, Headmistress."

Miss Wray peered at the frank mark. Cornwall. The headmistress hummed and hawed.

Miss Wray's secretary knocked on the door. "Miss Wray, Detective Brown is here to see you."

Chapter 34

A man in his late fifties, short, slight, with dark, intelligent eyes, surveyed the room. He smelt of tobacco and something else. Whatever it was, it didn't endear him to the headmistress. Miss Wray immediately made the introductions. Detective Inspector Brown did not appear to be bothered. A uniformed officer, po-faced, stood one pace behind.

"I think it must be my fault," began Mrs. Fuller, trying to explain the confusion. "The itinerary, the changes we agreed for Kathleen's summer break." She handed him the letter from Mr. Matthews outlining his expectations.

"Hmm." The detective gave it a cursory look. "Seems it's a simple case of a runaway." He sounded as if a missing girl were nothing more than a nuisance.

"But surely we should start looking. Send out a search party?" Mrs. Sellers looked shocked at his apparent total disregard.

"We need to do everything possible for her safe return. After all, the girl is only fifteen."

"Madam." He looked past Mrs. Sellers and out the window. "Seven weeks is a very long time for a trail to go cold. And there is a reported runaway every day of the year."

"Detective *Inspector*!" Miss Wray stepped in. "I *expect* you to make every effort to find her."

He returned a well-worn look. "Are there any financial issues you are aware of?"

Mrs. Fuller interjected quickly. "Her uncle, Mr. Matthews, has paid the school fees in full for the next two years. He also ensured his niece has ample money at her disposal. Thinking about it…" Mrs. Fuller was on her feet, pacing. "This is not a financial issue, but Kathleen mentioned she will become sole benefactor of the family estate once she reaches twenty-one."

Detective Inspector Brown, scratched his neck thoughtfully and began taking notes, moving his mouth as he wrote, "Inheritance." He automatically reached for his packet of cigarettes, tapping it until the tip rose from the box. "Are you absolutely certain you haven't received any blackmail letters or threatening telephone calls?"

The staff gasped.

Miss Wray eyed him firmly before checking with her staff for a negative. He put the cigarette into his mouth without lighting it.

"It is a fact," D.I. Brown continued, "if the girl is not pregnant, or a simple runaway, we will have to look more closely to home. Say, like her uncle."

The room went deadly silent.

"You will need to come to the station." The detective removed the cigarette from his lips. "Make it official. Each of you will need to provide a statement."

His mouth formed a paper-thin line, and for once he appeared to show a little concern, saying, "A young girl out there on her own, a lot can happen."

There it was, thought Miss Wray, her blood running cold. He was insinuating the dreadful things she already feared.

Chapter 35

New York City

Jack had one purpose in mind when he entered the board room in midtown Manhattan—to enlist the support of the board of directors. He couldn't help but glance across at the picture window. He never bored of Manhattan's East Side skyscraper skyline and the fantastic view of the art-deco-styled Chrysler building laid out before him.

"Good morning, gentlemen." Jack adjusted his stance, ensuring he could make eye contact with everyone in the room. The men were seated around a large oval chestnut table. Breakfast was arranged in the far-right corner, and a blend of roasted coffee beans percolated a welcome. Jack knew every man there, some more personally than others. Though the lawyer's name briefly escaped him, he knew the man had a fearsome reputation.

Frank smiled at Jack. He had met his bubbly wife and large brood of overly indulged children, and hoped to get him on side. He cast his eye at Carl Langdon, the older, more senior member, nodding in his direction.

Carl preferred to do business on the golf course. Word had it that Carl and the CEO, Bob Bateman, spent more time working on their handicap than on business.

Benjamin Fuller acknowledged Jack, shaking him

firmly by the hand, a tactic he always employed. The man took no prisoners, telling him once, when inebriated, that was how he assessed the mettle of a man.

Stuart and Howard were exchanging notes before business commenced, a pile of papers in front of them. They were younger than the rest of the directors, keen as mustard, and loved a challenge. Both were fair minded. Both were on their second marriage. Both would break your balls if they felt a deal was going sour. If they liked his proposals, they might be allies.

Jack confirmed he was keynote to the meeting and remained standing to face a barrage of questions. The air conditioning purred in the background.

"I am pleased to report that the initial issue at the mine has been resolved."

There was a ripple of smiles and clapping. Even Bob Bateman, CEO, got from his chair to shake his hand.

"Well done. I knew we could rely on you, Jack."

"Thank you, Bob," Jack returned. "As indicated, there's something I need to discuss. I know that visiting the mines is not something on your agenda, or a priority. So you may find the information a little difficult to swallow."

He had everyone's full attention as he handed out a large envelope to each man. He had his own copy keenly arranged to demonstrate his purpose.

"Before you open your envelopes, may I?" he asked Bob, indicating the flip chart.

"Go ahead," said the CEO, Bob, looking relaxed, comfortably leaning back into his padded chair.

Jack flipped the cover sheet over. It exposed a list

of emboldened headings: HEALTH, EDUCATION, MEDICAL CENTER, and finally SAFETY. Bob linked his fingers together, frowning. Jack caught the shift.

"I'm sure, gentlemen, you are informed if a serious injury occurs at your mines?" He glanced around the room. "Of course, mining is a dangerous occupation. One should be paid well for that risk, correct?" He raised a brow.

"Unfortunately, as you most likely are aware, there have been several deaths, and several people appear to have gone missing."

There was a definite shift in the air. Carl Langdon placed his coffee on the table and commented, "I'm assuming Van der Valk is taking appropriate action. That's what we pay him for."

"As you quite rightly say, Carl, Van der Valk is in charge." A muscle in Jack's cheek twitched. It was now or never.

"Would you be good enough to take the contents out of your envelopes, gentlemen?"

Everyone in the room, save the lawyer, looked appalled at what they found. Questions rose to a crescendo. Jack put up his hand.

"When I saw children as young as three years being exploited, it came as a complete shock. I can see it is the same for you."

"What about Van der Valk?" said Carl, now on his feet.

"I tried discussing the issue with him. He wasn't listening. And as to myself, well, let's just say I survived."

Jack's face was set grim, and his tone remained cautious as he gave them the whole story.

L. B. Griffin

"I believe you to be honorable men. You will do the decent thing. Van der Valk is a thief, a tyrant, and possibly a murderer. And as to the changes I propose, I am willing to plan, pay for, and oversee any construction to get this off the ground. All I need is your permission. Hopefully, you will consider the removal of your foreman and take appropriate action."

There came a knock on the glass door. A smart telegram boy stood outside with one of the secretaries. Miss Davis waited for permission before entering.

"Excuse me, sir, there is a telegram for Mr. Matthews."

"Can you excuse me a moment?"

URGENT STOP. TELEPHONE ME
IMMEDIATELY STOP. LILY STOP.

It was as simple as that. The boy politely stood to attention.

"Would you like to reply, sir?"

"No. Yes. No." For a second, Jack was unusually indecisive. He turned to the men in the room.

"I have outlined my proposals, but I need to deal with an equally pressing situation right now."

As Jack left, Howard tapped him on the shoulder, promising he and Stuart would follow his lead.

****

Jack caught the next available flight to England, having managed to contact Lily, the police, Mr. Gilbraith the solicitor, and enlist a private detective. By the time Jack landed in the UK, going over every possible scenario, he was beginning to flip from the rational to the irrational.

Van der Valk could be in some way involved, but then, if it wasn't foul play, why would Kathleen disappear of her own free will? Was it his fault? Was she pregnant? Jack instantly recalled the boy in her letter. He blamed himself, questioning all he had said and all he had not done.

His niece was a smart kid. Surely, she would have phoned him, given him a hint? He had to start unravelling the pieces, using everything and anyone at his disposal, and that would have to start with Lucy Latimer. If anyone, she might hold the key.

Chapter 36

October 16, 1955

Lucy sat down in the library, fuming. She could not write to her friend at home where she might be caught. And she felt truly caught, right in the middle of it all. Her mood was growing into a temper, something she'd never had before all of this.

First the police had bombarded her with questions, poking, prying, never letting up. Then her parents asked the same questions over and over, blaming themselves. The girls in her dorm had been questioned over and over, then began questioning her. If that wasn't awful enough, even her friends and teachers looked at her queerly. Why, even Miss Wray quizzed whether she knew more than she let on. And the worst of it was when Kathleen's uncle arrived, looking simply dreadful—even worse than her parents did, and that said a lot.

Lucy made sure she was alone as she wrote her ultimatum. Kathleen sounded so happy in her communications, but everyone else back home was not. How dare she! Her friend was being selfish, in every sense of the word. She picked up her pen, opened her workbook, and placed a sheet of paper inside.

Kathleen,

Lucy could not bring herself to put the word

"Dear."

You must have seen the newspapers. Your face has been splashed all over it. Everyone has been interviewed and re-interviewed, including me! Thousands of times. They think you might be dead, or that you could have been kidnapped. This is so selfish of you. I won't hold your secret anymore, but I will give you one last chance to do the right thing and tell everyone where you are.

One week, Kathleen, before I spill! Contact me, or better still, contact your uncle. He has camped out at Westfield.

Lucy stopped writing, sensing someone close by. She looked up to see the librarian peering over at her from one of the bookshelves.

"Is everything all right?"

"Yes, miss, I'm just revising." Lucy closed the workbook with the letter carefully inside and put it into her satchel.

"Terrible thing about your friend, Miss Latimer. Have you heard anything?"

"No, miss," said Lucy, crossing her fingers behind her back. Lucy left school after finishing off the letter and went straight to the post box with the fervent prayer that Kathleen would see sense.

Chapter 37

October 22, 1955

The private detective Jack employed had been worse than useless. It was now four months since Kathleen's disappearance. Having been interrogated by the police, he was finally released. Jack held the last letter from his niece in one hand, double-checking the time and instruction.

Impatient to cross over to Trafalgar Square, the constant tide of traffic belching sooty fumes and burning oil refusing to give up a space, Jack saw a gap and dodged between a hackney cab and a bus. He was rewarded with a blasting of horns and the angry yell of "Bloody idiot!" Jack waved apologetically without looking back.

Jack's need to scope out the area long before the agreed meeting time felt paramount. He didn't want to leave anything to chance. He'd arranged a couple of men to pace the perimeter. They had photographs of Kathleen.

A man stood in the middle of Trafalgar Square with his arms telegraphed outward, covered in pigeons. Even his trilby appeared to have taken on a life of its own. Jack shook his head, never understanding the fascination. He spotted a little girl, probably about five or six years old, wearing her Sunday best, holding a small brown paper bag. She squatted with bird food cupped in her hand. Hundreds of pigeons quickly descended in droves, pecking greedily. She shrieked excitedly. If only Kathleen were that small, she would never have been left to her own devices. He strode past the police phone box at the edge of the square.

Jack's heart skipped a beat. A young woman about Kathleen's age moved purposefully toward him from the opposite side of the square. He kept staring. Jack recalled Eve once wearing the same skirt, a poodle design, she called it. The girl turned at the last minute, away from him, and headed toward Nelson's Column.

"Kathleen?" He moved swiftly, calling out. "Kathleen!" He managed to catch her.

She turned, startled as he touched her shoulder.

"Please excuse me. I thought you were someone else." She gave a puzzled nod and resumed walking.

Disappointed, worried, Jack paced the whole of Trafalgar Square before deciding it might be easier to see her from the designated waiting area. He climbed the steps outside the National Gallery. Pushing his hand through his hair, he raised a brow. Clever girl, making him stand there in full view. If she wanted to back out at the last minute, she could. He hoped his men would be alert.

Returning Kathleen's letter to his suit pocket, he pulled a cigarette, staring into the ever-changing swell. The bitter taste of tobacco filled his mouth, reminding him why he gave it up in the first place.

Nine fifty-one and still no sign. Kathleen being late was nothing new, but more than twenty minutes? She would realize the importance, surely. In different circumstances, he might be relaxed about it. Not today.

London was a place that swallowed people whole.

Anxious, fearful, Jack shuffled from one foot to another, trying to see through the growing crowd. Clearly, if she arrived, it would be difficult to pick her out. If at all. But what if she didn't turn up? He couldn't bear the thought.

Jack's attention was diverted for a second by pigeons scattering into the air. His eyes flicked back to Nelson's Column, then to the fountain of mermaids and tritons. A young woman was standing there. He felt sure she had not been there before. She lifted a hand, as if in acknowledgement. But even with twenty-twenty vision she looked nothing like Kathleen. Jack, mesmerized, took in her apparel, a trouser suit, softly cut to fit curves, the sleeves of the jacket pushed partially up her arms. She wore a bright red ribbon around her neck, matching her shoes and handbag. He waited a second more to see if she turned her head. She lifted her hand again.

Frowning, Jack began descending the steps, the burning cigarette falling from his fingers to the ground. Had someone been sent in her place?

Closer now, Jack puzzled. There was something familiar about her stance, the tilt of her head, maybe? A little thinner, taller even, but the hair was completely wrong. As he drew nearer, he recognized the smile. Confounded, he realized it was her. With her beautiful hair cropped and dyed black, he would never have recognized her if he passed her in the street. Tears burned the back of his lids as his feet hurried him toward her. Arms outstretched.

"Kathleen? Thank God! Please tell me you're all right. Have you been hurt?" Words tumbled from his lips as he checked her over. There were so many questions. Kathleen smiled, almost too brightly, and they collapsed into one another.

"Why? Tell me why? Did I do something wrong?"

She looked up at him. "No, Uncle Jack. You did everything right. It was me."

"I don't understand. You need to explain yourself better than that, young lady!"

For the first time, anger replaced relief. "Do you have any idea? I've been out of my mind!"

Kathleen bit her lip. A glimmer of shame crossed her face.

"I'm sorry, but you need to understand just how stupid you've been."

"You have every right to be angry, Uncle Jack."

He noticed the edge to her voice.

Her sparkling green eyes darted this way and that. "Do you think we could walk? Please?"

Jack softened. She was just a kid, really. Everyone makes mistakes, even huge ones like this. He wasn't used to this parenting thing, and he certainly couldn't be mad at her for long. Kathleen was safe. She was alive. That was all that mattered. Jack suddenly realized his men would be watching. He raised a hand, the sign all was well. Kathleen frowned. Jack shrugged. He wouldn't tell her.

"How about St James' Park?" she suggested.

"Very well. But you will need to start talking."

Tourists and families with perambulators and pushcarts were wending their way along Pall Mall toward Buckingham Palace. The Queen's Life Guards came into view—scarlet-tunicked cavalry, haughty white-plumed helmets on beautifully groomed horses, clopped by, elegant, regal. The sight always took Jack's breath away.

"It's getting close to the changing of the guard. Its spectacular, isn't it?" They stopped, a moment of normality, and watched the procession.

"Apparently their dung is great for roses," Kathleen said as one of the horses let the side down, leaving a steaming heap.

Jack gave a half smile. At least her sense of humor hadn't changed. As they turned into the park, Jack began wondering what to do. He'd resolved to bring her home safely to finish her education, but he was already beginning to recognize just how difficult that might be.

They were lucky enough to find an empty seat, close enough to the bandstand but far enough away not to be disturbed. Jack caught Kathleen's hand and looked her in the eye.

"You can tell me anything. Anything at all."

Even with her right by his side he had a niggling suspicion she might take flight. There was a definite change in his niece, and not just her extraordinary appearance. Deciding to keep schtum, he would allow her to talk, with the hope she would begin explaining what really drove her to run away in the first place. The silence between them was eventually broken by the laughter of two small children chasing a pigeon. They glanced at one another in mutual amusement.

"I'm sorry, Uncle Jack, truly I am." Her mouth puckered. "I really didn't think about the whole picture. It was really thoughtless, wasn't it?" As she looked at his hand enveloping hers, tears began to fall.

"I don't want to upset you." He pulled a fresh handkerchief from his breast pocket and handed it to her. "I just need to understand why. So that I can at least try to make sense of it, and we can put this whole silly nonsense behind us."

He cleared his throat, looking at the world around him, not really seeing.

"In your letter, it said you didn't want to be a burden. I thought we had an understanding...*all for one*?"

Kathleen's eyes glistened, and she dabbed away tears. He had imagined so many terrible scenarios. Now they were together, they melded into one, nothing comparing itself to the other.

"I'm sorry. Do you mind if we walk to the lake?"

Jack reluctantly got up. She seemed unable to sit still for more than a moment.

Taking in the warm glow of the afternoon, they walked among lovers linking arms, parents strolling with their children, and ducks waddling along the path pecking between shoes, searching for treats. The trees were beginning to turn from green to burnt gold. If it had been any other day, they would have acknowledged their beauty and taken photographs.

"I heard you," she began, as the soft autumnal sun warmed their cheeks. "It was Christmas." She paused, painting the picture as if studying it from afar. "You were talking to Archie, out in the stalls."

She sighed. "I brought out the mulled wine and overheard what you said." She looked to the ground. "You told Archie you couldn't look after me. Archie said something about you needing a wife. You had mentioned Eve, and as she didn't come to England with you, I guessed I was the problem. I didn't want to be the one that stopped you marrying her and starting your own family. It's just not right."

Her voice had risen two octaves. "How could you possibly get on with your life with me in the background?" She was facing him now, defiant. "I know I'm right. You know I'm right!"

Jack frowned, puzzled, trying to put the pieces of a conversation long ago back into some semblance of order.

"Now, look here, young lady."

Jack, exasperated, stopped abruptly on the pathway, and a giggling little girl bumped into him with a piece of bread in her hand. Ducks surrounded her, pecking the half slice of bread out of her grasp. She began squealing. Jack shooed the ducks away, and her parents caught up, laughing, thanking him. A muscle twitched in Jack's cheek, waiting for privacy.

"In the first place, young lady, you shouldn't eavesdrop, and in the second place, you most certainly should not jump to conclusions."

"I'm sorry."

"So am I!" Jack let her stew, walking on ahead of her. Not too far. Just in case she decided to bolt. Jack stopped, waiting for her to catch up.

"So, Miss Nosey Parker, you haven't explained a thing."

"What do you mean?"

"Do I really need to spell it out?" He sighed deeply. "All that nonsense about me. Family. Eve. I don't believe a word of it."

"It really is the truth, Uncle Jack!"

"Hmm. Not a good enough reason to run away. Look," he said, "if I share with you what you *didn't* hear that night, I need you to be adult about it. Deal?"

"Deal."

Jack pulled out a packet of cigarettes and tapped the lid.

"Have you started smoking again?"

Jack raised a brow.

"Sorry, I didn't mean…"

"You're right. I was smitten with Eve." He put the cigarette to his lips and lit it. The tip glowed red. "Thought I was in love. Even had the ring. I planned to bring her over to England for Christmas. I even had a romantic proposal in my head." He stared into the distance. "I imagined the snow, a roaring fire, a bottle of champagne, and a box of sweets with a ring wrapped up inside." His laugh was hollow. "Imagine that." Blue smoke curled into the air. "Me getting all romantic and fluffy at my age! Turns out she had other ideas." The corner of his lip twitched. "I think you would have liked her."

"Why? What was she like?" Her eyes were on him.

"Beautiful, funny, charming."

"She didn't have much sense though, did she?"

"Pardon?" He turned.

"Well, she was stupid enough to let you go." Jack turned away, hiding the half smile on his lips.

"It's over to you now, young lady. I want to know everything. And I mean everything. Even if it's something to do with a boy." He placed his hands on her shoulders, his head full of D. I. Brown's dreadful insinuations of pregnancy. And that damned Eric in the postcard.

"What do you mean?" Kathleen looked baffled.

"What do you think I mean? You know…" He coughed. "Boys." Jack took another drag on his cigarette, wishing Lily Latimer were by his side, or better still, here instead of him, talking about these things.

"You know. I need to know…if…you know."

"What? Oh! You think I was…?" She looked shocked. "Bloody hell, no!"

"Good." He took a deep, relieved breath. Thank God that was over with. "Well, I'll have no more swearing, to start with, young lady, and I'd like to see your place of work."

"There's no point. It's closed."

She shut him down. He wondered if the job was just fabrication. He hated the thought of what else might be.

"I still want to see."

"Very well, if you insist, but I'm warning you it's a long way. And it *will* be closed!"

By now they were nearing St James' tube station. A beggar sat outside on the pavement, unkempt, stitches hardly holding his clothes together. One half leg, the empty trouser knotted at the knee. No obvious belongings. The man looked so cold. The area was dark and damp. Kathleen couldn't imagine why he would choose such a spot but immediately dropped a thru'penny piece into his cap. Jack saw thick black dirt embedded under the beggar's fingernails as he handed him a pound note and the last of his packet of cigarettes. He was so skinny and looked so sad. Jack took off his coat, and bent down with a quiet, sincere apology, offered it over, hoping it wouldn't offend. Kate stared in surprise.

"Thanks, guvnor, miss," the man mumbled, immediately secreting the cigarettes away under his old jacket and studying the note in disbelief. Straightening his back, he raised a light salute, and accepted the coat.

Jack felt sick to his stomach. Comrades and their silent stories.

"Uncle Jack, what do you think happened to him?" Kathleen whispered as they moved away. She'd seen him and others like him before. It made her feel terrible seeing him like that. "Isn't there help out there? Somewhere?" The words tumbled from her lips.

Jack guessed the man was a war veteran. There were so many like him. War crippled men. Not only their bodies, but their minds and their hearts. This man would have his own story to tell, but it was quite possible, that he, like so many, had lost his soul to the war. Jack drew a deep breath keeping some of his thoughts close, but Kathleen didn't need to be treated like a child, she needed a little honesty.

"There are some soup kitchens, I believe, and I guess there are hostels. If not, his bed will be a dangerous place to lay his head."

Kathleen sadly shook her head, but her thoughts remained private. His words had raised an idea, but she wouldn't say anything. Not yet. Everything now depended upon Uncle Jack and being able to persuade him she was better off living in London.

Chapter 38

While Kathleen confidently traversed them through the myriad of underground walkways, Jack quizzed her systematically about her life in London. There was no doubt in his mind she had changed since they last spoke. She sparkled with enthusiasm about her work and the famous people she met. But there was something else. Kathleen was no longer the child he remembered. She was confident, composed, self-assured, and unexpectedly relaxed in London's chaotic environment.

More doubt crept in. Taking his niece back home might be appropriate. It might be even difficult to execute, but would it be kind? Would taking her home only serve as a cruel reminder of the grief she'd tried to escape? Could he really do that to her?

They were standing on a platform, surrounded by the scent of a thousand dreams lost and found, as Kathleen talked animatedly about her goals and her ambitions. She reasoned London was the place to grow, to develop and hone her skills, and *the* place to showcase her work. Could he in all honesty destroy her vision?

A whoosh of air from the darkness hinted at the oncoming train. Waiting passengers shuffled into position expectantly. His niece had taken complete control. Jack knew right then she was in control of her own destiny.

Emerging into the paling autumn sunlight, Jack found himself surprised at how many London buildings still bore the scars of war. But London remained proudly holding its head high. His country and its people during wartime had stood united. He knew he and Kathleen should stand united.

They were nearing Kings Road when Kathleen spoke.

"We're here. This is where I work. Like I said, it's closed." She hinted mockery. The windowpane caught an ounce of the dying sun, and a large flower arrangement prevented viewing inside. The door reminded, "By appointment only." Jack looked at her wryly.

"Well, at least it's good to know exactly where you work. Do they know just how old you are, and your background?"

She fell silent.

"Thought not."

"There's something else. Don't get cross." She tipped her face toward him. "I'm not Kathleen anymore." She looked anxious. "I've got a new identity."

"Pardon?" He blinked in surprise.

"It's Kate. I'm known as Kate." She raised her frame, adding carefully, "My surname too. It's Westfield. After our home."

Jack gasped. With each revelation came a new twist, bringing more questions to his lips. Listening to her explanations, he could not help but find respect, admiration even. His niece didn't run away on a whim. Even though she got it completely wrong, he recognized her plans must have taken considerable thought and extraordinary patience.

"I think it's about time you took me to your place of residence, young lady."

Jack held his hat and rubbed his fingers along the brim, still thinking. Ideas were slowly beginning to come into focus.

"Very well." She looked downcast. "I know it's awful. But I am surviving, and," she continued pointedly, "*without* my allowance."

"The place is that bad, is it?"

****

The smell of stale grease and vinegar hit them before they opened the communal door. It wafted up the dark, dingy staircase and hung around the landing. Jack tried hard not to show dismay as they stepped into the bedsit and felt angry at the spineless landlord taking advantage of his young niece.

However, the bedsit was clean, which was not lost on him. Kathleen must have spent time trying to make it habitable. There was a bunch of lavender tied at the door, and slices of a dried orange stuck with cloves skewered onto a twig. And if he was right, the pretty patchwork coverlet on her bed was one she made.

A mouse peered out from under the one and only cupboard. Kathleen shrieked as it scuttled across the floor.

"Hmm, delightful." Jack bit his tongue, regretting he opened his mouth.

"You bloody thing, get out of here!" Kate grabbed a broom, chasing it.

"That's twice." He shook his head. "Do your famous clients mind you swearing?"

"Sorry." She continued to look for the mouse. "I didn't know I had a lodger. Maybe I should charge him rent."

Jack chuckled, watching her poking around the base of the cupboard with the broom.

"I know this place is vile, Uncle Jack, but it's a start," she said, giving up and plopping herself on a lumpy-looking mattress. She motioned toward a rickety chair in the corner. "I guess you have your view. So let's have it." She looked glum, waiting for his verdict.

The mouse ran across the floor again before disappearing under the skirting board.

"Well…" Jack rubbed his brow. "I can't say I'm impressed by your running away, and I'm certainly not impressed by your choice of accommodation, or the lodger." He paused. "But I am impressed by your tenacity, your will to survive, and the work you have."

Jack stood, and as he did a chair leg fell off. "Oops, sorry."

"Don't worry." Her shoulders sank. "I knew it was on borrowed time. I found it in the alley, going begging. Like most things in here." She took a deep breath. "But before you try to persuade me to come back home, and before you tell me this place is awful, let me say this is what I want. Even if I must share it with Roger the Lodger. I really want to try and make a go of my ideas. And to do that, I have to live in London."

"There you go again, making one and one add up to ten, young lady!"

Jack now towered over her. He sat on the bed beside her.

"Wow! Do you actually sleep on this?" He shook

his head, smiling. "I've found more comfort on a rock."

"Please?" she begged.

He shrugged. "Now, listen, I have an idea, but first we have to go to the police, clear my name, and let everyone know you are safe."

Chapter 39

Long gone was the tiny bedsit that smelt of fat and stale chips. Jack had secured a much larger and far more agreeable Victorian apartment which she shared with her friend Sarah, whom she worked with at the atelier. Uncle Jack had been right. Getting a fashion degree whilst working at Madam Raines' would support her goals.

****

Kate had become familiar with the beggars in London, but other than dropping the odd coin, she could only imagine the money would go on food and a bed for the night. Uncle Jack's word had struck home. She already had a roof over her head and was safe at night. What had happened to these people? How on earth did they end up on the streets? This was happening now. It was the fifties. Why? What was their story? It had played over in her mind more than once. She had seen a beggar outside Portobello Market. She would go back. Already she had a plan brewing. Uncle Jack had mentioned soup kitchens, and she wanted to find out more.

The day burst fresh and new, the air washed clean by last night's deluge, with the only evidence left being dark puddles between the cobbles. The market was already thronging with visitors and potential customers, its popularity evidently growing. A stall holder, purporting to have antiques, had arranged himself right at the opening of the market. Once more the fascination of each stall quickly drew Kate's attention. She was glad she had brought her camera as she took shots, observing from a quiet distance, framing photos just like her uncle had taught, for posterity, though her plan to find the busker again was to the fore of her mind.

After walking the length of the market, she heard the guitar and followed the sound. He was there, right by the corner. A deliberate move, Kate assumed, so that he could see the plods arrive and move on before they did for him. Kate, desperate to take his photo, surreptitiously studied the man. Head drooped, dirty, disheveled, weather-beaten brown. His beard a mat, long overdue for a trim, much like his hair. At a second glance, Kate found herself surprised. She initially had thought him to be old, but found his features were far younger than she'd assumed. Maybe twenty, thirty?

He was getting up. Quietly, silently, picking up his guitar and his begging bowl, a flat cap. He put it on whilst slipping a coin or two into his pocket. Kate wondered why he made the move. Then she saw a plod was on his way. Not drawing attention to himself, the man began to walk slowly, but with purpose, away from the policeman. Kate decided to follow. The policeman turned on his heels. No wish to confront the busker. He had done his job just by his presence. Kate kept a safe distance. Her interest in the man grew. She assumed he would be sourcing another spot.

Five streets on, there were fewer people around. The area appeared to be less inhabited. Then, to her astonishment the man disappeared between a crumbling church and its church hall. The front of both buildings met the street, no lovely long pathway to the front door like St Michaels Church back home. He was religious. Nothing wrong in that, but as she stood contemplating what to do, another man disappeared in the same manner. He also looked like he didn't have a penny to his name. Curiosity getting the better of her, she walked past. She could hear murmuring, quiet, low. Frustrated at her inability to find out more, Kate turned and walked even slower past the alley again. This time another man brushed past her, muttering under his breath. Her heart flew into her mouth at his unexpected proximity. But he did nothing more than disappear in the same way. Disregarding possible danger, Kate took a step into the narrow walkway. Five paces on, she found an open door. She peeked inside and saw a woman and man working flat out, using a trestle table as part of the kitchen. Men were lining up. The queue was becoming disorderly. The man working at the table called out for order.

"Hey, there's enough for everyone. Be patient. We've only got me and Jess on today!"

What Kate had found was exactly what she had hoped for. A soup kitchen.

Kate waited in the queue, as if she were one of them. The men gave her space. Some eyed her dispassionately. Some muttered incoherently under their breath. Some looked confused. Kate's heart had not steadied. She had put herself in a position she wished she hadn't and was about to leave, run even, when the woman called to her.

"It's men only here, luv. Go down to St Johns. They'll sort you out there."

Kate flushed, embarrassed. "No, I've not come for

L. B. Griffin

food." The woman shook her head, and, trying to get on with the job in hand, shouted, "Next!" She looked up to find Kate in front of her. "Sorry, luv. Didn't you hear? Go to St Johns. They'll sort you out."

A man pushed past Kate. The woman handed him a cup of tea and a sandwich. "Be polite to the lady, George."

He grunted a "Sorry."

"How are you, George? How's that cough of yours?"

He shrugged.

"I know there's no telling you, but really you ought to see a doctor." She smiled at his expression. "You know what to do, don't you now. Move along, let the next man in, find a seat you like, luv, and Fred will give you the rest, all right?" she sounded kind, her voice warm and friendly.

"Ta." The man took his food and moved on.

"I've not come for food," said Kate quickly. "I've come to see if you need help?" She stood firm. She was going to do this, and if they didn't want her, she would go to St John's. Wherever that was.

"What? You want to help?" The woman chuckled. "Well, I'll be blowed. Thank you. If you're sure, roll up your sleeves, and you can start right now by pouring tea."

Kate and the woman worked seamlessly side by side. She fitted into the routine as if she had been there forever, and at the end of the shift, Kate felt she had been hit by a bus. There were so many hungry mouths. So many in need.

"Carol, can I come again?"

"Are you serious? A young bit like you wantin' to

help?" Kate nodded. She liked Carol. A robust woman with a heart of gold. She spoke to all of her 'customers' and knew everyone by name, and it appeared she knew a little of their history.

"That would be fan-bloomin-tastic. How about a cuppa? Sit down with me and Fred, and let's have a chat."

By the time Kate got back home, she felt lifted. Pleased to be able to offer a little help and to do something worthwhile.

Chapter 40

1958

Madam Raines had begun to get a regular weekly visit from a man. He was burly and gruff and most certainly didn't fit in with the clientele. He came in the back way and disappeared into her office for a moment, then left. Forever curious, Kate easily worked out the pattern of his arrival and secreted herself behind a rack of material on one of "his" days.

She shouldn't have been listening, but even with the office door closed it was obvious Madam Raines was frightened. Kate retreated to the workroom, worried. He was extorting Madam for money. It was patently evident he was offering to either ruin her or keep her boutique "safe from exploitation." It appeared everyone else was oblivious to the situation, and she didn't know what to do with the information she had gained.

Not two minutes after Kate had set about her work, Madam Raines called for her. Spooked, Kate felt sure she had been found out. As she entered the office, Kate noticed how anxious Madam looked.

"Please sit." She licked her lips nervously. "I've some exciting news for you, Kate. We have a new client. If you do a good job, she will become your first exclusive client." Kate initially felt thrilled at the opportunity, but there was an underlying message, and she could almost hear the *but* before it arrived. "She will require the utmost discretion and will be visiting tomorrow." Madam dabbed a bead of perspiration from her brow before continuing. "I don't need to tell you to treat her with the utmost respect. If you have any issues, you must come to me at once."

"Of course, Madam…" Kate had a strange feeling in the pit of her stomach. "and her name is?"

"Miss Dorian Craddock. She was referred here by Lady Sutcliffe. She is expecting great things of us. Please don't let me down." There was a definite urgency in her voice, something Kate never heard there before. Who on earth was this Craddock woman, who had Madam Raines in such a tizz? Or was it down to the male visitor? Were they connected? Kate was quickly drawing conclusions she had no right to, but she'd met Lady Sutcliffe on a few occasions and certainly did not like the woman. She was rude, arrogant, and far too vile toward the girls, who did their utmost to accommodate her. Kate left the office concerned. She would not let Madam Raines down and wondered what tomorrow might hold.

****

It was early evening. Kate was sprawled on the floor, distractedly thumbing through a magazine, unable to get the woman's name out of her head.

"Sarah, have you ever heard of Dorian Craddock? She's a friend of Lady Sutcliffe?"

"What, you've never heard of her? Lor', she's a wrong 'un, Kate. Her father's a monster. Did for his son and was a part of the underworld. Thinking about it, I'm sure he's heading for the gallows. There was a huge piece about it in the paper not so long ago, don't you remember?"

Kate already had misgivings, and now she stared at Sarah.

"Well, she is coming to Madam Raines' tomorrow." She tried to play devil's advocate. "Just because her father's bad doesn't make her bad, does it?"

Sarah shook her head. "I don't know about that. They say a rotting apple never falls far from the tree. I've never heard anything good."

"Hmm." Kate rolled over and sat up, wrapping her arms about her bent knees. "Madam Raines is scared stiff. I know that much." Her mouth puckered. "She's told me that I'm to work with her."

Sarah puffed her cheeks. "Be careful."

****

Sarah and Kate arrived in good time the following day, discussing the impending visit. Madam Raines was waiting impatiently. Kate raised a brow at Sarah as she was pulled aside.

"You must do your very best, Kate. I'm relying on you." It was as if her employer hadn't slept all night. Kate certainly hadn't. By 10:05, the client had arrived and was shown into a private room. Kate was quickly introduced and immediately took in as much detail as possible without being obvious. The woman was tall, lean, with an aquiline nose and small, dark, unkind eyes that seemed to pierce right through her.

"Ah, Kate Westfield. Pleased to meet you." She held out a thin, gloved hand. "I believe you can design outfits for any occasion."

"I can certainly try, madam." Kate immediately

remembered her mother's professionalism. "Please, would you care to sit, and may I interest you in a beverage before we make a start?"

"No. I'm here for a fitting," the woman drawled. She looked at Madam Raines. "Are you sure this is the girl Margaux talked about, not one of your usual lackeys?"

"Miss Craddock," Kate cut in. "I apologize. The purpose of offering something to drink is to help make you feel relaxed in your surroundings. My aim is to ensure you enjoy the whole experience here. I'm sure you'll agree that having a new outfit isn't just about being measured or having the perfect fit. I think what we wear makes a statement." Kate paused, assessing the woman's body language. "I hoped to design something especially for you. Something that will not only make you feel amazing but will enable you to convey whatever you wish without saying a word."

Her heart was thumping so hard she felt sure it would pop right out of her chest. Kate put her hands behind her back, trying to control their shaking. "You can of course, if you wish, select from the haute couture already available, and I can adjust it to fit perfectly."

Dorian Craddock eyed her with surprise. She turned again to Madam Raines.

"Very well. Coffee. Black."

"I'll organize that myself, Madam Raines, thank you," Kate insisted. "Please, Miss Craddock, make yourself comfortable."

With the coffee arranged, Kate began working her magic. She asked Miss Craddock to walk around the room, already noting that any flapper girl of days gone by would have been glad not to have to bind her breasts. This woman was as flat chested as a cow pat. Kate also noticed that although she walked tall, her neck seemed to lean forward as if she were wearing an oxen yoke. Her hair was cut in a bang. It hung, short, glossy, and straight, and the fringe had been cut in the same manner.

"Curves." Kate eventually said. "You need curves." She had been sketching, as Dorian walked, watching her every move. "It's what every woman wants. That certain understated femininity that moves a man to desire and takes the eye of women who wish they had the same gift. I grant you the nineteen twenties had style. I personally love that era, but it doesn't give you the shape I think you yearn for." Kate offered it as a statement. Dorian Craddock rolled her thumbs one over the other.

"Your words are grandiose, but can you deliver?"

Kate smiled. Her hands still trembled ever so slightly, but she took a deep breath and quickly controlled the quiver in her voice.

She would not let Madam Raines down.

She showed her the sketches. "Shall we begin?"

Chapter 41

Dorian Craddock became Kate's regular client—so much so that she invited her to her home in Mayfair. They were discussing the new designs Kate had in mind when a man lumbered in through the garden doorway. His smock was covered in dabs of paint. He looked startled by her appearance. She noticed his co-ordination was slightly impaired.

Dorian swiftly made the introductions. "Davey, this is the Kate I've been talking about. This is my brother, Davey. I was thinking she might like to join our club. What's your view, Davey?"

"Don't you have enough girls?" Even though Kate understood the man, he struggled to articulate the sentence.

Dorian looked momentarily taken aback, then gave a little embarrassed laugh. Davey offered an indecipherable look.

"I was talking about a membership, darling. Not my girls."

Kate absorbed the information like breathing air. There was something unwholesome about the woman, and some of Sarah's rumors were difficult to ignore.

"Davey is a remarkable artist." Dorian continued, briskly, "He wouldn't say, but his dominant hand is useless, as you can see"—Kate flinched at the crass remark—"but Davey has relearned to paint with his

L. B. Griffin

left. Haven't you, darling? I round up life models for him." It sounded remarkably like a cover-up to Kate, as Davey shot her another strange look.

"Pleased to meet you." He held out his stronger hand, "I like art," he confessed. "Not so easy now, though."

Kate liked him instantly. Although there were familial similarities, he looked like the kinder version of his sister, and turned out to be far friendlier. To Dorian's amusement, Davey sat beside Kate.

"I'm going to brag a bit, Davey, and you can't stop me." Davey palmed his hand skyward as she dashed off to collect some sketches, while he valiantly put words together. "There's no telling her. I'm trying new styles. The latest, abstract, and I'm looking for a larger space—I'd like to do a mural."

By the time Dorian returned with the sketches in her hand, Kate and Davey were chatting like old friends, and her interest in the arts had not been lost on him. Dorian presented some of his work, and Kate looked through, thoroughly impressed.

"I wonder..." said Kate, quickly thinking on her feet. "You were looking for a large space to do a mural. I might have just the place—my apartment has...well, it's been what I've always considered as...missing something. It's a blank canvas, of sorts, a large expanse of wall...perhaps you would like to check it out?"

"Yes. Thank you." His face was wreathed in smiles. He turned to Dorian. "If that's all right with you?" Kate wondered why it wouldn't be.

"Of course, Davey." Though Dorian looked uncomfortable at her own response, she turned her attention back to Kate. "I suggested membership to

Club 59. We could take a tour right now, if you like. It would be my treat, the membership, that is. After all, one good turn deserves another. Doesn't it?"

Club 59, situated just next door to Dorian's Mayfair house, was simply fabulous. Kate could not fail to be impressed. The innocuous front door led the way to a grand entrance and five floors that were each as beautiful as the next. Each room was a glorious gem.

Dorian knew she would be impressed and proudly showed her the transformed cellar where she had brought in Turkish architects and imported marble for the fabulously constructed Hammas. Dorian walked Kate through her completed vision, conceived to attract only the rich and famous. A restaurant, a lounge, rooms for dancing and socializing. Then she finally took her to the casino.

The croupier came down a corridor toward them. She looked pale, drawn. Dorian took her to one side, and although there didn't appear to be a reason, there were angry exchanges. The girl looked beaten. Dorian turned back and politely showed Kate around the casino. Kate felt terrible. Was Dorian's anger meted out at the girl for her benefit? As an unspoken warning? She hoped not, as here in Club 59 Dorian had advised she could mix with the social elite, which would benefit her enormously. It was agreed she could market her trade without being presumptuous, and Dorian would help her to do so.

By the time they stepped outside the Club, they had come to another agreement—Davey would visit her Saturday next. Kate returned home and poured herself a glass of wine. She felt pleased with her work, but shattered by it. She now knew to be careful around

Dorian, who could fly off into rage so quickly. Today, Kate had learned far more than any speculation could have provided.

Chapter 42

Following Davey's visit to Kate's home, it was agreed he would begin work the next Sunday. Sarah was still in bed and wouldn't be moved even when the doorbell rang. Davey stood at the door armed with a boxload of painting materials. Dorian was right by his side. "Davey seemed to have it in his head he could manage to get here without me. I wanted to be sure everything was in order."

Davey gave her a half smile and raised a brow at Kate.

"I'm fine, Dorian. Stop fussing."

"Why don't you go on up, Davey, but I'd better warn you Sarah's still in bed." She glanced at the paraphernalia stacked at his feet. "I guess you want a hand with that lot?"

Davey nodded. Kate picked up the box and waited as he valiantly climbed stairs, holding tight onto the banister.

"You can go now." Davey instructed when he got to the top, clearly keen to get Dorian out of his hair.

"How rude!"

Davey sighed. Kate smiled. Dorian took the hint. "All right, you've made your point. Call me when you're ready, and I'll send someone to collect you."

Kate helped Davey settle in and offered him a drink.

"There's some food in the fridge. Help yourself to whatever you want. I'll be off soon, just for a couple of hours, so you'll be left in peace. Though I can't vouch for Sarah, that is, if she ever gets up."

Davey was already studying the wall, his new canvas. He passed a couple of drawings her way. "I thought something like this…"

"They're inspired. I love it!" Davey looked satisfied. "I brought some other sketches along—the girls Dorian spoke of…my life models?"

Kate took them from him in surprise and studied them carefully. There were two pencil sketches of each girl, the first posed fully dressed and the next nude. They were tastefully arranged, and he'd captured them in astounding detail. She puzzled, sure she had seen one of the girls somewhere before, but right now couldn't work out where.

"These are fantastic, Davey. Really wonderful."

He looked shy. "No one else, other than Dorian, has seen them."

"Why ever not?"

He shrugged and picked up a pencil. "Dorian suggested we didn't, not yet. CJ is thinking about taking me on a tour of the galleries, to gather interest first."

"CJ?"

"CJ Rutherford. He claims to be an art critic and antique dealer, and…" Davey muttered under his breath, "Whatever else Dorian wants him to be."

On that note, he frowned. "Sorry. Can I get on now?"

"Yes, of course. I need to go. See you in a few hours."

Kate caught the tube, heading to the soup kitchen, her mind covering just as much ground regarding Davey's comments about his sister and the mention of a CJ Rutherford. He sounded interesting. She was determined to ask more questions when she returned.

****

Unusually, Kate was keen to get back home, not only to see the progress Davey had made, but to study the sketches of his life models again.

Sarah was up, lounging around in her dressing gown. Kate was surprised. "You actually managed to get up?"

Sarah smiled enigmatically. "Davey wanted to draw me. Look. I'm in the mural. I always knew I was an angel in disguise, can you see?" Kate was flabbergasted. Davey had not only completed a comprehensive outline of his vision but managed to incorporate a tasteful nude of Sarah, resting within the heavens. "That's astonishing. How on earth?"

Davey shrugged his shoulders. "She insisted."

"Sarah can be very persuasive." Kate laughed. She spied the sketches. "May I keep these for a while? Just to study the detail?"

He nodded.

"I'll get us something to eat, then. I guess you didn't bother to feed our guest, did you, Sarah?"

****

Once Davey packed away and left, Kate picked up the sketches and squished next to Sarah on the couch.

"You don't happen to recognize this girl, do you, Sarah?"

"No. Why?"

"I'm convinced I know her from somewhere." She

217

studied the face again and pursed her lips.

Sarah began to thumb through the sketches. "But I'm sure I've seen this girl somewhere before." She showed her. "It was a long time ago, but I can't for the life of me remember where."

"Maybe I should ask Davey. He'll put me right."

"Yes, you should. You know how I hate mysteries. Now just remember, I'm an angel, and angels need communion wine."

Kate tutted and went to the fridge, returning with a bottle and two glasses. "Lazy oik!"

****

Davey returned early the following day, keen to get on with the mural. Kate was happy with the deal, and understanding his passion, offered the spare room to stay over whilst he worked on his project. Surprised by the offer, Davey contacted Dorian and checked that would be acceptable. He always rose early mornings, he told Kate, so the arrangement would suit him perfectly.

Kate found she loved Davey's company and looked forward to seeing him when she returned home from work. She could not fail to admire Davey's strength of character, his tenacity. He would not be beaten by his physical impairments.

Kate had quickly tuned into Davey's speech pattern and reveled in his quirky sense of humor. They bantered on their views of the world and discussed a wide range of topics. When she talked about the homeless, he was empathetic and appeared to understand their plight. Davey Craddock, for all his physical issues, remained an intelligent, reflective man, whom she believed would be a daunting adversary in any situation. In her opinion, he was an entirely different animal to his sister. He was kind, caring, and compassionate, whereas Dorian had a mean streak she could not disguise.

The night before he packed away, ready to leave, she knew she would miss him. It was then she had the idea.

''Davey, how would you feel if I took photographs of your mural? I think it should be displayed to the world, but as I can't have the world tramping through my home, perhaps it could be turned into prints or maybe even postcards? How would you feel about that?'' He was amused at the suggestion.

"You're a good friend, Kate Westfield. I like you very much."

"And I like you, Davey Craddock." And she meant it.

"If I say yes, I need a favor." He looked serious. "The sketches of girls." He pulled them off the table where Kate had left them. "Put them somewhere safe. I know Sarah has seen. But no one else. Can I trust you, Kate Westfield?" A strange look crossed his face. "Do not share—no photographs, postcards, posters. Promise."

She flushed. What was Davey hinting at? "Of course, I promise." He caught her hand, looking directly at her.

"Stay away from Club 59."

****

But Kate became a regular visitor at Club 59. Whatever Davey meant by his parting shot, she couldn't refuse Dorian's gift of a membership. It was an agreed opportunity to network and rub shoulders with the rich and famous. Whilst Club 59 offered rest and relaxation, she also found the steamier, wilder side attractive. She could take any amount of attention from super rich men, thank you very much. She would accept their insanely generous gifts, attend the wild parties mostly held at out-of-town locations owned by Dorian. Most of all, she could let her hair down and enjoy herself. And it all came without pressure. She chose what she wanted to do, and when to stop. When the drugs became a part of the scene, she dabbled, but didn't like it. As time progressed, the more she attended Dorian's special events, the more she saw. The more she saw, the more she understood, and didn't like, and a niggle of doubt grew. Then one evening everything seemed to slot into place.

Girls came and went. It hadn't been obvious, at first, but why she'd missed it to begin with she couldn't understand. One party they were there, the next they had vanished, and new girls replaced them. Kate couldn't work out who they were, where they came from, or why they disappeared. Forever curious, she just had to find out, and tonight was the perfect time.

A young girl had caught her attention. She was on a much older man's arm. It wasn't an unusual occurrence, but soon, after a few glasses of champagne, she was decidedly wobbly on her feet, and slightly distressed. He could have just been helping her to the powder room, but Kate doubted it. She decided to follow at a discreet distance. He escorted her into a private room. She saw a glimpse of beyond. A bedroom. The door closed behind them. A smartly suited man sentried himself outside. Kate, worried for the girl, tried to strike up a conversation, but it was impossible to gain his interest, or get past the door. He soon became irritated at her intrusion and unwillingness to leave. In one swift movement, he parted his jacket and revealed a gun, and with the action he gave a verbal threat. Shocked, with no choice left, she walked away.

Stunned, dismayed she couldn't do anything to help the girl, Kate now realized the underbelly of Dorian's business. Within the four walls of Club 59, meticulously carved out, Dorian had crafted such a wonderful experience for her clients. A Hammas, a casino, and other fabulous rooms for their leisure and pleasure. If the police were to raid her premises, there would be no evidence of wrongdoing. The darker, seedier side of her business was a well-constructed, carefully disguised high-class brothel.

Kate resolved to attend more of Dorian's events. Record everything. She trawled her memory, noted the days and times, and began sketching the girls' faces as best she could.

When she questioned Dorian, she was met with ice-cold denial, and a veiled threat to stay out of her business. Kate half expected the cool-handed reception and accepted Dorian's message with a profuse apology, but her fears were already on high alert. There was no denying Dorian had a fearsome reputation, and girls were going missing. She didn't have all the answers or evidence. Not yet.

****

Kate lay on the floor facing the ceiling, legs bent, reading the latest on the CND movement. She planned to join one of the growing Aldermaston marches against nuclear weapons, though her mind was on the upcoming bash. This would be the last of the parties Dorian threw that she would attend. She still had no idea what to do with the information she had. It was nothing to speak of. The police would have nothing to go on. If anything, they would laugh at her and call her a fantasist, plus she knew Dorian's connections reached far and wide.

"Mr. MacMillan is talking about a motorway system that will eventually cross the country," said Sarah, cutting into Kate's thoughts. Having finished her makeup and hair an hour ago, she sat on the sofa, reading a newspaper, and nibbled a biscuit. "Sounds like a good plan to me."

"Well." Kate rolled over with her dressing gown tucked under her. "I think we should be debating the bigger issues of the homeless and nuclear weapons, not extending bloody roads."

"Boring."

"Is it? I guess spending millions cutting into swathes of beautiful countryside for a road instead of spending it on people is a much better idea."

"It's called progress, Kate." Sarah rolled her eyes, then checked her watch. "Anyway, you agreed to take me to this party. And guess what, you're not getting away with it. Plus, we're late." Sarah dropped the paper to the floor and left a trail of crumbs behind her.

Kate, exasperated, called out, "It would be nice if you cleared up behind yourself for once!" Kate stretched her limbs, then glanced over the fallen paper as she picked it up. She really didn't want to go, but Sarah had nagged, and she ruefully relented.

A couple of minutes later, Sarah asked Kate to do up her dress.

"You're never going to wear that, are you?"

"And why ever not?"

"Breathe in." Kate groaned, tugging at the zip. "Well, if you don't mind me saying, I prefer the pale gray one. It's classier, and your breasts don't look like they're about to pop out."

"From what you've said, men like an eyeful," Sarah retorted. "Why else would I wear it?"

"Less is more, in my humble opinion." She huffed with one last tug. "At last!" She'd managed to pull the zip up, and Kate, brushing her friend aside, went into her bedroom.

"Here." She returned with a sable shrug. "It's cold outside." Sarah gasped at its beauty, threw it over her shoulder, and began prancing around the lounge.

"This is absolutely fabulous! Was this from the Russian diplomat, whatshisname Korsakov-itch, the man you *were* going to introduce me to once upon a time?"

"If I told you, Sarah, I'd have to kill you."

"Always with the secrets, Kate. Go on, you can tell me, was it him? I think it's gorgeous. *He* must be gorgeous, giving you something so beautiful. If you should ever want to…"

Sarah turned to find Kate had gone back into her bedroom, and she could only hear a muffled reply. She shook her head, happily stroking the softness of the shrug.

Kate selected an outfit while pondering over the Russian. She remembered the first time she'd met him, along with CJ Rutherford. It had been at Club 59. She frowned. That place had certainly given her contacts, but it definitely had its dark side. To top it all, she had never seen that girl again, and it frightened her.

Kate's thoughts returned to Nicolai. He'd been

the bar with a woman dripping in jewels when he spotted her. He dropped the woman like a rotten egg and made his move. Kate found his accent intriguing, and his interest in her flattering. He had been fun at the beginning. Generous, without question, but full of himself. His last gift to her had been an opal-and-diamond necklace. She opened a drawer and lifted the box out. The value she knew would be ridiculous. Embarrassed by the extravagance—unsure if she should have ever accepted it in the first place—she never wore it.

Nicolai was unpredictable. The man who initially was kind and generous became demanding things from her she wasn't prepared to give. When his sexual preferences began to grow more than a little risqué, she began to extricate herself from him. She took one more look and decided in that instant to give it back. Should he refuse, she would have a word with CJ.

"What are you doing in there? Have you gone to sleep?"

"Fat chance, with you hollering like a bloody banshee," Kate yelled back, and carefully stowed the box back in the drawer and slipped on her heels.

"So who else will be going tonight?" Sarah was standing in the lounge, her breasts hitched out of her dress, looking innocent. Kate began laughing. Sarah could be professional, demure, innocent, but she could also turn it all off like a tap.

"What did I say? I knew you'd pop out!"

"I was just wondering—if someone saw these babies, I might get me a mink, as well?" Sarah cupped her breasts and jiggled them around.

Kate laughed so much she was close to hysteria.

"Put them away."

"Spoil sport!" Sarah hooked them back inside her dress. "Better?"

"Better."

"Kate, what is it?" Sarah grumbled. "You look bothered."

Kate shrugged. "I'm not sure about tonight. I just want you to know that sometimes these parties can get a little crazy. I don't want you to get dragged into doing things you don't want to do. Okay? So be careful. Promise?"

"Okaaay. But everything you've told me up to now sounds exciting. I can't wait!"

"Right. If you're not listening to me, we're not going. That's the end of it." Kate kicked off her heels. Sarah looked mortified.

"I'm sorry, don't say that. Of course I'll be on my very *bestest* behavior and keep my wits about me. Honest, guv." Sarah saluted, with a wicked grin on her face. Kate, exasperated, sighed but remained worried.

Once outside on the pavement, Sarah produced an ear-splitting whistle at a passing taxi. The party was being hosted by Dorian Craddock in one of her many homes. This one was situated on the outskirts of London—reputed for riotous parties, and where the police would never be called in for waking the dead. Kathleen felt uneasy. She had no idea if Nicolai would be there and hoped he wouldn't be. Not tonight. She wanted to ease him completely from her life before he tried to ease her further into his.

****

Effigies of film stars were strategically arranged along the quarter mile driveway, giving rise for Sarah to

L. B. Griffin

shriek.

"Wow, Kate, just look! I had no idea it was a themed party, why didn't you say?"

The cabbie glanced in his rearview mirror and chuckled.

"I had no idea either," Kate replied dryly, but in the pit of her stomach, she knew she'd already seen too much of this lifestyle.

"My God! Just look at the size of this place, Kate. You didn't say. It's like a palace," Sarah shouted in her ear, now in her element. They stepped out of the cab and onto a red carpet leading to a huge door, high and wide enough to ride a horse through. Giant golden masks sentried the entrance. Men wearing only dinner jackets, bow ties, and black boxer shorts waited for their arrival, laden with trays of champagne.

"Heavens above, what next?" Sarah giggled. "Aren't you naughty boys?" She swiped a glass from one of the waiters as she passed by, grinning from ear to ear and virtually skipped up the steps.

Kate looked around, brooding. Sarah was trembling with delight.

"Clearly no need for decorum as you suggested earlier, Kate!"

Inside, a huge chandelier suspended in all its glittering glory shone its light upon a marble floor. This was flanked by two wide, sweeping staircases. The balustrades led to a gallery above, where a quartet played classical music. There was no sign of Dorian, though it would have surprised Kate if she saw her. Dorian apparently rarely made appearances at her parties, unlike Club 59, where she was highly visible. She could never understand why she would throw these ridiculously extravagant events and not attend.

"Kate this is absolutely extraordinary." Sarah was beside herself. "How the other half live, eh? You should have brought me before. I can't wait to meet your Nicolai. He is going to be here, isn't he?"

Just at that moment a scurry of people, a conga in the making, jogged past.

"The fireworks are about to go off in the park—come on, join us!" A male grabbed Kate by the hand and pulled her along. Sarah followed behind, laughing, through the entrance hall and into a massive lounge.

It was evident that the party was already in full swing. There was an orgy of snorting white powder, spread in regular lines on coffee tables. Lazy, crazy music blasted out from one of the hidden systems. Of course, Nicolai would be here, somewhere. He loved this kind of action. She hated the drug scene. Only once did she imbue in a stupid moment of madness, and she'd hated every minute and quickly learned the power it held over others.

"Come on!" The man was insistent. They had barged through the next door, and he was holding her hand even tighter. By now they were in a huge domed glass conservatory. The pool, designed to look like a conch shell, spurted a fountain of water. The pool also housed a swim-up bar, which encouraged the already naked, inebriated revelers. The place was fantastic, she had to admit, but she wanted a different, a more normal kind of life. A shuffle of people poured out to watch the fireworks, while the man let her hand go and began stripping off, whooping with delight. Sarah was already heeling her shoes off.

"What are you doing?"

"Joining the party, of course." Her dress came off remarkably quickly, considering the amount of tugging to get her into it. "Come on, let's live a little." And she flung herself into the pool, squealing as she hit the water, just as the fireworks exploded into the dark night sky. Kate watched Sarah splashing around and wondered what to do. There would be no telling her, not now. She'd better stay a while, keep an eye, let Sarah go mad, wear herself out, then take her home. Her eyes traveled back to the firework display. It was all so out of this world.

Kate wandered into a billiard room—men were potting balls, silently smoking huge cigars. They glanced up. She waved a hand and walked out. Next, she found a champagne fountain, and grabbed a glass, filled it, then hunted for something to eat. She didn't want to get drunk.

The next room was full of bodies, pressed together, writhing, sighing, pushing, pulsating in time to a throbbing bass. She rolled her head and stretched the tension from her neck, wishing the night were over already, wishing she'd never come. Kate slowly walked around the house, and then climbed the stairs. The notion of finding any more evidence on Dorian had been pushed to one side.

There were plenty of bedrooms. She hoped she might find an empty one, away from everything, a place to gather her thoughts and relax while she waited for Sarah to get bored. The quartet had vanished, leaving only their chairs as evidence they were ever there.

Every room she walked into heaved, a jumble of bodies moving as one, thrusting, groaning, pressing into each other. With no space to breathe or think, still in search of somewhere she could be quiet and maybe pre-book a taxi, she pushed open another bedroom door.

A threesome. No big deal. The minister, whom she recognized instantly, was loosely tied to a four-poster with black ribbons. He appeared to be loving every minute. She backed out of the room, throwing her hand up in mock apology. The next bedroom door was ajar. She peeked her head around to check she wasn't disturbing anyone. Her eyes adjusted to the dark. There was a man fixated on the matter before him. She thought she recognized the silhouette but couldn't be sure. He was using a tripod and camera, pressed into a peep hole drilled into the wall.

She instantly guessed it was a honey trap. He hadn't heard her. The MP would have no idea. Worried what to do, she crept silently away. She chewed her lip. None of this was right, or good, or even her business, but she couldn't leave it alone. Moments later, Kate, acting as if she were inebriated, staggered back into the honey trap. The girls encouraged her into their threesome. She giggled, allowing herself to be drawn in, and deliberately fell on top of the MP. She whispered, in his ear, urgent, low, "get dressed, you've been compromised. I'll call you a cab." She rolled off him, and, faking a tumble, pushed against one of the girls giggling. They fell off the bed together in a heap. Kate got up, and stumbled back out the room, laughing, as if in a drunken stupor.

A telephone farther along the landing caught her eye. She picked up the receiver and asked the operator for a cab.

"Hello." A voice from behind caught her off guard. Startled, she jumped. "Are you okay? You look bothered. I noticed you looked a bit lost, earlier. Perhaps I could get you a drink?" Kate's heart, still beating a drum in her chest, glanced up at him. She'd misplaced her drink somewhere, ages ago.

"Hmm. No, thanks." Her emotions were running riot. Dorian had already given her a warning. What if she got to hear about what just happened and put the pieces together? "I was thinking about going home."

"Really? Me too. Everything's getting a little, um…" He looked embarrassed.

"Wild?" she offered. "You say you saw me earlier. Are you a stalker?"

"No. Of course not." He was looking at her so intensely she blushed. That never happened.

"Kate." She held out a hand, gathering her wits. "Kate Westfield."

"Alex…"

"Alex Black. I know who you are."

He looked surprised. "I saw you earlier too—and in the paper—the motorway proposal?"

"Sharp-eyed and beautiful. I was only in the background in that shot."

Kate stared, instantly drawn to him but unsure whether he was flirting or being serious.

"Hmm. Are you here on your own?" he asked.

"No. I came with a friend, but she's kind of busy. I was looking for something, well, somewhere a little more peaceful."

"Maybe I could help you find it?"

"Maybe you could. But like I said, I'm leaving. I'm about to book a cab."

"I thought you did that already?"

"No. That was for someone else." She eyed him

quizzically.

"What about the friend you came with, then?"

"You ask a lot of questions."

Kate spotted Nicolai coming up the staircase. Her heart skipped a beat. Two young women were hanging onto him. It was obvious from their body language they were going to be on more than friendly terms.

"Do me a favor?"

"Anything…"

Kate pulled him into her so that her back was against the wall and his frame hid hers. She kissed him full on the mouth and stayed there until she was sure Nicolai and his friends had passed by. As she reluctantly pushed Alex off, she saw the MP emerging from the bedroom she'd found him in. He glanced her way and rushed on.

"That was a nice surprise, Kate Westfield. Do you often kiss would-be stalkers?"

"No. Only when I need to."

"The something you were looking for? I guess *he* was on the stairs."

"Yes."

"Ah. And here I was, thinking you were beginning to like me."

Kate gave him a wry smile. The kiss had been sensational. He knew it. She had melted right into him.

And now every breath she took betrayed the extraordinary hold he seemed to have over her.

"I'm on my way to find my *other* friend, to tell her I'm leaving. Are you coming?"

They found Sarah drying off by the pool. Alex watched, amused, as Kate unsuccessfully tried to coax her to leave. He stepped in, and Sarah couldn't resist his charm. Kate shot him a look that would have curled his toes, but he just laughed. He knew he wanted to spend more time with Kate. Now he'd found her, he wasn't about to let go.

Chapter 43

Kate was on her way home, it was dark. A cold breeze fell upon her cheek. Imminent rain, she thought, wishing she had her umbrella. Normally she and Sarah would go home together, but she'd stayed later at the atelier, and Sarah had plans to meet friends. She passed a pub. The King George's soft light touched the street. There were people inside, inviting to a warm welcome. It was tempting, but it was late. She crossed the road, and a cat hissed, then yowled. A streetlight flickered and died. The area seemed even more eerie without its orange glow.

When she heard footsteps, she checked over her shoulder but couldn't see anyone. The footsteps seemed to click an echo in time with hers. She glanced over her shoulder again. No, she couldn't see anyone. She sped up. A bottle tinkled, rolling along the ground to the left of her, a momentary distraction. A figure loomed out of the gloom and in two swift steps he had pressed a gloved hand around her mouth and wrapped a strong arm about her. Try as she might, she couldn't scream or escape his powerful grip. There were two of them now.

They hurled her against the wall, and she bounced off and fell to the ground before a sound could escape her lips. Winded, she gasped for air. She didn't get time to breathe before they began their assault.

With every punch and every kick, she was given a

message, the words grittily emphasized: "Stay away from things you don't understand, or the next time you and your friends will die."

Suddenly another figure loomed from seemingly nowhere. A guttural roar, and then the crack of splintering wood caught on the once-still air. It clanged a note in the alleyway. Someone else was there? One of her assailants was being landed blow after blow. Kate, bleeding, face against the ground, lay agonized, unable to move, unable to help. She could just make out shadowy figures. Now one of her would-be attackers was having to defend himself. Suddenly her savior was landed a hefty uppercut that lifted him straight off his feet. He landed beside her, groaning. Through her haze, Kate felt a vague recognition of the man. Another kick. The world turned black.

Just then a group of men, rowdy in their banter, wandered by. Disturbed, panicked, the thugs flew from the alley and, in their haste, knocked one of the men to the ground.

"Oi!" Two of them made chase, but they were soon lost to the dark. They returned to check on their friend. As they pulled him to standing, they heard a noise, a whimper, from the alley.

"Did you hear that?"

One struck a match and cagily moved into the passage. "It's a girl! For God's sake, quick! Get an ambulance! It looks bad."

****

Sarah and Alex arrived at the hospital. Kate's head was swathed in bandages, her eyes black and swollen, her lips bloodied and cut. She had two broken ribs. She struggled to sit up when they arrived but was thankful she was alive.

"What on earth happened?" Sarah flew to her side. Kate glanced away, trying to hide her tears, grateful to see them.

Alex took her hand and cradled it in his with a worried expression. A stream of questions poured from his lips.

"Did you see who did this to you? Was it a robbery? Have you spoken to the police?" She gave him a wan look. Her bottom lip wobbled as she tried to dismiss him.

"No, I didn't see anyone." She struggled to speak. "It happened so fast. Yes, I've spoken to the police." He kissed the back of her hand.

"I'm fine. It looks worse than it is, honestly."

"I'll let Jack know," said Sarah.

"No, Sarah, promise you won't. He'll just fret. I'm fine."

"Are you sure?"

"Yes, absolutely. I'll be up and about in no time."

Sarah looked at flowers arranged in a vase by the side of the bed. "Who on earth sent you flowers already? And who in their right mind would send you lilies?" She searched for the card. "Some people have no taste. My gran always said that lilies represented death—" She gasped. "I'm sorry, Kate. I didn't mean... I'm obviously mistaken. They're beautiful." Sarah had unwittingly confirmed Kate's suspicions. She was terrified. She tried to smile but failed.

Alex was quiet. Kate tried to read him but couldn't. He sat by her side. Her pupils were pinpricks. Her bravado didn't fool him. He felt sure there was more to the story than she let on.

"Well, all I want is my Kate back in one piece. No more walking home alone late at night. Do you hear?"

****

1959

Once Kate was fit enough, she resumed work and her Sundays at the soup kitchen. The regulars acknowledged Kate heartily as they arrived. She was thoughtful, sincere, and careful with her choice of words, so it had not been long before they began to trust her. To some, she'd become a friend, a confidante, someone they could talk to if they wished. She had become an integral part of the team, and since the attack, Alex had decided to join her. Kate loved him for that.

It was his way, he said, of "doing a bit for the community," but since the attack, he selfishly worried about her safety, and it was more for his piece of mind.

The busker she had originally followed to find the soup kitchen arrived. She looked at him. His face was a mess but repairing. Much like her own, only she could manage to disguise most of hers with cosmetics.

"Harry?" Kate stared. "What on earth happened to you?"

He shrugged.

She realized there was something missing. "Where's your guitar?"

He shrugged again.

Glimmers of the assault flashed through her mind. She shivered, the message indelibly printed on her mind. The sound of wood splintering, a flat ping of a chord. She stared at Harry in disbelief. Was she adding two and two and making five? "Please tell me—was that you who came to my rescue?"

He shrugged again.

She glanced over at Carol and Fred. "Can I take a few minutes out?"

Alex had been listening, and now he watched Kate move along the table, giving the man his food and then following him toward a chair. They sat down together. When Kate placed her hand on Harry's forearm, he winced. His face told a story as she spoke to him, and he raised a hand, trying to dismiss her questions.

Alex couldn't hear, but didn't dare interfere. He had prodded Kate for detail about her ordeal, but she played everything so close to her chest. Yet he couldn't help but notice she shut down whenever Dorian Craddock's name was mentioned.

It was as if she were afraid. But afraid of what? Alex continued to watch the scene, considering how the invitation to the party where he met Kate had come about. Was it a coincidence? Were they destined to meet? What was her connection to Dorian Craddock?

Later, after Kate's assault, he quizzed the colleague who had invited him to the party. He wanted to know more about Dorian. When his colleague disclosed that Dorian's father was none other than "Freddie the Fish Craddock," a notorious London gangster, Alex was furious. Furious at himself, for not being more aware. His mind raced. Kate was vulnerable. He did not want either of them to be connected in any way to that vile monster. He also knew a leak of that connection could easily put his political career in jeopardy.

He had no doubt in his mind there was every chance Miss Craddock followed in her father's very questionable footsteps. When he discovered Dorian Craddock moved in high circles, he felt it was without doubt the perfect camouflage to hide any dodgy dealings. Alex tried to find out more, but all he could turn up was that she was nothing but a very astute businesswoman—with a growing empire.

"It was you, wasn't it, the man in the alleyway?" Kate's eyes glistened with gratitude. "I can't thank you enough. But your poor face...your guitar..."

The man winced as she squeezed his arm. "Bastards."

"Let me take a look at you. Please?"

"No. I'll be fine. Had worse. It's just a bit sore." He shrugged again.

"How can I ever repay you?"

"I waited, you know. To make sure you were looked after..." He looked about. "We get accused of all sorts, attacking people, stealing, mostly when it's not true. So I hid. I didn't want the law to assume I'd attacked you. Though sometimes I decide, when it's too cold outside, a cell is the best place for a bed." He grinned, displaying three missing teeth. "Sometimes you even get a bite to eat."

"Dear God." Kate wrung her hands. "Did you know it was me?"

"No. Not until I landed on the floor right next to you. Fate, eh? Who would have guessed?"

Kate drew a deep breath. "I think I owe you more than a guitar, Harry. I owe you my life."

Chapter 44

Whilst Kate wanted to distance herself from Dorian, Madam Raines had other ideas, and nothing could dissuade her. Kate had swiftly learned the relevance of "Keep your friends close and your enemies closer."

Kate headed along the road with purpose, a sketch book tucked securely inside her bag and a plan neatly folded away in her head. Their flat had become a bit of a tip, thanks to Sarah's lack of domestic interest, and she wanted peace and quiet. A place to think, away from the clutter, and where better than the library. Sarah had been talking about moving out and was rarely quiet at the best of times. The thought occurred to her with surprise. Kate always considered herself the louder of the pair. But they were good friends, and sharing had been a bonus. Now their lives were moving in different directions. She and Alex had become closer, and Sarah was always out these days—well, nights.

The moment Kate arrived at the library, she swiftly began organizing books. She had spoken to Alex. He agreed her ideas were commendable, but she needed to think about her proposals more fully. She glanced around, her interest drawn to the architecture of the building.

The books began sliding from her grasp. A young woman about her age immediately hopped up from her chair and began gathering them up for her. The librarian gesticulated wildly to keep the noise down and pointed at the oversized QUIET notice.

"Thanks. It seems the head librarian is getting a little—irascible?" Kate jerked her head toward the desk, her eyes wide with amusement. "Like I'm a child." She grinned. "Uh-oh." The books began falling again and landed with huge thuds.

"Thanks for helping." She shot out a hand, once the books were safely on a table. "Kate. Kate Westfield."

"Harriet Laws." Harriet put her fingers to her lips, her eyes glancing in the direction of the counter. "I think you might find he's on the warpath again."

Kate quickly mouthed her apologies making a huge show of teeth and smiles, and the librarian silently turned on his heels. She could have sworn Harriet was giggling.

"What is it with librarians? Are they all born with 'Silent' stickers on their heads?" Kate wiggled her brows at Harriet, then took out a sketch book and a box of pencils. She pulled out a chair and comfortably swung herself backwards onto two legs and immediately stared upward.

Her mind was instantly transported to Paris with her uncle. The ceiling was covered in ornate gothic carvings. "Beautiful," she breathed in delight. So many ceilings across the world held such beauty, and seeing these treasures up close was far better than any picture in a book. She wondered how many people would miss such a treat with their eyes linear, traveling only to the bookshelves and their content. Pleased she'd made the effort to do some research beforehand, she quickly began sketching, her mind now completely focused.

****

Kate rubbed the back of her neck, a little stiff from the angle she'd been in, and checked her watch. She was surprised to find more than an hour had passed already. Her notion of writing a full account of her plans had vanished, and she felt a tad annoyed at herself for being distracted. Kate glanced across at Harriet and found she was staring her way. Kate waved a hand in acknowledgement. There was something about Harriet she couldn't quite put a finger on, but she liked her from first off. She called out, pointing upward.

"Have you noticed how great these arches are?" Harriet looked embarrassed. Kate laughed. "Your arches aren't too bad either." Harriet giggled. Kate checked her watch again, disappointed she didn't have more time. She was going to be late if she didn't get a wriggle on. She reluctantly put everything back into her cloth satchel and made her way over to Harriet.

"Here's my business card. Give me a call?"

And she clopped noisily out of the building with a beatific smile, waving her hand toward the librarian and loudly thanking him for his patience and the peace he'd created.

****

Two weeks later, Kate waited impatiently for a new client to arrive. She'd been told it was one of CJ Rutherford's lady friends. The message was clear—the woman could have anything she desired, and he would cover the cost. Kate frowned, wondering who his prey might be. CJ Rutherford had a bit of a reputation— particularly around women. Being attractive and wealthy made him a great catch. He'd once making a move on her. They were at Club 59 at the time, where she first met him, but she didn't fall for his charm. He didn't like her rebuttal, but in the end, they remained on friendly terms, and he agreed to pass her business card on to his well-heeled clients. Kate glanced at her latest gown, almost completed, and sighed with satisfaction.

The bell rang. Sarah answered it and brought the new client through.

"Harriet?" She couldn't believe it. "What are you doing here?"

"You know one another?" said Sarah, a little surprised. "Kate, this is the client we have been expecting."

"Why didn't you call me?" Kate ignored Sarah, pretending to look hurt, but she had a twinkle in her eye. "It's great to see you again. Come on, I believe you have a cocktail party to go to, and with the sexy Mr. Rutherford, no less."

"Kate!" Sarah pulled her up short. Even though her dalliances outside work were a little risqué, her behavior at work remained completely professional. Kate just laughed. "You don't mind, do you, Harriet?"

Sarah shook her head. "I'll get tea, then, shall I?" and she vanished somewhere out the back.

Harriet for some reason looked relieved to see Kate and smiled at her exuberance. They talked nineteen to the dozen like they'd known one another all their lives.

Harriet's choice of dress thrilled Kate—it was one of her own designs, and the little black number looked sensational on her. As Kate began adjusting the bustline for comfort, she still managed to ask a million questions, even with pins in her mouth, and constantly poked and pried for details—where were they going, and how long had she known CJ, where did they meet.

It was interesting, Kate thought, as Harriet keenly imparted the details, that she appeared to be seeking her approval. Kate, ever honest, and with a flash of the assault still fresh in her mind, wanted to give her a gentle warning about CJ and his friends, but decided against it. For the time being.

"Well, I insist you give me a blow-by-blow account of the evening, Harriet. We will have coffee, and I know the perfect place. Agreed?" Harriet smiled, happy with the arrangement.

Chapter 45

"Hattie!" Kate spied her at the back of the wine bar-come-café. She was perched on a stool and sipping coffee, looking bemused.

The crowd shouted back "HATTIE!" in a loud echo.

Kate laughed to see Harriet's face turn shy. The place was overflowing, and music played from somewhere, almost drowned out by the boisterous crowd.

"Come on, Hattie, let's go." Kate managed to push her way through the throng.

"I've saved you a seat. Don't you want to stay for a coffee, Kate? My treat?" Harriet still clutched the cup.

There it was again, something about Harriet that she couldn't quite put her finger on. An honesty. A connection. Whatever it was, they were already in tune, and she couldn't wait to show off her collection.

"No. I don't drink the stuff."

"Really? Then why meet here?"

Kate shrugged. "Our flat's not easy to find. Come on, drink up. I'd like to show you something and get your opinion. If you don't mind?"

Kate took her down a side road, and they walked down a narrow path. "We're over the casino. It's so quiet the dead would feel unnerved." She laughed at Harriet's expression. "Come on." She turned the key in the lock and opened the door.

"Tra-la. This is home."

Harriet gasped. Her attention had been immediately drawn to the back wall.

"The mural. It's fabulous, Kate. Did you paint it?"

"No. I wish I could claim the credit. Davey Craddock's the genius. It's amazing, isn't it? I'm surprised he can do anything so intricate after the beating he took."

"Beating?" Harriet glanced worriedly at Kate. "He's not related to Dorian Craddock by any chance, is he?"

"Yes, that's his sister. Why?"

A frown crossed Harriet's brow. For a moment she fell silent.

"Do you know her as well?"

"Yes, well, sort of." Harriet looked thoughtful. "Anyway, what happened to her brother?"

"It's a horrible story, Harriet, not for the faint of heart. It was all in the papers. I'm surprised you didn't see it. Apparently, Davey's father… Well, let's just say he was evil. I think, from everything I learned about that monster, even being hanged was too good for him." Kate wanted to say more about the Craddock family but decided against it.

Harriet recalled the story immediately. "I remember now—though I didn't know Dorian had a brother. Maybe if I'd been thinking I would have put the two together."

Kate scratched her neck, a little uncomfortable. "Do you mind if we talk about it another time?"

"Sure. Of course. Sorry. I just…" Harriet nodded slowly as if she had something to say but then thought better of it. "So what was it you wanted to show me?"

"Ah." Kate smiled and unlocked the door to the spare room. "Ta-dah! My collection. No one else has seen these. Well, only Sarah. Tell me what you think. Be honest. I would really value your opinion."

Kate's heart raced. Nervous, waiting for a reaction. Harriet hadn't moved. She could see her friend's eyes traveling over her collection of costumes but couldn't read her.

"I get it. Don't worry. You don't like them." Her face fell. She went to lock the door again.

Harriet sighed. "Don't be silly. Can I touch them?"

"Of course. I thought you might try them on for me. You've a great figure, Harriet, and I need to see them worn, not on a manikin, so I can gauge whether they flow, like I imagine they will." Kate rubbed her brow. "I need a drink." She went to the fridge and pulled out a bottle of wine and collected a couple of glasses. "There's one for you, once you've modeled for me."

She pulled the cork out of the bottle.

"Well? Will you try them on?"

Harriet turned to her. "You honestly got me here for my opinion, and to try them on?"

Harriet looked overwhelmed and shy at the same time.

"Of course. Now choose something, please? And don't spare my feelings. It won't be helpful." Kate sat on the floor outside the spare room, telling her about Madam Raines and how she had kindly given her the start she needed in the world of fashion. She explained how the contract between them had restricted her, with its provision that all designs done on the premises belonged to Madam Raines by right.

"I'll never move forward like that. My aim is to have my own fashion show. I guess you've heard about Mary Quant?" Harriet shook her head. "I'll take you to see her work. She's got a place in Markham Road. She's on the way to making it big. She's absolutely amazing." Kate waffled on, giving her all the details until Harriet stepped out wearing one of her designs.

"I love this, it's just like a shimmering waterfall."

"You look stunning, Harriet. Absolutely stunning. Your figure, the way you stand—you have natural deportment. Elegant. Beautiful."

"Kate, stop fishing for compliments."

Kate's face fell.

"I'm kidding. What you said about me is extraordinarily kind, Kate. But these designs? They are truly magnificent. Like a piece of fine art. Anyone could wear them and look amazing."

Kate's eyes glistened. "Seriously? Thank you, Harriet. You have no idea how much it means to me."

Harriet turned to stare at herself in the full-length mirror. "Fatty Hattie. Just look at you now."

"What do you mean 'Fatty Hattie,' you idiot? I'd say Slimmer Jimmer!" She laughed.

She poured Harriet a glass of wine. "For you, as soon as you've tried on all the rest, and you can give me the lowdown on CJ Rutherford." Kate could have sworn Harriet was blushing at the mention of his name.

"Well, was it good or what?"

"What?"

"The sex?"

"What are you talking about?"

"Come on, Harriet, CJ is reputed to be very good in bed."

"I really have no idea what you are talking about, Kate."

"The s-e-x!" Kate spelt it out.

"I think you've been drinking too much. And for your information, we haven't!"

"Seriously? That's not CJ's style." Kate shook her head, puzzled. "He must have it bad. I bet he's asked you out again." How could she possibly warn Harriet against CJ without sounding like a mother hen, or worse, jealous?

Chapter 46

1960

Kate paid the cab fare and stepped out at Club 59. Any passerby would be hard pressed to guess what went on inside the five-story Mayfair townhouse. Behind the inconspicuous door, the five floors were fabulously created for rest, relaxation, and recreation. The fifth floor, also decked out with the most luxurious of furnishings, had specifically been set aside for the most secret of business deals and private matters of the most intimate kind. All Kate knew was that she was sure girls went missing. She shivered, even though the air was warm. She hadn't been back since the attack, especially with the threat on her friends' lives.

Dorian Craddock also owned the two adjacent townhouses and sometimes lived in one with her brother Davey. The third-floor lights were on. The same floor where Dorian had let slip at an earlier fitting that she expected CJ at the Club tonight. She'd held that information close. Dorian was being tight lipped about Harriet and CJ—and nothing Kate said elicited any further details. It was as if she had something to hide, and Kate knew she didn't dare push her. She was worried. She hadn't seen Harriet in such a long time. She knew Harriet had become besotted with CJ, but it wasn't like her friend not to keep in touch. She hated that she felt so bothered about returning to the Club, so much so it virtually rendered her powerless. But right now, not seeing Harriet bothered her more.

Kate checked her watch. It was just coming up to seven fifteen. She knew CJ's appointment was for seven thirty. She also knew how fastidious CJ was regarding timekeeping.

Heart beating hard in her chest, she composed herself, smoothed down her suit, and was just checking her hair in her compact when she spotted him.

"CJ!" He ignored her call and kept moving toward the Club.

"CJ!"

He stopped, turned, and groaned at the sight of her.

"Kate. I have a meeting with Dorian. You know how she hates tardiness—almost as much as I do."

"I need just a moment of your time."

CJ cocked his head to one side.

Kate tried to sound neutral. She knew he could be devilishly difficult. "I just wondered if you'd seen Harriet lately. I haven't seen her for simply ages."

"Yes. Of course I've seen her. She's my wife, so I know exactly where she is."

"What?" A smart, gray-suited man patiently held the door open for them. They stepped inside, and she inwardly quivered. "What do you mean? You're married?"

"Kate." He sounded irritated. "You don't own the rights on Harriet, and it just goes to show she doesn't consider you a friend, as she would have told you. Wouldn't she?" His eyebrows rose impatiently. Something in his tone irked, and she couldn't let it go. He went to move. Kate grasped his sleeve. He tried to shake her off.

"When did you get married, exactly? Dorian didn't mention it."

"Kate, stop being so needy." Kate stepped back at the rebuke.

"Well, please accept my congratulation, CJ," Kate offered pleasantly, hiding her hurt. "Would you be kind enough to pass on my best wishes, and let Harriet know I've been asking after her." She looked at him carefully. "Harriet is all right, isn't she?"

"Of course, she is." He gave a low, sly, underlying chuckle. "Why wouldn't she be? She has the perfect life. With me. Her *husband*."

"Is she planning to come here any time soon?"

"Kate, my dear." He patronized. "My darling Harriet has no wish to be part of this scene. She's decided to be a stay-at-home wife. A wife who enjoys making me, *her husband,* happy, and that is as it should be." Kate frowned.

"Of course. I wonder, CJ. Could I pay her a visit? I'm sure she'd be happy to see me."

"Personally, Kate, I always thought you to be a bad influence on Harriet. But as I am the thoughtful sort, I'll mention it. Though don't get your hopes up. The last time we spoke about you, she didn't have anything good to say."

"Really?"

She caught a glint in his eye.

"Now, as I said, I have a meeting. Ahh, Margaux,

spot on time. Are you ready?"

"CJ, where are you living now?" But CJ ignored the question as Lady Margaux Sutcliffe, CJ's business partner, seductively linked her arm into his, and Kate could only watch the couple disappear into the lift. As the doors slid closed, Margaux looked back at her like the cat who got the proverbial cream.

Kate's eyes narrowed. If rumor was right, she was far more to CJ than a business partner. So why marry Harriet? It didn't make sense. But then why didn't Harriet let her know she was getting married? That really stung. There had been no hint of it. Nothing whatsoever.

Yes, CJ had been courting Harriet, she knew that. Alex wasn't keen on CJ, and it appeared CJ felt the same about him, so they never managed a foursome more than once. One other fact remained; Harriet had become more distant over the past months. She saw CJ at every opportunity, and their own regular outings had reduced to once a month at best, and their evening phone calls were often cut short because she was expecting to hear from CJ. Maybe CJ was telling the truth. Maybe Harriet had lost interest in their friendship. Kate had to admit some of the fault could be laid at her door. She had been extremely busy with work, and Alex, who had become a huge part of her life.

Kate coughed away a tickle in her throat as she thought about everything. Harriet had sounded excited about her developing romance with CJ. But had Harriet really become a stay-at-home wife? Was she the willing servant, as CJ implied? No. That wasn't Harriet's style. Was it? Kate's blood began to boil.

Unless…unless she was pregnant. That could be the only plausible answer. But surely, she would have confided in her?

A moment of sadness and doubt rested in the pit of Kate's stomach. They had been such good friends. How foolish to let that slip. But surely, though, no matter what, at the very least Harriet would have been excited about the prospect of getting married…failing that, becoming a mother, and she would have told her. But then, with CJ in control…and he had managed to dance around where they lived. He'd already implied Harriet didn't have anything good to say about her. That didn't add up. Did it? No. Harriet was honest. She would have told her if there was an issue. Wouldn't she? She sighed. How on earth could she possibly find out the truth?

Damn it! She would find her, and they would speak face to face. Have it out. There was no way she could believe Harriet would throw their friendship away because of marriage, or maybe a possible surprise pregnancy. Something didn't feel right.

Chapter 47

The following day, Kate stood outside Mrs. Gaffney's house, Harriet's old lodgings. She knocked on the door. Mrs. Gaffney answered. She was about to fix a cigarette into a long slim holder. Kate had admired her style before. She was smartly dressed, and clearly loved to be dressed in the latest fashion.

"Kate! How lovely to see you."

Kate quickly launched into her speech.

"Oh, my dear, do come in. I'm so pleased to talk to one of Harriet's old friends…" Though Mrs. Gaffney sounded happy to see her, she seemed bothered.

Mrs. Gaffney invited Kate into the front room and without hesitation lit up her cigarette.

Kate couldn't wait a moment longer.

"I'd love to see Harriet, Mrs. Gaffney, but I don't have her new address. I thought you might be able to supply me with it?" Kate's heart was now in her mouth, and she hoped the landlady would be good enough to give her the details.

Mrs. Gaffney shook her head. "I'm afraid I don't. Such a silly oversight, but then there were such peculiar goings on. That Mr. Rutherford, such a charming man. He came and went so quickly. Just like her. One morning Harriet went out and never came back. I've not had a word from her since."

Kate's mouth dried. "What do you mean, exactly?"

"Well." Mrs. Gaffney paused a moment as if recalling a conversation and tapped ash into a saucer. "You see, Mr. Rutherford, turned up a couple of days after Harriet…" She seemed to search for an appropriate word. "…disappeared. He was all smiles and politeness itself. Said they'd got married, and that Harriet had sent him to collect her things." Mrs. Gaffney blew out a pall of blue smoke. "I couldn't believe it. Getting married without a word? But Mr. Rutherford was so apologetic, so lovely, and insisted he pay her rent in full…" She looked embarrassed at the revelation. "Anyhow, he convinced me that Harriet was sorry she couldn't be there in person, but she, they, would definitely call, and very soon."

"And has she?"

Mrs. Gaffney frowned with a "no" upon her lips. "Of course, once you get married, circumstances change, don't they?" She looked Kate square in the eye, a disappointment lurking behind her glasses. "You are good friends, though. Harriet was clear about that. I'm surprised she didn't tell you they were getting married." Kate shook her head and smacked her lips together in frustration.

"No, it doesn't make sense. I confess, I'm confused, Mrs. Gaffney. Harriet was never secretive."

Kate's mind worked over the frustrating conversation with CJ the night before. He was always playing mind games. Always wanted the upper hand. She never really took to him for lots of reasons, and now she felt guilty for not keeping in closer touch or sharing her view of CJ with Harriet. Mrs. Gaffney broke her train of thought.

"Then there's Tom. Did you ever meet Tom Fletcher? The baker? Such a lovely man. Besotted with Harriet. So obvious, right from the start. He arrived on my doorstep asking after her. Worried why she hadn't turned up for her shift at the bakery. When I told him Mr. Rutherford and Harriet were married... Well, the poor man! You should have seen his face."

Mrs. Gaffney shook her head. "It was so obvious how much he cared for her. I felt sure he was going to propose once. Funny thing, though, come to think about it... I believe things changed between Tom and Harriet, and it was all down to an incident in which Mr. Rutherford was involved..." She tapped the end of her cigarette. "Harriet never breathed a word about getting married, and I thought she could tell me anything."

"So did I, Mrs. Gaffney. So did I."

Mrs. Gaffney let out a huge sigh. "When you find Harriet, and I'm sure you will, please tell her how much I miss her."

Kate left Mrs. Gaffney's more bothered than ever. When Kate arrived at Luigi's, the restaurant where Harriet worked her second shift after a first one at the bakery, she found a remarkably similar story about Harriet's disappearance. She simply had not turned up as usual, and they too were completely surprised to discover Harriet was married. Nothing added up. All it did was add to an inexplicable mounting fear.

Chapter 48

1960

"CJ's dead?" Kate, stunned, mouthed the words, reading the newspaper, just as the doorbell rang.

"Alex?" Kate rushed to the door with the newspaper in her hand. She stared between him and the postman, who offered over a small brown parcel addressed to her in the strictest confidence. Kate thanked the postman and pulled Alex inside.

"Have you seen the headlines?"

Alex took the paper from her. "Yes. I saw it first thing. Unbelievable. They seem to be linking Harriet and Lady Sutcliffe to Rutherford's death."

"I don't understand." Kate shook the paper in his face. "This report is not clear at all. In fact, it looks more like a hatchet job!" They walked through to the lounge, and Kate sat on the sofa pondering the details.

"I find it hard to believe any of it either, Kate. Especially from what I know of Harriet, and how close you were…"

Kate rubbed the back of her neck. "We've got to do something, Alex. I can't sit on my backside and leave her out on a limb. I wonder, could you possibly put some feelers out? Try and find out what's really going on? It has to be discreet, though." She had never told him what was said during the attack. She didn't want anyone implicated, not in any way, or be responsible for something bad happening to them. She looked pensive. "I can't ask. Dorian warned me off."

Alex looked curious, waiting for an explanation.

"There are things, Alex. Threats made to keep my nose out. I'm sorry I didn't tell you. But I was so scared. The mugging…"

He drew her into his arms. "All this time, and you've never said. Why?"

She let out a deep breath and pulled away. "I had been digging around. Trying to find out what was really going on at the Club. Then I saw something at that party where we met. Next thing I know, I'm in an alleyway being beaten up."

"What! Did you tell the police?"

She shrugged. "There's no proof. What would I say?"

"That's why you stopped going to the Club?"

Kate nodded, then leaned back against him. "Can you try to look into it? I'm really worried for Harriet's safety."

Kate tsked and looked over the small parcel in her hand. She noted it had been sent second class and thought she recognized the handwriting but couldn't be sure.

"I'm just popping to the bathroom, Alex. Pour me a drink, will you? Maybe we can talk more about this when I return."

The moment Kate locked the bathroom door she tore the paper off. Inside she found a parcel with a letter wrapped around it.

My Dearest Kate,

Things have taken a sad turning in my life. I am so

258

sorry to ask, but I need your help—you are the one person I trust with every bone in my body. Would you please—just in case my worst fears are realized—could you please follow these instructions. The enclosed package has some information. If it were to fall into the wrong hands, it would be disastrous.

Kate, I implore you not to be curious enough to open it or look at the contents, but should something happen to me, then please, please, destroy it.

One day, hopefully, this nightmare will be over, and when it is, I will be able to explain everything.

With much love and gratitude, Harriet x

Kate sat on the side of the bath and re-read the letter, shocked. She heard Alex calling—she couldn't tell him, could she? Should she? Kate looked about the bathroom, then stowed the package at the back of the medicine cabinet. She would find a better place later. Whatever was going on, this didn't sound like Harriet at all. But she would do whatever Harriet asked. Whatever it was, she knew Harriet would be innocent.

Chapter 49

Two weeks later, Harriet knew it was time. She made a call and prayed Kate would answer. A voice! Through the tears and whispers, her conversation was brief and to the point.

The following day, Kate arrived with chocolates, grapes, and a huge bouquet of flowers. She managed to upset Matron by sitting on the hospital bed, then immediately won her over with her personality and the chocolates, meant for Harriet. Matron, a bit of a softy as it turned out, pulled the curtain around them, whispering, "Just don't let everyone see."

They laughed, they cried, they hugged, and Kate bombarded her with questions.

"It is true? I'm so sorry! I asked about you so many times. I saw things in the newspaper. CJ gave the impression you wanted nothing to do with me. Though I never really believed it, and now he's…"

Harriet shook her head, with a sadness so deeply etched into her face it looked like it could never be erased. "I still can't believe he's dead, Kate." Harriet paused, wringing her hands together.

"I brought the parcel as you asked."

Harriet looked toward the visitors' lounge. It was empty. "Can we go in there? It's a little more private."

"Of course." Kate, puzzled, followed Harriet to the lounge. As they closed the door behind them, her nose twitched at the odd smell of tobacco and disinfectant.

"This is all a little cloak-and-dagger, Harriet."

"I know. But thank you, Kate, for being my friend," she said with a heartfelt sigh. "You'll never know how grateful I am." Her shoulders sagged. "I doubted my sanity so many times." Harriet bit her bottom lip and pushed her glasses back up her nose.

"So why not get rid of this before?"

Harriet looped her bottom lip over the top one. "It was a bargaining tool. Something I would never use, but had to have, just in case. Now CJ is dead." A tear pooled. I'm so sorry I dragged you into this. I can't tell you everything. I want to, but I don't think you'd believe me, even if I did."

Kate hugged her.

"Whatever you tell me, I'd believe you, you bloody nitwit!" They laughed.

"Then would you mind giving me a little more help?"

"Anything."

A short time later, Kate smiled indulgently at her ability to bamboozle a very irritating journalist who had been trying to get Harriet to give him an interview. She found her friend hiding behind a wall in the hospital gardens, where she was trying desperately to destroy the notebook.

A book burning seemed more in keeping with a ritual. What Kate knew was not to ask. Instead, she whipped out a box of matches and helped the process along.

As soon as flames had consumed most of the offering, Kate asked, "When are you being discharged?"

Harriet shrugged, looking lost.

"Well, come on then, let's find out, because you're staying with me for as long as you need."

Chapter 50

One week later, Kate arrived at Saint Mary's to collect Harriet.

"Good to have you back, Harriet." Kate sat beside her in the cavernous leathery interior of the hackney cab and held her hand. Harriet wound the window down and watched the hospital disappear.

London. Home. Well, almost. It had been a lifetime ago, or so it seemed. The streets were teeming. How could she have forgotten so quickly how things were? People were wrapped up against the chill—still weaving their Metropolis Maypole dance, never colliding, avoiding one another at all costs. Honking cars filled her ears, and black sooty fumes filled her lungs.

She spluttered and coughed and wound the window back up. It was nothing like the countryside, and nothing like the starched, disinfected cleanliness of hospital. Harriet shivered as she remembered when she turned up for work, at what would be her last day at Dingham's Department store. Fired for going to her grandmother's funeral. She sighed, still deep in thought, still staring out the window. It was Tom who saw her back then. Tom who saved her from certain death. Now she had been saved again, by the kindness of strangers and her good friend Kate. No. Nothing had really changed—maybe only her.

"Are you cold, Hattie?" Kate looked at her worriedly. "Here, I've brought a blanket, just in case. The damned weather, one minute warm, next minute freezing. It can't make its mind up!"

"Thanks, Kate. How thoughtful," Harriet instantly warmed as Kate dropped it around her knees. "I feel like a little old lady." She smiled, squeezed Kate's hand, and quickly returned to her private thoughts, not daring to think about her future. Soon Harriet realized they were not driving toward Kate's home. They were traveling along unfamiliar streets where traffic had petered out to the odd car.

They were in a small suburb cruising by a popular row of shops with names she recognized, Michell's, Bullen's, Perry's. The cabbie overtook a three-wheeled dairy van. *Express Deliveries* Harriet noticed written on its side. Different from the usual milk float, she thought and wondered idly if any of the milk from her Albert and Alice's farm ended up here. If Alice and Albert hadn't taken her in, she would have been wandering the streets homeless. They had been her savior in her hour of need. The day she finally escaped from CJ's clutches.

"Where are we going, Kate? This isn't the way to your flat."

"Didn't I say?" Kate looked innocent. "We're staying at my uncle's place for a bit. Sarah's moved out, and I decided to get the decorators in, to give the flat a bit of a spruce up."

"But?"

"Don't worry, Uncle Jack's expecting you. You'll love him. Promise."

Harriet turned to look out the cab window, hiding

her concern, her heart racing. This wasn't the agreement. She'd expected to go somewhere safe. Not to have to meet new people.

The cabbie pulled into a road lined with an avenue of monkey trees and double-bay-fronted Victorian houses. A little like Mrs. Gaffney's, she thought, but the area seemed somehow cleaner, smarter. Kate paid the fare, then whispered in her ear, "Before we go in, let me give you a tip. Whatever you do, don't gawk at my uncle."

"What?"

There was no need to press the bell, as the door opened before they got the chance. Harriet couldn't help but gawk at the handsome man standing there. Kate laughed. "Harriet, this is my Uncle Jack."

He just looked totally confused. How could she be here, at his front door, after all this time? He knew it was impossible, but the memory flooded back.

Chapter 51

Summer 1939

It had been at a dance in Brighton.

The moment Jack set eyes on her he was smitten. She stood only a moment alone. Men were lining up— and who wouldn't? She was beautiful. One dance after another, yet the girl never appeared exhausted. Instead, she seemed to relish each step as if she knew the music before it was played, and her body the instrument. She had an ethereal quality and a completeness about her, and there was something else. A smile that played across her lips as if the music transported her to another world.

He observed discreetly, at a distance, wondering who she came with and whether he could inveigle his way in to replace whoever it was. It took Jack less than ten minutes before he made his move.

They hit it off instantly. Taking her in his arms, he breathed in her scent as he whirled her around the floor, accompanied by tantalizing notes of apricot, vanilla, and sandalwood. She was intoxicating and as exotically delicious as she was light on her feet. She made dancing a joy. Even he was not his usual clumsy self.

Cassandra, Cassie, was enchanting, with her impish face and depths of genuineness in her sparkling green eyes. He remembered her laughter as it fell from her lips and gently upon his ears. She seemed woman, then girl, then minx—funny, serious, thoughtful—and he quickly learned she had an intelligence he relished.

Jack decided the moment he had her in his arms that no one else would dance with her, and he knew he was already falling for her long before the night ended.

Throughout the course of the evening he tried asking questions about herself. Cassie explained her friend brought her, but he had to be somewhere else and would pick her up later. Perhaps his chance of seeing her again was already thwarted. But why would a man friend leave her like that? He found the story a little odd but accepted the paltry explanation.

For now, he had her in his arms. Cassie was smiling at him. She was happy, he was happy. Cassie told him she needed to let her hair down. Work had been grueling recently, and she wanted to escape. When he asked what kind of work, she declined to say. Instead, she playfully drew him into her game of observing people, making up imaginary stories about their lives.

Jack, at first, found it amusing and became more intrigued as she refused to divulge anything other than that she didn't have a boyfriend. When he found she would be staying over, he was thrilled. One nugget she allowed—she was married to her job, whatever that meant.

Finally, Cassie agreed to see Jack the following day. They would meet at a café on the seafront. The next morning, he arrived early with a posy of flowers and paced the promenade for nearly an hour, waiting.

The wind was relentless, whipping along the seafront, sand-blasting his clothes, snatching at his face. Jack almost gave up, sure it had been just a ruse and he would never see her again. But then he saw her walking toward him. The relief he felt was beyond description. She was smiling, not at anyone else but him. Cassie was so graceful, commanding an elegance he had yet to see in any other woman. Poised, full of life, strong and yet vulnerable. As they sat in a café, she began humming a tune. Years later, he tried to recall what it was—the sugar plum fairy theme? Yes, that was it.

Their second night, they shared a bed. The affair lasted five blissful days and nights, not seeing anyone beyond themselves. Jack knew from the onset he had fallen for her, deeply and forever. He would have laughed if someone else told him that. But every morning he would slip out whilst Cassie slept, find the flower seller, buy her a posy, and hurry back. When it was to be their last day, he had a plan and left her as before, sleeping. Kissing her brow, wanting to give her so much more than a posy of flowers, he headed out.

If only he'd stayed, if only he'd waited for her to wake. When he returned, Cassie had gone, out of his life, as quickly as she arrived, taking his heart with her. Jack found a hurried message. An apology, a note left at the hotel reception. Her dear friend had been attacked. Hospitalized. She would return but needed to take him home. Him again. Who was he, and what was their relationship, really?

Jack remembered the pang of jealousy as he crumpled her message in his hand, wondering how she could leave him so quickly for another. But Cassie had been clear from the start there was only the friend. He just had to believe her. He slowly unwrapped the ball of paper. Cassie had signed the note with a capital C, and within the bottom half of the curve, like a moon, a smile, with a kiss. That day they had promised they would share their whole story.

All she knew was that he would be leaving for training that afternoon. He would be gone for three months—he couldn't tell her exactly why because of the official secrets act—instead, he had lightly touched upon being in the Air Force, who waited for no man. He waited and paced the room until he had to go, and left a note in reception, hoping she might return and contact him.

All he held in his head was that Cassie had shared four small pieces of information. She lived in London. There was a hint of a street name and a favored park. Then there was her photograph. He smiled at the thought of it. They were on the pier, Cassie laughing up at him as she tried to contain her hair flying wildly in the wind.

Three months later, Cassie had never been a moment from Jack's thoughts, and upon his return, he went back to the hotel where they'd made such wonderful memories. A schoolgirl had replaced the man at the reception desk. She was reading a book. She chewed on a toffee, twiddling her hair, and looked about like a wild animal with every question. Eventually she told him that her father had left her in charge. War had already brought chaos. It was no good—the girl could not hold a coherent conversation. He remembered wondering how she could ever read in that state.

When he saw the look in her eyes, the girl was frightened. No doubt he was handling things badly. Life was terrifying. He gently insisted she check with her colleagues. She went out the back somewhere and found an old man. He identified the clerk he had presented the note to—it was the girl's father, gone to join the army. Jack worried that if Cassie had returned, his note might never have been passed on. She would have thought him an absolute cad. The thought crucified him.

****

Jack quickly made his way to the remembered street. When he arrived, the shock of it nearly sent him over the edge. Everyone and everything were in turmoil. His world tilted, and he felt he was falling off. The bombings. A raid the night before had razed the whole street to the ground except for one house. A façade, no more than a sad lonely skeleton standing oddly erect amongst the carnage of rubble. He felt just like that, an empty shell, with nothing left inside.

He watched, dazed. People picked over mountains of debris, calling out. Grown men, women, and children, weeping in the growing light of dawn. He immediately set about helping in their pitiful search for lost family and friends. He pulled at torn and twisted metal matting the ground, cut his hands on glass, and picked at bricks, terrified he might find her broken body amongst it all. The dust cloyed. The smell of smoke permeated the air. Choking pockets of fire filled lungs. Fire wardens helping, moving people on, redirecting them to safety, dampening the flames.

He showed people Cassie's photograph, carefully asking questions, praying that someone would know her. Eventually, just as the smoke rose into the ether, so did the small draught of hope of ever finding her begin to fade..

He returned to the street in London as often as he could. He visited the park she spoke of, hoping one day he might chance upon her strolling through the trees or along its many paths. He walked the promenade of Brighton on the vague hope she would be there.

He searched for so many years. So many bombs hit London during the war, killing hundreds of civilians, devastating lives. So many displaced children. So much horror. No word, no hint, no death certificate. Nothing, and no one could tell him. The war was a bastard. It killed his friends, his comrades, and now quite possibly his love…

****

1960

"Uncle Jack?" Kate was shouting.

"What? Sorry." He regained his composure, blinking through Kate's persistence, coming to his senses.

"Pleased to meet you." He held out a hand toward Harriet. "Forgive me. You must think me very rude. Welcome. Please, come in. I'm Jack, by the way, Kate's uncle." His timbre warm, sincere, not clipped British, hinting of something else. He led Harriet through the hallway and into the lounge. A fire burned brightly, with warm soft furnishings in pale yellows and gold.

Kate looked on, bemused. She'd never seen her uncle behave so strangely.

"Are you absolutely sure you don't mind me

staying?" Harriet repeated.

"No. Of course not. Not at all." Kate was standing in the doorway, still puzzled at her uncle's odd behavior.

Harriet caught the newspaper headlines on the table: *"Grand Opening of Daisy's Bakery. The fifth in a rapidly expanding empire."* She smiled, instantly recognizing the pictures of Tom with Daisy right by his side. He looked just as she remembered. Fringe flopping, that quirky, lopsided smile. They were cutting a cake as if they were just getting married. How she wished things had been different.

Chapter 52

Two days later, Kate was busy, full of her fashion show and the work it entailed, and Jack, keen to give Harriet as much space as she needed, showed her his collection of music. He was going out and offered to get anything she wanted from the library.

When Jack came back from his walk, to his surprise he heard the Drifters on the radio and found Harriet in the kitchen humming along, doing arm exercises to the tune. He waved in the air the books she'd asked for.

"Thank you, that's very kind." She looked up at him shyly. "I need to keep working on my arm, to stop it going stiff."

"Like this?" Jack mimicked her movements badly, laughing. She liked his laugh. It was deep, warm, friendly. "What's in the pot? It smells great!" Jack had already lifted the lid and dipped in a spoon.

"I hope you don't mind."

"Mind? You have to be kidding! I haven't had a decent home-cooked meal in ages." Harriet, blushing, shrugged.

"I don't know about you, but I'm starving." Jack had already put the books to one side and was getting bowls and spoons out and putting them on the kitchen table. "I'm ravenous. Are we going to eat, or just smell it?"

Harriet grinned, happily ladling some into his bowl.

After lunch, they washed up together. Later, Harriet surprised Jack by suggesting a game of chess. Jack, pleased at the offer, immediately discovered she was no pushover and asked who had taught her. As a wistful smile crossed her face, he was startled by another distant memory. Quashing the thought more quickly than he had the first time he met her, Jack paid careful attention to her response. Jack was touched by her manner. He noticed the way she held herself, so proud yet so humble, and yet that niggle of a memory stayed with him.

"My grandmother taught me. I never managed to beat her. Well, sometimes I did, when I was small. I always wondered if she threw the game, feeling sorry for me."

Harriet called checkmate.

"Your grandmother must have been really smart. She taught you well." He leaned back, stretching his arms behind his head, and scrubbed his hands through his hair. "I'm going to have to watch you more carefully in future, little lady."

Jack enjoyed Harriet's company. She was easy to be with and asked questions without prying too deeply. She listened with an intellectual ear and posed questions he'd never really considered before. He even surprised himself by telling her about the mining debacle in Africa. Harriet wanted to know more, and he agreed to show her the photographs.

Each day Jack watched Harriet come out of her shell, seemingly more relaxed and alive. They fell into an easy routine of reading, chess, walking, preparing a meal together. At times he noticed her eyes glazing and wondered if the memory was good or bad.

One night, Jack had a recurring nightmare. There was no stopping it...

They were on scramble. Jack's heart raced as engines burst into action. Intel conveyed Balbo, a large formation of enemy aircraft, coming in from the east. As they took flight and gained height, he looked down upon the dreaming patchwork greens of Mother England and leveled off. The air had a pure crystalline quality, and the silhouettes of hills were crisply outlined in the distance. The Spitfires were now in formation, wingtip tight. He switched to Angels, high altitude coms. It would be ten minutes before radio exchange could be made.

Jack looked portside, acknowledging Henry, with Baby Chalky White and Ginger Gilbraith port and starboard. They signaled one another. Two fingers mimed, "Eyes out for bandits."

Five miles out. Nothing. Suddenly he heard the drone of engines, a roar above their own, and out of the rising sun poured Luftwaffe in tight military precision. The beauty of the bright blue morning sky behind the mighty force of Germany's finest caught Jack's breath. They were outnumbered. It took just one nanosecond before all hell broke loose. Planes were going down faster than he could count on both sides. He glanced across at Chalky, only to find horror. In that precious moment, the poor cheeky youth was lost. His chest bounced with bullets. Jack saw him flop forward as his plane poured ink-gray smoke and spiraled out of control.

Dear God! Jack signaled Henry. Suddenly their

radios crackled into action. "Do your bloody darndest, boys!"

Jack wiped his goggles, anger boiling. He held fast for one minute, keeping tip-to-tip formation with the few of his squadron that were left. He looked across at Henry, signaled, and banked steeply away as ack-ack continued to crisscross the sky from all directions. He had one of the enemy planes in his sights.

Rage still coursed through his veins at Chalky's fatal last moments. "Ready to play chicken?" His lip curled. He aimed his Spitfire directly at the German plane. "Not yet," he whispered, steeling himself. "Show me your guts!" Jack poised his finger on the trigger. There was an exchange of fire. At the very last second the German peeled and twisted away, exposing the fuselage.

Jack fired a volley of bullets directly into the belly of the plane and gated full throttle away from the expected explosion. He was not out of the woods. Flames scorched the air much sooner than he anticipated. Debris flew, hammering into metal. He was hit. Red-hot, searing pain burned into his shoulder. Then a flame of bright orange-gold blinded him. Automatically, he pulled hard throttle again, rising as far as his Spitfire would allow before it stalled. Blood coursed out of his jacket. Gritting his teeth, he quickly assessed the situation. Heart pounding, he saw a German plane tailing one of his squadron—Henry!

"Bandit on your tail, pal!" Henry banked steeply port and let off a volley of bullets, narrowly missing his target as the German, in a spectacular display of skill, twisted away. The German pulled up and rounded on Henry's tail again. Jack could see his best friend in

imminent danger. "Leave him alone, you bastard!"

Jack knew he couldn't get there fast enough. Another volley of ack-ack hit Henry. He heard the scream as Henry fought with his controls. Jack had the German in his sights and took aim, but as the bullets flew, the pilot once again twisted and rolled away.

"Bandits behind and above!" Ginger Gilbraith, their newest and brightest recruit came out of nowhere. In that instant, Jack became aware of their fatal predicament. With his attention diverted, they had been outmaneuvered. In a classic attack, the Germans were above and behind. The only survival possibilities were to drop out of the sky or to belly up against his pal Henry, to rise high and loop. They had done it before. Both Spitfires were badly hit and limping. The chances of rising to the right altitude were minimal, but falling away from the action would be pointless. He would rather die trying. He waved his wings, saluting Henry. The signal was clear.

"I've got it covered." Ginger sounded determined and cool.

"Ginger. No!" Before Jack fired out the order, Ginger came in under the Germans. Ribbons of white shot across the blue sky, hitting the belly of one of the German planes and then the second. They both exploded, leaving Henry and Jack free to veer safely away. Ginger banked steeply, but one of the planes spiraled straight at him.

"No! Watch out! Dear God!"

A volley of ack-ack and dragon's breath poured from Ginger Gilbraith's spitfire…

Jack woke abruptly, bathed in sweat. Slipping on his dressing gown, he padded shakily downstairs for a glass of water. Harriet, about to pour a glass of water herself, looked embarrassed, as if she had been caught stealing the family silver. She squinted at him.

"Did I wake you?" Jack felt awkward.

Harriet shook her head.

"I'm sorry." He guessed she was just being polite.

"Please don't be." She sounded genuine. "The women I stayed with had their fair share of nightmares. They told me I shouted out in my sleep, too."

It was the first time Harriet had come even close to talking about what had happened. Apart from the little Kate had shared and the newspapers with their skewed view, the details were vague. All he knew was that her husband had died in a car accident and that she, somehow, had been implicated in his death.

"Sometimes it helps to talk." She smiled, the gentle offer on her lips. Jack accepted the glass and swallowed the water in one gulp.

"I hope I don't sound presumptuous," she said, "but may I ask a question?"

Jack nodded, a little hesitant.

"It goes without saying the war had a profound effect on people's lives, not just physically but emotionally. We Brits are reputed to have the stiff upper lip and all that, but I always wondered if there was any kind of support for war veterans."

Jack knew his buddies struggled with their injuries, while others found themselves homeless or looking down the bottom of an empty glass, or worse. It was rare anyone spoke of the horrors they lived with. Most probably didn't want to or couldn't.

"The notion isn't without merit, Harriet. I'm sure

there is psychiatric help if one were to seek it. But for some that would be a difficult route to take." Jack stood a while in limbo, then, saying good night, took himself off.

He relaxed back into the dry, crisp coolness of fresh sheets. He thought about his nightmares, and Harriet's words. Perhaps talking would help him and others. Perhaps he could start to think how to do something positive about it. Harriet, it seemed, had her own demons to contend with. He reached for his wallet and took out the old photograph, loved, battered, and worn with age. The young girl laughing at him. Her long hair flying straight out behind her in the wind. Goodness, how impossibly alike they were.

Chapter 53

"Uncle Jack!" Kate hollered up the stairs. "Get up, you lazy sausage!" Jack sauntered downstairs and ambled into the kitchen. "About time." She tapped her watch. "Harriet and I have been talking. I need women. Real women."

Jack's eyebrows raised in mock amusement. "What, there are fakes?"

Kate ignored the response.

"What I don't want are a complement of professional models for my *special* collection, and Hattie-Cake's come up with a brilliant suggestion. We're going to visit some of her old friends and invite them to be the stars of my show. If they agree, they'll be my *natural* models. But what we need from you, Uncle Jack, is your car."

"You don't drive," he replied, falling straight into her trap.

"Exactly! It's so kind of you to offer, thank you."

Jack threw his hands up in the air, defeated. Harriet handed him a cup of coffee, smiling broadly.

"You may need some sustenance." She guided him toward the table loaded with steaming porridge and hot buttered toast. "It's going to be a long day."

"If I didn't know better, you two could be sisters. You're always in cahoots with one another."

Harriet and Kate looked at one another seriously

for a full second.

"Nah!" They burst out laughing.

Chapter 54

Kate was in the study with "Mack the Knife" playing on the record deck. The time had been well spent with Harriet's friends. All the measurements were taken, the fittings almost complete, and as she sang along to the tune, she put the last of the invitations in a pile. Her dear friend Lucy, her mother Lily, Treenie, the school, and a multitude of fashion gurus she wanted to impress had already accepted. It was thrilling. Her own show. Even Dorian Craddock had backed off lately.

Jack had gone to get his daily newspaper, and the decorators were finished with her flat a while ago. She could go home. Harriet was standing in the doorway, watching her.

"Hattie!" She slid the final invitation onto the heap.

"I've been thinking, Kate. It's time I went back." The word "home" stuck in her throat.

The front door opened, and Jack came whistling through the hallway.

"I wonder, would you mind coming with me? Just for an hour or two, just to air the ghosts?" The record ended, with the repetitious clicking of needle on vinyl, and she lifted the arm back into its resting position.

"I could do better than that, Hattie. If you like, I could stay over the weekend and help you settle in."

"You're just too much! Are you sure? What about Alex? Won't he be missing you?"

"Haven't you heard absence makes the heart grow fonder?"

"Please check with him first. Promise?"

****

The following day, Jack stowed their luggage into the tiny boot of his Mini and, knowing Primrose Hill well enough, navigated his own way there. As they journeyed, Jack filled awkward silences with childhood reminiscences. He spoke about his love-hate relationship with London Zoo, trapping animals for showboating versus the reasoning for conservation of rare breeds and educational value. He talked of his grandparents and his mother taking him and his twin sister to Regents Park, with its wide-open spaces and picnics, and how his sister Maury started his love of photography with a tiny camera the size of a matchbox. Jack spoke fondly of Lords, and cricket, and his father's evident passion for the game, but as they drew nearer to Primrose Hill, Harriet began fidgeting. Jack was about to cut short his dialogue when she pointed across his shoulder.

"We're here. If you can pull over and let me out, I'll open the gates," she offered in a tremulous voice. Before them, in the quiet residential setting of Wadham Gardens, stood an imposing, double-fronted, detached house. Jack followed Harriet into the driveway and parked.

"It's a great location, Harriet, and the house looks beautiful." Jack looked on appreciatively.

"Yes, the house might be beautiful, but sadly, not the memories." He and Kate exchanged wary looks as they stepped inside.

Harriet stood silently, seeming in contemplation, her eyes transfixed on the wall at the far end. There was evidence of a painting hook suspended from the picture rail, but nothing hung on it.

"Are you all right, Hattie?" Kate touched her lightly on the elbow.

"I will be." She turned to them. "Thank you for taking such good care of me, Jack. I don't know how I can ever repay your kindness, but please know that I am truly indebted."

"It's been my pleasure, Harriet. What do we say, Kate? All for one?"

Kate clapped her hands together. "And one for all!"

Harriet allowed the briefest of smiles, knowing a little of their pact, but her eyes traveled to a large bunch of keys resting on the hall table. A jailer would be proud. Memories flooded back. She picked them up. They weighed heavily. Seeing the study door, she flinched at another memory.

"Please, why don't you both look around while I prepare a light lunch, and perhaps you could choose which bedroom you would like, Kate? Mine's first on the right."

Whilst Jack and Kate meandered through the house, Harriet began unpacking the groceries, looking out the window and into the garden. She needed to get outside, to get some air. When she stepped into the garden, she couldn't believe how overgrown it was and began pulling at vine weed furiously, angry for everything that had happened. Angry and hurt that her husband could be so cold and calculating. Angry she could be so gullible.

As Kate peered out from the back window of one of the bedrooms and saw Harriet below, Jack came to her side.

"It looks like Harriet's having an argument."

They were watching her flinging great clumps of vegetation attached to large clods of earth. "Maybe she needs a little more time to herself. How about we sort out something to eat?"

Jack lit the fire just as Harriet came in through the kitchen, her hands muddied from her efforts, her hair in disarray. "I'm sorry, I'm not a great host, am I."

"No, silly. Uncle Jack's sorted out the fire, and I've made lunch, so whenever you're ready…"

Chapter 55

Harriet and Kate stood on the porch watching Jack squeeze himself into the Mini. Once inside, he raised his hands to the heavens with a comical smile. Then he was gone.

"Come on," said Kate, "let's get a hot toddy and blankets. We can snuggle up in front of the fire."

They huddled together on the floor, using the sofa as a back rest, and talked at length. Eventually Harriet, exhausted, fell asleep with her head resting on the cushioned sofa. Kate wrapped her up in a blanket and stared into the flames, flickering, lulling her to think. She had such wonderful parents. If only they had been her real parents. If only she knew what happened to her natural mother, and why she had been given away. Perhaps, if she knew, she could move on with her life and try to put all the not knowing and sense of abandonment behind her.

Early next morning, Harriet found herself on the floor with a cushion under her head, covered in an enormous blanket. She could only assume the arrangement, with the fire still burning, was Kate's doing.

Kate made tea and placed the tray on the small table by the side of the sofa.

"Don't tell me you slept here as well?" Harriet yawned and stretched.

"I can't say the floor is that comfy. I slept on the sofa." Kate grinned.

"Thanks for staying with me, Kate."

"All for one, eh?"

"And one for all." Harriet smiled, scooting up close. "Funny, witty, talented Kate, with a marvelous uncle who adores you."

Kate pressed herself against Harriet, with a distant look on her face.

"What's up?"

Kate shrugged and looked at her palms. Harriet took her left one in hers.

"Let's see your lifeline." Harriet traced it from the base of the thumb to just below her forefinger.

"Ah, a long life. And I see many children." Harriet hid a grin. "One, two, three, four, five—no, six!"

"Oh, bloody hell, Hattie, don't say that!"

"Don't you want to get married and have children?"

"Yes, maybe, one day, but six?"

Harriet nudged her. "Come on. Tell me what's going on. Let me in."

Kate's face plucked a dimple of doubt. "Maybe, another time." She looked at the palm of her hand, brooding. "Six children? You've got to be kidding!"

Chapter 56

Dorian Craddock sat on the white kidskin sofa, staring at the tiger rug with its teeth bared in his last growl. She wondered how to approach Harriet. The matter was a delicate one.

She recalled how Harriet had rescued her at school, literally saving her life from the brutal hands of George "Silver Smith" Blaney, her father's rival.

Now Harriet held information on her that could ruin her. The letter Harriet had sent some weeks ago held a promise, but it was not a guarantee. Dorian rolled her thumbs one over the other as she thought about CJ. He had been blackmailing her and others before his death. She wanted the notebook and photographs like nothing else before. Margaux had failed her in trying to claim it and in the process had followed up with her instruction that CJ would meet with an untimely death. Now it was up to her. She needed to see Harriet face to face and deal with the issue herself. She would persuade Harriet to hand over everything. She had the means.

****

Harriet arrived at Dorian Craddock's five-story home in Mayfair. She shuddered as she spied the door to Club 59, having no idea Dorian lived so close. Memories flooded back. Dorian had only one motive for inviting her, she was sure of that. She would have to be on high alert.

Dorian had expected to find a meek, mild woman beaten into submission due to recent events, but instead, to her surprise, she found Harriet quite transformed. Bold, determined, and with a new air of confidence about her. She was nothing like the girl she'd once bullied at school, or the woman CJ married.

As Harriet was invited to take a seat, Dorian introduced her to her brother Davey, then arranged drinks.

"Dorian…" Harriet began, "The painting over the mantlepiece." She pointed toward it. "Have you had it long?"

Dorian eyed Harriet carefully. She loved the painting almost as much as her tiger skin rug that stretched across the marble floor.

"You like it?"

"I've always loved it. It belonged to my grandmother," Harriet replied dryly.

If there had been any surprise in seeing the painting, Harriet did not show it.

"Then we will get down to business." She turned to her brother. "Davey, I'm sure you'll have better things to do." Harriet noticed how Dorian's voice softened around him. He knew how to take the hint and rose a little unsteadily to his feet and left them. The moment he walked out the door, Dorian rolled her thumbs one over the other in contemplation, already certain she had victory over Harriet.

"I believe Margaux explained CJ was in debt to me?" She jerked her head toward the painting of geese waddling toward a ford.

Harriet eyed her coolly. "Yes."

"Would you like the painting, Harriet?"

"I would. But can I assume it covered CJ's debt?"

"Yes."

"Good. Then we are all square."

Dorian's eyes widened in surprise. "We could come to some arrangement...Say the painting for the information you have."

"No, thank you, Dorian. If you wished to give me back what is rightfully mine, fine. But it will not be in part an exchange...for anything."

Dorian smarted. Her eyes narrowed as she contemplated her next move.

"Like I said in my letter, Dorian, you are safe. However, I have secured everything with my solicitor. Should *anything* happen to me, he knows what to do."

For the first time in her adult life, Dorian had little left other than empty threats. The fait accompli was laid at her door. Harriet rose to standing, proud and erect.

"Everyone deserves to love and live life without fear, not to have their lives destroyed by other people's disgusting greed. Even someone like you, Dorian."

"You saw? You know?"

Harriet pulled on her gloves. "I'm assuming we have nothing further to discuss."

Harriet left Dorian with her head held high, though inside she felt like a trembling jelly. It wasn't until she turned the corner, out of sight, that she leaned against a wall and took comfort from its strength. Dorian was formidable. Even when she didn't try. Her brother, on the other hand, appeared to be a gentle giant—kind, thoughtful, and nothing like his sister. Thank God she didn't crumble. If Dorian knew she had destroyed the evidence, Lord only knew what havoc she would wreak.

Dorian descended the back stairs to the garden. Her mind churning. Harriet's parting words left a hole as deep as a well, full of anger. Harriet was smart. She safeguarded herself. She would never be able to get the evidence from her, not now. Dorian stepped out into the sunshine. It was a beautiful day, but she couldn't see the beauty of her walled garden past her temper. She went to find Davey. Davey, her beautiful brother Davey, who had tried to save her from her father—and ended up like…

"Davey?" Dorian found him in the art studio. "I've brought lunch. Would you care to join me?" Davey wiped the paint from his hands with a rag, then checked he'd screwed the tops back onto the paints before putting his brushes to soak. He never said no to food.

"What did you think of her?"

"I liked her. She's kind. Honest." He ambled beside Dorian, a little more lumbering than she would have cared for, but he was alive, he could still paint, and his speech therapist was doing wonders. She looked into his soft brown eyes, just like their mother's. He had the same gentleness she had. Even the same stupid belief everything could be rosy.

They were sitting under a shady tree on a wraparound bench as Davey began munching on a sandwich. The gardener was in the distance, mowing the lawns, the sounds far enough away that usually would soothe her. Dorian rolled her thumbs, still infuriated with Harriet. She hated being beaten.

"Give her the painting, Dorey. It belongs to her." It was as if he read her mind.

"You've always been soft, Davey. Like the girl you were soft on." She knew how to push his buttons. She wanted to hurt someone, even him.

"Which girl?"

"Irene."

Davey stopped eating. He heard the inflection in her voice. "She went home to her parents. It was the right thing to do."

"Did she? Or was she just another whore I took off the streets, and went to the highest bidder?"

"You're selling girls?" The sandwich fell from his grasp. He turned to his sister, an impossible truth staring him in the face. His face burned.

"Like I said, Davey, you're soft and sometimes a little stupid. Why else would I feed and clothe them? For my health? For you? For your artwork?" She shook her head, laughing. "They're worth a fortune when they're tarted up. Especially the pretty ones. Like Irene."

She got up and began to walk away. He wanted to kill her. Davey saw a hoe propped by a tree, left by the gardener. He lumbered over and held it in his hand ready to strike. He had loved Irene. He'd believed Dorian when she'd said she had given her the money to get back home. Dorian was right. He was stupid. How could he have believed her? How many girls had fallen for her lies? How many girls had there been? Why had he not seen what was going on? His eyes shimmered with fury. Now he knew the truth, he had to put the wrong right. Dorian had no right to steal their young lives away. No, he reasoned, her death would be too simple, too kind. A thunder in his heart raged as he watched Dorian disappear back into the house. He knew exactly what would hurt Dorian the most.

Chapter 57

Kate heard the doorbell—buzzing continually, as if someone were leaning up against it.

"All right, all right, I'm coming. Keep your toupee on."

She opened the door.

"Davey. What's wrong?" He looked distraught. "Come in."

Davey was breathing heavily. "We need to talk. Is anyone else here?"

"No."

"Good."

They went into the kitchen, and Kate got him to sit down.

"Whiskey?"

He nodded.

She poured him a glass and placed it on the table. He took a swig. It fired his throat. He downed the rest. She topped him up.

"You have the sketches? The girls?" He sounded panicked.

Kate stared at him for a moment. "Yes. I'll get them."

"No. Wait. First, I need to ask you questions."

Kate sat opposite, her mind whirring. This wasn't the Davey she knew. He was usually calm. Centered. Easygoing.

"You used to go to the Club. You saw the girls?"

"Yes."

"Do you know what happened to them?"

"No." Her heart pounded. She wasn't entirely proud of herself, having never managed to get concrete evidence to take to the police.

They spent the next hour talking. Davey was shattered from the effort, by the end. He looked broken. Kate couldn't believe what she heard and felt sure it was just the tip of the proverbial iceberg.

"I can't let her carry on like this, Kate. She's turned into my father. I always prayed she had a good streak in her, somewhere. I've given her the benefit of the doubt for too long."

He put his head in his hands. "It's all my fault, for believing in her, wanting to trust her." Moments passed. Kate remained silent, patiently waiting for him to speak. He looked at her with desperation on his face. "Will you help?"

"What do I need to do?"

"Can you make sure the sketches are hidden somewhere really safe? When I'm ready, I'll let you know what to do."

Kate swallowed. "You know I was beaten up? Threatened?"

"No? Her?"

"I couldn't prove it. But yes, I'm sure it was."

"Sorry." The guilt in his voice said it all.

She reached a hand across to his. "Don't be. You weren't to know. Besides, she's your sister, and she can be very plausible. And yes, of course, I'll help in any way I can. Just tell me what to do."

****

Sunday, two weeks later, Kate had just put her apron on and was plating up food at the soup kitchen. She knew everyone who came these days, but today someone new stood in front of her. His face was mostly hidden by a flat cap pulled down over his eyes and a scarf drawn up under his chin almost to his mouth. She smiled, "Welcome." Her eyes traveled over his clothes. Ragged, torn, disheveled, with one hand stuffed heavily into a jacket pocket that hung with barely a thread holding it together.

"Is there anything you don't like?" Kate asked as she picked up a plate.

"No." It was the first word the man spoke.

"I'll bring it over. If you can collect your cutlery at the end," she pointed, "and find somewhere you would like to sit." She glanced over to Carol and Fred. They nodded. When newbies arrived, Kate tried to take them under her wing. She'd learned very quickly not to offer advice. People were homeless for many reasons and would not take kindly to being judged. Instead, if they needed anything, or were to ask for help, she would attempt to point them in the right direction. Mostly, all they desired was the safety of a roof over their heads, warmth, food in their bellies, and clothing. On occasion, a friendly, listening ear was appreciated, and she was happy to provide it.

Alex, who was in charge of the clothes store and had done marvels getting donations, was busy making tea. He didn't see the exchange.

Kate dished up his meal, then calmly walked toward the man. She had watched him find a seat. Her heart thudded. She knew that walk anywhere.

"How are you?" If anyone overheard, it would be

a reasonable question. Nothing untoward that could cause questions.

"I'm doing fine." He grunted, taking the plate from her. "Thank you."

"You're welcome."

"Is there anything else you need?"

"Maybe a million quid and a place to put my head for the night." He gave a wry laugh.

"Well. I'm afraid I can't run to a million pounds, but I do have a spare bed."

"No bed. Too dangerous." He ate the food slowly, savoring each mouthful as if it were his last.

She checked over her shoulder before whispering, "Are you all right?" Silly question, she thought the moment she spoke it.

"I'll be fine, thanks," he whispered back. "Your offer of help. The church, fourth pew down, taped underneath."

She frowned.

"I'm leaving. Disappearing. I'm sorry to burden you. Parcel it all up with the sketches. Post it to the police, anonymously. Can you do that? For the girls?"

"Of course. Anything."

Someone sat down close to them.

"Have you finished? I'll take your plate, shall I?"

"Thanks miss. For everything." And Davey walked out of her life forever.

Kate felt flustered. She couldn't wait for the shift to be over. She asked Alex if he would mind stacking the chairs, saying she'd found something she needed to do. Alex had no idea of the exchange she'd had with Davey, and she had no intention of drawing him in. Not yet. Wiping her hands on her apron and taking it off, she folded it neatly, ready to wash, then hurried out the door with her bag. The local lay preacher had been a joy, and not only in his empathic non-preachy sermons. He'd also managed to persuade the district council to allow the disused church next to the church hall to be opened Sundays. Anyone could join in. She had spotted him doing his usual rounds in the soup kitchen, so she knew he wouldn't be there, but was conscious there might be hangers-on still in the church.

Kate studied the huge oak doors wide enough for three people to walk abreast. The familiar smell of dust and dank reached her nose even before she stepped a foot inside. The next set of doors was propped open. The only remaining pane of glass was at the top right-hand side. The stone font remained intact, and the beautiful stained-glass window, over what was once the altar, glowed in beautiful reds, blues, and golds. It took her breath away as the sunlight streamed in and shone to the floor.

Kate quickly checked there was no one around. Over the years, people had stolen anything they could sell from inside the church, until the council did a better job of securing it. She counted four pews down. Only one side of pews remained. She counted nine rows. The rest most likely had been used for firewood. Sacrilege, she thought, as she sat down and checked around again, just in case she'd missed anyone kneeling. No one was there.

Kate put her hand under the bench. Nothing. She scooted along trailing her hand underneath. Finally, she found something. She tugged at it. At a noise from behind her, she dropped to her knees on the pretense of praying.

Alex arrived and slid along the bench beside her. "I wondered where you were. Is everything all right?"

"Of course, silly. Just thought it might be a good idea to confess all my sins."

"Really?"

"Yes. Is that so strange?"

"Shall we get married here, then?"

"So romantic, Alex!"

"Well, a man can only keep asking, and in so many ways, for so long."

"Please, Alex." She could think of no decent response. There were too many things going on in her head right now. And to cross that other threshold, confess why she couldn't marry him? The thought of losing him...

Alex watched, bemused, as she placed her hands in supplication and prayed silently for Davey's safety whilst Alex waited to lock up. She would have to leave the package for now and try to claim it next Sunday.

It was around sixish when Alex got a call from his boss. There were some matters he had to attend to. "I'll be back as soon as we're finished," he promised, giving Kate a kiss before he left. Not two minutes later, the bell rang. Kate leapt down the stairs, laughing, assuming it was Alex having forgotten his key.

Instead, it was Dorian who greeted her.

"Good evening, Kate."

Her heart dropped to the pit of her stomach.

Dorian was flanked either side by two of her henchmen. One she recognized from his visits to

Madam Raines. It was as if they had been watching, waiting, until Alex left. Had they known he was being called to work? Was she being paranoid?

"Dorian?"

"Where is he?"

"He who?" Kate, terrified, couldn't take her eyes off the men. One had put his foot in the doorway, preventing her closing the door.

"You're not being very polite, Kate. Aren't you going to invite us in?"

Kate, heart in mouth, tried desperately to stand her ground but was left with little choice as she was manhandled to one side. The men went ahead.

"If he's here, I'll find him."

"Alex isn't here."

Dorian's eyes narrowed. "I'm talking about Davey. He's disappeared."

"Disappeared?"

"What are you, stupid?"

Kate could hardly hear her next words over the racket the men were making.

"Seriously, Dorian, I don't know what you're talking about. Is Davey all right?"

Dorian was on the top tread of the stairs, with Kate following quickly behind. "I thought he may have stayed over, left word, or…" Her eyes glinted. "Or given you something?"

Kate's heart stopped. Thank God she didn't have the package, but the sketches— What if they were discovered?

They found doors flung wide open. The men were throwing everything out from drawers and wardrobes in heaps. They had just smashed open the door to the room in which she'd locked her costumes prepared for her fashion show.

"Nice," Dorian purred, fondling her designs. She plucked from its hanger the one Harriet had called a shimmering waterfall. "I think I'll have that one. It would suit me nicely. I'm disappointed at you, Kate, for not bringing this to my attention."

"But they're for..." Kate stopped. She didn't want anyone to hear the pleading in her voice. She knew it would be handing bait to Dorian.

The men were in her lounge, tipping up the sofa, checking underneath, destroying everything in their paths.

She changed tactics. "What do you want? What are you looking for? Perhaps I can help."

She'd hidden both their sketches inside the old fireplace where a painted fireguard had been placed in front. One of the men was walking in that direction. She thought wildly, then suddenly yelled at Dorian to distract him.

"Keep the bloody dress, if you must, Dorian! But I don't have anything that belongs to you." She took a swipe at the man. He shoved her aside, but in doing so he caught his foot on the coffee table and stumbled.

"Clumsy oaf!" said Dorian irritably. She snapped at the other man. "Have you found anything?"

He grunted a "No."

"Don't forget, Kate Westfield, I own you and everything you do at Madam Raines. I helped you get on the first rung of the ladder, and I can knock you off just as easily." She held the dress aloft. "Thank you for this." And she disappeared back down the stairs and out into the street, laughing, with her men trailing behind.

Kate, shaking, trembling with rage and fear, looked out the window, then ran back down the stairs and locked the door behind her. Unable to compute what had just happened, she slid to the floor in a shivering heap, unsure whether to call the police, Alex, or anyone. Life was not that simple. The warning was clear. Thank God, she thought, the thugs didn't do a thorough enough job and find the sketches. Thank God she had not brought the package home. Thank God Davey had declined her offer of a bed.

Kate wrung her hands together, hating herself for her cowardice. Not demanding the dress back. Not telling them to get out of her home. Gathering her composure, fear turning to anger, she started clearing up. Each item not destroyed she cleaned and put back in its rightful place. The broken items went into the bin while she formulated what she must do—or in this case, not do.

She stared out the window, seeing a dark fog had descended, and it felt like her mood. She would have to tell Alex. After her flat had virtually been destroyed, she was left with no other option. All she knew was that whatever Davey had entrusted to her must be incredibly important, for him to go to such lengths and for Dorian to be so determined to get him—and it—back. She could only pray he was safe somewhere and Dorian wouldn't return.

****

When Sunday arrived again, the day turned murky with another heavy fog that left a blanket of damp gloom all around. Kate and Alex went to church after doing their usual duties in the soup kitchen. They joined the small congregation in the freezing church, and patiently listened to the sermon and joined in prayers. Once the church was emptied, Alex stood at the door, promising to check no one was left behind and he'd lock up.

Kate, heart racing, swiftly began the search. For one heart-stopping moment she couldn't find it. Then she realized that in her haste she had counted five pews down, not four.

She breathed a sigh of relief, and when she turned to Alex, he tipped his head in question. She gave an affirmative and hid the item in her bag. Then they returned to their clear-up duties in the soup kitchen.

All Kate needed to do now was send everything to the police.

Chapter 58

December 1960

It was nearing Christmas, and the verdict of Harriet's husband's death had been agreed by the courts. The lawyer had done a brilliant job of getting Margaux off the hook, which came as no surprise, as Margaux's father, Lord Sutcliffe, QC, undoubtedly pulled many strings. Lord Sutcliffe was also true to his word. The same lawyer also advocated for Harriet, and Lord Sutcliffe met all costs, as promised.

Harriet sighed a breath of relief. It was over. No longer would she need to look over her shoulder. Or worry that her life was in danger. The life insurance CJ had taken out on her in case of accidental death before her twenty-first birthday was nullified. And, as per her agreement with Margaux, she never spoke of the woman's duplicitous hand in its preparation.

She was also financially sound. Harriet was surprised to find CJ's business had been doing remarkably well under Margaux's careful eye, and the lies he told were just that, lies.

His estate was worth far more than she could ever have imagined. Harriet could not believe that during all the time she'd scrimped and saved, all the time CJ berated her for being frivolous with the housekeeping, making her life a misery and trapping her at home, all that time he had been out enjoying life, carefree and with a spend, spend, spend attitude. CJ had soundly played her.

The painting that once belonged to her grandmother but had been "stolen" to supposedly cover his debt remained with Dorian Craddock. At least, she consoled herself, it was safe, and loved by Davey, her brother. Harriet could start her life over. No longer would CJ be able to torture her physically or mentally. In the new year she would sell up. The house would go to auction, and CJ's businesses would be sold. She would be able to afford something smart, small, and comfortable, maybe somewhere in the countryside. Then, with the rest of her funds, she would put her plans into action.

The phone rang. Harriet had moved it from the study and into the hallway, as she was spirited to make small changes over time. CJ had always controlled her. He'd never let her use the telephone and kept it locked away in *his* study. The forbidden room. Now the door stayed permanently open, even with its secret still to be shared with someone. But not yet.

Harriet took a deep breath and picked up the receiver.

"Hello, Kate." Harriet smiled down the line. They had reinstated their agreement—to speak to one another every night since Kate went back to her apartment.

"Are you okay?"

"Yes, fine, thanks, and you?" Harriet decided not to share her dealing with Dorian. Instead, she asked about Alex. It seemed Alex, an upcoming back bencher, was making a name for himself, and Kate always breathed his name like a schoolgirl with a crush. It made her smile. Alex seemed to be ying to Kate's yang. He was the calming influence when she got a little crazy.

And she did get crazy at times. Harriet often thought it must be her creative genius that made her go off on one of her wild tangents, especially concerning her upcoming fashion show. But every time Kate spoke of Alex, she sounded happy. Gloriously happy. Strange, Harriet thought, that Kate had said Alex asked her to marry him but she had refused. Nothing she could say would persuade Kate to share why the refusal.

"I was thinking…" said Harriet, the smile still on her lips.

"Oh, no, there you go again." Kate giggled.

Harriet sighed. "Can I speak? I wonder if you and Alex would like to stay over for Christmas. I love to cook, and I know Jack's off to Africa in the new year. Do you think he might come as well? I hope so. It would be lovely to see him again." She couldn't stop talking. Like a child who ate too many sweets, she fizzed. The thrill of the idea. Just the thought of doing something nice for her friends already gave her pleasure. "Please say yes."

Kate, laughing, caught up with her enthusiasm, shouted down the line, "Yes, of course! You know how I hate cooking. Count us in."

Harriet was pleased, excited. A time to air the ghosts once and for all. Plus, if Kate could come earlier, to stay with her, all the better. If they were alone, it might be the perfect time to talk about her plans to open a safe house for battered women.

Harriet replaced the receiver and made her next

call. Mrs. Gaffney, her old landlady, was in floods the moment she posed the question. A little holiday away? Time spent with lovely people? A Christmas meal? How could she possibly say no?

Next, Harriet telephoned Jack. His deep voice came across the line, polite, courteous, until his likeable comical tone caught Harriet's ear when he realized it was her. Jack's answer was a resounding yes. He loved her cooking. Couldn't get enough of it. *Yes, please. Thank you. What time shall I be there? Who else is coming? I can collect Mrs. Gaffney.*

Harriet exhaled. Pleased. Happy. There were another couple of calls she would need to make. When Daisy and Tom agreed to come, she couldn't have wished for more.

****

Christmas Eve, and Harriet's lounge was awash with a heap of fashion magazines. Kate was sprawled out on the floor. Harriet had left tea for her on the table and muttered something about going upstairs. Kate sat up to take a sip when she saw the newspaper by the side. It was folded over, the headlines face down. She flicked it open, and the unmistakable photograph of Dorian Craddock stared back. The headline read:

Daughter of Gangster "Freddy the Fish Craddock"
Held for Questioning.

The doorbell rang, and she started. "Get that, Harriet, will you?" she hollered, desperate to finish the article, her eyes not leaving the paper. She quickly read on.

Miss Dorian Craddock—daughter to London gangster Frederick Craddock, hanged for murder, is facing charges of her own...

She quickly read on.

Fifteen women have been rescued. Thirty-one people arrested for trafficking young women...

Tears welled. A deep nausea sat heavy in the pit of her stomach. She had been beaten and left with a message and no room for doubt to keep her nose out of Dorian's business. Then Davey had vanished, leaving her with information. She'd posted everything as instructed. She couldn't believe barely a month had passed. Maybe there was still a chance he was all right.

The bell rang again.

Kate got up and walked down the hallway. No sign of Harriet. "Harriet?" she hollered. There was no answer.

She opened the door. A huge parcel had been left on the doorstep. Looking around, expecting see the Royal Mail, she just caught sight of a black van pulling away down the road.

"Harriet!" Kate called out again.

She arrived, looking flushed.

"About time!" Kate wanted to get back to the newspaper.

"Where did that come from?" Harriet puzzled at the parcel.

"Father Christmas, who else? He couldn't get it down the chimney, so he thought, hey, why not drop it off early."

"Really?"

Kate turned serious, the news of Dorian and worry regarding Davey's safety had not been a second from her mind.

"Sorry. I guess you weren't expecting anything, by the look of you?"

Harriet shook her head.

"Well, it's got your name on the front. Are we going to bring it in, or leave it on the doorstep?"

Kate helped Harriet carry the parcel through to the lounge. She licked her lips before speaking. "Harriet, have you read the newspaper?"

"Not yet."

They propped the parcel against the sofa, and Harriet's gaze never left it.

Kate placed the newspaper flat onto the dining table and drew Harriet's attention to it.

"Look."

Harriet flew from hot to cold all at once. Bile rose in her throat the moment she saw the headlines and photograph. "Good God! Tell me it isn't true. Is it?"

The details were vile. Extortion, blackmail, prostitution.

Harriet puffed out her cheeks, her mind whirring over possibilities. "Why do people have to be so evil? Why can't they just use their talents for good? Dorian has built up an empire she should be proud of. Not something so vile!" She slammed her fist on the table, surprising herself but furious she had not seen through Dorian. She had shown her compassion. Where was Dorian's compassion?

Kate could only feel relief. Dorian was being held on bail. The one person she worried about right now was Davey.

Kate could see Harriet's mind had refocused on the parcel. Unable to think further for the moment, she found scissors and a sharp knife and handed them over. "Come on, then, what are you waiting for?"

Harriet paused. She needed just a moment longer to gather her composure before she began cutting away the string.

Three layers in, they came across a large cotton covering constructed like a pillow. As its content were slowly revealed, Harriet gasped.

Kate watched Harriet's every expression but said nothing as she helped lift the painting off the table and prop it upon the couch.

"I never thought to have this, ever again."

"Who is it from?" Kate stepped back, admiring it. "It's beautiful, Harriet. Funny thing, though, it looks so much like the place where I grew up…" She eyed Harriet curiously. "This isn't the painting, the one you told me about, is it? The one that was stolen?"

"Yes. I discovered a little while back that Dorian Cradock had this painting all the time." Harriet's face was set grimly.

"What?"

Harriet's eyes flicked over the painting, her chin jutting out. "It just seems so out of character for her to return it. Unless she has ulterior motives. Maybe she knew the police were onto her and wanted to get shot of it."

"Okaaay," said Kate slowly. "Harriet, there's something I need to tell you."

Harriet looked puzzled.

Kate explained a little of her dealings with Dorian and Davey, while Harriet looked on in amazement. Then she asked, "Are you going to tell the police about the painting, Harriet?"

"I will, but not until after Christmas. It's mine, by

rights, and it's going to stay with me, in my bedroom. If Davey has been kind enough to return it, then all I really want to do is thank him from the bottom of my heart."

After a moment of thought, Harriet reached out a hand. "There's something I want to show you."

Kate, curious, followed her into the study.

"Have you ever seen a priest hole?" Not waiting for a response, Harriet walked Kate straight over to the huge wall of books.

"I don't think I could do this without someone else being here," she whispered, running fingers along the lower half of one of the shelves until she found it—*Tail of Two Cities*.

Kate spotted the misspelt cover as Harriet lifted the base of the book, and she immediately let out a low wolf-whistle. "That book, my lady, is worth a small fortune."

Harriet just nodded. "I know." But when the door to the priest hole silently swung open, Kate couldn't believe her eyes.

"Just before I ran away from CJ, I discovered this. I found out the burglary was down to him. All the stolen paintings were hidden here, with one exception—the one that has just been delivered."

"Bloody hell, Hattie!" Kate exclaimed. "No way!"

Harriet pulled her inside the small room and tentatively switched on a light. The door swung closed.

Kate gave a low groan. "I hope you know what you're doing and how to get us out of here." Seconds later, the light went out. Kate groaned again.

"It'll be all right. Just a minute." Harriet was still fumbling along the wall, her breathing coming in short rasps, not inspiring confidence. "Just bear with me. We'll be fine, but before I do anything, Kate, allow your eyes to adjust to the dark. Now. Can you see through into the study?"

"Well, I bloody never!"

Harriet laughed despite everything.

"I thought I was going mad when I lived here with CJ. When I came upon this priest hole, it explained so much about the strange noises I heard when I was alone. Doors closing, a draft of air..." She had found the switch and flicked on the light. The door slid open.

"Phew!" Kate sounded relieved. "I was beginning to think we might miss Christmas Day altogether!"

****

Harriet was preparing a bite to eat, whilst Kate fiddled with a tea cloth, meditating.

"You've been through a lot, haven't you, Harriet?"

"You could say that. I reckon I could write a book on it. Though some of it I'd rather forget." She turned to Kate. "But you've been through a lot as well, haven't you?"

Kate breathed slowly, deeply, as she recalled the day she learned her family were killed in that dreadful accident. It wasn't a story she cared to share with people. It raked over so much hurt, but she felt Harriet deserved to understand everything—her life, her adoption, her parents, the mother she never knew, her dealings with Dorian, and now her fear for Davey's safety. "I don't know where to start."

"I always think starting at the beginning helps, Kate."

Kate smiled. It was something her uncle always said. Her eyes misted. Her memories and thoughts had rarely strayed from her family, even after all this time.

"What were your parents like, Kate?"

"Simply wonderful." She allowed herself a moment to gather her composure and reflect upon her life. "Without question they were wonderful, and I'm so lucky to have Uncle Jack. He epitomizes their kindness of spirit and generosity of mind." She took a deep, shuddering breath. "I was very lucky to have them, even though it was only for a relatively short time." She frowned before speaking again.

"There are things I've never told anyone. Not even Alex." She looked at her hands in contemplation and shame. She shook her head, her eyes reflecting embarrassment.

Harriet reached out and hugged her. "What on earth!"

Kate shuddered a deep spasm that traveled through her body. "Dorian," she said flatly. "I'm not blaming her for my greed. From the day I met her I knew she was bad, but I was just as bad. A selfish child looking to better herself. When she offered me a free membership to Club 59, it was a perfect opportunity to network. Greed. That's where all of this has stemmed from."

Kate looked at Harriet wild-eyed. The words began to tumble from her like huge waves crashing into rocks. Sometimes they fell with relief, other times blasted out in desperation, and all the while Harriet listened.

"I've done some things I'm not proud of." Kate brushed her fingers through her hair before continuing. Sighing, with an expression of remorse and shame, she said, "Going with men I really shouldn't have, just for the thrill of it. If Alex were to find out...I haven't told

Alex I'm adopted, either."

"Why ever not?"

Her eyebrows rose. "Prejudice? I'm frightened of losing him." Her head dropped. "He works for the Government, after all."

"Goodness, Kate. We're not living in the dark ages. Alex loves you. It won't make one iota of difference. Honestly." Harriet held Kate's hands in hers and drew her to a chair. "The rest of it, well, does he really need to know?"

"No."

"Well, then." Though as the words left her mouth, she understood. She knew how unkind adults could be, blinding their children to their own bigotry. She had heard children being hateful toward children who were adopted, and had endured similar abuse having been born to an unmarried mother.

"Tell him, Kate. Trust me, you've nothing to lose or to be ashamed of. Honesty is the best policy. He's a decent, wonderful man. There is no way he would walk away from you."

That evening they sat in front of the fire, exhausted. The preparations for Christmas were completed. Tomorrow was Christmas Day. They would relax and enjoy it with friends and family.

Chapter 59

Christmas Day 1960

Waking to a cold Christmas morning, Jack read over the last communication from Africa. Naidoo had a contract delivering Coca-Cola, and his business was growing. What pleased Jack just as much was the gang sticking together. He knew the boy would make good. He was proud of him and glad the Rolex had afforded them the opportunity.

Jack jotted notes and decided to make the journey to see Naidoo while he was in the country next month. There should be time, even though he had to be back in time for Kate and Harriet's joint twenty-first birthday. It came as such a surprise to all of them when they discovered they were born the same day and year. If he missed their party, he would never live it down.

Jack finished his coffee and put the cup in the sink. Slipping on a warm coat and scarf, he jumped into the car, looking forward to sharing Christmas with his niece and Harriet. It would be different. A good kind of different.

He knew Kate would already be at Harriet's home with Alex. Kate had sworn to help with the Christmas preparations, although, he mused, Harriet most likely would fuss over her like a mother hen and let her lounge around instead. Jack chuckled at the thought.

And as he drove Mrs. Gaffney to Harriet's, they talked, and both agreed how kind it was of her to include them in the festivities.

****

When Tom arrived with Daisy, Kate could see the joy in Harriet almost spill over, and from that moment on, the day morphed into fun and frivolity.

Kate felt heartened to see Harriet looking more relaxed, lighter in mood, less reclusive, happy to be sharing Christmas with the people she loved. She noticed how Tom couldn't keep his eyes off Harriet, and vowed if he didn't do something about their relationship soon, she would have to box his ears and knock some sense into him. She needn't have worried. As he and Daisy prepared to leave, Tom took charge and kissed Harriet full on, and in front of everyone. For a moment, Kate saw Harriet's face—she couldn't read her expression. Tom must have felt the same, as he looked mortified and apologized profusely.

When Harriet dragged him back and told him off for waiting so long, then gave him a slow, lingering kiss, Kate whooped for joy. "About bloody time, Mr. Fletcher!"

Tom glanced across at her bashfully, holding Harriet in his arms as if he would never let her go again.

Kate breathed a long happy sigh of relief. Harriet deserved to be loved. Harriet was a good friend… No, she thought, Harriet was far more than just a friend.

Chapter 60

February 1961

Sarah had dropped in for a catch-up and found a pile of letters on the floor. She waved an envelope around. "Mail for Miss Popularity."

Kate, lounging on the sofa, feet up, wondered whether she could face her coffee.

"It's from a firm of solicitors. Gilbraith & Son. Ever heard of them?" Sarah squinted at the frank mark.

"Nope, should I?"

"Oh, Kate, for goodness' sake, read it and put me out of my misery."

"If you insist." Kate happily put her coffee down. It smelt much stronger than usual, and not in a good way. Tearing the envelope open, she pulled the letter out. The paper was classy, heavyweight, with embossed lettering across the top. Slowly standing, she read.

"It seems a Mr. Gilbraith, of Gilbraith & Son, is under instruction to meet with me on my twenty-first birthday."

"But that's only a week away."

"Like I don't know. I even get to vote! But my show—it's so close, and I've still got loads to do." She fanned the letter backward and forward, cooling her brow.

Life didn't usually bother Kate, but the letter felt odd. It weighed heavily in her mind as she considered the facts. What did a solicitor need with her? Not only that, how did he know where she lived, and what did he need to say that was so important it could not be addressed within a letter? Intrigued, Kate made the call and spoke to the receptionist, who either could not or would not divulge the purpose of the meeting. She accepted the offered appointment set for ten o'clock, Friday 14th February, the only time available.

Kate put the receiver back, frustrated with herself for not having found out more. Sarah was close by, pressing for news. Kate shrugged. "I'm none the wiser," and popped the place and time into her diary.

Chapter 61

February 14, 1961

A little birthday shopping, then lunch at Luigi's at two thirty with a few friends. Harriet checked her watch. An hour or so surely would be all that was required? Harriet allowed herself a smile. It was amazing to think she and Kate shared the same birthday. They got on so well, like peas in a pod. Maybe she should have told Kate about this unexpected appointment. Too late now.

Harriet stepped into the offices of Gilbraith & Son exactly on time. Miss Fry, the receptionist, requested she take a seat, apologizing that Mr. Gilbraith was occupied at the moment but would be with her shortly. Harriet ran a cursory eye around the room. The air was still, with no sounds except the exacting tick of the walnut grandfather clock on the far wall. Even Miss Fry didn't seem to breathe.

Ten minutes later, bored and wriggling around in her chair, Harriet checked her watch again. She instantly felt stupid. Had she not looked at the clock not moments before, showing exactly the same time? A range of newspapers lay on a coffee table, and her eyes were drawn to a headline:

British Authorities Announce the Discovery
of a Large Soviet Spy Ring in London.

Harriet drummed a beat on the arm of her chair, considering the intrigue, then remembered Kate had told her about wild parties, an opal-and-diamond necklace, and a Russian diplomat. The though startled her. She hoped there was no connection. The receptionist moved just enough to attract her attention. Harriet stopped tapping for a second. She felt trapped. Was that the right word? Nothing else sprang to mind. She certainly didn't feel able to leave. The day was all mapped out. She hated being late. This appointment had already gotten in the way. Harriet absently rubbed the face of her watch, consoling herself that Kate would most likely be late anyway.

Harriet stood and walked to an imposing bookshelf on the same wall as the clock. "May I?" she asked, indicating she would like to peruse the law books hidden behind glass. The woman gave a look of surprise.

"I'm afraid not, they are precious. Hence the lock."

Harriet spied the mechanism and walked back to the chair, pondering over her house move. With the conveyancing almost complete and only contracts to sign, it would all be over very soon. Her research of specific areas, wanting somewhere discreet yet large enough to house a minimum of five women and possibly children, she had to ensure there would be ample room.

A door opened from somewhere, and muted voices drifted out, breaking her train of thought. Miss Fry dropped a book, which landed with a thud on her desk, and the receptionist looked at Harriet, who caught her worried expression.

"I'll see if Mr. Gilbraith is free." Harriet overheard a gentleman thanking someone for their understanding. He enunciated the woman's name in a well-educated voice.

"I will look forward to your decision, Miss Westfield."

Miss Westfield? Moments later, Kate appeared from the corridor, her happy smile instantly turning to astonishment.

"Harriet?"

Harriet, equally flabbergasted, checked her watch. "I have an appointment. But more to the point, what are *you* doing here?"

Miss Fry interrupted.

"Mr. Gilbraith is ready for you now, Mrs. Rutherford."

Kate raised her hand. "Just a moment, please." Turning back to Harriet, Kate thrilled with excitement. "I've just had some amazing news."

"You have?"

Miss Fry cut them off.

"Mrs. Rutherford, I'm so sorry, but if you would be so kind, Mr. Gilbraith is ready for you now?"

"Wait here, Kate, and hold that thought. You can tell me when I'm done. All right?"

Kate's nose wrinkled in frustration.

"If I must."

Harriet put her finger to her lips.

"I guess you're the reason my appointment has been delayed. So just be patient." She left Kate stewing.

Chapter 62

Mr. Gilbraith quickly introduced himself but was unable to disguise his surprise at Mrs. Rutherford's appearance. It was uncanny. He watched her every move as she elegantly placed one hand over the other on her lap and gave him a hint of a smile that spoke of interest. Her clothes were smart and far more conventional than those of Miss Westfield, who, in his mind, had a very exotic taste, her outfit being all pink and yellow, with an oddly huge red bow planted in her hair.

"I presume you are curious as to the matter that brings you here?"

Harriet nodded.

"Very well, I will proceed." He gave a polite cough before beginning. "I have a letter you are required to read in my presence." He passed it over.

Harriet swallowed, nervously accepting it. Mr. Gilbraith had a friendly face, and his manner she could not dislike, but Harriet was more alert these days, assessing body language, gathering information of her surroundings—CJ's legacy of self-preservation.

Harriet noticed a photograph of a young man in uniform on his desk. He looked a lot like Mr. Gilbraith, and she guessed he might be his son, or maybe even himself when he was younger.

"Do I have to read this out loud to you, or just to

myself?"

Mr. Gilbraith steepled his fingers under his chin. "Whichever you choose, Mrs. Rutherford. I just need to know how you would like to proceed."

Harriet tentatively peeled back the lip of the envelope and pulled out the contents. She gulped. It was like going back in time.

"This is…" started Harriet immediately, turning the pages over, already recognizing the handwriting, not really needing confirmation of the signature at the end.

"This is from my grandmother, but how… Why?" she exclaimed, stunned.

Selfishly, Mr. Gilbraith wished he could turn back the clock. But then only if he could have been less of a coward. He pursed his lips together, blinking owl-like, adjusting his glasses.

Harriet's brow furrowed.

"Naturally, you are shocked, but she wanted to ensure you received it. We planned to see you together." He indicated the letter. "If you would be kind enough to read?"

Harriet's gaze darted back to the letter, to travel over the words. A sentiment, an apology, an account of her mother's last day on earth. Things she never knew. Decisions Nana made that day, to which she could never reconcile herself. Shocking, terrible, and all so very sad. She wiped a stray tear with the tips of her fingers, remembering that last night with Nana, still so vivid and painful in her mind. Nana wanting to tell her something about her father, her history, but never having the chance. Now some of the answers were laid out, but if she wanted to know more, it depended on someone else. She was shaking.

"I'm so sorry, Mrs. Rutherford."

This was it. If they both agreed to the conditions, then the truth would be out. George Gilbraith prayed with all his heart that he could manage it appropriately, kindly, honestly. He would deserve every bit of hate and condemnation thrown his way, regardless.

Harriet looked at the letter incredulously.

"Did you know my grandmother?"

"Yes."

"Did you know her very well?"

"Enough to know she was an intelligent woman with a difficult decision to make at a very difficult time." Shame crossed his face as he spoke, unable to meet her gaze.

"Did you know my mother?"

"Yes."

"Very well?"

"Not as much as I would have liked." He would keep his sentences short. He wanted to gather his composure and thoughts. The day was already turning out messy, and he knew it could get far worse. He poured a glass of water. "Would you care for some?"

Harriet declined. He took a sip and slowly placed the glass back onto the desk.

"Mr. Gilbraith, I have so many questions, but I need some air. To gather my thoughts. May I return in a moment or two?"

Not waiting for an answer, she walked out of the office and along the corridor, her head fit to burst. Her mother had died giving birth. She already knew that, but the burning questions for which she'd wanted to know the answers, throughout her life, now depended on some mysterious person's agreement. Did she want to know? Of course she did. But Kate was waiting.

Chapter 63

Kate saw the letter still held in Harriet's hand. Confused, she delved into her handbag and thrust a similar letter her way, comparing the two.

"What are you doing with a letter from my grandmother?" Harriet blinked, momentarily mesmerized.

"I could ask you the same thing," replied Kate. "But I'm sure as hell going to find out. Coming?"

Miss Fry called after Kate, who was already marching back toward Gilbraith's office. Harriet hung back just a moment, giving Miss Fry a slight, apologetic shrug. She had begun calculating an almost certain possibility, and with a hint of excitement pulsing through her veins hurried after Kate.

Kate had entered his office without knocking, and he stood up in surprise.

"Miss Westfield? Mrs. Rutherford?"

"We'd like you to explain these." Kate propelled her letter in front of his nose.

"Ah, I see."

Trying to appear composed, he indicated the chairs, hoping to gather a modicum of control.

"Ladies," he began, as they took their seats. "We have a dilemma. I am unable to divulge information unless the other party agrees to the conditions."

"Would you kindly reiterate the conditions for the

benefit of us both?" asked Harriet.

A little whistle of air caught the back of his throat, and he sat, pressing himself into his chair as if seeking much-needed support.

"Very well." He moistened his lips with his tongue. "Should you wish to know more about your lineage, you are to independently make that decision. The other person, or persons, must then acknowledge or decline that opportunity, and advise me of their decision. Until then, I am unable to proceed."

"Are there others beside myself and Miss Westfield involved?"

"No."

"Can we assume the contract will reveal who our birth parents are?"

"Yes."

Harriet reached out a hand for Kate, wide-eyed and smiling.

"Then I can assume we're related."

Without giving an answer, Gilbraith's eyes flickered with a hint of worry.

Harriet twisted in her seat toward Kate, pushing her glasses up her nose. "Do you want to know more? Do you want to find out who your natural parents are? If you do, now might be the time to agree."

Harriet waited, watching Kate closely, praying for an affirmative, ignoring Mr. Gilbraith's obvious nervousness.

"If you need time to think, Kate, or don't want to find out, then I will respect your decision, and we will leave it at that."

"Yes, I want to know." Kate caught her hand, a tear in the corner of her eye. "You have no idea."

Harriet turned to Gilbraith, smiling. "Then I think, Mr. Gilbraith, you have our answer."

Mr. Gilbraith stood, providing him a level of superiority and control, as he might wish in a courtroom.

"Very well, as you have both agreed. But please be aware that you may find the information distressing. I advise you to try to prepare yourselves as best you can." He adjusted his glasses, waiting for a reaction. There was none.

"Very well. If you are sure?"

Kate edged forward on her chair expectantly. Harriet remained composed, calm, elegant, like the young woman he'd met briefly all those years ago. The beginning of a strategy began to form as he spoke, though he could barely make eye contact.

"You are sisters. To be precise, twins." The statement was delivered so matter-of-factly that at first nothing registered.

"But we can't be!" Kate exploded. "Okay. We share the same birthday, but that's just a coincidence, surely? Besides, we look nothing alike!"

Mr. Gilbraith glanced between the women, his lids fluttering.

"I think perhaps you, Miss Westfield, take more after your father, and you, Mrs. Rutherford, are more like your mother." Though truthfully, he could not see a likeness in either of them from his side at all.

He spread his arms wide, palms up in submission. Harriet and Kate looked at one another, totally bemused. He reached across his desk and picked up the photograph, holding it a second before passing it across.

"This is my son, Johnnie." They looked at the picture blankly. "My son Johnnie is—was—your father."

"What?" said Kate. "But that means you are…"

"I don't understand. Please explain," asked Harriet, dumbfounded. "Slowly, so we can both catch our breath."

Mr. Gilbraith took a sip of water.

"I admit I should have been in your lives and been proud to be called your grandfather. But life is rarely easy." The whistle caught in his throat.

"The photograph you have in your hand, Mrs. Rutherford, is my son Johnnie. Your mother and he…" He paused just a beat. "Your mother and Johnnie were friends. When she discovered she was…" He took another sip of water. Twenty-one years to get this right, and he was bumbling.

"You see, the fact of the matter is…" His gaze darted to the photograph. "When your mother found she was in the family way, my son—your father—did the decent, honorable thing and asked her to marry him."

He hated himself. It was nothing like what he'd wanted to say. Not slick. Not considered. And certainly not thoughtful. He could see it in their faces, a look of disquiet, shock, and something else he could not quite read. Sweat bloomed under his armpits.

"Well, that's bloody rich of him!" Kate shouted, sparking flames.

"So?" Her voice grew louder, her eyes boring into him. "Your son, my father, decided he couldn't cope with two girls?"

Kate didn't give him room to maneuver. "You're

saying that *your* son got *our* mother up the duff, and *sooo* generously offered to marry her, and then backed out of the deal—and *I get adopted*, and Harriet gets to live with *my* grandmother!"

If she were a child, she would have been stamping her feet in a tantrum.

Miss Fry tapped the door and poked her head around. "Is there anything I can do?" she asked, looking worriedly at the people in the room.

"Maybe tea, Miss Fry. Thank you."

"Like tea is going to make it all better, or change the course of history," mumbled Kate into her hankie, a little shamefaced.

With one glance from Mr. Gilbraith, Miss Fry backed out.

"Please, ladies. This is all so very difficult. Please, would you mind." He indicated the chairs. "So that I may try to explain more clearly."

Harriet obediently returned to her seat. Kate remained stubborn and stood, occasionally dabbing her face, which by now was blotchy and red.

"I can understand your frustrations and confusions. But it is fact. When your grandmother drew up the contract, it was such an exceedingly difficult time, so very sad." This time he drew confidence in his words.

"Cassandra and Johnnie were devoted to one another. They were excited at the news of having a child. Johnnie had compassionate leave to marry your mother. Sadly, it was not to be." He looked between them. "I'm unsure what your grandmother wrote in her letters, but my Johnnie was a daring and very brave pilot in the war. Before he could return home and marry your mother, he was killed in action."

His words hung suspended in the air as his bottom lip wobbled with the grief flooding back. He swallowed, knowing they deserved to know the whole truth. He almost relented. But what good would it do now? How would it change things? They were his granddaughters. He'd let them down. He could not bear their hatred. He could put a better slant on all of this. Make himself feel a little better. They would feel better. Of course, they would, it would be kinder.

Harriet had stood and put her arms around Kate. She was trembling, wringing her hands, wiping her tears.

"Miss Westfield, Mrs. Rutherford." He needed to say it out loud again so there would be no mistake, or misunderstanding. Expelling a deep breath of air, he continued, "My son died before he had the chance to marry your mother. He died a hero. I'm sorry. I truly wish I could tell you otherwise."

A thousand bombs could have dropped in that room and not one would have been heard.

"I've wanted to know about my father the whole of my life," said Harriet, turning to Kate. "Don't you think he looks kind, gentle, and so handsome in his uniform?" Kate succumbed to the question, twisting the frame toward her, gazing at the picture, shaking, unable to speak.

Mr. Gilbraith took charge. His panache in a courtroom now held in his own office. It took a full thirty minutes to go over that dreadful night, ensuring credibility in his story.

Kate and Harriet understood Mr. Gilbraith to be their grandfather, and they understood his role in

Kate's adoption. His wife, Marjorie, was too unwell to have even one of the twins. The shock of losing her son...her nerves, you see. Their maternal grandmother, Molly Laws, a widow, had to make a difficult choice. Her daughter had died, leaving her with two baby girls. As a result, she devised the contract, and he, George Gilbraith, promised to make good. The adoption agency, an intermediary, found a good home with a childless couple. Kate was selected because of the color of her hair. Her adoptive mother had the same coloring and felt she would look to be more naturally theirs.

"Your grandmother drew up the contract just a few hours after your mother died. The law did not, and to this day does not, allow adopted children, or their natural parents, to seek one another out. The contract was her legacy to you."

Kate rose to her feet, clenching her fists. "And all this time I blamed myself for not being good enough." She bit back a sob. "I want nothing to do with you."

The burst of fury left Harriet reeling, and she went to put her arm back around her, but Kate shook her off, pointing a contemptuous finger at the solicitor.

"You could have helped, stepped up, done something financially, or looked after us, especially Harriet, but did you? No!" She flew out of the office.

Chapter 64

Harriet's emotions were everywhere. She looked at Mr. Gilbraith. Kate was disappearing through the door. Horrified at Kate's outburst, she rushed after her, catching up with her in the street. The thought of losing her was too dreadful to contemplate.

Kate felt wretched. How could this be true? She wanted to know her family, have a mother, father, grandmother—but the hope of ever meeting them had been stripped away in just a few short minutes.

"Please," Harriet called after her. "Don't do this. We have to talk." Kate stopped and turned. Her eyes were wild, red-rimmed, her face full of indignity.

"I'm sorry, Harriet." She flung her arms about her. "I didn't mean to hurt you. None of this is your fault." She stared—tears both happy and sad went rolling down her cheeks. "You're my sister, Harriet. We are sisters. Can you believe it? It seems so unreal."

Harriet gave a shaky laugh, agreeing. "Look, I really don't think we can air this in public, do you? It's miles to find anywhere suitable. The closest place is Gilbraith's office. What do you say?"

"You've always got your head screwed on, Harriet." Kate's voice rang loudly. "But I don't want to bloody well see *him*."

A bowler-hatted gentleman gave her a look of disgust and, stepping up his pace, passed by.

"And you can stop bloody well eavesdropping!"

"Really, Kate?"

Kate scratched her cheek, looking marginally embarrassed.

"Maybe you'd better check if there is somewhere private? I don't want to bump into *him*. If I see *him* again, I might say or do something I will really regret."

When Harriet stepped back into the waiting room, Miss Fry flapped as if a thousand flies were buzzing around her head.

"Can I help?"

"My sister..." She began rolling the new, impossible but wonderful word around in her head. "My sister and I have just been given some information we would like to discuss. I'm sure Mr. Gilbraith would understand that we require a room where we can talk without being disturbed?" She gave a half-hopeful smile.

Miss Fry stopped blinking. "Yes, I'm sure I can arrange that."

Harriet stepped back outside and held out her hand. "Come on."

They were shown into a large, well-lit office smelling of wood polish hinting lavender.

"I'll bring tea." Miss Fry quickly bustled back out of the room while they stood deciding where to sit. Harriet folded her hands across her lap, her mind working furiously.

"It's not fair," Kate began. "Gilbraith tells us his story, gives us an '*I'm ashamed of myself*' act, and thinks he's as good as got away with murder. What does he expect? I fall into his arms and forgive him and say, 'Hello, Grandpa, so lovely to meet you at long last'?"

She was still ranting when Miss Fry arrived with a tray and the unmistakable smell of Earl Grey. Miss Fry looked between them, placed the tray down, and quickly retreated.

"I agree," said Harriet. Nothing could give her one good reason to exonerate Gilbraith's behavior, but what she loved was the contract. She smiled to herself. Nana was so forward thinking, so smart, and she had pushed Gilbraith to do the next best thing—even if it was against the law.

"Just think, Kate, how many hundreds of adopted children there are, just like you, wondering about their birth parents and never able to find out."

But the hurt of being an unwanted child still festered in Kate's heart. All those years she believed she'd done something wrong, though there was never a hint or suggestion of that from her family. In fact, quite the opposite.

"I don't care about other people. I care about me. I should have been kept, not sent away!"

Kate walked to the window and stared out with her arms folded. "You were the *special* one. The one she kept. How do you think that makes me feel?"

"I really can't imagine, Kate. The decision must have been impossible." Harriet tried placating her. "Did your adoptive mother really have hair like yours?"

Kate grudgingly acknowledged the fact.

"From what Gilbraith said, it seems your coloring made you the obvious choice."

"Bloody marvelous!" Kate sniffed crossly. "Just

as well my hair wasn't pink. I might have been sent to a fairground and made to sell candy floss, to fit in."

"You idiot!" Harriet, standing by her side, could not help but laugh.

They were looking through a window into the shaded sun of a simple walled car park, as Kate began talking.

"My adoptive parents were wonderful, Harriet. They loved me, like I said before, and I loved them right back. But when they died…" She wrapped her arms tightly around her body in a hug. "I curled into myself. It was so difficult. It was like being abandoned all over again."

She shook her head.

"When I ran away, at first I thought it was to make a name for myself." A dimple plucked her cheek. "I realized some years later, as you already know, the other reason why. I was kind of searching for my identity."

"And Jack, he seems so very kind. You said they were like him?"

Kate was beginning to calm, stemming the flow of tears with her damp handkerchief.

"Yes, he's always been quite amazing. Please don't misunderstand me. I know just how lucky I've been."

Harriet still found it difficult to believe Jack wasn't Kate's actual uncle. There were so many similarities. Maybe, she reasoned, there was more to the nurture versus nature debate after all?

Kate spoke fondly of Jack and the support he gave her through that terrible time and since. Then Harriet shared her own life in a little more detail, a life in a tightly knit community, and her spirits lifted. It was a good childhood.

"I really can't imagine what Nana must have gone through when we were born."

Harriet, distracted, accidentally spilt some of her tea and watched it pool in the bottom of her saucer.

"We said, didn't we, that we both felt there was something missing." She poured the tea back into her cup. "For me, I guess, it wasn't what Nana said, it was more what she didn't say." Then guilt flushed so hard it hurt her chest. "If only I hadn't kept pushing her for answers."

Kate placed her arm about her shoulders, clucking that she was being melodramatic.

Harriet shook her head, a half-smile on her lips. "Me, melodramatic?"

Suddenly Kate rushed out of the office with her hand to her mouth, leaving Harriet bewildered. Five minutes passed before Kate returned, her face flushed.

"Are you okay?"

"I don't usually suffer with nerves, but what with my upcoming show…"

Harriet glanced at her watch. "Shall we cancel Luigi's? He'll understand."

Kate had forgotten all about it. There was just too much going on in her head. There were so many people they would let down.

"No, why should we let *him* ruin our day? Let's go, have a drink or two, get sloshed. After all, for the first time in my life, I can enjoy booze *legally*, and *he* can go to hell."

Harriet hugged her. Kate seemed a little more herself. Harriet's eyes flicked to the door. There was still so much to learn. She asked Kate to wait a few moments, and then Harriet and Kate clasped hands as they left the solicitor's office.

"Happy Birthday, Kate." Harriet nudged her the moment they stepped outside into light, smiling sunshine. "I still can't believe it."

"Happy Birthday, Hattie." Kate nudged her back as they walked toward the tube.

There was so much to tell her, so many new emotions to deal with. Thank God she had Hattie. Kate wanted that even more now.

"What a strange birthday," Kate murmured.

"Yes, very sad, but wonderful," said Harriet. "We have one another. A new beginning. A coming of age. Finding that I have you, of all people, as my twin sister could not be more perfect!"

"I wonder if you're older than me. I think you look *waaaay* older." Kate smirked, a semblance happier. "It would make bloody sense. You've always got your head screwed on and giving me orders."

They smiled at one another. They knew there would be a long road ahead of them, but they would get through it, somehow, together.

Chapter 65

They found Alex outside Luigi's restaurant, the place where Harriet once worked. Alex had a huge grin on his face as he wished them happy birthday.

"As always"—he winked at Harriet—"our late Kate has finally turned up!"

To their absolute astonishment, there were friends from all over, waiting, with shouts of "Surprise!"

"Was this your doing, Alex?"

"I can't take all the credit. Others had a hand in it, Tom being one."

Kate laughed, and Harriet began moving through the gathering, smiling, giggling, talking. Kate was amazed and thrilled to find Lucy Latimer, her old school friend, there. And Uncle Jack, with Françoise. How wonderful! She quickly made her way over, reuniting with hugs, kisses, and apologies for not keeping in touch.

Kate turned her attention to her uncle. Was that a twinkle in his eye, or was she imagining it? Were he and Françoise more than friends? She hoped so.

Françoise drew Kate in toward her, mouthing her thanks for the invitation to her upcoming fashion show and the party, pressing an envelope into the palm of her hand, insisting she open it later. This was not a gift, but business. A polite cough from behind their little group interrupted them. Tom, smiling, pulled

Harriet in close to him.

Kate, wide-eyed, gave him the onceover.

"At last. It's about time you've got your act together, Tom." She winked. He flushed, embarrassed.

A tra-la rang out, one of Luigi's little tricks to get everyone's attention. He held the note at the top of his voice, holding the last "laaaaaaa" so long his face reddened and contorted, getting every ounce of air out of his lungs, and had everyone laughing. In the end, he threw up his hands.

"Time to eat? Come, come, sit. We celebrate the birthday girls."

Jack raised his glass. "I would like to make a toast to my lovely niece Kate and her very good friend Harriet."

Kate elbowed Harriet.

"Friend," she whispered. "Little does he know. We'll tell him later, after the party, together, agreed?"

"Agreed."

Chapter 66

When Harriet ventured back into George Gilbraith's office and then left, he knew that would be the last of it, at least for today. He pressed the button on the office intercom.

"Elizabeth, there's something I should have done long ago."

George picked up his coat and his felt trilby. Walking out of his office, he looked at the woman— his secretary, his lover, and his confidante for nearly twenty years. He would do the right thing by her. Everything else in his life had been a lie. At least she should not continue to suffer the humiliation of being a kept woman. He placed a kiss on her forehead.

"I promise I will make everything up to you."

George felt shame for allowing his wife, Marjorie, to bend him so willfully. She had insisted long before Cassandra gave birth that it would be better to distance themselves. Far better than facing the social stigma and humiliation of being connected to an unmarried mother. Far better than allowing it to reflect upon his legal practice and the repercussions thereafter.

Weary and anxious, he pondered the events. His lies. His deceit. Feelings of doubt and guilt had weighed him down for twenty-one years. But even now, faced with an opportunity to redeem himself, he had taken the easy option and lied again. The only truth he'd uttered that morning was that Johnnie had died a hero before he could marry Cassandra. Life, he thought angrily, was not so different. Even now bigotry ran deep.

George asked the taxi driver to stop outside the gates of Heardsley Park, their home. The spittle in the air reminded him of the first time he and Marjorie viewed the place.

"This will be fine, thank you." George paid the fare, got out, and stood a while before walking up the quarter-mile driveway. Refusing to wear his hat, he hoped the walk and damp air would help him ease his mind and prevent a full-blown headache, already pulsing in his temple. As the rain fell, it cooled his brow, and he continued along the gentle sweep of the bend lined with oaks, until the red-brick mansion with its columned porchway came into view. It was certainly imposing, he thought wryly, but nothing more than that. He hated the place and had told his wife so the moment he saw it. In his opinion, it was better suited to a Vincent Price horror film.

George's mind went on to play over that dreadful night, the call from the hospital, all those years ago. His behavior toward Mrs. Laws had been truly disgusting, after Cassandra, that poor, sweet, beautiful girl, died giving birth to Johnnie's girls. They were his granddaughters. Mrs. Laws was grief-stricken, poor, and alone, and he didn't raise a finger to help. How he hated himself for being so weak. Mrs. Laws' contract was her last desperate plea. He was glad he had finally agreed to it. George strode the last few steps toward the house, needing to vent his feelings. His wife was the best natural target in the world.

He stood a while in the hallway, listening for familiar sounds. It was silent, no usual half-hearted off-key humming from the girl who did, and he remembered it was the maid's half day. Marjorie, he guessed, would either be taking a nap or out spending his money without a care in the world. He slowly climbed the wide mahogany stairway, allowing his hand to glide up on the smoothness of polished wood and its natural curve. He found his wife in her dressing room, sitting in front of the mirror.

"You're home early." Marjorie held a slim gold container between her thumb and index finger, ready to apply ruby lipstick. "I assume you're going to one of your *business meetings*?" Her sarcasm was unmistakable.

George looked at her. "Would it make any difference if I didn't?" Marjorie shrugged, taking on the look of her sour-faced father.

"Are you really asking me if I mind, George? No. You can fall under a train, for all I care."

"Well, let me tell you that color lipstick suits you perfectly, the tart you are!"

Tears sprang to her eyes, and she hung her head, mumbling how he would know all about tarts. George pulled his tie and flicked it to the floor.

"That poor woman." He shook his head. "Why we put her through all that, and for what?"

"What woman?"

"Mrs. Laws. Cassandra's mother. Do you remember her? Oh, of course not, you refused to meet her!" He eyed his wife distastefully, shaking with rage. "Do you know, she had more integrity in her little finger than you could conjure up in a lifetime. The girls,

L. B. Griffin

our granddaughters, are twenty-one today, Marjorie. Bright, lovely, intelligent young women." He jabbed a finger at her. "Even without our support."

"You agreed it was for the best, George." He heard a tremor of justification in her voice.

"Best for whom?" He massaged his temple, choking back anger. "I'm ashamed I didn't support that poor girl's mother in what must have been her darkest hour. I already knew what it was to lose my son, and she had just lost her daughter."

"George. Please."

"The truth is you're a bloody rotten snob, just like your father. It's all about money and social standing with you."

But as he yelled, he felt sick to his stomach, every bit as guilty, and every bit as much the snob. George thumped the door. It rattled in response. His voice broke. "I wonder, Marjorie—did you ever really love our son?"

Marjorie shot out of her chair and struck him hard across the face.

"How dare you!"

"At last, an ounce of passion from my frigid wife!"

George stormed out of the room as she berated him through her sobs. He tore open his top drawer containing the one item he claimed of his son's last moments and took out the posthumous Medal for Gallantry. He paused only a moment to think how cruel life had been. He held the medal out in the palm of his hand toward Marjorie, wavering in her dressing room door.

"Our son was the only true and decent thing that came of our marriage. Johnnie was brave, kind, loyal,

344

and honest. He died with honor. Thank God he was nothing like us. We will be divorced, Marjorie. Another piece of shame to add to your list. I'm ready to face my disgraceful behavior. Are you?"

Chapter 67

Marjorie stared after her husband as he left the room, his broad back stiff, upright. She turned to see herself in the mirror and hated what she saw. Screaming in frustration, she threw her lipstick so hard it struck the glass, which splintered into a tiny web in the angle of the hinge. The sticky blush hung just for a second, embedding itself, before sliding down, leaving a blood-red trail.

Marjorie cast her eyes to the dressing table. She heard her husband on the telephone.

George was wrong. No question she loved Johnnie. If only George knew. Her mind worked over the secret she had so desperately wanted to tell her husband long ago.

When Johnnie mentioned he'd met a girl at a party, her heart had lifted. Marjorie prayed she had been wrong about her sensitive son. After several months of their being together, Johnnie told her that he and Cassandra were going to a dance in Brighton. They were staying over at a friend's. Her heart lifted again.

Marjorie pulled a photograph album from the drawer, a record of her son. She smiled at the baby photographs. Johnnie—so cute, so sweet, so sensitive. Johnnie reaching manhood—debonair, handsome in his uniform. Who would have guessed?

But it was the brutality of the attack in Brighton

that finally brought the truth out. It would stay with her forever. Cassandra brought Johnnie home, his fine-looking face pulverized. The girl had tried to protect him, of that she was sure, making feeble excuses. They somehow had become separated. When she got word, he was in hospital.

When Cassandra left, Johnnie confessed what she'd long suspected about her son's secret life. He loved men. If it ever got out, it would mean prison, shame upon the family, destroy them all. As he cried, she listened. He would be vilified. Suffer the humiliation of vile tests. Injections. Shock therapy. Cassandra was a dear, dear friend, nothing more. But during his confession he made her promise never to tell his father.

Marjorie breathed slowly, steadily, in through her nose, calming herself, a quiet mantra in her head. Breathe in, breathe out. Twenty-one years. Was it really that long ago?

She'd always believed in her refusal to support the notion of Cassandra marrying Johnnie after his confession. After all, it had been the kindest thing to do, for the girl's sake. How could she endorse a marriage when it could only ever be a sham?

Marjorie withdrew a letter from Johnnie, placed carefully at the back of the album, made more poignant as it was written on the day of his death, arriving with his personal effects one week later, addressed for her eyes only. Not one word was obliterated by faceless operatives like all the rest had been.

Mother Dearest,

Cassandra is expecting a child. You will understand that whilst I know it is not mine, there is no sign of the father, and I have asked her to marry me. She has finally agreed. I have arranged the marriage license and have been given special dispensation to come home for one whole week.

Please understand, Mother, the child can only bring light where there is dark. I believe marrying Cassandra and bringing up a child will help bring stability, normality, and love into all our lives. I hope by doing this, the right thing, it will bring us all closer together.

Marjorie could not bear to read on. As she rubbed her brow, guilt spread across her chest. A tear splashed onto the paper, and the ink fanned out over her son's signature. Desperately blotting it with her fingers, she let her tears continue to flow.

Johnnie had seen a way out, a cover story for him. Cassandra would have a husband and a father for her child, and financial support. Marjorie trembled. George needed to know. He thinks he is their grandfather. She would have to tell him. A kindness, or a kind of madness?

Oh, God. What had she done? If only she had shown George the letter straight away and explained the truth. Her son wasn't sick, he just didn't care to love women. George would call her all sorts. He would never believe it. She would make him understand. She—they—would have to deal with it.

"George," Marjorie called. "There's something I must tell you."

Chapter 68

February 14, 1961

Kate nudged her sister, a smile of sunshine on her face and the scent of Chanel drifting in the air.

"We've so much to talk about, Hattie." She shot her a meaningful look. "Are you still okay with Alex and Uncle Jack coming over?"

"Yes, of course."

In truth Harriet would have preferred it to be just her and Tom tonight but felt selfish and ungrateful.

Jack was propped up against the doorway, chatting with Luigi. They must have shared a joke, as they both laughed at the same time. Jack was a rock and, in her mind, an important part of their lives. Though not blood related, he was family. Family—what a wonderful word!

Kate hooked her arm into Alex's. She looked drawn, and something else Harriet could not identify.

"Kate's going with Alex," said Jack, now at her side. "I see Tom's already taken Daisy home. Will he be joining us later?"

"Yes."

"Good. I've arranged a taxi for Françoise to take her to the hotel. It's been a long day, what with the journey from Paris. I've a spare seat in my car. Want a lift?"

L. B. Griffin

Harriet caught a fleeting glimpse of apprehension on Jack's face. There had been a few more of those lately, though she never asked why.

"You don't need to come back, not if you don't want to, Jack."

"Of course I do. Thank you." His right cheek twitched, giving away that something was playing on his mind. Jack squeezed himself into the tight hug of the driver's seat, muttering under his breath how right the girls were and that the Mini really was too small for his build. He began focusing on the belching traffic. Weaving in and out of queues as expertly as a hackney cab, they moved ever forward toward their destination.

They drove in amiable silence until he pulled into her driveway. To Harriet, the house was still filled with hard memories of mistrust and hurt, though she took small comfort from the success of Christmas. At least she knew the sale would mean she could leave the house forever.

Stepping inside, Harriet issued a private thank you to the heating system and asked Kate to give her a hand in the kitchen whilst the men settled themselves, hoping to find a moment when they were undisturbed. The telephone rang. It was Tom, full of apology and worry. Daisy was unwell. He felt it only right to stay with her.

"Of course you should, Tom. Maybe call the doctor?"

"I knew you'd understand, Harriet. I'll keep in touch if there are any developments." Harriet put the receiver down and wandered into the kitchen. Kate was pacing the room.

"Daisy is unwell. Tom's staying with her, and if she gets worse, he'll get the doctor." She sighed; a frown crossed her brow. "Maybe I should go and check on her. What do you think, Kate?"

Kate appeared to be in one of her flighty moods.

"Stop fussing, Harriet. I'm sure Daisy will be fine, and Tom's with her, isn't he?" The response was so unlike Kate, it shocked her. Kate picked up the tray of cheese and biscuits and marched into the lounge. Harriet arranged a tray of glasses, thinking about what to do, and found Jack hanging around in the hallway, where Harriet had decided to re-hang her painting.

"Where did you say the painting came from, Harriet?" Jack asked, following behind her into the lounge. The question surprised her. There was so much she and Kate needed to talk about, and now she worried about Daisy's health. She chewed her lip.

"The fact of the matter is, Jack, it belonged to my Nana. The painting was stolen from here, and someone delivered it to my door just before Christmas."

Jack looked astonished.

"Stop it with the painting, Uncle Jack." Kate had arrived in the hallway. She sounded jittery and cut her uncle off. "I have something I need to say."

"We *both* have something we would like to *share*, don't we, Kate? Let's go through to the lounge first, shall we?" Jack eyed them curiously and followed behind. Kate sat on the arm of the chair next to Alex, fidgeting.

Harriet was just about to speak when Kate jumped up, her eyes shining brightly. Alex's hand fell away from her back.

"I'm pregnant!"

Chapter 69

Just those few words and everything seemed to change. Alex looked dumfounded.

"Pregnant? What? How? When?" Already he was on his feet, holding Kate gently, studying her face, drying her eyes.

"Well, as you were part of the bloody action, Alex, I guess I don't need to go into the details. Do I?"

Jack looked on in half-surprised silence.

"Oh, Kate," said Harriet, "it's wonderful news."

"Seems history has a way of repeating itself," Kate mumbled, her words meaning everything to the pair of them but nothing to the men. Kate went to pick up a glass of bubbly, but Alex intervened.

"Maybe milk would be more appropriate?"

Kate huffed. "Don't you want this? Don't you want us, me?"

"Do you?"

Kate's lips wobbled trying to contain her emotions.

Alex wrapped his arms around her, tutting. "You're a real idiot, Kate. Isn't it obvious? I love you."

"I'm going home. You both need to talk." Jack was already on his feet. The couple hardly noticed Harriet following Jack out and closing the door behind them, bewildered.

"Don't worry, Harriet. It'll all come out in the wash."

She sighed, as she watched Jack reverse out of the driveway. When she entered the house again, even with the lounge door shut tight she could hear Kate talking between sobs. Alex, she felt sure, would not let her sister down. There would be no way any child of Kate's would not be loved or taken care of.

Exhausted, bothered by the unexpected unraveling of events, Harriet went to bed, worrying about Daisy, worrying about Kate. She plumped pillows. Listened to the hum of the boiler and the creak of a pipe as it contracted. She listened for the telephone and to the soft patter of hypnotic rain against the window, and she counted sheep. Sometime later, maybe in her dreams, she heard the muted whisper of a giggle. It sounded a bit like Kate. They would talk tomorrow.

****

Harriet rose early the next day. The cold nipped at her ankles. Pulling on her slippers and dressing gown, she peered out the window. There was no other noise in the house other than the back boiler chugging into life. Frost stars clutched each other on the windowpane. She smiled, fondly recalling the days when she could scrape frost off from the inside, long before radiators. But the pressing matter was Kate. Her sister was pregnant. A good thing, she hoped. Harriet slipped downstairs and found the fire already lit. Puzzled but grateful, she phoned Tom. Everything was fine. A chest infection. The doctor had given Daisy some medicine, and she felt much brighter already.

Tom would be coming over later. He had

something to talk about, he said, but needed to see her face to face.

Harriet breathed in relief and decided a long soak in the bath might help her put yesterday's events into perspective. She added rose bath salts, swishing them around, watching the water turn murky before slipping in. Five minutes later, there was movement outside, and a tap at the door.

"I need to pee. Is it okay if I come in?" Harriet exhaled. She'd forgotten to lock the door.

"Close the door. I don't want Alex in here standing to attention!"

"Alex left early, around five. Something big is going down in Parliament."

Kate looked different, with her hair set free. No longer dyed black or cut spikey short, it hung in glorious natural waves of burnt umber down to her shoulders. Kate flushed and washed her hands.

"Have you heard from Tom? Is Daisy all right?"

"Sounds like everything is fine." It was good to have the old Kate back again.

"Well?" said Harriet, flicking bath water Kate's way. It landed on her dressing gown. "What's the verdict with you and Alex?"

Kate grabbed a towel and patted herself dry. Harriet flicked more water her way.

"Really? You're such a child at times."

"Well, tell me!"

Kate sat on the edge of the bath and talked like waves rushing to the shore. The proposal, the agreement to marry Alex, and their love. She apologized, but she'd already told Alex the news that she and Hattie were twins. She couldn't help herself. It all came out—her adoption, her behavior, her connections with Dorian Craddock. Every single little detail. If they were to be married, she had to be honest, and he had to know. She knew how her pregnancy and her background would be frowned upon in Parliament's tight circles of prejudice. But Alex was right on it. If there was a problem, he would find work elsewhere.

"You've a good one there, Kate," said Harriet, asking her to pass a bath towel over.

"It took ages for me to realize my monthly had stopped." Kate looked so sweet, so innocently childlike, sighing. "And I thought Alex and I were careful." She gasped. "Hattie! What if I'm carrying twins! What if history really does repeat itself?"

"Now, stop that nonsense." Harriet caught their reflection in the bathroom mirror—and sensed Kate's fear. She wrapped her arms about her. "That was twenty-one years ago. Things have moved on. But, if you're worried, I'll find a specialist to help put your mind at rest."

Kate smiled, her mood changing like the wind. "Thanks, Hattie. Can I use your bathwater?"

"Still living in the dark ages, Kate?" Harriet pulled the plug, tutting.

A little later Kate sauntered her way into the kitchen, a towel turban wrapped around her wet hair.

"Tea?" Harriet offered mismatched cups and saucers. One of those things she did since coming back to the house. Placing tea towels at jaunty angles, leaving cupboard doors slightly ajar, piling dirty crockery on the side, or leaving crumbs all over the table. A virtual smack in CJ's eye, instead of her own.

Rubbing the dents in the sides of her nose made by her glasses, she felt stupid. No one would understand. Did it matter?

The doorbell rang, and Kate answered it to find Jack, with two small posies in his hand.

"I'm sorry, I know it's early," he said, rubbing bristle, a little shame-faced. "I was just so worried."

"Oh, Uncle Jack, you're so sweet." The telephone rang. "I need to answer that, but Hattie's just getting breakfast. Why don't you go on in?" Kate picked up the receiver and waved him toward the kitchen.

"Hello?"

Jack heard Kate murmuring to someone and stopped a moment to study the painting in the hallway before going into the kitchen.

"How kind, Jack," said Harriet accepting the posy and pushing plated toast his way. "I guess you'd like a cup of tea with that?" She smiled and arranged the flowers into a vase.

"Great, thank you." He quickly dolloped marmalade on the side of his plate, just as Kate arrived, looking coy and with one word on her lips.

"Alex."

"Alexander the Great?" said Harriet, prompting her to eat and tell Jack the outcome of last night.

"Alex has asked me to marry him." Kate's eyes sparkled, but she refused food.

Jack polished off a slice of toast with an air of relief. "I presume congratulations are in order, then?"

"Well, Uncle Jack, there's more. Harriet and I have an announcement to make."

Harriet held up her hand.

"Could you give me a moment? There's

something I need to get first." She began to rummage around in the glory hole. Jack put his tea down with a wink.

"Sounds mysterious."

Eventually she emerged with an old shoebox. One corner had been battered in, and a sticker on the side of the box, marking a size three, was peeling off. Kate looked puzzled.

"That's the one Mrs. Gaffney looked after for you, isn't it?"

Harriet nodded. "It's the one thing I have left of my mother, and it means the world. Let's go into the lounge. I don't want it on the table."

"Didn't know you were superstitious, Hattie."

Harriet allowed a glimmer of a smile. "I'm not, but just in case."

Kate, still having no idea, caught her uncle's hand with an air of excitement, and while Jack sat on the sofa, Kate and Harriet, like little schoolgirls, sat on the floor, either side of his legs.

Harriet suddenly realized she was holding her breath and exhaled before untying the string and taking off the lid. Then, lifting the pink satin pumps out one by one, like a private ritual, she handed them across to Kate.

"They're hers." Kate sat mesmerized and measured the ballet shoes against her own feet. "She must have been tiny."

"I guess so. All I did was grow into a full-size elephant."

Kate shook her head. "Idiot!"

Harriet watched Kate for a moment with the ballet shoes, her mind was churning over the events of yesterday. So much happened, so much to tell. She took a deep breath.

"We had letters, from the same solicitor, Gilbraith and Son," said Harriet quietly, turning to Jack, wondering how to begin. Harriet got up and went to the fire and poked it, turning over the coals.

"Yes," Kate joined in. "Was it really only yesterday?"

Jack, curious, leaned forward.

Kate cycled the pink ballet pumps along the floor as if they were dancing. "We were surprised to find one another there, trust me."

With Kate now in charge, it confirmed what Jack suspected—her appointment with Gilbraith had been about her inheritance. The Westfield family home and its entirety had become hers. What came next was an astonishing string of coincidences.

"We're twins, Uncle Jack," said Kate. "Harriet and I are twin sisters."

"Pardon?"

Harriet laughed at his face.

"No one was more surprised than we were, I can assure you."

As Kate marched on, describing how the color of her hair determined why she came to be the one adopted, Harriet began interjecting with her version of events. Jack hung on their every word, trying to put order to the jumble. He could hardly take it in. The girls were looking at him, eyes shining. Harriet reached out a nimble hand, her laughter light, like rain falling gently upon earth, and he had to stop himself from gasping, trying to push the distant, impossible memory away.

Harriet's animated face softened as she removed tissue paper from the shoebox, revealing newspaper cuttings, though yellowing with age, still intact. She smiled fondly at one. The article was glowing. Her grandmother had read it to her a million times, and she knew every word by heart. But it was the photograph of her mother delightfully caught mid arabesque that she really loved. Harriet handed the cutting over to Kate.

"This is our mother."

"This is her?" Kate studied the grainy image of a young ballerina closely. "She's beautiful." Kate gently held the scrap of newspaper between her fingers, reading the article. Harriet sat beside her. It was then the second bombshell was delivered.

"It's terrible to think she must have found she was pregnant just as she was beginning to gain fame."

When Kate passed the image to Jack, the blood drained from his face. He didn't need his wallet. He knew, instantly.

Misery froze his heart. She was dead. Anything would be preferable, so long as she were alive.

He put his head in his hands. He could hear talking, but the world tilted on its axis. His temperature soared from hot to cold and back to hot again. Ice pricked the hairs on the back of his neck, and perspiration ran down his spine. He couldn't breathe. He had to get out. Grabbing for the sofa for balance, he caught Harriet's shoulder.

"Sorry."

"Jack?"

Rushing out through the front door, Jack began hammering the roof of his car. Cassie had landed the leading role in *Giselle* just before they met? A prima ballerina? Why didn't she divulge something so fantastic? He'd asked to know more about her so many times, but she insisted they play the silly game throughout their glorious week together. The only hint of her background, perhaps, was her poor disfigured toes. They were so imperfect compared to her beautifully crafted body. When he asked, she told him it was because she was married to her job. Worried she might be a nun, Cassie only laughed, still refusing to reveal the truth. Why?

That last morning, the game over, their truths would be outed. With Cassie asleep, not wanting to disturb her, he'd searched for a flower seller and a plan to ask her to marry him. When he returned, Cassie had gone.

Jack shuddered. The ground sparkled with frost. A flurry of tiny snowflakes swirled and swept along the ground with the promise of more to come. But Jack saw none of it, angry at himself. A fat tear rolled. Nausea welled with the same terrible loss he'd felt all those years ago. There was no doubt in his mind. The timing. The dates. It all added up. It just had to be.

Jack doubled over. Because of him, she was dead. This was all his fault.

Chapter 70

Harriet and Kate, shocked, flew after Jack, but the door slammed in their face. Harriet saw him through the viewing pane.

"Jack's hitting seven bells out of his car! Does he do that?"

"No!" Kate went to open the door. Harriet stopped her. "But?"

"Don't."

"It's bloody freezing out there. I'll get his coat."

"No. Whatever it is, he needs space. Let's put the kettle on, give him time."

When a blast of cold air hurried along the passageway like an unwelcome friend, Kate was on her feet in an instant, rushing to greet him.

"Are you all right?"

Jack looked disheveled. His eyelids held a bluish tinge, his face ash white. She saw the hip flask protruding from his trouser pocket and smelled whiskey on his breath. It was not yet ten.

"I'm sorry, I…" Jack's shoulders sagged. "It's just so…" A chance sigh, and his eyes could not meet hers.

"What is it, Uncle Jack?"

He reached for her hand. He started to say something, then came out with, "It's nothing."

Kate decided to let it lie.

Jack went to freshen up, but they all knew he was hiding something.

While Harriet made tea, Kate sat on the sofa with the shoebox on her lap. She finished reading the articles and was just about to put them back when she noticed something poking from under another layer of tissue paper. She lifted the tissue and found an envelope.

"What have you got there?" Harriet asked, bringing the tea tray through.

Kate, spellbound, showed her. Harriet's eyebrows furrowed, accepting the envelope, and opened it just as Jack arrived, looking bothered.

"Uncle Jack, are you all right?"

He exhaled and sat heavily upon the chair as if a huge weight bore down upon his shoulders.

"I don't understand." Harriet was looking through the contents of the envelope. "We could never afford to have photographs taken."

She proffered one toward Kate. The shot was of a little girl standing on a front porch, her nose all puckered up, smiling at the camera. "She looks kind of familiar."

Kate gasped. "No! It can't be!" She turned to Jack, encouraging him to look. "Do you remember the clematis? Pops said it would grow purple because the fairies knew I loved the color, so they put a magic spell on it." She had been five years old and believed every word. Shaking her head, "I don't understand..."

"Harriet?" Jack swallowed. "You haven't seen these before?"

"No."

Jack turned the image over. It was dated. He instantly recognized his sister's distinctive looped handwriting. His hand trembled as he ran his hand through his hair.

"Do you have more?" Harriet handed him the small pile. Thirteen in total.

"Look closer, Kate." His voice ached with emotion. "Remember how your mother insisted I take photographs on your birthday?"

He still had the old camera kept for posterity, in a box somewhere, dispensed for more professional equipment.

"Always scrunching your nose up. You could never relax."

"But why thirteen? Why stop?" Kate's face suddenly turned ashen, catching a whisper of back then. "Dear God!"

"What am I missing? Please, tell me. I don't understand," said Harriet.

Kate fell silent. Her head bowed, sadness sucking her right back into her past. Jack placed a tender, knowing hand on her shoulder. Her parents had died just days before her fourteenth birthday.

Chapter 71

"There are a few things I'd like to share, if I may?" began Jack. The girls perked up. "My sister and Henry. They were so grateful when you arrived, Kate. We all fell in love with you the moment you entered our lives."

The events gathered speed as he spoke, memories flicking through time. Jack could never understand why his sister Maury was so finicky when he took the photographs. Every pose and angle had to be perfect. If his guess was right, it might make sense.

"I'm wondering, Kate." He pointed to her five-year-old self in the photograph. "What do you actually see?"

"A cutie, obviously me?" A dimple of laughter.

"Look again." Harriet and Kate squeezed close together, studying the shot, so crisp a professional would be proud. The child held a small trowel, helping plant the clematis.

"I can see the name of the house!" exclaimed Harriet.

"I think, if I'm not mistaken, you will find little clues in every photograph. And every photo has been dated."

Jack, with heart in mouth, watched the girls' pore over the pictures, noting the tiniest detail. A signpost at the end of the lane. The driveway. Chaz and

Treenie's farm. Jack held his breath. He wanted so much to tell them about Cassandra. Did he dare go down that road? How would they feel? Would they believe him? Would they hate him?

"I still don't understand what you're getting at." Harriet frowned.

"My guess is my sister wanted to give your grandmother clues as to where Kate lived, to show her she was safe. Maybe even a hint to try to find them. From what you've told me, the contract was between your grandmother and Mr. Gilbraith the solicitor. Everything would have to go through Gilbraith & Son to pass on to your grandmother. My sister would never have known your address, Harriet. He would never have been able to allow it."

"Gilbraith!" Kate shouted. "What did I say? He's been the bloody pig in the middle through all this!"

"Kate, I almost forgot!" Harriet cut her off, her eyes wide as she rushed out and moments later returned with a framed picture.

"Jack, this is our father. He was going to marry our mother, but he was killed in the war just before their wedding day."

"Johnnie? Johnnie Gilbraith?" Jack blurted.

Harriet and Kate blinked in complete surprise.

"You knew him?"

"Kate, Harriet…" Jack looked worriedly between them, taking one of their hands in each of his. He had to tread carefully, do this sensitively.

"I found some information when I was going through Henry's paperwork."

Kate began twisting her hair.

"I really don't know where to begin." He looked

uncomfortable.

Kate gave him a half smile. "You always say the beginning is the place to start."

"Yes, usually," Jack responded gently. He had their full attention. "It was after, well, just before the funeral, I discovered a file in your father's study. Your adoption papers pointed me in Mr. Gilbraith's direction. However, he couldn't give me any details at the time. While I was in his office, I saw the photograph of Johnnie on his desk.

"I couldn't believe it. Still can't, it was such a shock, such a coincidence." Jack's cheek twitched. "You see, your father—Henry—and I flew with Johnnie in the war." Harriet and Kate were speechless. "You're right. Johnnie was a hero. He saved my life, and Henry's."

Kate remained on the floor, staring at her uncle in disbelief. Harriet fiddled with something on the mantelpiece. Jack could see everything slotting into place. The girls had been told their father was Johnnie Gilbraith, the handsome, dashing pilot, a hero to be remembered. Johnnie was indeed a hero, but could he in all honesty allow the girls to believe their father was dead?

Chapter 72

Jack knew Johnnie, and he knew Cassandra, but what Jack had not known, until now, was that they knew one another. Had Johnnie been the best friend Cassandra alluded to all those years ago at the party in Brighton? Was he the man she rushed to take home from hospital that fateful day when he lost his love forever? There were things that added up, but other parts didn't.

His watch indicated twelve minutes past eleven. He wanted another drink. His tea had gone cold, a good excuse. He indicated his cup, getting up.

"If it's not too presumptuous, could I make another?" Harriet nodded absently as he went to the kitchen. There was something Jack was holding back. She was sure of it.

"I feel sick," moaned Kate.

"You need to eat. Just a little something. You promised."

"All right, all right." Kate groaned, turning up her nose, nibbling on a piece of dry toast.

"Do you have a cracker, maybe, and eggs? I fancy a boiled egg, and have you got some of that piccalilli left over from Christmas?"

"Pickle. Seriously?"

Kate, curling her feet under her, reached for the shoebox, clearly in no mood to get it herself. Harriet sighed, exasperated, and followed Jack's path into the kitchen, only to find him pacing the room. He stopped the moment she entered. He looked bothered.

"Kate's decided to have a boiled egg and piccalilli." She put two fingers to her open mouth as if to gag.

"Not together?"

"Who knows." Harriet shrugged. "Pregnancy apparently does strange things."

Jack half smiled and disappeared. All this time. If only he had known. What could he say?

Harriet heard Jack calling to Kate as she busied herself putting on eggs and searching out the jar of pickle.

Kate huffed. Feeling tired and working on empty did her no favors. What did her uncle want? Reluctantly she put the box down and found him in the hallway, by the painting. He switched the light on for closer inspection.

"I recognized this the moment I saw it. Do you?"

Kate gave an almighty groan, but Jack took her hand and led her to stand back so they could view its magnificence.

"What do you see?"

"I think it looks like the ford at Westfield."

Jack's eyebrows rose, nodding in surprised agreement.

She gulped. She'd thought it the moment she first saw it but dismissed the idea. How long ago did she last visit? How long ago had she dipped her toes in those very waters?

"If my memory serves me right, the painting went missing around the time your parents brought you home. I never did ask Maury what happened to it. My guess now is that your mother sent the painting and photographs via Mr. Gilbraith, like I said, in the hope your grandmother would know you were safe." Jack rubbed his head, never feeling more certain he needed to tell them everything. "Kate, there's something else."

"Harriet, come see!" Kate shrieked excitedly, ignoring Jack. Harriet came running, and she dragged her toward the painting.

"This view, it's on Westfield land! I told you Westfield would be the ideal place, you know, for your *project*." She refused to say "battered women" because to her that made the women sound like deep fried fish. "We will go and look it over, to see what you make of it!"

Harriet's eyes widened in disbelief.

"It's perfect, don't you see?" Kate's excitement bubbled over, and she laughed with satisfaction. "I've got loads of ideas, Hattie. Loads of them!"

Forgotten were Kate's feeling of irritation at Mr. Gilbraith, and that empty nauseous feeling of early morning pregnancy, and even—for the moment—the shoebox. Together she and Hattie could do anything if they put their minds to it, and the ideas fell from her lips like water from a fountain.

Jack watched the delight sparking between them. He was happy for them, but worried. He wanted to tell them everything, but how could he prove it? How would they react? He hoped—he prayed—they would understand.

Suddenly there was a loud pop and the smell of something burning. Harriet, squealing, rushed to the kitchen. The eggs had boiled dry, burnt black. Grabbing the pan from the hob, Harriet flooded it with water, it hissed back, and she dumped the pan outside the back door, closing it quickly against the freezing air.

"Sorry. How about crackers and piccalilli instead, Kate?"

"No, thanks." Kate retched theatrically. "I'll give it a miss."

Harriet glanced at Jack, leaning against the door jamb. He looked paler than a gray winter's day. Just then the telephone rang.

Kate moaned, "What now?" and instructed Harriet if it were Alex, he would have to call back later.

Harriet virtually danced to the telephone, praying it might be Tom telling her he was on his way, but Kate hurried into the lounge. Something was drawing her back to the shoebox. It felt heavy, even when empty. It didn't make sense.

Sitting on the sofa, she studied it inside and out. For a moment it revealed nothing, but upon closer inspection, to her surprise she discovered there was a piece of card tightly fitted at the bottom, on the inside, as if it had been placed there…maybe to hide something? Excited, she dug her fingernails into the edges and began to pry at the sides. The card eventually gave way and underneath she found a notebook, so old and worn most of the paper had become separated from its spine. As she lifted it out, cotton strands dangled from the edge of the book like fine white hair. Kate knew this was something private. Something hidden from prying eyes until now.

She turned the notebook over in her hand and

gently opened it. Inside, to her delight, she found wonderful sketches of tiny ballet dancers and notations of choreography. But then as she turned the pages, she found something else, not quite a diary, but a story, starting in 1939.

She gasped. Her heart began to race. She became more breathless with every word. Jack came into the room without her being aware, but a small movement from him startled her. She looked up and stared at him in disbelief. It couldn't be…?

"That was Mr. Gilbraith." Harriet arrived, pushing her glasses up her nose, her face a picture of confusion, her voice betraying her emotions. The information still playing a dance in her head.

"Kate…"

"Forget Gilbraith! There's something here I need you to see…" Kate held the notebook out in her hand.

"Please, Kate, I need to tell you. You're not going to like this one bit, but…" Harriet wrung her hands. "In a nutshell, Mr. Gilbraith was full of apology but says he has proof his son was not in fact our father!"

Kate bunched her lips—she knew already. It was all there, within the pages of the notebook. She looked at Jack, flustered, wanting to show him, them…

Jack drew a deep breath—maybe they would understand. He'd calculated the dates, over and over, and the information he had been presented with could only mean one thing. There could be no other explanation.

All for one and one for all?

He hoped their bond would be enough for them to remain united. Taking the wallet from his breast pocket, he gently lifted the creased photograph out and smiled sadly. How he loved her. How he wished she could see her girls. They were such wonderful human beings. How proud he would be to continue to love and cherish them as his daughters, to be known as their father. He'd always dreamed of sharing his life with Cassandra. It was not meant to be, but something good would come of it after all. A tremor of breath caught his throat.

They looked at him as he held the photograph of their mother in his hand, her hair flying wildly in the wind, her face so very young and bright, her cheeks flushed with such love in her eyes as she looked at the man taking the photograph.

"Harriet, Kate, there is something so wonderful, so amazing I need to tell you. I can only hope you will understand."

He paused. "I need to tell you about your mother and me."

A word about the author…

Lynn B. Griffin was born, raised, and married in the City of Bath, UK. Between being a College Lecturer, bringing up a family, and writing, her passions are travel, art, reading, sport, and socializing with friends.

Her writing has always been inspired by stories of courage and survival. Her debut novel, *Secrets, Shame, and a Shoebox*, the prequel to this book, is entirely a work of historical fiction.

Happily married and surrounded by her family in Wiltshire, she would love to hear from you online:

www.facebook.com/lynngriffinauthor
www.WifeInTheWest.com
www.instagram.com/lynngriffinauthoruk/
https://twitter.com/LBGriffinAuthor/

Thank you for purchasing
this publication of The Wild Rose Press, Inc.

For questions or more information
contact us at
info@thewildrosepress.com.

The Wild Rose Press, Inc.
www.thewildrosepress.com